PRAISE FOR ALAYA DAWN JOHNSON

Love Is the Drug

2014 Nebula Award winner for best young adult novel

★ "Utterly absorbing." —*Kirkus Reviews*, starred review

"Equal parts character study and thriller, *Love Is the Drug* offers a gripping study of identity, sly social commentary, and a chilling glimpse of a dystopia that's just around the corner." —*NPR*

The Library of Broken Worlds

"Mysterious, sweeping, wholly original, and anchored by an extraordinary heroine as wily as she is vulnerable. Johnson has crafted a story so immersive it will leave you drunk with visions of strange worlds and new gods, so compelling you'll be happy to drown in this dizzying, bloody brew of technology, lore, and world-shaking conflict." —Leigh Bardugo, *New York Times* bestselling author of *Shadow & Bone*

"*The Library of Broken Worlds* is an ambitious, multilayered, multidimensional exploration of power, selfhood, freedom, and love. Alaya Dawn Johnson writes with fluidity and precision about mind-bending ideas and gorgeously imagined worlds, but also with tactile specificity about food and ritual. This novel rewired my brain." —Malinda Lo, *New York Times* bestselling and National Book Award–winning author of *Last Night at the Telegraph Club*

"One of the most haunting and lovely tales I've ever read. Modern epic poetry. Wow." —N. K. Jemisin, *New York Times* bestselling author of the Broken Earth trilogy

"With *The Library of Broken Worlds*, Alaya Dawn Johnson immerses us in a genderqueer-friendly universe filled with space travel, gods, and AI that we want to cheer for. Readers will be transported into a wholly unfamiliar and completely fascinating new spacetime." —Chanda Prescod-Weinstein, author of *The Disordered Cosmos: A Journey into Dark Matter, Spacetime, and Dreams Deferred*

The Summer Prince

Longlisted for the National Book Award

A *Kirkus Reviews* Best Book of the Year

★ "Like leaping into cold water on a hot day, this original dystopian novel takes the breath away, refreshes, challenges, and leaves the reader shivering but yearning for another plunge." —*Booklist*, starred review

★ "With its complicated history, founding myth, and political structure, Palmares Tres is compelling, as is the triple bond between June, Enki, and Gil as they challenge their world's injustices." —*Publishers Weekly*, starred review

★ "An art project, a rebellion and a sacrifice make up this nuanced, original cyberpunk adventure . . . Luminous." —*Kirkus Reviews*, starred review

LOVE Is
the DRUG

ALAYA DAWN JOHNSON

Scholastic Inc.

Copyright © 2014 by Alaya Dawn Johnson

Photos © Shutterstock.com

This book was originally published in hardcover by Arthur A. Levine Books in 2014.

All rights reserved. Published by Scholastic Inc., *Publishers since 1920*. SCHOLASTIC and associated logos are trademarks and/or registered trademarks of Scholastic Inc.

The publisher does not have any control over and does not assume any responsibility for author or third-party websites or their content.

No part of this publication may be reproduced, stored in a retrieval system, or transmitted in any form or by any means, electronic, mechanical, photocopying, recording, or otherwise, without written permission of the publisher. For information regarding permission, write to Scholastic Inc., Attention: Permissions Department, 557 Broadway, New York, NY 10012.

This book is a work of fiction. Names, characters, places, and incidents are either the product of the author's imagination or are used fictitiously, and any resemblance to actual persons, living or dead, business establishments, events, or locales is entirely coincidental.

ISBN 978-0-545-41782-2

10 9 8 7 6 5 4 3 2 1   24 25 26 27 28

Printed in the U.S.A.   40
This edition first printing 2024

Epigraph on page vii from *On Drugs* © 1995 by David Lenson, University of Minnesota Press. Used with permission.

Book design by Phil Falco

To Frank, Tibbs, Ms. Schindele,
Mr. Wood — and the old fiction room.

"It is said that once the back of a fine watch is opened for repair or examination it can never again run in the same way, for a fleck of dust will always lodge invisibly in the works and provide a stress, albeit incalculably small, to the functioning of the mechanism. So too when a drug opens the clockworks of consciousness for examination, that awareness thereafter becomes ever so slightly more self-aware. Self-consciousness becomes a slightly greater part of consciousness. And so the question finally becomes: how intimately do we want or need to know ourselves?"

— David Lenson, *On Drugs*

[androstadienone]

$C_{19}H_{26}O$

Bird wakes up.

The walls aren't white, but close, the color of a cracked egg. She turns her head on the pillow and looks through a window to the street below. Deserted, not a single car parked on the side, and she stares at that until a solitary tank grumbles down the road, guns steady.

Her head aches. She raises her arm to feel it, and sees a needle taped down to the vein in her elbow. She tries to count the stitches on her forehead and concludes ten or eleven. A hospital. But the silence of the room, the hush in the hall, the jarring rattle of a tank outside —

"What happened?" she says, and finds her voice rusty but functional. It has never been particularly melodic. She tries to remember. It's like trying to follow a conversation in a language you barely speak — whatever meaning lies buried there, she can't reach it.

Outside, the sun turns orange and limp violet, silhouetting the bare branches of the trees lining the street. Something about those branches makes Bird sit up and push her hair away from her forehead. *I need a relaxer*, she thinks, feeling the dense, wiry curl at her roots. How long has she been here? There are flowers on the side table — white and pink lilies wilted around the edges and swimming in cloudy water. A note hangs from the vase but she doesn't read it. She wants to believe they're from her parents, but she knows they aren't. Her head aches with the effort of not thinking about him.

She looks back out the window. The trees still had their leaves at the Robinsons' party. Yellow and red and brittle brown.

And so Bird remembers the last thing she can.

It goes like this —

Coffee was in the basement doing lines. Paul was upstairs with the Robinsons and their guests, capital-N networking. He wanted a national security internship this summer, and there were at least two senators and one highly placed government contractor drinking martinis who could help him. Bird had known the second she saw Coffee smoking by the mailbox outside that she would make her excuses, but for now she filled the slot that Paul expected: supportive girlfriend, enjoying the party.

"I think that guy over there is with the *Washington Post*," Paul said, and nudged Felice. "Weren't you saying the other day you were thinking about journalism?"

Felice looked up from her phone and glanced over. "Isn't he the film critic or something? Honestly, you'd think Pam Robinson could get some better guests. I mean, Bob Woodward is a family friend. I haven't decided what direction I want for this summer, but if it's journalism, I'm sure my dad can just call Bob."

"Bob Woodward, like from AP US History? Deep Throat?" Paul said.

Felice smiled gently and combed her fingers through aggressively blunt-cut bangs. "My dad is very well connected."

"My dad knows Adrian Fenty," Charlotte said. She glanced at Bird as she said this, her look a soap bubble of pride that popped under Felice's dismissive shrug.

"What's he, the old mayor of DC? I mean, great for your dad, but the local political scene is low rent."

Paul jumped to Charlotte's rescue. "You really think that, after 8/16? That terrorist flu is practically a pandemic. Venezuela has oil money, a rogue government, and biological WMDs — they're a world threat. And the most important people in the world live here. Local politics are national politics." Bird stepped closer to Paul and squeezed his hand, though she felt a jolt of some repelling force she didn't want to name when he continued, "And that makes it a very good time for me to get in the game."

Charlotte wound a braid around one finger and said nothing. Behind her, Trevor Robinson stood beneath an early-period Warhol that had probably cost six figures. He was speaking with Cindy de la Vega and an older white man who was gesturing, for some reason, at the ceiling. The Robinsons' dining room and foyer swarmed with people, mostly adults with a few young hopefuls like Paul, Bird, Felice, and Charlotte.

"Forget the stupid flu, the guy that Trevor's talking to is the head of Cornell admissions." Bird jumped to hear Gina's voice behind her. Gina was a friend of Felice's, the daughter of someone very rich whose profession seemed to consist of spending money (most recent purchases included an exact replica of the Christopher Nolan Batmobile and a third château in the Loire Valley). Somehow the transitive properties of friendship never seemed to extend to Bird and Charlotte, whom Gina alternately tolerated and ignored.

"I didn't know you wanted to go to Cornell, Gina," Paul said.

"Well, I *want* to go to Harvard, but Ms. Vern says that it's a real reach for me after that shit show in geography last semester, so right now as far as my dad's concerned any Ivy will do."

"But still, I mean, *Cornell*? You can definitely do better," Felice said.

Bird usually stayed out of Gina's money-scented orbit, but she couldn't let this go. "I don't think Cornell is really —"

Paul twisted her hand just as Gina pivoted and smiled. "I know you'd be really glad to get in there —"

"Actually, I want to go to Stanford —"

"— but some of us have parents who hold us to very high standards. And *anyway*, we all know that you guys are lucky. You've got, like, a free pass to any Ivy you want. The other day I heard that even *Marella*,

3

who hasn't done an extracurricular that didn't involve fucking the freshmen girls since sophomore year, is applying to Princeton. Like, my dad actually told me I should check the Latino box on my apps because my great-grandmother came from Puerto Rico, I mean she was white, but still, Puerto Rico, but I decided that it wouldn't be right to get in on anything but my own merit."

"Gina," Felice said after a silence filled by a John Coltrane trumpet solo and Pam Robinson's laugh, "I think everyone is getting in on their own merit."

Paul and Charlotte looked at once exhausted and uncomfortable, precisely how Bird felt; they had all heard this shit with different tunes since sophomore year. Still, usually Felice managed to avoid it when Bird or Charlotte were around.

"Sure," Gina said, smiling at them. "Of course you guys are. You're so smart and talented and, like, pillars of the school. But, come on, Marella's another story. If she was white, she'd be off to UDC."

Paul and Felice laughed. Charlotte wound another braid. Bird realized that she was about to throw her Diet Coke in Gina's face.

"I'll be back," Bird said, and jerked her hand from Paul's grip. Had she seen Coffee standing by the French doors? She pushed through the crowd, heart jumping when she saw a tall man from behind, but he turned out to be Trevor's father. Coffee wasn't upstairs.

The invitations to this party had been limited and coveted, but only by a certain type of student at the brother-sister prep schools of Bradley Hall and Devonshire Academy. Trevor Robinson was one of the richest boys in school, which was saying something in a place where the category of "parents" included the vice president and the secretary of state. His mother was a senator and his father worked on K Street. His mother was also Black, which put her on Bird's mother's radar as a potentially valuable ally in the ongoing campaign to turn her daughter into a model of successful Black womanhood. Pam Robinson was throwing this party ostensibly in honor of a new scholarship she was funding, which would give three "underprivileged" DC students four free years of the world-class education on offer at Bradley and Devonshire. Carol Bird had complained for a solid week about having to miss this party, but she and her husband had been called away to Georgia for work. For the space of a breath, Bird had thought that meant her deliverance as well. Attending this party would make all her mother's plans for Bird's summer as inevitable as a hole in the ground. How could she possibly refuse that prestigious K Street internship, facilitated by Pam Robinson and her husband, in favor of some cashier job at a gift shop on U Street? Never mind that when she walked past Cici's Handmade on her way to the Metro, Cici always waved at her from the register. Never mind that the smell of their handmade shea butter cream and incense always made her smile. Two days ago, Coffee had found her crying about it in the rose garden. It was the first time their acquaintance had crossed that particular threshold, but it happened easily, naturally. He put his arm around her shoulders; she wiped her nose on her jeans. *Just don't go*, he told her. *Stay home, and tell her you forgot. How much longer can you do this to yourself, Bird?* She knew exactly what he meant. And she had promised him. But then Paul had called her this morning, so sure of her support. Her mother had called this afternoon, and between the fire on one side and the hot iron on the other, she had protected herself the only way she knew how. She went along.

She hadn't known that Coffee would be here too.

She found Coffee in the basement. Hiding from the crowd or waiting for her — she didn't know, but the game required that she didn't guess. He lifted his face from powdered remains on the glass coffee table and wiped his nose.

"That's some excellent company you keep, Bird. What was it you were all laughing about? Marella screwing the freshman class? And here I believed you when you said you didn't want to come to this party. But I'm sure the homophobia adds spice to your friendships."

Bird shivered. So she *had* seen him upstairs. She felt a profound moment of regret for not having thrown her Coke in Gina's face, never mind the consequences. His withering smile, his condescension, they made her run hot and cold with shame and anger.

"They're not that bad," she said, though she knew they were.

"You honestly think that?" He shook his head. "No wonder you came here. So what do you think," he said, "are we all dead by Thanksgiving or Christmas?"

He tapped his left foot nervously against the wrought-iron table leg and flipped the snuff spoon between his fingers, so fast it looked like a magic trick. Her heart beat very fast, like she'd actually snorted his powder, but she knew that was just Coffee. They had met at another prep school party more than a year ago, and whenever she saw him she felt the echo of that first galvanic shock.

He snapped his fingers and tossed the silver spoon to his other hand. His eyes were a little green and a little yellow, and right now they made him look alien. They narrowed like darts, and they drew blood when they landed true.

"Well? Head up, Bird, or do you care about anything besides getting into Brown?"

"Stanford," she corrected automatically.

He laughed — she hated that laugh, short and brittle. It made her feel as if she'd been strafed with bird shot. Her breath rattled out of her.

"What, you mean the terror flu?"

"It's not just a flu, Bird," he said, making a stupid pun of her last name. Only he ever used it — everyone else called her Emily.

"Then what is it, genius?"

She walked over the plush carpet, so she felt the slight advantage of looking down on Coffee's swamp-colored eyes and dirty-blond hair, which grew in curls thick and discrete, like fat worms against his scalp.

"A pandemic," he said quietly. "The CDC called it an hour ago. And California's ground zero. You sure you'll have a school to get into this spring?"

He let her tower above him, but she felt awkward in her heels and short skirt, and so she knelt.

"Don't be melodramatic," she said, even though upstairs Pam Robinson and the other politicians were talking about quarantines and travel restrictions. "It isn't that bad."

"Five to ten percent death rate," Coffee said, punctuating each word with a swipe of his snuff spoon, like a junkie conductor. Not that Coffee was a junkie. He was something more complicated. "We're talking Spanish flu bad. SARS bad." He paused and let the spoon fall to the glass tabletop with a clatter. Bird wondered what Trevor would think if he came down just then — but he must have been the one who invited Coffee in the first place. Boys like him sometimes liked playing sides like that: CIA contractor upstairs, prep school dealer in the basement. Martinis and coke lines, shaking hands and smiling politely.

"Start a war bad," Coffee said quietly, and leaned a little closer to her. She sucked in a breath. "You think so?"

"Suits upstairs say the drones are already flying over Caracas."

"Caracas? Already? But isn't Venezuela still denying that they hired those FARC generals?"

"And FARC claims they haven't even laid eyes on those guys for years. But the drug lords say Venezuela paid them and gave them the flu, and of course that means we're safe to ignore the mountain of evidence that even when Chávez was alive Venezuela barely spoke to the FARC."

FARC, the *Fuerzas Armadas Revolucionarias de Colombia* (Revolutionary Armed Forces of Colombia), had been staging an armed rebellion against the Colombian government for decades. They were notorious for brutal kidnappings and world-scale cocaine operations, and speculation had bubbled for decades in the US press about their ties to Venezuela's socialist government.

Bird chewed her lip. "Venezuela's been supporting terrorists for years. Colombia says they've been harboring them in training camps. Maybe there's special intelligence, like in Afghanistan. . . ."

"And bombing some poor city to rubble is really going to save us? Come on, don't you ever think about the opinions you regurgitate?"

She glared at him, though sometimes she thought half the reason she talked to Coffee was because he would call her out. The way he said it, more wearied than angry, somehow made it better.

"You're the next Thomas Paine, yeah? Where are your original opinions?"

"I didn't say they were original. But at least I think about them."

"How do you know I don't?

Coffee smiled, close-lipped. He gave her one of those long looks, the ones that made her wonder why the hell she'd ever liked Paul, even though she knew that her life would be over if she dated someone like Coffee. It made her feel like she wouldn't care.

"Because you're smart, Bird. If you thought about it, you wouldn't believe it. And you *know that*, somewhere deep inside, and so you make sure you never really examine what other people say. Because then you wouldn't be the perfect Devonshire Academy girl, and you might do something that disrupts your parents' government careers, and you might realize you won't actually like the life you're headed into like it's a goddamn firing squad, and then, Bird, where will you be?"

"Back in Northeast, living with Nicky."

It took her breath away, the things she would say just to see his reaction. Thoughts she'd never told anyone, thoughts she never even knew she had, laid out like his little blue pills on a designer coffee table. And that, she knew, was the real reason why she talked to him. Every semi-accidental encounter at a party or after class or in the rose garden — all so that she could feel the profound relief of his presence. Coffee was the only person she had ever met who seemed to like who Bird really was, beneath all the layers of expectation and achievement and failure. Even if Bird had told Charlotte and Felice about her uncle, they wouldn't have understood. *That* was Coffee's magic — despite being prickly and judgmental and occasionally insufferable, he understood. He was the one person who didn't need her lies.

Coffee leaned back. Bird was aware of an uncomfortable, unprece-dented silence between them. As though her confession had stopped the world. Then she understood: For once, Coffee had gone motion-less, his habitual jitters stilled.

"Why is it you don't try that more often?" he said softly.

"Try what?"

"Honesty."

She shrugged. *I try with you*, she could have said. She loved Nicky, she admitted that in dark nights of furiously planning the exact steps of her future — Stanford, Harvard Law, K Street. All of it to avoid turning out just like her favorite uncle. All of it to avoid seeing disgust smother the reserved pride in her mother's eyes.

"I take it Nicky is your deadbeat uncle?"

"He's not —" She shook her head, the turn of the conversation so close to strained confrontations with her mother that she felt nau-seous. It was her particular hell, always having to defend and love the person she'd give anything in the world not to be. "Nicky is a good guy. He's just a poor, unambitious loser."

"Like me?"

She stared at him. Something tapped an irregular tattoo on the glass, and when she looked down she realized it was her own hand, her own ring from her debutante ball a year ago.

"You're not poor," she said.

He flashed his teeth, though she wasn't sure she would call it a smile. "Two out of three," he said. "No wonder you like me so much."

She didn't tell him that she knew Nicky had dealt on and off for years. Never got caught at it, thank God. Coffee was a diplomat's son at a prep school with the vice president's kids — the worst that could happen to him was probably getting deported back to Brazil. But a Black dude in Northeast selling dime bags of coke on the street cor-ner? She wouldn't see him for years.

Maybe Coffee had first intrigued her because of how he seemed like Nicky's photographic negative. But that wasn't why she knelt on the shag rug and grit her teeth against a shiver more violent than a chill. That wasn't why she could tell him things she would never breathe to anyone else.

That wasn't why she wanted to scream when Paul's voice hit her broadside from the stairs.

"Emily," he said, "why don't you come up? There's someone I want you to meet. Oh. Hi, Alonso."

Paul insisted on calling Coffee by his real name. It was one of Paul's things — he didn't believe in nicknames. He found it faintly offensive that Coffee called her Bird. She savored her secret like hard candy: She liked it better.

"Olá, Paulo," Coffee said, raising his right eyebrow so gently only Bird would notice it. She laughed once, like a yelp.

Paul had generous lips, which now drew back in clear disapproval. "Seriously, Emily, everyone is upstairs. The Robinsons were nice enough to invite us, the least you could do is show your face."

Between the two, Paul easily won the ribbon for best-looking. Not that Coffee didn't have a certain appeal — she had admired the compact strength of his wired frame more often than she would admit to anyone, even him. But Paul had the broad chest, the kissable lips, the chiseled jaw, and the killer smile. He was light-skinned, which her mother approved of, though she would never say so. When he laughed, she wanted to laugh with him. When Coffee laughed, she wanted to hit him. Paul would never think of neurotic, schizo, drug-dealing Coffee as competition.

He wasn't, of course. Coffee didn't compete. Though lately she had begun to feel a tension in his presence, along with the relief. She thought of him when he wasn't around; she noticed the way he looked at her; she refused, categorically, to consider what that might mean.

Paul helped her up. "Remember that security firm I was telling you about?" he said, lowering his voice. "One of the guys up there practically promised me a paid internship this summer. I know I said I wanted the CIA, but I've been thinking the private sector is really where the action is."

Bird's stomach lurched for no good reason, except that the hand Paul kept on the small of her back felt so proprietary and demanding. Like she had no choice but to follow him to the stairs and make nice with the people the Robinsons had invited to get their son's friends internships and job offers.

Coffee stood abruptly and fished a tin of rolling tobacco from his vest pocket.

"Hey, Alonso," Paul said, pausing on the steps. "Friendly advice, there's someone who works for the DEA upstairs. I'd be careful."

Coffee's honey eyebrows drew together in a scowl that looked almost dangerous. "Nicotine is a fully legalized narcotic, Paulo," he said — the last, mocking syllable almost swallowed.

Bird knew when Paul was pissed, but unlike Coffee he considered it a sign of weakness to express it. He smiled. "Shit will kill you too, *Alonso*. Have fun."

She had one last glance at him before Paul propelled her the rest of the way up the stairs. Coffee stared at the space where she had knelt a minute before, the tremor of his hands spilling tobacco onto the rug like pollen.

"Roosevelt's on the porch," Paul said. "Here, do you want a drink?"

"Trevor's parents are letting us?" she asked, surprised.

Paul laughed and grinned at her, revealing the perfect teeth his parents had purchased at great expense during middle school. "Like, a Coke. Don't get too excited."

"I'm cool," she said. "Who's Roosevelt?"

"Roosevelt David, recruiter with Lukas Group. They're private contractors with the CIA and Army Special Forces. Serious national security shit. They don't even have a website."

She forced down a smile. "So how do you know he isn't just a freak with a business card?"

"Senator Robinson invited him, remember? And anyway, this isn't the first time we've met. These guys are legit, believe me."

Bird didn't know what to make of this information. It implied that Paul had been less than truthful about his strategizing for the all-important post-graduation internship, and this disturbed her. For the past year, his approved ambitions for the future had protected her own half-formed hopes from her mother's scrutiny. They were the reason why she let him steer her around the party like she was more dirigible than girl. The reason why she hadn't broken up with him six months ago.

Some days she didn't understand how she put up with Paul — physical attraction can only count for so much. And then she contemplated the breakup conversation with her mother, who Bird swore loved Paul more than her own goddamn husband, and she panicked and recalibrated. Bird was an excellent recalibrator. Adjust a screw here, prop an unraveling lie there: Paul is a great guy, goal-oriented just like she is, and does she really want the hassle of a breakup now, when it will all happen so naturally once they go to college? She thumbed this rosary of self-justification until she felt calm and steady again. Until she felt safe in the conditional penumbra of her mother's approval. Forget dating Coffee. Forget it. He wouldn't want her anyway, as she damn well knew.

Paul, of course, hadn't noticed her abstraction. He stared through the glass doors that led to the back porch and frowned.

"Crap. That dealer of yours is out there. Smoking with Roosevelt. I hope he doesn't think he's getting anything out of him. That job is *mine*."

"I doubt he wants it, Paul," Bird said, rubbing his arm in a habitual, placating gesture. A boy who said things like *the principle agent of terror around the world is the US government* wouldn't exactly be eager to sign up as the CIA's newest waterboarding trainee.

Paul shook out his shoulders and smiled. "Of course not. You're right. That druggie asshole couldn't get within fifty yards of Langley."

He caressed the back of her neck without looking at her. She shivered. "I don't know what I'd do without you, Emily. Thanks."

Her wobbly smile felt genuine. Paul *was* a great guy. She didn't have to want him for the rest of her life to be happy with him now.

"I'm going out there," he said suddenly. "Coming?"

"You hate cigarette smoke," she said, but he was already propelling her forward, and her words seemed to get lost somewhere between the tilted edge of the Warhol and Cindy de la Vega's peroxide-blond split ends.

Coffee leaned against the marble banister, smoking down one of his hand-rolled cigarettes. He must have walked outside from the basement while Paul led her through the house. It didn't look like he was actually speaking to the man Paul had called Roosevelt, though they shared that quiet smokers' camaraderie. Roosevelt was younger than she'd have expected for a high-level government contractor. No more than thirty-five, though he could just be thirty and a smoker. He had brown hair and eyes of the exact same shade, and a muscular build that indicated some, but not too much, time in a gym. He looked unassuming, but something about the set of his mouth made her instantly wary.

"Oh, Paul. I didn't know you smoked."

"I don't," Paul said, smiling with a bit too much gum and spreading his hands in a you-got-me shrug that made him look like Alfred E. Neuman. "It was just a little stuffy in there. Emily wanted some fresh air."

Oh, did I? Bird thought, and caught Coffee's raised eyebrows. She tried to glare at him — she didn't want to screw this up for Paul — but it came out with a trailing edge of an embarrassed smile.

"So *this* is Emily," Roosevelt said, and flicked the stub of his cigarette over the railing. Bird thought of the Black or Hispanic gardener who would probably be picking this asshole's cigarette butts out of the azalea beds tomorrow morning and sighed.

"I've heard a lot about you," he said. "I worked with your parents a few years back. Your mother's a brilliant woman."

Bird struggled to keep her mouth curved in a polite smile, her eyes bright and interested, her hip jutted in a casual contrapposto. She did not so much as flick a glance at Coffee, and yet she felt him burning in her peripheral vision like the glowing ember of his half-smoked cigarette.

"She's a difficult act to follow sometimes," she said, and though she felt reasonably proud of her effort, she knew Coffee, at least, would be able to read her confusion. Maybe even see the deep pit of anger and hurt that gazed up at her when she contemplated her parents and their all-important jobs. She had no real idea what they did. When asked, she told teachers and friends that they worked in public health with various government agencies. But all she really knew was that her parents were scientists: her father's PhD in chemistry, her mother's in molecular biology. They did not encourage her curiosity, and abandoned her for weeks at a time on business they would never discuss. Still, over the years she had gathered her clues and hoarded them as carefully as a KGB spy. A careless letterhead, crumpled in the trash instead of destroyed in a shredder. A late-night phone call her father took in the backyard, when she was supposed to be visiting a friend. The remembered Wi-Fi signature of a private airport in Virginia, frequently used by Pentagon contractors.

That they would work with a man like Roosevelt confirmed all of her worst suspicions. She felt queasy and smiled to cover it.

"Emily! You never told me your parents were in . . ." Paul trailed off, suddenly unable to describe what precise field Roosevelt might represent.

"You work for Synergy Labs?" Bird said, each syllable hanging heavy from her lips.

Coffee's cigarette tumbled to the ground. He stubbed it with his heel and then retrieved the remains with shaky fingers, white with cold. Did he *know* something about that place, or was he just jumpy from whatever he had snorted? Roosevelt's lips tipped upward. He reached inside his coat pocket. For a hard second she was sure he was going to pull out a gun. But like a magician's trick, the danger she sensed in his posture transformed into something utterly pedestrian: a business card in sharp blue and red, printed on heavy stock.

Roosevelt David
Director, Analysis and Recruitment
Lukas Group

"Not Synergy Labs, no," he said. "I'm not sure where you would have heard that name, Emily."

She took the card with a hand she forced to be steady, and shrugged. She had found the name on ripped stationery one afternoon years ago while rummaging through the trash. She'd Googled it exhaustively, but hadn't found anything more than a couple of rumors on anarchist message boards — the kind frequented by people who thought rockets had hit the Pentagon on 9/11.

"My parents don't talk about work much," she said. "But I overheard stuff a bit when I was younger." She didn't know why she added that last qualifier — except that Roosevelt's blandly interested smile intimidated her with logarithmically increasing intensity. She began to wonder if there was more to this meeting than just Paul wanting a killer internship. Had Roosevelt used Paul to get to her?

But that was nuts. No way anyone like Lukas Group or Synergy Labs, whoever they were, would care about Emily Bird. No matter where her parents worked.

Her self-deprecation seemed to have dispelled some of his interest. He shifted his attention from Bird to Paul. "It's understandable," he said. "You can never be too careful in matters of national security. I think you can appreciate that, right, Paul?"

As Paul rushed to reassure anyone listening how highly he valued discretion and the value of knowledge to protect our country, especially given the new threats of bioterror, blah blah, Coffee flicked his wrist in the direction of the house. Without another word, he walked down the porch steps and went through the sliding glass doors to the basement, where she could see a dozen or so fellow students had retreated, driven back at last by the drunken, power-hungry socializing of the adults above.

Bird waited through a full minute of Paul's monologue — she would have to warn him later not to confuse desperation with enthusiasm — and then excused herself.

"I'm a little chilly, but it was great to meet you, Roosevelt. I'll let my mother know I ran into you when she gets back from her trip."

For some reason, Roosevelt laughed. "You do that, Emily Bird," he said.

Cindy de la Vega and her Gonzaga boyfriend had trapped Coffee between a Chinese vase and the eighty-inch flat-screen television tuned to *South Park*. Cindy was telling him how much she needed Adderall to help her study for *four fucking APs* in the spring. The Gonzaga boyfriend grimaced and rubbed sweet circles on her back, but Bird had heard that whatever-his-name was getting recruited by Cornell to play football. Officially, of course, Cornell was interested in his well-rounded academic profile, but everyone knew what it meant when certain admissions officials dropped by a game. Only people like Gina distinguished between Harvard-Princeton-Yale and the other Ivies, so he was unlikely to be too concerned about AP cramming.

"I understand that, Cindy, I do, but I don't have much on me."

Gonzaga boyfriend had never seemed very bright. He had a nice body, but his looks weren't much: His teeth could have used braces and a spray of acne scars marked his high cheekbones. Nothing compared to Paul, Bird knew that, and yet that unself-conscious, adoring smile he gave Cindy made jealousy burn with the endless heat of napalm fire in her gut. Everyone told Bird she was lucky to have Paul, but she knew she was just a coward. *Cindy* was lucky.

Gonzaga boyfriend pulled his wallet from his back pocket and handed Coffee a hundred-dollar bill.

"She'll take what you have. And when you get more, let me know?"

Coffee eyed the bill a second longer than felt comfortable, shrugged, and took it. He pulled out two sandwich bags, one with pills.

"Eight Adderall," he said. "And this is Hindu Kush."

"Hindu what?" Cindy said, grabbing the pills like they were the last of the Halloween candy.

"Weed, babe," Gonzaga boyfriend said, and put the second bag in his pocket. Bird hoped that Cornell didn't drug-test their football players.

"Now," Coffee said, with diction just precise enough to take a mocking edge, "if you'll excuse me —"

He caught Bird's eye, and they stared at each other for a moment that made her feel tumbled and stoned.

"Wait," Cindy said. "Are you sure you don't have something else?"

"Not unless you want some coke," said Coffee baldly.

But Cindy just shook her head and leaned closer. "No, I mean your own stuff. I hear you make shit way better than Adderall in your basement."

Bird had heard this too, not as though she'd ever seen any evidence for it at these parties. But a month ago she'd overheard Mrs. Cunningham, their AP Chemistry teacher, saying that she thought "the Oliveira boy" was an actual genius and knew more about organic chemistry than your average first-year grad student.

"Not for sale," said this purported genius. And then, "Cindy, keep those safe, all right? People are already talking like every Latino in the US is a druggie terrorist-in-waiting."

"I don't see what those Colombian assholes have to do with us."

"Neither do I. The Republican party has other ideas, though."

Cindy laughed like he'd made a joke. She let her boyfriend pull her away for a solid make-out session on the couch. They weren't alone —

two students Bird vaguely recognized were getting into it against the wall behind them.

"If it's going to turn into that kind of party," Bird said, knowing without looking that Coffee had approached her, "I hope Trevor keeps his parents from the basement."

"Trevor has plenty of experience keeping his parents from the basement," Coffee said somewhat cryptically. She turned to him. He smelled like shag tobacco and ironing starch and vulcanized rubber and a little sweat. She hated his cigarettes, but she loved the way he smelled with the mindless passion of an insect hunting its mate. This was one of the things she would never tell him.

"Listen," Coffee said, "I think you need to stay away from that guy."

She knew who he meant. "Why?" Though maybe she already knew, maybe she already agreed, thinking of Roosevelt and his strange laugh and disturbing insinuations.

"He's an asshole." With his accent, it sounded more like "arsehole."

"You think everyone's an asshole."

"Okay, a dangerous asshole. Synergy Labs is nothing you want to mess around with."

He spoke very quietly. No one was paying them any attention. And still, Bird felt for a moment like she had stood up too quickly and the room glowed white and hazy around her. "You *know* what they are?"

Coffee was very tall. He hunched over and pinned her with his eyes. "Everything your parents do is classified, Bird. Top secret. Did you see Roosevelt when you mentioned the name? He nearly shat himself."

Bird hadn't noticed much at all, but she was willing to concede that a dealer might be better at gauging reactions to illicit information. "But what is it? If it's so classified, how do you know anything?"

"I don't. But sometimes things leak. There's other sites like WikiLeaks now, though they never last long. Cyber attacks, probably by the government. But if you're paying attention . . . so I was paying attention. I saw the name crop up in a few places. They're involved in national security, mostly bioterrorism. They're private, but work with the CIA. They . . ."

She didn't know that she'd ever seen Coffee swallow his words before. He was more the type to deploy them like depth charges. His right hand drummed the wall, out of rhythm with his tapping foot. He looked jumpy enough to clear his skin.

"What? What is it?" *Who are my parents, really?* Bioterrorism sounded heavy. It sounded like hazmat suits and contamination procedures and deadly viruses that caused zombie plagues.

"They might be involved with the new flu."

"Involved?"

His breath stuttered like a machine gun in his chest. "No one believes any of those terrorist groups could have done this on their own. They had help."

"Yeah, and the secretary of state said that the help came from Iran."

"You really think they have that kind of expertise in biological warfare?"

Her eyes snapped open. She hadn't even realized she had closed them. She was angry enough to spit. "Oh, you almost had me, you know that? You're telling me a CIA contractor, working for the government of the US-of-A, helped terrorists deliver a virus that's *killed fifty thousand people*? Really? What else? Roosevelt personally sent the rockets into the Twin Towers?"

Coffee's fists clenched and unclenched. He looked away from her. Though his voice was just as low as before, it trembled and cracked with strain.

"I don't believe that shit about 9/11, Bird, but please tell me you're not such a conservative, conformist, privileged US —"

"Oh, *hells* no. Some preppy Bradley boy telling *me* about privilege? Dude, you're bathing in it."

He ran a trembling hand across his forehead. It came away slick with sweat. Some of Bird's anger twisted, and turned to fear. "Bad choice of words," he said. "But there's good reason to believe that someone other than terrorists are involved in this flu."

"The president —"

He rolled his eyes and cut the edge of his hand through the air beside her. "Screw the president," he said, and for a moment Bird nearly crumbled in laughter at the thought of anyone saying something like that in a place like this. Only Coffee. "He says the evidence is classified. His officials leak unsupported accusations in the press and then the administration uses the leaks as evidence for their war. It's bullshit, Bird. We have no idea how this happened. Hell, maybe it's natural. Mother Nature screwing us over."

"But you don't think so. You think the government, *my parents*, helped spread this flu that's killing its own citizens. That's mind-control drugs in the water nuts, Coffee. Serious tinfoil hat time."

She knew she was telling the truth, and yet the bleakness of his expression as he regarded her made her shift uncomfortably. She had upset him, so effectively penetrated his wall of disaffected cool that she felt exhilarated and humbled by it. But until now she hadn't realized how thoroughly disconnected Coffee was. She felt untethered, almost sick with the knowledge of him.

"Ever heard of the Tuskegee syphilis experiments, Bird?"

"You mean that case from the seventies? Some kind of medical discrimination against Black people?"

"The government of the US-of-A watched four hundred Black men die slowly of syphilis for decades after they'd developed a treatment. For an experiment. History, no tinfoil hats required. Look it up if you don't believe me."

She remembered the offhand mention of the case in her history textbook. She didn't say, *But that was probably a long time ago*, because she knew better. The government continued its excellent record in selling Black folk down the river, as her grandfather would have said.

But Coffee wasn't done. "And for good measure, the US also sent some infected prostitutes into a Guatemalan prison to give syphilis to around a thousand inmates so they could study them for a couple more years."

She shook her head, as if that would make the things he was telling her less believable, more comprehensible. But still — "Fifty *thousand*, Coffee."

His honey eyebrows drew together sharply, like he'd been burned. "Two hundred fifty thousand. At least. You don't *have* to forget the rest of the world, you know. It's not a test of US citizenship."

Her cheeks surged with warmth, and he was close enough to see her blush. She couldn't deal with this. She couldn't stand to be around Coffee and his conspiracy theories for another second.

"Do you have a point? Because otherwise I should find Paul."

"My *point* is that Roosevelt is dangerous. He moves like he's packing, though he isn't, which should tell you something. He tells you about your parents like he knows all about you, and you've obviously never met the guy before. You can argue with me all you want about Synergy Labs, but you said that name like you *knew* it was bad news and wanted to know what it meant to someone else. Well, here's what it means: You just told Roosevelt that you knew something that you shouldn't. So I strongly suggest you stay away from him."

Bird's feet ached in her stupid heels, but it felt too vulnerable to take them off here. Coffee stared at her with an air-sucking, chest-heaving intensity. She looked away. "He's giving Paul an internship."

"So?"

"Paul *is* my boyfriend."

He flicked his fingers against his palm. "The obvious and unavoidable. But I understand. How could you have resisted his scintillating wit, his insightful political observations, his clear respect for your intellect? Or, wait, did I mean his finely toned abs? I get confused sometimes."

Bird took off her shoes in two jerky, furious movements and waved one of the stiletto heels in front of Coffee's nose.

"*You* are no prince either. You're a crazy, lazy, nicotine- and pot- and

God-knows-what-else-addicted freak. You're a *diplomat's son,* for God's sake, you could do anything you wanted, but you're just a dealer. And a conspiracy nut."

He knocked her shoe away. It smacked against the wall beside them, loud enough to make a few of their classmates stare. She had to stop this. This would be all over Facebook in a second. With video, if she wasn't careful.

"So he's the suck-up and I'm the druggie. But you, Emily Bird. You're the worst of us all."

He looked so sad as he said it, though his tone was angry enough. She had every intention of turning away, but the open end of that sentence called for completion, for the terrible verdict to be elucidated and explained. *Is this what Coffee thinks of me?*

"The worst?"

He closed his eyes, and did not open them even when he started to speak. "You're an iconoclast whose highest aspiration is K Street. You're a Black DC girl determined to run away to a California suburb with barely any Black people. You have a heart, Bird, but you only use your head. You try as hard as you can to be conventional and unoriginal and unthreatening, but somehow you always fail. Just a little bit. *Because you know better.*"

She picked up the shoe with one trembling hand and wiped her eyes with the other.

"Fuck you, Coffee," she said, feeling like she was cracking in half, riven by a fissure spreading from somewhere north of her belly button. "I never want to see you again."

He nodded, as though to acknowledge the fairness of this, but then she saw that his own eyes were too bright and he had sagged against the wall. She took some pleasure in this, but not much. She must have imagined whatever she felt with him.

Or perhaps he was just the first person who cared enough to see her clearly.

22

She climbed the steps in her stockings. Nearly at the door, his voice stopped her.

"Bird."

He sounded hoarse, desperate. She didn't turn around. He pressed something into her palm. A piece of paper with a phone number scrawled across in a nearly illegible hand.

"In case something happens. I've never . . . you're the most . . . sometimes it kills me, what you could be."

"If you don't like me for what I *am*, what good is it?"

He fell silent. She balled the paper into her fist, shoved it in her pocket, and pasted a pleasant smile on her face. Then she went to find Paul.

This part is hazy, broken, half-intelligible. Strange, with the rest of the party indelibly burned into her memory — *Somehow you always fail. Just a little bit. Because you know better* — that the end would fuzz out like a radio station out of range. Bird lies in the dark, alone in a hospital, and forces the pieces into something like a shape —

Her saying, "I want to go home, Paul," while keeping her voice pleasant with an effort that felt like lifting a car.

Paul giving her a panicked shake of his head and hurrying off to confer with Roosevelt. Her feeling Coffee's number in her pocket, nearly throwing it away, and finally smoothing it out and tucking it back. What if something did happen? Who else would believe her?

Trevor talked to her then, she thinks, something about the track team, which they did together in the spring, but she can't remember more than that. Then a disjointed wash of noise and color and shape: Pam Robinson standing by the door to thank people for coming, Paul waving her over to the leftovers on the dessert table (painted marzipan and chocolate ganache, and the sweet, fizzy smell of spilled champagne), Roosevelt making some comment . . . some comment . . .

Her head throbs.

"Emily," he said. "Emily, we need to talk, I think, but somewhere more private. Paul, could you drive . . ."

And then she's in the car. Paul is strapping her in, she doesn't understand why.

"She's drunk?" someone said — not then, in the car, but earlier. Outside. Her mouth tastes of peach schnapps and vomit. The wind kicks up clouds of orange and red and brown leaves. She raises her hands unsteadily to catch them. She recognizes the voice — Trevor, sounding worried and bemused. Trevor, whom she used to crush on like anything back in ninth grade, before Paul. Trevor, who has never seemed very interested in Devonshire girls.

Paul's arms around her. She squirms to get free, but he holds her close. "Had a bit too much, I guess," he says. "I'll get her home."

Paul half carries her to the car. The Robinsons' house looms over his shoulder, pale bricks and amber wood and glowing glass, a tasteful fortress nestled in the enclave of Rock Creek Park.

"Paul," she says. "Paul, Paul, Paul!" Each time more insistent. He fastens the seat belt. He doesn't look at her.

"Emily, honey," he says to the dashboard. "Emily, we're just going to talk to him for a few minutes. I don't . . . you don't have to worry. I'll take care of you."

I should have broken up with you, she thinks, then and now, a clear peal of regret. She can hardly feel her limbs. She is sinking, melting into the leather interior of Paul's new Land Rover.

Then the car starting, then the house receding, then her heart in her throat as a shape falls down the driveway, a boy in an uncoordinated, headlong, screaming fit of a run. She can't hear him. She feels the peach in her throat again, pushed up by the sudden pressure of her desire, her happiness, her sharp and fractured panic. He will not make it. He can't possibly. But he still tries.

Paul curses. "Not *that* asshole! Emily, what did you tell him?"

He guns the car and takes the driveway corner on two wheels. Bird knocks her head, hard, into the window. When she can lift her head again, there's blood on her face and Coffee is gone, gone, gone.

Beyoncé starts to sing, and Bird realizes it's Paul's phone. He stares at the caller ID. Unavailable, it says, which means Roosevelt.

She's going to be sick again. She's going to pass out. She has to say this first. It is important, more important than anything that she say this first.

Clearly, articulately, as though she isn't holding her head together with her fingers, she says, "Tell him what? He's just a freak with a thing for me, Paul."

And then Paul takes the call, and she closes her eyes and imagines Coffee's footsteps, unsteady and quick, following her into darkness.

Subject:

Bird, née Emily, seventeen years old.

Appearance:

Dark brown skin, wide nose, medium lips. Her hair is shoulder-length and brittle from years of drug-store relaxers. There's a revolution at the roots, though, where it grows thick and nappy. Small breasts, small hips, big thighs. An athletic build, if I were being generous. Fairly tall at five foot nine, though far from the tallest girl in her class. Still a head shorter than Coffee.

Disposition:

Narrowly ambitious. In possession of a serious Mommy complex. Probably a Daddy complex too, but Mommy takes enough energy as it is. Secretly longs to own her own shop in a friendly, not-too-gentrified DC neighborhood and feel embedded in her community in the sort of small, holistic way her mother would never understand. So she compromises by aiming for the farthest mother-approved school she can find: Stanford. In her snarly subconscious, Bird understands that this is a final gambit, a desperation tactic designed to prevent her outright suffocation, her mother's ambiguously intentioned asphyxiation of her daughter's spirit.

In her pocked and abraded conscious, she thinks this is because she wants to attend a top-tier university in a well-cultivated suburban setting.

In the liminal space between the two, she imagines the shapes her shop might take: bookstore, lending library, soul food restaurant, natural hair salon. Hell, a few months after meeting Coffee, it occurred to her she could even run a head shop. The thought of what her mother would say about that sent the notion fleeing deep into her overstuffed subconscious, but it hasn't left her.

Verdict:

Capable of an astonishing degree of self-deceit. Prior to the disaster of the Robinsons' party, would have described herself as "happy" with her home and school life. Prior to the revelation of that last ride in his car, would have indicated she was "mostly satisfied" with her relationship with Paul.

How stupid can a girl get? She's in love and she doesn't even know it. You're in deep, now, Bird. Wake up!

[nicotine]

$C_{10}H_{14}N_2$

A nurse comes in an hour after dark. She's an older Black woman with short, natural hair and purple scrubs. Her eyes seem tired but kind above a baby-blue surgical mask.

"You're awake, hon?" she says, startled, when she leans over the bed to check Bird's IV.

Bird swallows, but it doesn't give her much moisture. "What happened?" Her voice is a hoarse whisper. The nurse looks worried, though it's hard to tell from just her eyes.

"You hit your head pretty hard. And you took some stuff you shouldn't have. You've been out of it for eight days."

Eight days. The tank in the street, the nurse's surgical mask, the hushed silence of the hallways all seem to indicate that something has happened. Something more than the strangeness with Roosevelt and Paul and Coffee — her chest tightens in sudden panic. Something beeps. The nurse straightens.

"Take it easy, okay? Deep breaths. I'll get you some water. There's someone waiting for you. I'm sure he'll explain everything."

"My parents?" she asks. Though she knows, somehow, that the answer is no. Whatever that tank means, her mother and father will be at the heart of it. Not at home. Not caring about her. "Uncle Nicky?" she asks, desperate and hopeful.

"Honey, I'll give your uncle a call and let him know you're awake. But there's an . . . official. He said to make sure he talked to you as soon as you woke up. It's about the — well, you know, why don't I just get you that water."

She hurries out, but flips the light on her way. Bird squints and pushes herself up against the pillows. The room has an empty bed on the other side. The sight of its clean-tucked white sheets fills her with disquiet. She wishes she weren't alone. Alone means vulnerable. As if she weren't vulnerable enough with stitches in her head and a needle in her arm.

She forces herself to turn back to the side table. Behind the withered lilies is a small teddy bear holding a box of dollar-store chocolates. There's a card attached to a cord around its neck. The prefab message reads: *Get Beary Better Soon!* and beneath it, in her uncle's careful, blocky hand: *I luv you like crazy, Em!* She bites her cheek and opens the box. One of the chocolates is missing — her cousin Aaron probably got into them. Or maybe Nicky did.

"You're so damn tacky," she says, smiling at the bear. It has a faint musk of bleach and hazardous chemicals from some unregulated factory. She wonders if she should throw out the chocolates before Nicky gets here. He didn't grow up in a world where boxed chocolates had distinctions like "decent" and "complete shit." He buys Aaron and Monique all their toys at the dollar store, that land of mysterious provenance and distinct olfactory delights. And yet, she can recall her excitement at seeing the yellow glow of Lin's Everything Five Dollars spilling across the sidewalk on Benning Road late at night. When she was five, a visit with Uncle Nicky was an adventure better than going through a looking glass, an entire world called Northeast, with narrow houses and laughing people on doorsteps and strange men who nodded hello at Nicky as he herded her along the sidewalk. He would take Monique and Bird to the dollar store as a treat some summer nights, after getting three-colored popsicles from the off-brand ice cream truck. Once, she remembered insisting on buying a pink colander for a whole three fifty. Monique had gotten a plunger, and they played knights and armor while running through the heavy spray of a jacked hydrant. Nothing is like DC in the summer. The rich smell of humidity and baking asphalt, the sharp-sweet of cut grass and the sulfurous fumes of spent fireworks, all swept away in the ferocity of an evening storm that pounds the city, rich and poor, white and Black, Northwest and Northeast, with its harsh equality.

Bird's mom helped Monique get into college, a small place in New York, but Bird can't help but think that her cousin feels lost up there, with the wrong accent and the wrong skin color and the wrong high school. Bird should do fine at Stanford, God knows her mom and dad made sure she could play in the white sandbox as well as anyone, but sometimes she feels as lost at school now as Monique does when they talk on the phone.

A Black DC girl determined to run away to a California suburb with barely any Black people.

It aches to hear his voice, even in her head. She shivers and grabs the card for the flowers, reads the note in one quick rip of the Band-Aid.

For my Beautiful Girl. Get better soon, Emily. — Paul

She presses the back of her fist to her mouth to hold back a cry. He was taking her somewhere. Something to do with Roosevelt, but then she hit her head. And after . . . what happened after?

Her memory feels like a bruise, painful to the lightest touch. *Nothing, nothing, nothing. Keep yourself safe, Bird.*

Safe from what? Safe, how? Had she said that or had Coffee? But how could he have, running hopelessly down the driveway after Paul's car — too, too late?

The nurse comes back with a cup of water and a choked smile. "There's someone here to see you, honey, like I said. Now if you're too tired, just let me know —"

But before she can finish, Roosevelt comes through the open door. He's holding a box of artisanal chocolates and puts them on the bedside table with an apologetic smile. He's different than she remembers from the party — bags under his eyes a little more pronounced, his demeanor subtly more aggressive.

"This won't take very long, Cynthia," he says. "I'm sure Emily will be fine."

Bird feels as if she might faint when she looks at him, so she fixes her gaze firmly on the nurse and takes the cup. She drinks slowly, gathering her courage against the onslaught of formless dread.

"Will you stay?" she asks the nurse when the water is gone. She feels a little better, but not much.

The woman looks nervously between Roosevelt and Bird, but Roosevelt shakes his head in a firm negation.

"I'll be right outside, Emily," she says finally. "Just holler if you need anything."

"You've got nothing to be worried about," Roosevelt says, getting up to shut the door. The click resonates within her like a firecracker burst. "I just need to talk to you about a few things. A lot has happened since your accident. I wouldn't want you to get confused about anything. Especially with your parents . . ."

Her paper cup clatters to the floor, spilling its last few drops on the scuffed rose-colored linoleum. "What's happened to them?"

"They're safe," he says. "And doing important work. I can't tell you where, Emily, but I'm sure you're used to that." He pulls up a chair and straddles it backward, trying to look casual and reassuring. But something in his face makes her think he knows it isn't convincing. She dislikes Roosevelt, distrusts his expensive-casual clothes and carefully bland features. He's like the worst of the Devonshire girls, a garish shellac of approximated sincerity masking a face whose hints reveal only bare cruelty.

"Can I talk to them?" Conversations with her parents are always strained, especially over the phone, but she wants to make sure they're (she makes herself think the word) *alive*.

Roosevelt nods slowly, though his eyes say no. "We'll see. The phone lines have been pretty busy this last week, given, well, why don't I start at the beginning?"

The bite of her untrimmed nails against her palms feels like a kiss. She never knew fear could be like this, a gripping, needle-fingered horror that strangles even her thoughts. She never knew you could want to cry from it, or hide from it — as if she would flee her goddamn skin if she could. She understands with sudden clarity that bravery has nothing to do with the absence of fear, but the response to it. She could let Roosevelt terrify her into doing anything he wanted.

Or she could stare him in the eyes and bide her time. She'll get out of the hospital. She'll understand what's happened to her. She'll find ways to protect herself.

"Okay," she says, her voice like blowing leaves, "why don't you tell me."

Roosevelt adjusts his watch, pushing up his sleeve so she can see that it has a microphone attached. Someone is listening; he wants her to know.

I hate you, she thinks, and smiles, and feels a breath of calm.

"Well, Emily, the Venezuelan flu has gone critical. The president declared a national state of emergency the night of your accident, in fact. The DC metro area is under protective quarantine, essentially everything inside the Beltway. All suspected cases have been isolated, and no one else is allowed inside. If you want to leave, it's a one-way ticket. So far, we're safe. The news is not so good on the West Coast, I'm afraid to say. I heard you wanted to go to Stanford. I'm sorry."

Bird opens her mouth, then closes it. He would know about Stanford. He probably knows everything about her. He's trying to keep her off-balance.

"Naturally, there's a lot of security in the city right now. There's a curfew and restricted vehicle access and other precautions. But your uncle can tell you about all that. Now, Emily, I'm sure you're wondering why I'm really here. You're Carol Bird's daughter after all. This might come as a surprise, but I'm here to apologize. I'm afraid I'm partly responsible for your accident after the party. They tell me you were doing some drugs and drinking, which you probably regret right now. It impaired your judgment. You wanted to talk to me about your parents, and I agreed to do it in a private place, which I regret, in hindsight."

Drugs? Drinking? She remembers the regurgitated flavor of peach schnapps, but not drinking any. And the strongest stuff she's ever done is pot, and certainly none at the party. She wishes she could form a clearer memory of that last hour.

"Didn't Paul drive?" she says, her voice small and confused. Not on purpose, but she can see that Roosevelt appreciates any opportunity to display paternalistic sympathy.

His left eyebrow twitches and he pats her hand. "Ah, I see you remember that much. We had wondered. The kind of drug you took was probably a dissociative. They tend to make it difficult to retain memories, especially with your head trauma. But yes, Paul was driving. He says you started having a paranoid attack when someone started to chase you both down the driveway. You grabbed the wheel to get away, and nearly crashed the car." He pauses and leans the chair forward on two legs. "Do you remember anything else?" he asks, close enough that she can smell the coffee and menthol cigarettes on his breath.

His eyes are the dullest, flattest brown she's ever seen. Duller than mud, two discs punched from an old wood plank, so bland she almost thinks he wears contacts to make them that way. Beneath the mask his eyes must be cherry red or charcoal black. She focuses on the depilated remains of his receding hairline, a hint of something human and vulnerable, and thinks of what to say.

"What sort of drug?" she asks.

His lips tighten and then relax, like he might have caught and strangled a smile. "Well, I can't say we're so sure," he said. "You got away from Paul and only turned up the next afternoon. You don't remember any of this?" He shakes his head slowly. "Your blood tests were suggestive of a number of drugs, but we're just not sure. Personally, Emily, I think that you saw a very ugly side of a designer drug. And I think we both know the only person who could have synthesized it for you."

He means Coffee. He thinks Coffee gave her some of that stuff they say he cooks in his secret lab, and that it made her go nuts and crash the car and end up here. Only she doesn't even know if those drug-cooking rumors are true, let alone that he would give her some the night of the party. Let alone that she would take it.

But then she remembers the putty-softness of her muscles when Paul strapped her into the car. She'd hardly managed to turn her head to watch Coffee sprint down the driveway. She was on *something*. Paul told Trevor she was drunk, but being drunk had never felt like that before. Like her limbs were hardly attached to her body, and moving involved a complicated set of levers and pulleys only vaguely connected to bone and muscle. And if Coffee had let her try some of the stuff he refused to sell Cindy, and if she'd done too much or it had hit her too hard, and if she'd persuaded Paul to take her home or take her to Roosevelt, and if Coffee had known . . .

Why did he chase her? Why sprint after the car with that desperate, furious, agonized grimace?

Because he had done something he shouldn't have, and realized it too late?

Now, Roosevelt watches the confusion ripple over her face and lets his smile show through. "You're friends with Alonso, aren't you? Paul told me so. But Alonso certainly betrayed your friendship. I hope you can see that. If it weren't for him, you wouldn't be here. This may shock you, but my colleagues in the police department had to put out a warrant for his arrest, given events at the party."

"If you don't know what he gave me, how can it be illegal?" Maybe she shouldn't be defending Coffee at this point — she doesn't know what to believe — but annoying Roosevelt seems worth it.

"We have testimony from someone at the party."

She wonders who would have cut the deal. Cindy? Her Gonzaga boyfriend? Maybe even Trevor, trying to save himself once his parents got wind of the disaster?

"Why are you telling me this?" She wants Roosevelt away, so she can try to stitch together the bloody wound of her memory. She doesn't want to believe Roosevelt's story, but maybe Bradley Hall's most notorious druggie was never someone she should have trusted. She feels light-headed at the thought of her mother's reaction.

"Well, Emily," he says, letting the chair fall back on its legs with a heavy thump, "your friend Alonso is evading police custody. We strongly suspect that he will try to get in touch with you, and we'd like you to let us know the moment that he does. It's very important. Just so you know, for your mother's sake I have convinced my colleagues to overlook the . . . circumstances of your hospitalization, but if it seems like you won't cooperate with us, well, illegal drug consumption has its penalties."

He puts his business card, the one she remembers from the party, on top of Uncle Nicky's bear. She wonders, in deep panic, if this is some subtle signal, some hint that he knows about Nicky's occasional street-corner deals and will hurt him if she doesn't cooperate.

"You're not a cop," she says. She's never trusted cops. Some ignorances are just not available to a Black DC girl, no matter how assimilated.

"I can get in touch with the proper authorities. This case involves some sensitive issues. Alonso is affiliated with the Brazilian embassy after all. If you don't want this to go badly for him, I suggest you use that number."

Bird looks at the card, but can't bring herself to pick it up. Snitch on Coffee, whose designer drug might have almost killed her, or get indicted for possession? Not much of a choice, but she hates herself for making it. "Okay," she mumbles, unable to look anywhere but at her hands, ashy and stiff on the white hospital sheets.

Roosevelt stands up. His posture radiates satisfaction, but his mouth turns down in something approximating sympathy. "I should let you rest. I hope you take this incident to heart. I'm sure Paul would hate to see anything else happen to you, Bird."

He taps his wrist, where his sleeve covers the recorder, and then walks out of the room.

It takes her a full, paralyzed minute to realize that he called her Bird.

Her Uncle Nicky takes Bird home that night, though the doctor suggested she stay until morning. Her head is fine, the doctor said, no swelling on the brain, which was a worry when she didn't wake up at first. "Whatever you took, it was a doozy," she said, and Bird tongues the word "doozy" all the time Nicky fills out the forms and never once asks her the obvious. She loves and hates him for it. Her legs feel unsteady at first; she staggers when Aaron rushes her for one of his bear hugs. Aaron is a giant of an eleven-year-old, just like his daddy, but he hasn't realized it yet. She gives Aaron both boxes of chocolate, and he smiles at her and then frowns.

"You don't want it, Em?" he asks, and where Aaron got to be so considerate, she doesn't know. She hugs him, her left arm aching from the IV needle.

"I'm not hungry yet," she says. He attacks Russell Stover and Jacques Torres with equal dedication, and she smiles.

"Looks like we're done here, hon." Cynthia the nurse takes the clipboard full of discharge forms back from Nicky. "Let me get your things, and you can go."

Nicky looks at Bird and clears his throat. "I brought you some clothes. Thought you might want something more comfortable."

He would. Nicky wears what he always does: baggy jeans, a Hoyas jersey, and the same old black do-rag he's had since she was a kid. His shoes, on the other hand, are always bright and shining Nikes. His big concession at Monique's graduation was to take off the do-rag and cornrow his hair. Bird's mom complained for a solid hour in the car about appropriate behavior, and embarrassing "poor Monique." Bird had cringed in embarrassment herself to watch her uncle fumble uncertainly among the Jack and Jill parents at the reception afterward, but Monique hadn't seemed to mind at all. If anything, she seemed proud of her broke-ass, college dropout father.

But the clothes Nicky brought for her are fine, a pair of boot-leg jeans and a cable-knit sweater. They leave while she changes out of the faded flower-print hospital gown. The nurse gives her a bag, and then they're heading into the elevator and out into the parking garage. Bird feels like she's holding her lost memories in a plastic gift shop bag, and they might explode if she doesn't handle them very carefully. She can't bring herself to look inside.

She takes the front seat in Nicky's black Impala, at least twenty years old and looking like it, though he does his best to keep the monster running. Nicky brushes the crumbs and wrappers — one of which looks disturbingly like a Trojan — off the seat and onto the floor.

"Sorry about the mess," he says, like he always does. The car smells like hair oil and Circus Peanuts — Aaron's favorite. It smells like family and home, and though in his way Nicky scares her almost as badly as Roosevelt does, she relaxes into the worn leather seats and lets him drive.

It's Aaron who notices him — Aaron, with a smear of chocolate on his cheek and dirty fingers that smudge the glass when he points. "Hey, Daddy," he says. "That's the guy who wanted to know about Em."

Bird's head snaps up so quickly her stitches throb. At the edge of a crowd of people waiting for the bus, someone about Coffee's height scuffs his shoes on the pavement. His hoodie is a nondescript gray, pulled low over his forehead, but she swears it's his eyes that follow the Impala as Nicky pulls out of the parking lot.

"Quiet, Aaron," Nicky says, and stares straight ahead like someone's paying him to do it.

"But —"

"Aaron!"

Aaron scowls at his dad and takes a vindictive bite of a chocolate, pink ganache dribbling down his chin.

Even looking feels dangerous, but she can't help herself. If the feds are after him, what business does he have standing there? Can't he guess that they asked her to inform on him? She wants to tell him to get away, to protect himself from professional assholes like Roosevelt. But maybe she also wants to scream at him to tell her what the hell happened that night, what exactly he did to her. Instead, she puts her hand against the window. His lips curve in a bare, sad smile that she holds in her sight until a bus roars between them. Nicky shakes his head.

"Nicky," she says, "do you know anything about . . . did Coffee —"

"I don't know nothing, kid," he says. "Except when to keep my head down."

He waits until they're almost at his place to drop the news.

"Em, you won't like this, but your mom's house is boxed up. Quarantine. You can't go back there. I got what I could, that CIA dude who was at the hospital helped me, but you won't believe what it's like out here. Like a goddamn war zone, kid."

Nicky never worries about things like cursing in front of his kids. Bird's mom swears that "shit" was Aaron's third word. But actually her cousin is pretty good about keeping his language location-appropriate. Monique, on the other hand, used to love to curse in front of Bird's parents. Bird's father, when home, would just turn up the volume on the football game, filing down the sharp edges of family dynamics with smooth male voices discussing passing stats.

"Why's the house quarantined?" she asks. "Mom and Dad aren't sick, are they?"

"They're safe, wherever they are. I talked to Carol yesterday. She's cool. But that man at the hospital said someone in your maid service came down with it, so they boxed up the house. The whole thing's gotten pretty serious. There's quarantines all over the District."

Bird looks up at the steps and stoop of the house, covered in the same green Astroturf that has faded more each winter of her life. Grandma was always on Nicky to change it, and he always promised he'd get around to it, right until she went to the hospital. Bird hates the familiarity of that fake grass and the large brass numbers by the door; she hates how much it feels like home, despite her parents' house on an appropriately tree-lined, affluent street in Northwest.

Nicky helps her out of the car, and she shivers in her light coat while Aaron takes the stairs two at a time. Nicky lives in a squat row house on Twenty-first Street in the Kingman Park neighborhood, the same house he grew up in, the one his dad bought in 1945 for thirty thousand dollars. Today it'd be worth quite a bit more — farther down Benning Road, white families have been buying up houses in these old middle-class Black neighborhoods like overpriced, fixer-upper candy. Every time her mother or aunt comes back, they talk about how much the neighborhood has changed. But this street looks the same as it always has to Bird — until she notices the police tape on a house down the block.

"What happened to the Gibsons?" she asks. She and Monique would play with the Gibson kids in the fire hydrants of young summers. She remembers the oldest, Tyrone, got involved in some gang stuff and spent three years in juvie. Heroin possession, she heard. Coffee doesn't deal heroin — too dangerous, he says. But then, it turns out that even Adderall was dangerous enough.

"The youngest got it," Nicky says.

"Is she all right?" Bird can't remember the kid's name — a granddaughter, she thinks, because another one of those hydrant playmates had a kid when she was just fourteen.

Nicky purses his lips and looks up at the door, but Aaron's already inside. "No," Nicky says, quiet. "Won't even give them the body for the funeral. I haven't told Aaron yet, so —"

"It's okay," Bird cuts in, suddenly sick and light-headed. "I won't say anything. Jesus. How old was she? Six?"

"Five."

In the sickly glow of the streetlight, she looks down the deserted road and counts each stoop blocked off with yellow police tape and red stickers on the door: two, maybe three, if she squints into the dark at the other end of the block. Her home, her uncle's neighbors, her whole city, stricken by the flu they say came from narco-terrorists.

Bird shudders, and the headache stabs her again. She drags herself up the stairs and inside her grandparents' house. Uncle Nicky's house. Her house.

Bird takes Monique's room, which Bird's mom shared with Aunt Grace when they grew up here. Bird liked staying here overnight with Monique, but by herself she can't help imagining her mother at her age, staring up into the glowing city night through the grimy skylight and dreaming of the day when she escaped — to college, to a fancy Northwest address, to a Jack and Jill husband and a skyrocket career in national security. Bird knows even her mother probably hadn't figured everything out by seventeen, but she imagines it anyway: Carol Bird in miniature, the prototypical, soft-dough, wet-paint version of the brightly plasticated wonder woman she's known all her life. Young Carol swears on the stars to get out, to be the one who goes places, the one who rules the world of her rich classmates at School Without Walls. She will have a daughter who will go even further, even higher than she, and that will be her solace and joy at the end of a long life filled with the pleasures of a sharply imagined wealth.

Only, the daughter emerges wrong, resembling neither father nor mother but *uncle* — a nappy-headed, wide-eyed, crooked dart of fate. And though the daughter is neither as smart nor as pretty nor as ambitious as the mother, she tries her best every day to be someone her mother can stand to look in the eye across the breakfast table. To be someone her father can bestow a smile upon when she brings home a 2200 on her SATs. To be the girl who loves her uncle but will never, ever let herself be like him.

Never, ever, Bird says to herself, even though Nicky is glued to the television downstairs and Carol Bird is in some undisclosed location, saving the world. Bird's head hurts and so she fumbles through the bag for the prescription pain killers. She finds them wrapped in the black skirt she wore to the party. Bird pulls it out slowly, and lets it drop to the bed. Sweet alcohol and vomit perfumes the air for a moment. She grimaces and pushes the skirt from the bed and takes the pill.

She doesn't remember vomiting. If she doesn't remember that, what else could she have forgotten about that night? Maybe taking some of Coffee's drugs in a fit of reckless idiocy? *Just like your uncle?*

The Vicodin starts its work a few panicky minutes later, making her languorous and sleepy, dulling the pain in her head. Vicodin is an opiate, the sort of pill that Coffee sells, alongside perennials like Adderall and Oxy. She wonders how much he gets for it, and why he needs the money in the first place. She strips to her underwear and tosses it all near the gift shop bag. She sits on the edge of the bed, aching with exhaustion. But she doesn't turn out the light. She stares at the bag, fascinated and terrified of its contents. What else might she discover about that lost night? Emily Bird wants to go to sleep and forget about it. But she knows that Carol Bird would confront whatever frightens her without hesitation. She would pull taut any errant strands of her life and brush them down with good oil.

Bird gets on her knees and upends the bag onto the carpet. Out tumble her cell phone, her pink shirt, and her black bolero jacket. Her shoes are missing, she realizes, though she finds the stockings stuffed into the jacket pocket. They have a run as large as her hand on the left leg, and dried mud on the feet and knees. She's wondering why she kept them even as a small, crumpled paper falls from the tangled mess.

She picks it up.

Coffee's number. *In case something happens,* he said. Did he know? Had he already given her the drug without her knowledge, or was that later? Or maybe he has nothing at all to do with her fractured memory. Only, why is his number crumpled in with her stockings? She put it in the pocket of her skirt, she distinctly remembers, carefully smoothed out. Had she called him? Was *that* the reason why she caught him skulking outside the hospital? And what about the strange words beneath his number? She could have sworn they weren't there when he handed it to her.

She stares at the paper a moment longer, then shakes her head and puts it on the bedside table. She woke up in a hospital because of whatever happened that night, but even her most basic memories seem suspect. There are only two people who might tell her truth: Paul and Coffee. She flinches from the thought of Paul, but Coffee — her desire to speak to him is sharp, undeniable. But should she? She's not in the habit of distrusting authority figures, a space that Roosevelt, however odious, clearly occupies. If she finds Coffee, she ought to turn him in. There's a quarantine in the city after all. Congress is one declaration away from starting another war. It's not safe for him out there. He would forgive her eventually, right? But first she has to find him, she has to hear his side of the story.

Because if he *didn't* give her the drug, it means that someone else did.

It means that Roosevelt is lying.

Aaron runs into her room early the next morning. He would have startled her awake, but she's been staring through the skylight since four. Her dreams were dark and frightening, but she can only feel their sticky residue. Shouted threats, locked doors, blurred shadows.

She aches for sleep, but sits up when Aaron pushes his head under her chin.

"Glad you're awake, Em," Aaron says. "Dad was worried."

He means that he was worried, but even at eleven Aaron has learned better than to express his emotions directly.

"I love you, Aaron," she says, and where normally he would groan, he just blinks and hugs her tighter.

"Dad says to tell you Aunt Carol's on the phone."

Bird lurches from the bed and follows Aaron downstairs. Nicky is sitting at the small, round table where she remembers her grandfather dumping Liquid Aminos on his runny eggs Sunday morning before church. The phone cord stretches from the receiver on the wall by the fridge, and Nicky hunches over it like a kid cowering from the playground bully. But it's just her mom on the phone, and that's Nicky all over. He's weak-willed, her mom says. Goes along to get along and never goes much of anywhere. He doesn't have a natural drive, and so he's doomed by his circumstances to his lazy, shiftless existence. Bird has better circumstances, but her mother is convinced that this central flaw will overwhelm her better qualities without constant vigilance.

"It's been rough, Carol. Okay? You don't always need to rag on the —" He glances up from the phone and jerks. "Hey, kid," he says, not very happily. "Your mom's on the phone. You want to talk to her?"

Bird doesn't see how she has a choice, but she appreciates even this paltry spark of defiance from her uncle. Nicky is the oldest, but you'd never know it from the way they act around each other. Carol Bird likes to call herself an old soul.

Bird just shrugs and pulls up a chair. "Hi, Mom," she says.

"It's good to hear your voice, Emily. I won't ask how you're doing. You're awake, and that's enough for the moment. Are you settled in at your uncle's? You don't know how much your father and I wish we could have come back there to be with you, but given the circumstances . . . well. You know we'd do it if we possibly could. Our work here is too important."

"Yes, Mom," Bird says, obedient. "Of course. I understand." Though she doesn't, and she never has. From the vaguely portentous tones in which her mother discusses their work, you would think she and her father were superheroes, saving the world each day from an international team of villains. And, hell, maybe it's true. Maybe right now, Carol and Greg Bird are searching for the origins of this so-called v-flu, and will change global politics with their discoveries. *What exactly is so important?* She could ask, but she knows that she won't. She never does. She can't bear her mother's disappointment — *No impulse control, just like your uncle,* Carol Bird would say, and sigh, and turn, turn away.

"I want you to know, Emily, that things are going to be difficult for some time. It might seem frightening, but you're in the absolute safest place right now. The security measures in place within the Beltway are very impressive. And the school has assured me they're doing everything they can to protect you students from the flu. Just follow the rules, Emily. Do you understand? It's *very important* that you follow the rules, and do everything that your teachers tell you to do, even if it seems strange. Mrs. Early is very well connected. She . . . well, suffice it to say that I feel safer with you there than anywhere else."

"Mom," Bird says, a little baffled. "Do I *ever* break the rules?"

Bird's mom takes a breath, as though to launch into another of her speeches, but then stops. For a full five seconds, Bird hears nothing. She wonders if the line has gone dead. Then:

"Sometimes I wish you would, sugar. You know, I swear I do. The doctor had to force you out, and I remember exactly what he said: 'Your girl doesn't want to leave.' But sometimes I wonder if you just didn't know how. You've always waited for someone to tell you what to do. But I guess I'm grateful for that, now."

Bird gulps, chokes on her own saliva, coughs sharp and hard, each exhalation strobing through her stitches. She tries so hard. But she's never the right kind of smart, the good kind of ambitious, the admirable kind of popular. Nicky shakes his head and herds Aaron out of the kitchen. For a moment she hates him; would it kill him to stand by her, even once? But Carol Bird is the immovable object, the unstoppable force. Carol Bird will break whoever goes against her — brother, husband, daughter. Carol Bird is not to be crossed.

"Do you even know why I was in the hospital, Mom?"

A hasty and riddled defense, but it's all she has. "Well, Emily, you know I heard quite a few things. Some disturbing things. Pam Robinson called me herself, I'll have you know, to apologize for having that drug dealer at her party. I told her that I'm sure you understand that you are responsible for your actions. I hope that you have the decency to apologize to her, Emily."

Bird almost laughs. Apologize for almost dying? Apologize for Roosevelt? For Coffee? "I'm sure I was just asking for it," Bird mutters, and then clenches her jaw in horror when she realizes she said it aloud. She braces herself for the lecture, the just-like-your-uncle acid bath, but her mother doesn't even respond.

"Well. Would you like to speak with your father?" Carol Bird says with icy calm.

Bird knows herself dismissed, recognizes it by her own signature response of fury and relief and longing.

"Sure," she says, as if this is a normal conversation, and hers is a normal family. She and her father talk about the Redskins losing again.

"It's bad luck, that name," her father says, in his slow, careful way. "Could they go around calling themselves the Washington Niggers and get away with it?"

"I agree, Dad, it's a terrible name. But the universe is punishing them?" she asks, comfortable in this familiar territory.

"I don't know about the universe," he says. "But I know about fair. It's just bad mojo."

"Okay, Dad," she says. "But I still think the defensive lineup has something to do with it."

"Oh sure. Sure. They really need to work on that for next season. Em?"

"Yeah?"

"Take care of yourself, okay? Listen to your mom. She's a smart lady. It's dangerous out there. Don't mess with anything you aren't supposed to. Whoever this dealer kid is, let him be."

What do her parents know about Coffee? What did Nicky tell them — or Roosevelt? She thinks of the paper on her bedside table and presses her palm to her stomach.

"Don't worry, Dad," she says, and he lets it go. He always does.

Her cell has thirty-five new text messages. Twenty-two are from Paul. The rest are from Charlotte and Felice, asking if she's okay — more from Charlotte than Felice, of course. It's Sunday night, three days after her release. She has to go back to school tomorrow; she's already so far behind. She dreads the questions and innuendo, the inevitability of her notoriety at school. But for now she stares at the paper with Coffee's number and the cryptic message. *The writing on the wall.* The handwriting is blocky, possibly her own, but only if she were trying to disguise it.

If Coffee did write it, he could explain what he meant. Coffee could explain a lot of things. She types the number into her phone, ten, fifteen times, but then deletes it. What if Roosevelt is tracking her calls? She *should* help him, she knows that, but she can't quite bring herself to do it before she knows more. She looks at the clock — three in the morning. How long does it take to die from insomnia? She hasn't managed to sleep for longer than two hours at a stretch since she left the hospital. Each time she wakes up, swaddled and perfumed in an inexplicable grief, she struggles to remember her dreams, the faintest hint of her lost hours. But she is always gasping and alone, slowly bleeding out from a wound she can't find. She asks the skylight who she is now, this memory-free girl, this unhappily newborn orphan, adrift in a world of armored cars and military checkpoints and endless miles of quarantine tape.

You are Bird, the skylight tells her. Emily fears the world. Bird can solve it. Bird will find her memories and break up with Paul and buy that store she's always secretly dreamed of, and damn what her mother thinks of goals as humble and unambitious as shopkeeping.

Bird will, Bird can, Bird might, but what Bird does is pull on her coat and sneak down the stairs. Nicky has passed out in front of the television. He doesn't even stop snoring when she shuffles past, and the sound of McCoy lecturing one of his endless string of female DAs about a case covers the creak of the front door. Outside, the street is dead quiet. The District has been under a strict curfew since the Beltway quarantine. It's illegal for her to even walk on the sidewalk without a permit, and this is the sort of neighborhood where the police love to harass people for no reason at all, but she hopes she'll get lucky. She can't leave this any longer. Her mother thinks that she never does anything without permission? That she'd never dare to break the rules?

"Well, watch this, Carol Bird," she whispers. Her words turn to cloudy vapor and dissipate into the dark, though they ought to shatter. She pulls the hood over her ears and hurries to the one pay phone in the neighborhood that still works, four blocks away. This isn't *The Wire*, she knows that the government doesn't need much of an excuse to bug every pay phone in the city if they want to, but she hopes that this will be safer than her cell.

She pulls *The writing on the wall* out of her pocket along with some change. She doesn't really need the paper anymore, it's probably dangerous to keep it, but lately she feels as if it's the only thing keeping her sane. The last object that she remembers from that night; the last time she spoke to Coffee and he told her . . .

What did he think she would say to that? What she *could be*? Maybe she wouldn't mind it if he stopped doing stupid shit like dealing drugs, but she never bothered him about it.

She dials the number and holds her breath while it rings. She has to gasp for air before she acknowledges that she won't even get voicemail. The phone rattling in the receiver makes her wince and she looks up and down the street. A few blocks up ahead, on Benning Road, a tank slowly trundles into view, mounted rifles swiveling. She crouches out of sight and shakes so hard that her head knocks like a maraca against the metal of the phone box. What if she gets caught breaking curfew? Should she call her mom? Should she call Nicky? She tries to pray but finds her mind empty of even the most rote appeal for divine favor, for the most workaday intercessions. She's reduced to closing her eyes and humming under her breath a song that she's forgotten most of the words to, a song that her grandmother would sing to her when they went to church together. *Oh happy day,* she sings over and over to herself, and if the irony bites her, she doesn't suppose it bit her grandmother any less.

The rumble of the tank fades to silence. In the distance, a siren starts to wail, but that's a city noise that she understands, the reassuring banality of someone else's disaster. She rests her head against her knees and watches her breath cloud the hourglass between her ankles. Safe. She's still safe.

The phone rings. She jerks and smacks her elbow, hard, against the phone box. Cursing, tears in her eyes, she swings her head around. Is anyone watching her? Is that a faint light she sees in the window across the street? A second ring. Shit, she can't let it do that, but does she dare pick it up?

Bird is scared out of her mind, but she doesn't want that tank with its big dick guns to come back for her either. So Bird dares.

"Hello?" she whispers.

"You're really awake," he says. "I wasn't sure."

She rests her forehead against the polka-dot inside grille, *oh happy day, oh happy day, oh thank you, Jesus.*

"I can't sleep," she says, though in all her looping anticipations of this conversation, she had never imagined this would be her opening gambit.

Coffee lets out a shuddering breath, second cousin to a laugh. "I'm so sorry, Bird."

"So Roosevelt is right? It was your fault?" She didn't mean to say that either. Carol Bird has never encouraged emotional vulnerability in her daughter, and Emily Bird learned very early not to show it. But the kingdom of sleep demands its forfeits, and the world looks very different through eyes cracked and yellow with its denial.

"My fault?" Coffee says. His normally resonant voice is thin and pressed with anger; her hand tightens around the receiver. Shouldn't *she* be the angry one? The girl who woke up in a hospital with a ghoul by her side? "Maybe so, Bird. Maybe in the end." He sounds more sad than angry, she realizes. "But do not deny that I *warned you*. And I'd say I'm in enough trouble without you punishing me."

"I never told you to deal, Coffee," she says, and worries too late about using his name.

That aborted hiccup could be a laugh or a sob. "If you think that's what this is about, we should stop talking."

"What it's about? What the hell *is* this? Because no one is telling me anything. What happened to me? What drugs did I take? What did you give me? What did Paul do? Why was Roosevelt waiting in the hospital for me to wake up? Please, Co — tell me. If you know, tell me."

He's silent for a long time, nearly a minute, but she knows that he's there by his breathing on the other end. She doesn't mind waiting for his answer. If anything, his labored breaths, an echo from somewhere else in the city, are a comforting mirror of her own. She always did feel safer with Coffee than anywhere else. From the first moment that she saw him, alone and contemplative at that Landon party a year and a half ago, she had known she would find him again. She hears the faint click of a lighter and the relieved breath of carcinogens delivering their payload deep into alveoli.

"You don't remember," he says finally. His voice is flat, soft, uninflected. Even Bird, an adept in the mystical art of Coffee, can't read anything into it. Another deep breath, another exhale.

"Tell me," she says softly. "I can't stand this. Everyone knows something but me."

"How do I know you're not working with him?"

For a nonsensical moment she thinks he means Paul and his endless texts. But of course he means Roosevelt. He's asking if he should trust her. Which he shouldn't.

"No way," she says. "With *Roosevelt*?" She's almost sure she avoided any obvious tells, and yet in her head her voice fluoresces with the lie.

"You asked me if he was telling the truth. It's even a question? If he's got to you . . . Bird, the precise last thing I want to do in my life is rot away in a US prison. This country is not a very good place at the moment for Latinos."

"But you're Brazilian. And your mother —"

"Do I want to risk her too? Bird, Roosevelt is . . . I'd say he's inhuman, but he's too human in all the wrong ways. I wouldn't blame you for working with him, but you can't believe him either."

"Then give me something else to believe! He knows my parents. He works for the government. If he's so evil, I need something else to go on than your word."

"Where will you be tomorrow?"

"School," she says.

"Of course. I bet your mother made sure you'd be safe there."

"My mother? What does she —"

"I'll try. For you, Bird, I'll try."

And his sudden absence is a busy signal and a frozen gust of wind, bringing with it the musk of garbage and cigarettes — organic tobacco, she imagines, hand-rolled by fingers that shake with need.

The summer before Bird's senior year, three very important events dominated the news. The first — though US newspapers managed to focus on this far less than papers based elsewhere — was an unprecedented global heat wave that had caused droughts all over the world. Climate change became part of daily conversation, even while Congress debated anemic emissions targets with dates decades away. There were food riots in Hawaii, the Philippines, Singapore, and Venezuela, the latter of which lasted the longest and caused the greatest crisis. This lead to the second, far bigger news story: the sudden hike of the Venezuelan oil windfall tax to eighty percent on all oil sales over fifty-five dollars a barrel. A temporary move, according to its socialist government, to raise money, "to help alleviate poverty caused by the CO_2 emissions from other countries."

France, Germany, Canada, Saudi Arabia, Bahrain, and Colombia joined in condemnation of their "unprecedented destabilization of global markets." The irony of this coalition of the willing at the same time discussing their great concern for the impacts of global warming went largely unnoticed.

Venezuela soon eclipsed Iran as a country subject to focused, open US hostility. Two weeks before Bird would tour the Stanford campus with her mother, the third story began to bubble from the bottom of the first two. It began with calls from certain senators for a "tougher foreign policy." It included some speculation about the size of Venezuelan oil fields (potentially the largest in the world). Stocks went so low that Wall Street froze trading two days in a row. Congress fast-tracked a sanctions regime against Venezuela. They promised stronger action if the windfall tax wasn't immediately cut to a quarter of its current rate. Venezuela refused.

Two weeks later, a pair of disaffected FARC generals, allegedly paid and supplied by the Venezuelan government, deployed a deadly virus on a private jet leaving from the San Francisco airport.

The same day, Bird toured the Stanford campus with her mother. That this tour occurred in early August, nearly two months before students returned to campus, had been a bone of resentment between Bird's teeth since the moment her mother had conceded to the trip. Carol Bird had tried everything but outright disapproval to steer her daughter away from her first choice: pamphlets for Harvard and Yale helpfully placed on her bed, Jack and Jill alumni currently attending

East Coast Ivies casually invited for dinner, promised meals at expensive Providence and Cambridge restaurants. And then this Pyrrhic victory: a visit to her top-choice school during the depopulated summer intersession, because otherwise Carol Bird had "absolutely no time" to accompany her.

That morning Bird forgot her wallet at the house; they had to turn back on the highway to get it and nearly missed their flight. Her mother did not speak to her for the first half of the trip, a supposed punishment that perhaps came as a relief for both of them. And yet, by the time they landed, something had changed. Perhaps it was the weather, air that smelled of dry ocean and rosemary after weeks of suffering through the heat wave, that made Carol turn to her daughter at the taxi stand, start to speak, and then just smile.

They arrived on campus an hour early for the second of the day's two tours. To Bird's astonishment, her mother suggested they go exploring. "It's gorgeous here," she said. "Very different from the District. And yet . . . did I ever tell you I did my freshman year at Spelman?"

Bird stared at her mother. "But, didn't you graduate from Georgetown? Isn't that where you met Dad?"

"I met him in Georgia, actually," Carol Bird said quietly. She was watching two students sunbathing topless in the grass. "We transferred together. It was the right decision, but that year at Spelman . . ." She sighed. "I felt like I belonged. Do you think you'll be happy here, Emily?"

Bird glanced again at the pair of unself-consciously topless girls, a game of Ultimate Frisbee on the lawn, a group of students speaking in rapid Japanese and taking a few puffs on a cigarette that smelled, as they passed, pleasantly of pot. Carol Bird sniffed, then shook her head and smiled.

Later, after a tour led by a student who gave every impression of recovering from a hangover ("Thank goodness the campus speaks for itself," said Carol Bird, and her daughter could not help but agree), they stopped by the library. They walked the stacks, through the main reading rooms and smaller areas with couches and carrels and students crouched inside them in ignorance or defiance of the beautiful weather. They stopped at a desk beneath a tall window, where one of the few Black students they'd seen that day was sleeping on an open chemistry textbook.

"Orgo," Bird's mother said, something strange in her voice. "Nothing quite like it to teach you what you want —"

And just like that, she was crying. Bird stared, frozen. She didn't offer her mother comfort; perhaps she couldn't, and perhaps, this once, she was as selfish as Carol claimed.

"God, Georgetown," her mother whispered over the gentle snores of the sleeping chemistry student. "The things they called me. My accent. In the middle of the District, and I felt like I'd landed on Mars. I never wanted that for you, Emily. I wanted you to have what I didn't. I wanted you to *belong* in those places I could only visit. And you do, don't you?"

And Bird realized what she could do: "I'll be happy here," she said.

The next day, the president announced to the world that the FBI had prevented a devastating act of bioterrorism, and that they would no longer allow a state supporter of terrorism to strangle global oil markets. The target had been a private jet carrying the Bahraini and Saudi Arabian ambassadors. Bird and her mother had been in the same airport at the same time, though she didn't know it then. No one knew those details until the second, far more somber presidential announcement nearly two months later: The terrorists had not hit their targets, but they had deployed the virus anyway. A deadly flu was even now spreading across the West Coast and other parts of the world. "Incubation time" became the byword on the cable news channels, to explain the impotence of the CDC and other health agencies around the world at stopping its spread. Other phrases circled like prayers: ten to fifteen days before symptoms appeared, five to ten percent death rate, worse than the Spanish flu.

Her mother disappeared back down the black hole of work. We were left alone to remember that last normal summer day, that glimpse of her mother's humanity that has made some things better, and some things worse.

[hydrocodone]

$C_{18}H_{21}NO_3$

Nicky apologizes that he can't drive her to school, but she understands. Between the checkpoints and the driving restrictions, he couldn't get her there and make it to his doorman job on time. Bird's mom calls Nicky a deadbeat, but it isn't really a fair word for a guy who's worked shit jobs most of his life. It's just that he can't manage to keep anything for very long, and what he does get is soul-killing. So she takes Aaron to the school bus, all the kids inside alien and wide-eyed with face masks and gloves. She checks Aaron's value-sized bottle of hand sanitizer and reminds him not to touch his face. If the v-flu spreads to his school, she honestly doesn't know if even that will save him. Right now, the Beltway quarantine is holding the disease at bay, but she wonders how long the White House can keep the rest of the world out of its sacred bubble.

She takes the Metro to school, and it's more of the same: adults with face masks and gloves and poison glares for anyone who so much as clears their throat. She keeps her hands from her face and feels as if she's dreaming every time she blinks. She's exhausted by the time she arrives. It turns out that eight days in a hospital bed really do a number on your muscle tone. She's early, and surprised to see a line winding into the side lawn from the upper school entrance. A few soldiers in fatigues stand by the entrance with bulky automatic rifles. She stares; the nearest one gives her a wary nod and gestures her to the line.

The whispers start as soon as she walks past. For this, at least, Charlotte prepared her with a text this morning:

Felice and I are getting in early. Meet in senior room? Everyone's really excited to have you back.

Bird has not been a student to occasion excitement. She is solid, dependable, moderately popular: an uncontroversial extra body to warm a seat at a lunch table that might look awkward empty. But she knows what Charlotte means with that nonconfrontational sweetness: Everyone's talking about you, you need to show your face. There's a reason why she and Felice made sure they weren't here to meet her out front.

Girls she hardly recognizes whip out their phones and start texting, whisper through covered mouths to their nearest neighbors. She wishes that Charlotte, at least, could have been here for her. But even the specimen-in-a-jar effect of an exclusive all-girls school doesn't seem like much compared to the specter of Roosevelt and his shadowy Lukas Group.

She looks past the ravine and the bridges to the other side of the campus, where she can just make out the wrought-iron spire of the great chapel at Bradley Hall, where Paul is probably already parking and checking his texts. The ones that will tell him Bird is back in school. She's decided that she has to talk to him before making any decisions about what to tell Roosevelt.

For now, she tries to ignore the silence, the weight of their curiosity, but her head throbs and it's all she can do to avoid touching the long row of stitches that her hair has abundantly failed to conceal. It's easy to avoid the squat and cloudy mirrors at Nicky's place, but what she can see of herself reflected in the girls' faces does not reassure her.

There's a group of freshmen at the back of the line. They give Bird nervous smiles and then array their backs against her; a couple hastily reaffix brightly patterned face masks. Do they think she caught the flu in the hospital? Or maybe they fear a more social sort of contagion. The line is slowly moving past the armed guards and into the sanctuary of the school. She doesn't understand what this is for, but she imagines it has something to do with the quarantine and constant terror alerts, and the reason why her mother felt "very secure" with the idea of Bird continuing to go to school.

Bird closes her eyes against a rush of nausea, takes deep breaths of dewy late-fall air. There's a crispness to it that she only recognizes from Shenandoah vacations. The roads are almost empty aside from buses, police vehicles, and dark cars with tinted windows that hint at some secret official purpose.

"Hey, Bird."

"Hey, Marella."

Bird opens her eyes. Not a difficult guess; there's only one other person who calls her that. She and her copresident of Africa Club have been classmates since fourth grade. She knows that Marella's father is from Guyana and her mother from PG County, that she's managed to keep a scholarship since middle school, yet Bird can't say that she knows her very well. They're perfectly cordial, they work together for the club, but it's never gone any further than that. Marella has a white girlfriend from Holton-Arms: a model-gorgeous blond with a trust fund and an occasional unplaceable accent. Bird once saw them together in the rose garden, tangled together and laughing, and she blushed and turned away though they weren't even kissing.

Marella is the only out lesbian in their grade, the only one with an obvious girlfriend in the entire school. The girls pretend they're okay with it to her face, but when the gossip turns vicious in the senior room, Bird's kept silent more times than she wants to admit. Gina isn't even the worst of them.

"It's good to see you back. We were — I was worried."

Bird's throat suddenly feels too warm to speak. She's always admired Marella, wanted to be her friend since they played tennis together in summer camp. But Marella never seemed to like Bird much.

"Thanks," she says finally. "I didn't realize I'd gotten so notorious." Her smile feels as though it's been peeled back from her teeth, and so she abandons the effort.

Marella puts a hand on Bird's elbow, a simple gesture of sympathy that draws astonished stares from the closest girls in line. Marella, normally so composed, so determinedly disdainful of the homophobic fog that fills the school, snatches back her arm and takes a gulping breath.

"Yeah. Well. You know how this place is. Just when I thought I'd escape, they call in the army."

Bird looks at soldiers not much older than her hoisting their automatic rifles with a disturbing combination of awkwardness and flat-eyed determination. She thinks of massacred wedding parties in Afghanistan and shudders.

"We'll get through it, Marella," Bird says, surprising herself by sounding so strong and sure.

Marella smiles. "One sanctioned extracurricular activity at a time."

They finally reach the front of the line. Bird lets Marella go ahead. Beyond the glass doors of the upper school foyer, three sets of soldiers pat students down and go through their bags. Looking for what, Bird doesn't know. A man and a woman in scrubs, gloves, and full surgical masks take temperatures and inspect open mouths. When it's her turn, Bird tries to accept the intrusion stoically, but she can't help but flinch when a soldier who looks like he could be her cousin pats down her legs. She grits her teeth and wonders why sleeplessness makes her feel every touch like a needle. All the influence this school has, and they couldn't bother finding a few female officers for the pat downs? Then again, the vice president's daughter goes to the lower school. It's probably a five-star quarantine in the building across the bridge.

The soldier inspects the set of keys in her pocket and the pencil case in her backpack like he can actually see errant colonies of v-flu lurking on their surface. She feels a glare rising like a sneeze, and so looks down at her feet until he gives them back. At the medical station, a white man in purple scrubs searches for her name on a tablet, then pauses.

"Emily Bird?" he says, his eyes inscrutable above the mask. He turns to an older Latina woman wearing a lab coat. "Dr. Granger, you'll need to take her back."

The doctor frowns at the surly nurse and takes the tablet from him. "This won't take very long, Emily," she says with a tired but genuine effort at a smile. "Will you follow me?"

Medical facilities have taken over two lower school classrooms. She follows Dr. Granger across the Woodley Bridge and down the path to the newer redbrick building quietly. The desks are gone in both rooms, but in the one on the left a line of young girls in uniform wait to receive shots from three medics in scrubs. Secret Service agents — she recognizes them by their clear earpieces and boxy suits — stand impassively behind the students. Bird stops to stare until the doctor pulls her past the open door and into the second, empty room. The tall windows are draped in white cloth. Cloth partitions hang from the ceiling, separating three empty medical cots from a wall of medical machinery.

"What's all that?" Bird asks, pointing to the next room.

The doctor jerks her head to the door and bites the inside of her cheek. "Immune support. Just a precaution. We'll be rolling it out for the upper grades in a week or two."

"So what do you want with me?"

"You were in the hospital recently," she explains, pressing Bird firmly onto a cot. "It's a frequent vector of infection. We need to run extra tests."

Bird looks at her watch just as the five-minute bell rings. She's going to be late.

"We'll write you a note," the doctor says. "Now raise your left arm."

She draws three vials of blood and tests them in a large machine crammed into the corner. To her surprise Bird falls asleep on the cot while she waits for the results, a reprieve that feels like five minutes but turns out to be an hour when the doctor shakes her awake.

"Your tests are clear." The doctor removes her mask, lets it dangle from one ear. "Emily . . . how are you doing?"

"Doing?" Bird glances at the machine and wonders if they tested for anything besides the v-flu. Like designer drugs. "I'm fine," she says.

"You seem tired," the doctor tries.

Bird feels a breath of panic. She feels as though if she says or does something wrong, they'll put her back in the chair, and this time she'll never get away.

Back in the chair?

"I'm just having a little trouble sleeping," Bird says, smashing her voice flat with an effort that leaves her feeling bloody.

The doctor nods. "You were in a coma?"

"I guess so."

"Did the hospital run tests before you left? Insomnia can definitely be a consequence of stress, but you might need a more thorough checkup."

"They did an MRI and some other stuff," Bird says. "They said I looked fine. Do you think you could give me some sleeping pills?"

The doctor sits on the cot beside her. "Tell you what," she says, "I'm going to give you a brochure on ways to change your sleeping habits. It might take a while, but it will help. And if you're still having trouble after a week, it should be okay to take some melatonin. But sleeping pills just aren't safe after a head injury."

The doctor climbs off the cot and riffles through a stack of brochures piled on the corner of her desk.

"Here," she says, handing Bird a brochure with a picture of a white woman sleeping soundly beneath the words *Sleeping & Your Health*. "It's a stressful time for all of us, Emily. Don't be afraid to ask for help if you need it."

She looks as exhausted as Bird feels, which makes her advice seem a little absurd.

"You should too," Bird says, surprising herself.

"What, ask for help?" She shakes her head. "I'm *venezolana*, Emily, and I'm working with very paranoid security officials. Either I'm perfect, or I'm a —"

Dr. Granger's laugh is so bleak that Bird winces. "It's not easy here, is it?" Bird says.

"No, not really. But we both have to stay. Especially you, Emily. This school will keep you safe. Whatever else it does."

Bird wonders about this as she puts on her coat and heads for the door. Dr. Granger doesn't even say good-bye — she stares into space at the side of her desk, lost in some private, adult drama that gives Bird an uncomfortable feeling of half familiarity.

Bird opens the door and runs outside, across the lower field, and only stops at Woodley Bridge, in sight of the pale brick and limestone upper school building. She drops her bag on the wet wood and bends over the railing until all she can see are the bare trees and rocks lining the bottom of the ravine.

Her breath laces her lips white and the misting rain beads her hair — it'll take an hour in the shower to comb it out at this rate — and she wonders what Coffee is doing now. Huddled away from the rain? On a plane to São Paulo? Will she ever see him again? *For you, Bird, I'll try.*

She cries for the first time since the hospital, fat tears that for a moment comfort her with their warmth.

The Bradley athletic center received a world-class addition and a new name three years ago, much to the satisfaction of the trustees and distinguished alumni who funded it to a fifteen-million-dollar tune. The old wing, still determinedly called Nagler by most students, has become a tide pool for the anti-varsity sport, the requirement fillers, the Stage Fighting III, Fitness Yoga, and After-School Pilates that Bird has carefully avoided after a ninth-grade brush with Adventure Club nearly destroyed her nascent social credibility. In a typically perverse twist, the older building, while social death as a location for athletic activity, is a destination hangout for the cool and not quite, and Felice loves to go there and flirt while pretending to do her homework.

The location of this activity, which has a smell as distinct, if not quite as unpleasant, as the Devonshire senior room, is called "the pit," and was once some kind of varsity lounge down the hall from the old locker rooms. Why the elite of two elite schools would prefer to gather on couches with leather so worn Gina likes to draw animal faces onto the patterns with silver Sharpie, Bird does not understand. The inexpungible smell of a century of teenage male sweat and foot powder follows her for hours afterward, and yet she still dutifully accompanies Felice and Charlotte across campus on the days they make the trek. Felice made perfectly clear that her attendance in the pit today was expected. And so Bird sits on the arm of the couch closest to the varsity wrestling trophies of '64–'67 and watches Carter Crumb juggle Gina's pencil case just over her head while Gina shrieks and jumps half as high as Bird, her teammate during a winning season of JV basketball two years ago, knows she can.

Beside her, Trevor reads a battered copy of *The Secret History* with every appearance of complete absorption, while beside him Felice works on AP Calculus and glances at him every third problem, like a little reward to keep her focused. On the floor beneath Felice, Charlotte looks wistful and sad, but then pulls out a copy of *Martha Stewart Weddings* from her bag and circles the floral arrangements she likes best with a purple ink pen.

"How are you feeling, Emily?" she asks, more to her magazine than Bird's battered face.

Bird plays with the zipper of her hoodie. The steam heat is on, but she can't get warm. "All right," she lies, like everyone.

Charlotte nods. "What do you think of this necklace? It's more a mother-of-the-bride design. When Valerie got married last summer her mother wore something like this, do you remember?"

Valerie graduated Devonshire three years before them, another Jack and Jill kid, a future young African American leader. She was one of the first people Bird met when she began attending gatherings of that select African American community organization. And Valerie actually married the boy who escorted her at her debutante ball. A little early, sure there were some looks, but a National Cathedral wedding was enough to turn most of them to shrugs.

"Damn that was a boring wedding," Trevor says without looking from his book. "How long did that service last? An hour?"

"Don't even, Trevor!" When Charlotte's armor of placidity cracks, something interesting leaks out. "It was beautiful. You'd be lucky to have a wedding half as beautiful."

Now Trevor looks up from his book. "That's a fascinating argument, Charlotte Andrews."

Felice straightens and then cants her head so her hair brushes Trevor's shoulder. "What argument?" she says, as though she hasn't monitored every syllable and gesture of his conversation.

Trevor does not appear to have heard her. "Speaking of fascinating arguments, have you seen Paul yet, Emily?"

Bird nearly falls into his lap. "I — not yet. I need to talk to him." Bird has texted Paul to meet her, but he said he was busy until eight. Doing what, he did not explain. "We're not arguing," Bird says.

Felice reaches behind Trevor's back to give Bird's arm a friendly pat. "Emily and Paul are the *perfect* couple."

Trevor glances at Felice now, his eyes twin lasers of critical examination submerged in a laugh that just touches his lips. Felice pulls her hand back and squirms a few inches.

Bird considers Felice. "Were you still there when he took me . . . I mean, when I got in his car?"

Charlotte grimaces around the back of her pen. "My dad picked up me and Felice right after the toast, Emily. They said you didn't remember everything. I'm sorry we can't help you."

Felice glowers at the mutineer at her feet. "Well, Paul *told* us, Char. Right, Trevor?"

"And Coffee told me something a little different."

Gina, gasping on the floor after an apparently taxing wrestling match with Carter, claps her hands. "Oh my God, you did *not* hear from him? Trevor, like, there's a manhunt on. Denise thinks he's patient zero. You'd better tell someone before you get arrested."

Trevor carefully creases the corner of his current page and closes his book. "I'll take that under advisement, Gina. But he told me this at the party, not after he went on the lam."

Carter laughs. "On the lam? Dude, that sounds so gay."

"Do you think Marella would do it with a lamb? What's a female lamb? A ewe?"

Trevor stands, upsetting the delicate balance on the couch; Felice, who had been in the process of casually resting her arm on Trevor's thigh, falls to the side, knocking into Bird, who actually does tumble off the edge.

Trevor catches her. His hand on her elbow hauls her upright just as she braces herself for the fall. He doesn't even look down as he does it, and that confidence and unconsidered strength is what lets him get away with saying things like, "A lamb, Gina, is a baby sheep of either gender. A ewe, though, I bet that could refer to a lot of things. I'm getting a Coke. Want one, Emily?"

Everyone stares as Bird follows him into the hall.

"Thanks," Bird says when the noise of middle school band practice drowns the conversation from the pit.

"Anytime." Trevor punches a code into the Coke machine. Only the janitor and the principal are supposed to use it, but being Trevor Robinson has many privileges, some more obvious than others. "Diet?" he asks.

It's a simple question that hides a declaration of loyalty. Bird hates the taste of aspartame, but never drinks anything with sugar at school. Felice and Charlotte are always on some diet, and it's easier to avoid any pointed comments about her thunder thighs if she pretends to be too. But now she feels disgusted by that scene in the pit, by its familiarity. Now she feels the hanging sword of Roosevelt's threats and the awful moment she'll have to snitch on Coffee —

"Regular," she says, and Trevor knows. His smile is a thin crescent of approval.

"Coffee told me Paul took that curve like Bruce Willis. Paul says . . ."

He shakes his head and hands her the soda. Trevor and Paul have been friends since kindergarten. She doesn't know what kind of relationship he has with Coffee, but they've been talking after school more and more often. That hint of burgeoning friendship has helped Coffee's reputation maintain its razorlike balance between cryptic-freak and weird-but-cool.

"Talk to Paul," Trevor says, and walks away before she can ask him anything else.

Back in the pit, a bunch of guys from varsity soccer are playing Street Fighter on their iPads, hair still damp from quick after-practice showers. More Devonshire girls have come too, including some socially forward freshmen, and so she doesn't see Paul until she nearly bumps into him.

He's sitting on the couch in Trevor's spot, holding a smartphone with a blue case and a picture of the Lincoln Theatre on the back.

"Emily!" He stands up and hugs her.

"What are you doing with my phone?"

"Giving you some new numbers. Here, let's talk outside."

She notices Felice's hard look as she packs her stuff. "You can't have them both, you know," Felice whispers, barely audible in the din of the pit after practice.

Bird swallows. She thinks of Marella, one of the coolest people she knows, who has never had any time for Felice. "Maybe I don't want either," Bird whispers back. She nods at Charlotte's sympathetic astonishment.

Outside, Paul pulls her against the band lockers and kisses her while his fingers find her stitches. She can't think of a way to refuse quickly enough, so she submits for a minute and tries to feel the way a girl should feel being kissed by her boyfriend. But her heart won't stop pounding, and finally she pulls away.

"We need to talk," she says.

Paul kisses her nose. "I know, babe, but I'm so glad to see you —"

She takes a step to the side. "Please."

"Emily . . . you're okay, right?"

Bird finds within herself a reservoir of anger, unexpected and welcome. "Do I look okay?"

Whatever he sees in her expression makes him take a step back, and she is stabbed with joy and then regret, because once she almost loved him. Once her breath caught to see him loping across the rose bridge. The sight of the muscled veins in his forearms, revealed when he so-casually rolled up the sleeves of the blue Bradley blazer was enough to make her drag him into the rose garden, desperate for the beautiful boy taste of him.

Paul cracks his knuckles, what he does when he's nervous. She normally hates the sound, but now a thrill pricks through for each pop. This is her power, doing this to him. This is her revenge.

For what, Bird? Revenge for what? She doesn't know.

"Roosevelt said he already told you what happened with the accident."

Her stomach lurches. "You're chatting with Roosevelt now?"

"That's what I was going to tell you. I got that internship. I've been working with Roosevelt since all that shit went down. I'm supposed to be your contact in case you hear anything from Alonso. You just let me know, and I'll take it from there."

"You? Roosevelt? You want me to turn in Coffee?"

Paul models his perfect grin. "Pretty slick, huh? Anyway, don't worry about that junkie, he's safer with my people than he is out there." He shakes his head.

I talked to him last night. She could say that. She tries, "Last night, Coffee —"

"He's contacted you?"

He looks so eager. His fingers hover like water bugs over the screen of his phone. Even if it *is* for Coffee's own good, it will also ruin his life, and she hates the thought of Paul using that just to get a good college rec.

"No," she says. "I don't know why you guys are so convinced he will either."

He shrugs. "Like you said that night, he's a freak with a thing for you. Not that I blame him."

He brushes her hair back from the scar and winces. "If this doesn't fade, my sister knows a really great doctor who helped her after her C-section —"

"Tell me what happened at the party," Bird says, because otherwise she's afraid of what she'll say to him. "Your version, not Roosevelt's."

The hand withdraws. He fiddles with his phone to stall, but she waits. He clears his throat. "You got drunk. They all . . . we went to the woods. To drink, you know, so Trevor's parents wouldn't catch us. And you drank too much and it got a little crazy and I took you home, but then you . . . I mean, that asshole, Alonso, maybe he gave you something, because he was chasing after us and, I don't know, I turned and you grabbed the wheel and . . ."

"I hit my head?" she asked.

"We nearly crashed."

"Where's your car?"

"In the shop."

But she is sure of it: his panicked flooring of the gas, the turn on two wheels, her head smacking hard against the window. She never took the wheel of the car. How could she have hit her head if she wasn't close to the passenger window?

If she trusts Roosevelt, she should trust Paul. If she trusts Coffee, she shouldn't trust Roosevelt. If she trusts Paul . . .

"So how's it going with Lukas Group?" she asks.

He doesn't even catch the sarcasm, just purses his lips while his eyes go wide in excitement. "I can't really talk about it, but . . . well, damn, Emily, you've always understood. This is my break! I get this right and I could be doing reconnaissance work before I'm out of college."

"You'll be like the LeBron James of national security," she says, and it isn't as though she's never had these thoughts before, but she's never said them out loud. The Bird of her thoughts has never escaped into the Emily of her words. It's like a wall cracked when she hit her head against that window, and bits of herself have been leaking ever since, a phosphorescent trail leading back to Paul's Land Rover.

Paul has finally realized she might not be overcome with happiness for him. "Emily, I didn't *do* anything. If you want to be mad at someone, try that druggie."

He fumbles in his pocket and pulls out a pink silk jewelry bag, drawstring pulled tight. "I got this for you. Listen, I get if you're upset, I really do. What happened to you was shitty. I'd be confused too. But don't blame the good guys. I've heard some things from Roosevelt that, well, let's just say this shit is going to get worse before it gets better. Don't push me away now. Not when you need me."

He drops the bag into Bird's palm. His hands are warm, and she's surprised at the comfort she derives from his familiar, dry touch. He catches her eyes with a lift of his curly lashes.

"I love you, Emily," he says. "I'll take care of you. I promise."

Big guns, she thinks, even as she closes her eyes against a shiver that pops right against the seam of her True Religion jeans. She doesn't believe him, but it feels nice anyway to hear someone say it.

He doesn't kiss her. By the time she opens her eyes again, he's heading down the hall to the exit.

She opens the bag. It's a bracelet of braided silver with leaves of rose gold, studded with tiny rubies. He removed the price, but left the store tag of a boutique in Georgetown she knows of only because Charlotte is obsessed with fancy wedding rings.

Charlotte would love this bracelet.

Bird stuffs it in her pocket. At the end of the hall, Paul's phone rings.

"Yeah, we've talked," he says. Whatever else follows is swallowed in the slam of the exit door.

*　　*　　*

Bird is in religion class, checking the commercial real estate listings on the *Washington Post* website while occasionally alt-tabbing to make some notes on the Eightfold Path (detachment, enlightenment, she knows she'll never find either), when the drill bell rings loud enough to make Charlotte shriek. Mrs. Parker sets down her PowerPoint remote, her wandering right eye nearly pointing at her nose in distress.

"All right, girls, you hear the alarm. Get up, to the door, single file. Remember your face masks! I'm sure this is just a drill, but . . ."

The dangling conjunction does more than the bell to get them out of their seats. Bird hastily stuffs her computer in her backpack and then waits for Charlotte, who has to pack away the twenty different colored pens she brings out for each class. Charlotte likes writing her notes, she says it relaxes her and helps her focus. Charlotte has a note from her doctor that gives her extra time during exams — ADD, the note says, though clearly thumbed-over copies of *Martha Stewart Weddings* and *Ebony* inspire more concentrated attention. Charlotte knows the going rate of an ounce of jewelry-grade platinum the way an aspiring senator knows the price of a gallon of milk. By the time Charlotte has finished her careful-hasty rearrangements, the front of the line has already filed out of the classroom.

Mrs. Parker pulls her gray-and-green knit cardigan tightly over her wide belly, though the heat hisses through ancient steam radiators. "Hurry, girls," she says again, but faintly, and she's looking out the window to the stream of lower school students across the lawn heading into their basement. Armored cars and tanks clog streets around the school — she remembers seeing tow trucks drag the last of the residential cars away a few days ago. She counts dozens of soldiers and Secret Service agents, alien invaders in rubber gloves and black gas masks.

"That's a lot of security for a drill," Bird says, walking to the window.

Charlotte gives her a panicked, wide-eyed glance, but Mrs. Parker just sighs and looks, for a moment, older than usual. Behind her, a green-and-gold mandala glows like a halo on the projection screen.

"The vice president has insisted on maximum security for his daughter, as you can imagine."

But there's something else in the way her fingers grip her elbows. Like she's just as disturbed by the reflected glare off tinted car windows and tank guns. Is Roosevelt down there, in one of those anonymous boxes?

"What do they think is going to happen?" She is hardly aware of having spoken aloud, until Mrs. Parker gives her a sharp shake of her head.

"We'll see soon enough, Emily. And Charlotte, perhaps you could take this opportunity to work on your extra-credit project."

Religion is not Charlotte's best subject, but Bird suspects that Mrs. Parker mentioned it as a perverse reassurance: The world could not possibly be ending so long as the matron of the senior locker hall hounds you about religion assignments.

So they hurry to their designated drill rendezvous, the fifties-era bomb shelter in the basement of Nagler. It's just barely large enough to hold the upper grades of Devonshire and Bradley. A team of gas-masked soldiers guards them in relays. Four tanks idle on the street, two helicopters whir overhead, for what purpose she can't imagine. Charlotte looks up from her cell as they start down the metal stairs to the basement.

"It's a mess down there, but Felice says she's saved us a spot. She's with Trevor."

"And Paul?" Bird asks, trying to keep the tremor from her voice.

Charlotte stops abruptly on the step below her and looks up. She reaches, as though to touch Bird's arm, but draws back when Bird flinches. She hasn't asked about him since Bird came back. "It's okay," Charlotte says quietly. "Felice says he went somewhere with one of the medics."

"Okay" is all Bird can trust herself to say.

On the landing above them, an unmasked soldier glares down and waves his gun. "You girls, hurry —"

Sirens drown out the rest of his words. Harmonious, simultaneous wails from a dozen different mouths, sweeping across the empty city.

"What the hell?" she says, but she only knows she spoke from the vibration in her throat.

"Terror alert!" the soldier shouts into a walkie-talkie. A few others join him up there and they slam the doors shut. Bird would have stood paralyzed with fear and the strangest, bleakest sort of curiosity if Charlotte didn't push her forward. The shelter opens up at the end of a short, claustrophobic hallway that smells like cockroach bait and lemon-scented floor cleaner.

It's a room about the size of a gymnasium, with folding chairs set up in what must have been neat rows. Now, her classmates sit on the floor and against the walls, backpacks disgorged and media devices glowing. It feels like every upperclassman from Devonshire and Bradley turns to look at them when they come bursting through the door. The silence deepens and Bird thinks she ought to be used to notoriety. Charlotte blushes to the roots of her braids.

From the center of the room, Mrs. Early, Devonshire headmistress, turns her helmet-gray head and raises her eyebrows.

"Thanks for joining us, ladies. Next time, I expect you all to respond to our early-warning bell promptly and quietly. The situation is too serious for anything else."

Mrs. Early has dismissed them, but they still don't have a place to sit. The floor is packed, and Charlotte finally sees Felice fluttering her fingers from the far back of the hall. They're still climbing over chairs and bodies when Mrs. Early resumes her speech.

"I want you all to understand that this is just a precaution. We have no word of any actual attack, but in this environment we must take these threats seriously, and that's why you're down here until we get the all clear. I want you all to take the opportunity to study, not social-ize. The noise should be kept to a minimum."

The ensuing rush of conversation echoes in the musty shelter like an avalanche. Charlotte and Felice start talking over each other and

Bird, who normally would try to pretend like she's part of the conversation, sighs and looks around. Marella sits by herself in a corner of the room, near some juniors. She catches Bird's eye and smiles slightly. Bird remembers what Marella said that awful day Bird came back to school: *Just when I thought I'd escape.* Marella doesn't belong here, Bird knows. She should be in Paris or Berlin, smoking in a café and arguing about art and the sort of radical politics that Coffee likes. Bird tried to belong, for a long time she felt like she *almost* did. Now she feels her grown-out roots and wonders how she ever fooled herself. Nearby, she hears Coffee's name at least three times, and tries not to jump. Trevor is telling a wide-eyed Charlotte about anthrax spores and fatality rates — he glances at Bird while he speaks, a look heavy with indecipherable meaning. What could he tell her about that party, if not for his loyalty to Paul? She closes her eyes, torn between screaming and sleeping.

She's saved from either by Roosevelt.

"Ladies, gentlemen," says a man she recognizes after a beat as the headmaster of Bradley Hall. "We have someone from the security services who are helping us out who would like to speak to you for a moment. Please give him your full attention."

But Bird's already noticed Roosevelt, and Roosevelt has sure as hell already noticed her, though he hides the smile he gives her inside a broad one directed at the group of wary, wide-eyed teenagers.

"As I'm sure you've all heard by now, we're looking for one of your classmates, Alonso Oliveira."

Bird has braced herself, but still she flinches against the considering heat of three hundred pairs of eyes. In her peripheral vision, she sees Felice blush and scoot closer to Charlotte. But Bird forces herself to look straight ahead, to keep all the heat and fury of her pounding heart trained on Roosevelt, whom she now hates more than anyone in the world.

"If *any* of you have had any communication from him, or know anything about his whereabouts, I need to know about it. Just talk to

Mr. Levenson here or Mrs. Early and they'll let me know. This is for his own safety, guys. The situation out there is dangerous, and he's much safer with us than he is on the run in a quarantine zone."

He doesn't even look at her, the balding asshole with his gray blazer and his jeans, that sort of California look that Coffee would tease her for wanting at Stanford and, God, how could she give this guy anything, let alone a creation as unprecedented and unique as her patron iconoclast? Even if she should, even if it's right?

She looks down at the bracelet, which she has worn for the last three days on her right wrist. The appropriate people dutifully admired it, Charlotte most genuinely; Bird could practically see the bridesmaid dreams drifting across her gaze like organza cataracts.

"Emily?"

It's Charlotte, tugging on her sleeve, whispering in her ear.

"What?"

"You haven't seen Coffee, have you?"

For a moment, Bird almost tells her: about their conversation on the pay phone, about her obligation to turn him in, and her doubts. About the silence that has stretched since that moment, how every night she falls asleep with her phone by her ear, praying that he'll never call her.

"No," Bird says.

Charlotte looks back at Felice and bites her lip. "Are you going to break up with Paul?"

I wish, she thinks. "Why would you ask that?"

"Felice said something. I know he gave you that bracelet, but no one's seen you with him lately. I don't think we should care one way or another, but Felice . . ."

Bird understands: Paul has been her social passport for almost two years. And she's about to see it revoked. Bird sighs.

Cindy de la Vega squats down beside the two of them, surprising because she normally hangs with the sportier girls.

"Hey, guys," she says to Bird's shoes. The last she saw Cindy, she was buying prescription drugs to cram for exams. Did she rat on Coffee to get out of trouble? "You guys have any tampons? Left mine in my locker."

"Oh, you know, I might. Hold on...." As Charlotte rummages through her giant backpack and Bird shakes her head, Mrs. Early raises her voice above the din of the shelter —

"Just to be clear, not cooperating with the authorities about Alonso will be a matter for the honor board, ladies."

Charlotte shakes her head. "I used my last one, I guess. Sorry, Cindy."

Roosevelt whispers something in Mrs. Early's ear. The folds of her neck quiver as she shakes her head, and her pencil-lined lips collapse to a straight pink-and-brown smear on a pale face. Bird has never thought much about Mrs. Early one way or another, but she is sick with dread in the long moment that follows, watching the headmistress of the school walk through a sea of girls to where Bird huddles beside friends who don't want her anymore.

"Emily?" she says. "Come with me for a moment?"

And there's nothing for it but to brave the stares and the whispers, to collect her things and avoid Cindy's gape-mouthed squeak, Charlotte's awkward wave. Only Marella looks at her like she gives a fuck — a tensed jaw, a flash of rage, one lost outcast to another — *we'll make it through.*

Bird follows Mrs. Early silently. She wishes she could be as strong as Marella. But she can only be as strong as Bird.

"I'll take it from here, Molly."

Roosevelt stops at the base of the steps. Mrs. Early has replaced her face mask, as though there's more danger from a door to the outside than three hundred crowded kids and teachers. The skin at the corners of her eyes is crumpled paper, powder concealer following the crevasses like drifted snow. She seems far too old to have ever been the sort of person you could call "Molly," but she just nods sharply at Roosevelt and turns to Bird, arched eyebrows denoting some sort of false smile spreading beneath the mask.

"Mr. David would like to speak with you about Alonso, Emily. Your mother has assured me you'll give your full cooperation, but . . ."

"Honor code violation, yes, I heard," Bird says, even as she feels a spike of bile beneath her breastbone at the thought of her mother speaking with Mrs. Early. What did she say? In ninth grade, when she overslept one too many mornings, her mother parked the car instead of dropping her off, put her fist into the small of Bird's back, and marched her up the stairs to the administrative offices. Back then Mrs. Early had been the upper school director, and she maintained her eyebrows at a careful angle of sympathetic concern for the entire agonizing encounter. As Mrs. Early listened to Carol Bird number the sins of her ungrateful, lazy daughter who did not fully appreciate the opportunities rained upon her, only the slightest tremor of her lower jaw indicated that she found anything awkward about this impromptu public shaming.

But today a mask hides that telltale jaw muscle, perhaps by design. Perhaps Bird imagines the sympathetic slow blink as the headmistress turns away from them both.

"Well, Emily," Roosevelt says. "Come on up."

He doesn't wear a mask, and so Bird leaves hers in her pocket.

"What is this about?" she asks when they push through the gymnasium, away from the exit closest to the upper school.

He pulls out a key ring instead of answering, though he gives her a considering look, as if her hostility were an object of potential utility. He smiles.

"I don't know if you understand the stakes," he says. "I thought I might explain them to you."

They exit into a garbage alley. A few soldiers guard the opening to the street; he exchanges quick greetings as he goes to one of four sleek black cars with tinted windows. This one is a Beemer, the others are Audis.

"The stakes? Like, incarceration and death by pandemic disease? I got that, thanks," she says, and bares her teeth at him.

He rests an elbow on the top of the car. "Do you know how many people have died in Haiti?" he asks, strangely intent.

"A lot?"

"Fifty thousand."

Bird's pulse skitters. She feels as if she should have known this, but the numbers scrolling across the bottom of the news channels have blurred into an almost uniform horror. Or, at least, she has allowed them to blur. "That's awful," she says. "But what . . ."

"I'm just saying that you should be grateful for this country. You people always complain about what was done to you, but you never acknowledge everything we gave you. Well, just think about what would happen if you caught this flu in Haiti, or Zimbabwe, or —"

"Some other scary place with Black people?" she says, facing him over the hood of the car. He thinks she should be grateful her ancestors were slaves? That people of color in other countries have to continue to deal with the toxic residue of colonialism? Her stitches start to throb, but she's getting used to that, even feels grateful for it sometimes. At least it means she's alive. At least it means she survived.

"Get in the car," he says. For a moment, his shoe-polish blandness falls aside. There's something dark beneath it all, something sharp and angry. Terror shoots through her so strong she has to lean against the door to stay upright.

"No." Her throat is dry; her voice scratchy and soft.

He glances sidelong at the soldiers, facing away from them. "I really think you should." His calm has returned, but she's seen the threat beneath it. She fumbles for her cell phone and dials Nicky's number.

Whatever's going to happen she needs witnesses; she's done with going along willingly.

"Are you taking me to one of those black sites? Where you torture people?" It's a shot in the dark, a vague memory of a conversation with Coffee, but it makes his eyes go wide for a moment.

"*We* don't torture people."

"You just pay other countries to do it."

"Terrorists who want to hurt America don't deserve your pity. The people they hurt do. You have no idea how much our operatives sacrifice to keep you safe. Now, get in the car."

She gets in the car, but she texts Nicky: *If you don't get a message from me in forty minutes, call Mom ASAP. Mention Roosevelt. Love you, Em.*

Roosevelt watches this precaution with no discernible reaction except a fleeting smile. He starts the car.

"So how are things with you and Paul?" he asks, pulling out of the alley.

"Why, you'll have to ditch me if we break up?"

He turns smoothly onto Connecticut Avenue, one of the busiest streets in the District turned into a ghost town by quarantine and terror alerts. The only people on the sidewalk are soldiers. A few faces peek out from behind shopwindows, and Bird slouches in the leather seat, irrationally worried that someone might assume she's working with Roosevelt.

"Why aren't you wearing a mask?" she asks. "What about the terror alert?"

"There's no threat," he says. "False alarm. The all clear will go out in a few minutes. In the meantime . . ."

He switches into a higher gear and the engine drowns any conversation as they tear down the road, traffic lights blinking a stream of forlorn red behind them. The tires squeal when he makes the turn onto Military Road, and she wonders why her knuckles ache before she sees her hand gripping the handle above her head like she's hanging from a cliff.

"Could you slow down?" she says, clipping each word hard against the back of her teeth, not quite a scream but close enough.

He knows what he's doing. He sees her stitches. He visited her in the hospital, for God's sake. He's doing this to intimidate her, to show off, because he's a rich white dude who can, and —

He downshifts and glances at her. "Sorry, didn't mean to scare you."

"What the hell do you want?" He's still driving too fast, both hands on the wheel, every movement perfectly controlled and perfectly terrifying.

"I was wondering if you remembered any more about what you did that night of the party."

"Slower?"

"Because there was a period of time when no one knew where you were, Emily. You ran away from Paul while intoxicated, with a head injury. And next thing we know, Alonso is fleeing the authorities. It's very important that we find him."

The black line on the speedometer creeps to the right, steady as a clock. "I don't know where he is."

"Why did he run away? How did he know we were coming for him?"

Because I called him. That's what Coffee said, though she doesn't remember that or anything else that Roosevelt wants. And she wouldn't tell him even if she did.

"Slow down."

"You're holding something back, and you need to tell me what it is. Now. Did you contact him that night? Did you tell him something?"

"I don't know."

The line creeps past seventy; the car's engine grumbles and Roosevelt presses the clutch.

"Did he see you after you took the drug? What did he say?"

"Slow the fuck down!"

He releases it. The line falls left; she breathes and swallows. "I don't know anything about Coffee," she whispers.

"Paul is a good guy, you know. You shouldn't be so hard on him. He cares about you, and he's trying. You're better off with him than Alonso."

"Maybe I can take care of myself," she says, though lately she's started to wonder.

"Okay," he says. He signals, though they're alone on the road, and turns onto Sixteenth Street. "But think about what I'm saying. I trust you, Emily. I know Carol Bird's daughter will see things the right way, but maybe not all of my associates have the same, ah, faith. If you're with Paul, I might be able to ditch you more often."

"Why do you care so much, anyway? Do you think I could hurt you? That Coffee could?" Her heart races from the drive. She feels carsick.

"This isn't about a threat. It's about a *precaution*. Your parents have very important roles in the current crisis." He pauses, and turns down a side street. "What you call 'black sites' we call 'special operations.' But there's a reason some secrets need to stay secret. Nobody wants another WikiLeaks. US interests — the *good* that we can do around the world — depend on secrecy sometimes."

"Are you saying that my parents are going to leak something?"

"Of course not. I told you, this is a precaution."

"So I'm just insurance? So they keep quiet?"

"And you have a connection to a fugitive."

"But what does he have to do with my parents?"

"Because he's a criminal connected with you, and you are a person of interest."

Maybe, Bird thinks, but why ask her so much about that one night? As if they're terrified of what she might have told Coffee during her lost hours? As if it's *her* they're worried about leaking secrets, not her parents?

He parks. "So how about it, Emily? The more you hide from me, the more you hurt your parents."

The car reeks of his expensive cologne and cedar air freshener and leather and she's going to puke. She throws open the car door — unlocked, all this time? — and falls to her knees on the front lawn. *Her* front lawn. Only now, clutching her stomach and coughing up vomit, does she recognize where Roosevelt has taken her. The yellow quarantine tape swims in her vision, disguising and changing the stucco house where she's lived most of her life. *There's something hidden there, there's something terrible*, she thinks, but she doesn't know what.

Roosevelt squats beside her. She ought to vomit on him, but the threat has passed. He offers her a bottle of water, and she takes it after checking to make sure the seal is intact.

"Are you always so distrustful of authority?"

Not according to Carol Bird, but she doesn't tell him that. She just spits a swish of water onto the lawn, close enough to his pants that he flinches back, and wipes her mouth with the back of her hand.

"Distrustful of assholes," she says, and hauls herself to her feet on the pure, brass-balled faith that they will hold her up. They do.

She squints up at the house, but it makes her stomach lurch again, and so she looks down the block instead. No other quarantine signs in this upper-middle-class neighborhood, not like Nicky's stricken Northeast streets.

"Is that maid okay?" she asks. "The one with the flu?"

He just shrugs, a simple gesture that dissolves, finally and completely, any lingering hope that he might not be so bad after all.

"This is some flu we've got," she says. "It only kills poor people."

"I wouldn't believe everything he tells you."

She keeps her eyes on his shoulder. "I wouldn't believe he tells me anything."

"We know you've talked to him."

She shrugs, an elaborate mimicry that wins her a frown and a restless toe tap. Somewhere in the distance horns blast a single high-pitched pulse. The all clear, she guesses.

"If you knew something, you'd have arrested him by now," she says. She takes a step back — an involuntary twitch to put distance between them. He reacts with unexpected speed, grabs her upper arm in a firm grip that would hurt if she pulled away.

"So I take it you don't remember anything."

Her blood pounds beneath his fingers; the cigarette stench of his breath would make her puke again if she weren't so afraid. She's pushed him too far. By the time Nicky calls her mother, it'll be too late.

"I told you I didn't."

He holds her for a moment longer, then lets her go.

"I'll take you to your uncle's," he says.

"I'm not getting in that car again."

He hesitates. "The bus is pretty slow these days."

"I'll do my homework."

He nods and gets back in his car. She waits until he's pulled from the curb and turned the corner to Sixteenth Street before she takes a full breath. Then she picks up her backpack, feels every one of its thirty pounds, and walks to the bus shelter. The yellow bottle they gave her at the hospital has never been far from her reach since she returned to school. The last three pills rattle like a toy maraca, and the woman on the other end of the bench looks away pointedly as Bird dumps all three in her mouth and swallows.

Coffee dubbed her Bird the first time they met, a presumption that she didn't much remark on at the time, but in the end, changed her life. We can't know who's going to change us — least of all me, this lonely crier in her mind's dusty corners. I only know that the sight of him struck us like a supernova, with the violence of beauty. For-ever changed, though that chemical reaction still has yet to fully balance. I keep trying, but it takes more than a spell to change lead to gold.

It takes chemistry. And who would know more about that than Alonso Oliveira?

Witness our moment of reaction: Emily Bird has escaped a lecture from her mother to attend the party of a Landon boy Felice has been crushing on for the last two months. It's the start of junior year, and while Felice has landed the boy in a lip-lock beside the refrigerator, Emily has taken herself into the balmy early-September air on the back porch of yet another Bethesda mansion. A boy leaning against the railing has handed a bag to a pair of girls and taken some money in exchange. Alone now, he pulls a straight battered metal pipe from his pocket and flicks shaky fingers over the wheel of a lighter.

Catalyst: I see you standing there. I don't bite.

Reagent: You're a *dealer*.

C: I know, a dealer at a *Landon* party? [He lights up, takes a drag.]

R: You go to Landon?

C: Nah. Bradley. And you're at Devonshire.

R: How do you —

C: Seen you around. [Breathes out] Want some?

R: [Steps closer] Is that crack?

C: [Coughs, laughs] *Foda-se!* It's sweet opium, straight from a den in Chinatown. I'll be Greene if you'll be Hemingway.

R: [Looks down] Oh, it's pot. Weird pipe.

[Smiling, he offers her some. She takes it after glancing over her shoulder.]

C: It's a heavy Indica, mixed with a bit of hash. A fine, mellow high.

R: [Sucks on the pipe, coughs] You sound like a sommelier.

C: Nothing like prep school girls for SAT words.

R: It's a —

C: I know what it means. And English isn't even my first language.

R: What is? [Takes a second toke]

C: Organic chemistry.

R: Teach that along with the alphabet in . . . Portugal, do they?

C: Close. Brazil.

R: Wow. What did you say this stuff was?

C: You like it?

R: I think the last pot I tried was actually oregano.

C: I can see why I got invited to this party. Should I sell your boyfriend some?

R: How do you —

C: I told you. I've seen you around. You're Bird, right?

R: Em — Emily.

C: Emily Bird. I'm Alonso Oliveira.

R: Alonso the dealer.

C: But Betty, if you call me, you can call me Coffee.

Bird: What kind of a name is that?

Coffee: The one that fits, Bird.

[melatonin]

$$C_{13}H_{16}N_2O_2$$

Nicky is hysterical when she finally calls him, saying he's been trying to get through to her mother for the last ten minutes and what the hell is going on, anyway? Bird tells him the truth, as far as it goes —

"This asshole cop keeps harassing me," she says. "I'm trying to handle it."

He pauses. Then, "Well, *shit*, kid."

"I know."

Another pause, and then a distant voice shouting on his end. "I've gotta get back to work. You okay? You sure?"

"Sure," she says, slouching against the bus window and bunching her feet above the heater. The shivering has almost stopped. She jumps every time she sees one of those black cars zip past the bus, but she knows intellectually that Roosevelt wouldn't bother following her.

Which doesn't mean somebody else isn't. She looks around the street when she gets back to Nicky's, but if someone has staked her out, she can't see them. She hunches her shoulders against the memory of Roosevelt's greedy eyes and unlocks the door. She knows Aaron's home from the strains of Muddy Waters pulsing through the basement. Last year, Aaron uncovered their grandfather's album collection and dusted off the record player to go with it. He was just eight when their grandparents died, but they'd helped raise him since he was a baby and she figures that this is his way of reconnecting.

"Aaron," she hollers down the stairs, "did you eat?"

Muddy moans his way through another verse of "Trouble No More," and Lord, but today is the sort of day she can use the blues.

"Not yet," Aaron calls back. "Could we have pizza?"

In this neighborhood, "pizza" means Domino's or Papa John's. She sighs; she has complicated feelings about Northwest, but it sure as hell has better food.

"Okay, but I'm making a salad first."

She ignores his groan and heads to the kitchen. The music is soothing, a sound track of afternoons cooking with her grandmother and gossiping about the latest family scandals. The fridge is bare compared to those days, but the hunk of romaine lettuce is just good enough to use. She clucks her tongue; if she's going to keep living with Nicky, she might have to take over grocery shopping. She brings the salad and silverware down to the basement with her, where blues chord progressions and that rich, careworn voice surround them both like a blanket. She sits with Aaron on the floor and sets the salad bowl between them.

"Do I have to?" he says, taking the fork.

"I got you stuffed crust, and my mom would kill me if I let you get scurvy."

"What's scurvy?"

"A vitamin deficiency from too much pizza. Eat. It's got ranch dressing."

This seems to ameliorate his horror of lettuce. The needle hits the end of the record a few minutes later, and Aaron hurries to change it.

"I'm starting to like Lead Belly," he says. "But Robert Johnson is the best." He puts the latter on the turntable, a record that looks old enough to have belonged to her great-grandfather.

She shakes her head. "You are awesome, you know that?"

He grins at her and turns the volume up so loud she couldn't hear his response if she wanted to. Then he scoots beside her and puts his arm around her shoulder.

"That guy, that one from before," he says into her ear, still barely audible. "I think he gave me this for you."

He slides a piece of paper into her hand. Bird stares at his uncharacteristically solemn face. He knew this was dangerous. He knew people might be listening.

That guy from before. Coffee, slouching in a gray hoodie in front of the hospital bus stop. Coffee, who said he would try. For you, Bird.

She looks down at the grenade in her hands.

CANAL LOCK 7. I MIGHT HAVE SOMETHING. DON'T CALL, JUST COME IF YOU CAN. TOMORROW, MIDNIGHT. THEY'RE WATCHING.

She chokes on her saliva when she finally remembers to take a breath, and coughs painfully while Aaron frowns at her.

"You okay, Em?" he asks.

God, when did Aaron get so smart and wise and musically precocious? And with Nicky as a father? But then, look at how well Monique turned out too. Maybe it isn't as much of a fluke as her mother likes to imagine.

"Fine, Aaron," she says when she has her breath back. "I'm great. Thanks for showing me this. Where did you get it?"

"I found it in my locker."

Coffee hasn't skipped town. Her heart pounds, like it knows what she doesn't want to admit: He stayed for her.

And if Roosevelt is right? If he was the one who gave her the drug that so thoroughly screwed up her life?

"You going, Em?" Aaron asks, low against the plaintive high timbre of a man who sold his soul at the crossroads.

The idea of sneaking out under Roosevelt's nose terrifies her. But she wants to see Coffee. Because she wants to know what happened. Because she wants him to say to her face that he gave her that drug. She wants to be brave. Be brave, Emily Bird!

"Don't know, Aaron," she says, and he wipes her cheek with his beloved, dirty sleeve.

Her mother calls just after Bird has swallowed two of the over-the-counter sleeping pills that are definitely against Dr. Granger's recommended sleep hygiene program. She prays for merciful unconsciousness throughout the five-minute conversation, the duration of which she is painfully, prickingly awake. Her mother's words fall like water on her forehead:

"Your uncle called me today. He was very concerned."

Plop.

"Didn't I tell you to follow all the instructions your school gave you? That includes speaking with Mr. David. He'll have told you that we know each other."

Plop.

"I'll admit he can be a bit . . . trying at times, interpersonally. But the man is quite competent and good at his job. There was no reason to panic."

Bird looks down at the bruises blooming on her upper arm, four long, livid smears of purple.

"Your uncle's reflexive distrust of authority is the sign of a less evolved, childlike consciousness, and I understand that. But you, Emily, I expect you to know better."

Plop. Bird presses a finger against a bruise.

"I thought you said I always need to be told what to do. That I couldn't think independently."

"Don't talk back, Emily." Her mother's cool voice is an efficiently delivered slap. "I know perfectly well what I said, but now is not the time for you to stage some belated teenage rebellion. Employ your situational intelligence —"

"My situation —"

"Girl! Do not cross me. This is a phase six pandemic. There's a war about to start. There's rumors flying around about a draft! I thank Jesus every day that you're safe at Devonshire inside the quarantine, and I have paid my dues to keep you there. Do not do anything to jeopardize that. Cooperate with Mr. David. If you hear anything from that drug dealer, tell him immediately —"

"Mom, what does Coffee have to do with any of this? Why do they care so much?"

She braces herself for an explosion; her mother does not tolerate unfinished paragraphs, let alone interrupted sentences. But all she hears on the other end is a strange, high-pitched wheeze, like an overfull balloon grudgingly releasing air.

"They say he's a drug dealer."

"So are a lot of people."

A pause. Then, very carefully: "You've always known when to stop asking questions, Emily."

Bird closes her eyes. It's not about the drugs at all. Of course it isn't, why would Roosevelt, why would Lukas Group, why would *Synergy Labs* bother with some prep school pill pusher? Because they're afraid he knows something. Because of that night.

"I guess so," Bird finally says, and she could swear that her mother sounds grateful.

She falls asleep within minutes of hanging up the phone, dreams dragging her under like lazy sharks. She doesn't even have time to change into her pajamas, just slumps against the pillows in her underwear and bra.

She wakes up an hour later, panicked and shivering with cooling sweat. But the sleeping pills want her back, the dreams she can't remember demand her attention, and so she only manages to claw some covers on top of her before falling back inside the well of her own mind.

Remember, Bird, she tells herself, even as another part of her, an Emily part, flinches at the prospect of palpating those seeping wounds.

She dreams of Coffee without ever seeing him. He's on the other end of the telephone, or just around the corner, or calling her name in the dark. She repeats his telephone number to herself while she tries to dial it with shaking fingers. She presses the wrong buttons, endlessly. She won't get in touch with him in time. She will be too late.

In her dream, his phone rings.

Bird wakes up.

The shrine to Lara Swan in the senior room has acquired new flowers — plastic roses, in this case, after the Crenshaw twins complained about fresh flowers aggravating their allergies. Bird hardly remembers Lara, though they were classmates for all of lower and middle school, before the Swan family moved to San Francisco.

The picture above the plastic flowers looks recent, but a little fuzzy, as though someone swiped it from her Facebook page. Lara had been a petite, round-faced white girl everyone thought looked ten at thirteen, and would probably be carded until she got gray hair.

At least, she would have been. But Mrs. Early announced her death, along with that of her younger brother and father, at assembly that morning. Charlotte cried right until the start of second period. Bird stayed with her before the first-period bell, but then Felice came and texted Gina, and Bird's presence became subtly, emphatically redundant. Bird thumbed the clasp of Paul's bracelet, wondered if this was the sound of the wind rushing past her ears, and retreated. Charlotte has always been nicer, but Charlotte has never cared about Bird enough to stand up to Felice.

Bird doesn't look up from her history homework when Felice and five of her friends burst into the senior room, even though something about that bright, warming laugh sets her ears back like a dog's. Rupa Patel and Cindy de la Vega have been watching the news — reports from California, reports from Caracas and the "narco-terrorist battle-front" — but Felice marches straight to the television and changes the channel. She smiles at Cindy and shrugs in Rupa's general direction — assuming forgiveness, as though not giving a damn about anyone else were just an endearing quirk.

Rupa snorts and rolls her eyes, but no more: She's not high enough on the ladder to get away with it or low enough to not care about the consequences. Cindy just stands and walks over to Lara's shrine.

They have switched to a romantic comedy about two doctors, so cosmically inappropriate that Bird feels words rising out of her like an emetic.

"Honestly?"

Felice brushes down her bangs and smiles over her shoulder. "Emily, I didn't even see you! What are you doing over there by yourself? Denise, move over so Emily can sit down."

Bird hesitates, but the invitation is irresistible. The inner circle has been her safe space at Devonshire for most of high school; what kind of decision would it be to give it up now, when every other part of her life is crumbling like pounded sandstone?

So Bird sits where she has been directed. The bracelet feels heavy and cold on her wrist, but a half hour passes before she learns the real reason for Felice's unexpected gesture.

"So you and Paul?" she says.

Bird presses her palms into the carpet. "The perfect couple?"

"Sometimes even perfect has its problems."

"What's it to you, Felice? Do you want him?"

Felice laughs softly and shakes her head. "Why make this so hard? I'm just trying to help you. Paul is . . . important to the dynamic of the group. You know that."

Bird wants to rip off the bracelet and throw it at the sixty-inch flat-screen television that Gina's parents gifted to the senior class at the start of the school year. It's horrible to see body bags and helicopters in high definition, but it's somehow even worse to see Owen Wilson.

"So, what, you'll ditch me if we break up?"

They stare at each other, shocked by the rawness of Bird's words, by the clarity with which they are very nearly done with each other.

"I'd be sad, that's all," Felice says, recovering first.

Bird takes a deep breath, another, and lowers her head. She and Felice can use each other amicably, they always have. She just has to get back inside the line. She just has to survive, and get into a good college, and satisfy her mother —

"Sorry. Shitty day. It's my cramps, I think."

Felice pats her hand and smiles in beneficent forgiveness. "Oh, no worries. PMS totally sucks."

Bird retreats, sits in a bathroom stall for fifteen minutes before forcing herself to go back. But when she does Felice and her posse have gone, leaving the two awkward costars to grimace at each other in images so sharp and saturated they make Bird feel fuzzed out and gray. The only person left is Cindy, writing a message on Lara's shrine. Bird walks over and studies the photograph again. An arm drapes casually over Lara's shoulder, but whoever it is has been cut from the image. An ex? Boyfriend? Girlfriend? The dead brother? All that is written beneath Lara's name are dates, so close together they look more like a mistake than an epitaph. She was eighteen, but just barely. Three months older than Bird.

"It's so sad." Cindy's infamous peroxide hair is twisted into a messy bun that reveals roots as untended and overgrown as Bird's.

"Yeah."

"I was thinking of starting a memorial wall. Like, for parents and relatives and stuff. There's a sophomore whose brother just died. And look at everyone who's missing school, I bet there's a lot more."

Her expression is an earnest wince, but she still focuses anywhere but Bird's face. Just like Charlotte, never quite looking her way as she sat in a different desk during religion class. But Cindy isn't part of Felice's circle, so why bother freezing Bird? Did something happen between them that Bird doesn't remember? Bird remembers her at that party. She might have stayed after Felice and Charlotte left. She might have seen something. If Bird can corroborate Paul and Roosevelt's story, then she won't have any choice but to trust their judgment. She'll tell them about Coffee's letter. They'll meet him on the canal, at lock 7 in her place — he'll be there, she knows it in her teeth, nothing could keep him — and he will hate her forever, for his own good. She'll probably stay with Paul and wear his bracelet and sit with Felice in the senior room, and all the steady lines of her life will realign, unto infinity.

And Coffee will be in jail, or deported.

"Cindy, at Trevor's party, did you see me and Paul . . ."

She doesn't know what to ask, but Cindy jerks and stumbles back. She meets Bird's eyes for a searing moment, a lash of shame and horror Bird can't quite understand, but seizes upon.

"You did," Bird whispers. "You know something."

Cindy looks around the senior room, but they're alone with the white plastic flowers and white people endearingly misunderstanding each other and the mustard-yellow couch that reeks of hasty teenage sex.

Cindy bites her bottom lip, smearing pink lipstick on her teeth. Her eyes are bloodshot, tired, and a little wet. Bird doesn't flatter herself into thinking this has much to do with her, but she hopes she might be a contributing factor.

"I'm not, I mean, listen, if you want to talk to someone about it, I get it. You have" — she takes a deep breath and wipes her eyes — "no idea how much I get it, but I'm not, like, the one. There are professionals. I'm no good at this. Why don't you try Ms. Riley?"

Cindy turns to leave, but Bird steps in front of her. "And tell her *what*, Cindy? Don't you get it? I don't remember! Paul told me something, but . . ." *But it doesn't make sense.*

Cindy's shoulders slump, then shake with a sob. "There was something in the drink, wasn't there? In his canteen. I wondered, you got drunk so fast. But I didn't . . . I couldn't just accuse Paul like that, what would Byron say, they go to the same church, and everyone knows you and Paul have been together for ages, I mean, they didn't believe *me* when I barely knew him . . . what could I do? I feel sick every time I look at you, Emily, but what could I do?"

Bird finds a breath in her throat and forces herself to suck it the rest of the way in, filling her chest with stale chips and musty carpet and the bitter stink of what she imagines must be both of their terror.

"You think he raped me?"

Paul strapping her into the car, telling her everything will be okay.

"I told you, I didn't actually *see* anything. If I'd seen that, believe me, I wouldn't have given a fuck who Byron went to church with."

Bird's breath rattles out of her like one of Coffee's laughs, brittle as ossified bone. But relieved, so relieved. There's more to this story, she knows it. She remembers that unavailable call on Paul's phone moments before she passed out. Whatever Paul did, Roosevelt was involved. And Coffee? Well, there had to be a reason for him to chase after her like that.

"But you saw me drinking something from a canteen?"

"Yeah. Peach schnapps. Everyone was drinking it, but Paul poured some into this canteen he brought and you two went off into the woods. Then you came back, I don't know, fifteen minutes later? And you were smashed, Emily. I mean, sure, he poured a lot into that canteen, but fifteen minutes? You were falling all over yourself and crying and laughing at the same time. You could hardly string a sentence together."

"And Paul?"

She crosses her arms close to her body, fierce and on guard.

"He came for you a little while later. Said he was taking you home. You didn't seem like you wanted to go — at least, you kept saying something about needing to call Coffee. And then I thought it was probably okay, because maybe you'd taken some crazy drug of his in the woods with Paul, like you'd meant to get like that."

"I didn't." She's sure of it now, though there's still so many lost hours. But she knows herself, and she knows how she left things with

Coffee in the basement. She would never have gotten smashed on one of his designer drugs in the woods behind Trevor Robinson's house.

"I'm *sorry!*" Cindy shouts, loud enough to be embarrassing if they hadn't gone far past the point where such things mattered.

"Did something happen to you . . . like that?"

Cindy reaches for the doorknob, but doesn't turn it. "There's drugs," she says hoarsely. "That are supposed to . . . make it easy. Rohypnol. GHB. I'd say you should ask Coffee, but . . ."

"Otherwise occupied."

"If it happened, I'm sorry. I won't tell you Paul is a good guy. The ones they think are good guys do it too. And no one will believe you, so I hope for your sake that he didn't. And . . ."

"And?"

"I won't talk about this again. I can't."

Bird nods, up and down, up and down, with a painful jerkiness it takes conscious effort to stop. "Okay. Okay." She takes a deep breath. "Thanks, Cindy."

Cindy shakes her head and opens the door, brushing past someone in the hallway. Bird stumbles out behind her and bumps into Felice.

"Oh, there you are!" Felice smiles her tight-lipped smile. "Where'd you ghost to?"

"Bathroom," Bird manages.

"I couldn't help but overhear. Is Cindy going on about David Upton again? You know you can't believe anything she says about him." David Upton graduated Bradley last year, and now Bird recalls the vague rumors about him and Cindy last summer.

"I can't?"

Felice's lips stretch like pale, rose-colored putty across her face. "She's a slut. Everyone knows it, and I think we can safely say that Upton was way out of her league. Like she didn't want it. It looks bad, saying things about people that everyone knows are lies. I'd be careful, Emily. Friendly advice."

She and Felice have learned to get along over the years, for the sake of Charlotte. But Bird is watching that door close and all she can think about is what Paul might have given her that night, what he might have done with it, and what kind of monster wouldn't care.

"I'll do what I have to," Bird says.

"So will I. Oh, and Emily?"

"Yes?"

Felice reaches out and pats her head, very gently. "Is something wrong with your hair? It's a little . . . puffy."

Bird stares at her, shamed into silence. Felice seizes her victory in her delicate, manicured hands and walks into the senior room.

Alone, Bird slumps against the wall, buries her hands deep into her puffy, unacceptable roots, and waits for the knife in her heart to hold still.

Six Things Coffee Has Told Bird and She Almost Believes

(1) A million Iraqis died in the war. If asked, she'd have said it was maybe 80,000, but he told her those lower numbers were from the US government, which only acknowledged someone dead from the war if they were reported in the newspaper. And since it's a war, how is it possible for the newspapers to have counted every single dead person? She says that doesn't actually mean the US Army is responsible for all those dead people, obviously the insurgency and stuff caused most of it, but Coffee just flicks his fingers and asks if there would have been an insurgency in the first damn place, without our invasion? She doesn't know what she thinks, but whenever she sees these implausibly low numbers tossed around in newspaper articles or on television, she flinches. Eighty thousand is a lot of people, but a million is so large she can hardly wrap her heart around it.

(2) He doesn't sell the drugs he makes himself. They're too danger-ous, he says. If that's true, she asks, then why make them at all? "I'm a

94

spelunker in the caves of my own psyche," he said one evening after school. "And a master craftsman of my tools." She told him this was some self-aggrandizing bullshit, and he laughed and blew smoke in her hair.

(3) She already knew that one in three Black men will go to prison in their lifetime, most of them for nonviolent drug offenses. But it was Coffee who told her that the work they did there was for private corporations. One prison in Louisiana is actually located on an old plantation, and the Black men there pick cotton and corn for pennies an hour, just like their great-grandfathers.

In 1969, right before he launched the war on drugs, Nixon told one of his top aides: "You have to face the fact that the whole problem is really the Blacks. The key is to devise a system that recognizes this while not appearing to." Watching half of her Northeast acquaintances disappear into the maw of the system, she has to believe it. Carol Bird doesn't, but morality is the change that falls from your pockets when you climb up the ladder.

(4) She's too good for Paul. He doesn't rag on Paul all the time, but often enough, especially when Paul calls him Alonso and gives them dirty looks for hanging with each other. He thinks Paul is a controlling freak who lacks empathy. She thinks Coffee is contemptuous of ambition because he doesn't have any himself. "So why not admit Paul and I are perfect for each other?" she asked. He just shook his head. "Don't you want something better?" *Like you?* she thought, but didn't — couldn't — ask.

(5) Venezuela is now an official enemy for the same reason all the rest were — opposition to US interests. He dismissed the windfall tax crisis of the summer entirely. They're sitting on trillions of dollars in oil wealth, why *shouldn't* they keep it for their own people instead of giving it to multinationals? Especially since oil caused the global warming that caused the droughts in the first place?

Sure, their socialist government isn't a shining example of political morality, but who is? The US supported a coup against Chávez in 2002 and only the mass popular uprising of Venezuelans put him back in office. Sadly, that isn't true for at least nine other US-supported coups of democratically elected governments in Latin America in the last hundred years. And we wonder why "they" hate us?

(6) Ignoring your subconscious is like neglecting the termite infestation in your basement. Sooner or later, the consequences of neglect will far outweigh the momentary unpleasantness of clearing the nests. He thinks Bird doesn't do enough "self-examination." He thinks her parents are "pieces of work" and she's going to have a breakdown in college if she doesn't slow down and smell some roses. The irony of him saying this while skipping class in the rose garden was not lost on her. She brushed him off, but his words knotted in the pit of her stomach — what if she did break down in college, what would her mother say? It would prove Carol Bird right, for her daughter to fail the modestly rigorous course laid out for her. So she told Coffee not everyone could feel satisfied reading novels and chemistry journals and occasionally handing in papers two weeks late. He shrugged and told her to ask him for some shrooms when she was ready. "You're such a hippie," she said, and his eyes sliced into her like lasers. "Do I look like a hippie? I'm right, Bird."

He was right, Bird. The foundations are nearly gone. If you don't find me soon, I can't tell you what's going to come down.

[tetrahydrocannabinol (THC)]

$C_{21}H_{30}O_2$

Bird is brave, she tells herself, *Bird can dare.* Emily is terrified to go find Coffee at the canal lock, and only Bird can help her.

For now, she prepares her armor. She sits in the basement bathroom, the one with her grandmother's claw-foot tub, and unscrews the lid off the jar of Nicky's Hawaiian Silky. He offered to help, but her hands shook when she took it from him and all she could do was tell him no, she was fine by herself.

The smell of perfumed conditioners and relaxing chemicals is familiar to her, though she's always had the help of her mother or her aunt or a stylist. Her mother's preferences are old-fashioned; she's used Hawaiian Silky for years and won't hear of trying any of the newer brands. Let alone anything more radical: Bird has always wondered how she'd look with a more natural style. Once she asked if she could get her hair braided like Charlotte, and Carol Bird just frowned and said, "Charlotte's more Howard than Harvard. Don't make it easy for them to dismiss you."

But which "them"? Bird wonders now. White admissions officers? Or Carol Bird?

She dips the brush into the white cream and waves it experimentally over her head. She'll only have fifteen minutes to cover her roots once she begins. She last thing she needs right now is bald patches from an overtimed relaxer. She's taken off Paul's bracelet and slipped on the plastic gloves a little gritty from past use. She should probably smear more Vaseline between the careful parts in her thicket of hair, but it's getting late, and it will take her at least two hours to walk all the way down the canal to Lock 7. If she goes.

"I'll go," Bird says, holding the cream-laden brush like a sword. After what Cindy told her, how can she miss the chance to ask him what he saw? To find out what sent him sprinting down that driveway, too late to save her? She's thought a lot about what happened to Cindy, and what Paul might have done. She feels sick with the possibilities, and though her empty memories ache each time she presses them, she isn't sure that Cindy's suspicions are right. Ambition is the fuel that runs Paul's engine, and whatever happened that night had something to do with that endless, combusting need to get ahead. She can't say it's impossible that rape came into it — not with Roosevelt involved — but she thinks, she feels, she hopes that it didn't.

Coffee might know for sure; at least, he knows more than she does. But to sneak out in defiance of curfew, of common sense, of her mother's explicit prohibition — that's nothing Emily would do. But it's not Emily who's desperate to see him.

Sometimes it kills me, what you could be.

The brush falls from her fingers, smearing cream on her thigh and down the side of the tub. She stares at it longer than she should, even after she feels that slow tingle that will lead, inevitably, to burning. The smooth, glistening finish, the lumps like globs of rice pudding, the hair salon smell that has so anchored her most intimate interactions with her mother, it leaves her light-headed and gasping. She's lost everything already. On her laptop upstairs an email from Ms. Vern, the college guidance counselor, informs all graduating seniors that college application deadlines have been deferred for three months. The news from California looks worse every day. Who is she doing this for? For the Devonshire girls, wondering what's happened to Emily since she left the hospital? For her mother, who couldn't be bothered to leave her undisclosed location even when Bird was in a coma? For Stanford, who can't have her even if they did want her?

The tingle crosses the line into pain slowly enough that she only notices when her body jerks, as if of its own accord, and she reaches for a towel to wipe it off. Her arm knocks the bracelet into the sink, and the burn from the relaxer bleeds into the sight of those needle-sharp gold leaves and their drops of ruby fruit. Without thinking, she drops it into the Hawaiian Silky tub, watches it sink and disappear into the glistening white, and screws the lid tight.

She finds Aaron outside, looking through the record collection.

"You done, Em?"

A pair of scissors glows like a cartoon pirate treasure on the table behind him. "Aaron," she says hazily, "what about some LaBelle? 'Something in the Air'?"

Aaron nods, though he's only lately discovered his father's seventies R and B collection. To the anthemic determination of "The Revolution Won't Be Televised," Bird takes the scissors to her hair. With each snip she discards not the roots but the floss, not the Bird but the Emily. She cuts and cuts until the hair surrounds her, until her head floats from her shoulders, until she laughs with the Bird in the mirror, the badass diva with a tight fro who can do anything at all.

"Em?"

She gasps and turns around. Aaron takes a step forward and then hesitates. He looks afraid.

"Are you okay? You . . ."

Seeing his reaction sends a lump of fear into her gut; familiar, but not, this time, insurmountable.

"I'm cool, Aaron. I think it's better this way, don't you?"

Aaron smiles. "You're always cool, Em."

The C&O Canal runs from the heart of DC to deep rural Maryland, and Coffee's meeting place is a deserted lock a few miles over the DC–Maryland border. Bird sneaks onto the towpath in Georgetown before the ten o'clock curfew, dressed in a hoodie, baggy jeans, and a pair of Nicky's old Nikes laced tight. This disguise takes her over her neighbors' fences, until she reaches Rosedale Street and saunters onto the sidewalk like she owns the thing. No cars follow her. She only passes a few hardy runners on the towpath, but they vanish a half hour before curfew. She jumps at every squirrel scampering through rotting leaves, at every duck paddling through the water, but Coffee knew what he was about: They've probably secured the canal at the border to the quarantine, but here she can't see a soul.

Lock 7 is one of the smaller outposts, which she only knows from the times she cycled past it in the summer on her way to the more famous (and scenic) Great Falls. She sees no one by the abandoned lockhouse, so she walks a little farther, to where the water pools high behind the gates that once upon a time would open to allow barges through. He's not at the lock either.

"Coffee?" She dares a whisper, her breath a wisp of white. The coldest night of the year so far, but until now she hasn't felt it.

Did something happen to him? Is he even now in some anonymous cavity in the bowels of the Pentagon, specially interrogated by Roosevelt David? She tosses her hood back and buries her fingers in her shorn hair, forcing herself to concentrate on the texture of kinky curls coated with coconut oil, forcing the panic out with each lacy breath of air. Maybe he just ditched her. Maybe he's halfway to Brazil right now, a daring escape before they lock him away, and could she blame him? She's more terrified of Roosevelt than the v-flu, and no one is trying to arrest her.

And then, "I didn't recognize you."

She spins around to see him in the lee of the trees by the path, his long limbs folded against the cold or some deep ache. His fat worm curls are covered with a dark gray ski cap and his fair skin is smudged with dirt. Only his eyes shine in the cloud-obscured glow of a gibbous moon, green and gray and gold and full of wonder.

"Are you okay?" she asks softly.

"Is anyone? Are you? Nice do, Bird."

She takes a breathless step closer. She didn't really believe that she would see him again. She didn't dare. "Don't mock me."

Wide lips stretch into a smile. A Coffee smile, full of broken glass and finely ground pepper, but genuine for all that. "I'm not," he says, and on his long legs a step out from the trees brings him a handbreadth away. "You look beautiful, Emily Bird."

"I look like a boy."

He laughs. "No. You don't."

One raised arm would touch him, pull him close, obliterate everything but the two of them and the desire she has felt since the moment they met. Surely he's felt it? Surely he cares, even a little?

"So do you know something? Can you tell me what happened that night?"

He tilts his head to the side, regarding her silently while a few late crickets sing and the Potomac River gurgles distantly. He lifts his left arm, and she notices the sleeve of his sweatshirt is torn and stained a dark color she hopes, insists, is just mud. His long fingers hover an inch from the side of her face.

"You're alone."

"Who else would come with me? Nicky?"

"Roosevelt?"

She flinches, nearly chokes on the memory of just how close she came to proving him right. Coffee's hand drops.

"You nearly did. Oh, of course you did."

His weary certainty galls her. Especially because, in the fullness of his presence, she can't think of anyone she trusts more. "If you didn't trust me, why go through the trouble of asking me here? Why the hell aren't you halfway to Brazil by now?"

She leans forward, greedy enough to inhale his familiar scent, now tinged with the earthy musk of mud and sweat. Why does Coffee have to be Coffee? Prickly and sharp and unfathomable. There's nothing easy about him.

"I needed a reason to stay."

She raises her eyebrows. "Don't let me stop you."

"Oh God, Bird." He rips the cap off of his head and grips it tight in his fist. She swears he shines in the dim light, anger leaking incandescent from his pores. "Do you hate me so much?"

"It's not about that."

"Then why? Paul — no, he did something else, didn't he? You flinched. Bird has finally figured him out."

"Bird is . . ." She shakes her head. She's ashamed of how Roosevelt and Paul have threatened her with that relationship. She doesn't want Coffee to see her like that — a soft girl who can be bent and pressed into service. "Anyway, it's not Paul, it's Roosevelt. You don't want to get within a thousand miles of him. Go home, Coffee."

He rubs his wrist where the sleeve has torn and smiles sadly. "This isn't my home?"

"You know what I mean."

"I've lived in Brazil, what, four years total? I've spent more time in DC than Brasília."

It's true that his accent is strange, some polyglot mix of American and British and Brazilian Portuguese, a linguistic palimpsest of places lived and abandoned. It warms her, somehow, that he wants to claim the only place she's ever called home. But still — "Only one of them is going to kill you."

A dismissive flick of his fingers. "Anything can kill me."

"Like you're some badass? Please. You weren't even smooth enough to deal Adderall."

"It wasn't my fault!"

"Then get away! Leave! Whatever happens there can't be worse than Roosevelt."

A wind whips the trees, dislodging the few remaining brown and withered leaves from their branches. It feels like the end of the world out here, like the two of them are unlikely survivors of the apocalypse.

Coffee takes a step back. "Bird. What the hell did he do?"

"You gonna defend my honor?"

She regrets her words immediately, so punchy and vulnerable. She's had too little sleep and too much trouble, and now she's hurt him. She can see him take a breath and hold it, see his wide eyes, his open palms hanging in the air like they only want something to grab.

"Bird?" His voice is tight as a piano wire, his eyes are wet. A trickle spills out onto his cheek and she grabs his hands without thinking.

"No. No." She shakes her head, but her voice drifts out again, quiet, unsure, "At least, I don't think so."

His grip hurts her, but she doesn't even try to pull away. "I tried to stop him," he whispers. "Do you remember that, at least? When you called the next morning, I knew I'd been right, but it was too late. . . ."

"What?" She stares up at him, baffled and terrified at the hollow, windy place inside of her where all her memories should be. "The writing on the wall? Did you write that?"

"I didn't write anything. I didn't see you after the party."

"What did I say? Did you learn anything else?"

He hesitates.

"You promised you'd tell me, Coffee!"

She rips herself away from him, furious and taking it out on the nearest willing target. She wants him to scream back at her, but he doesn't — just walks to the bench overlooking the lock gate. Bird has loved sitting on the canal in the summer, light streaming through the trees and the soft gurgle of water flowing past. Even in the stink of July, when the algae floats die in one great Malthusian jamboree, she has loved flying down the towpath on her bicycle, geese scrambling out of her way and clouds of gnats bumbling in confusion behind her. She would go with Nicky and Mo and little Aaron toddling behind on his tricycle. They would barbecue by the river and avoid the geese and complain about the mosquitos as the sun went down. Then Aaron would beg for "Papa's music," and Nicky would put on some scratchy Motown CD, the one where "Mr. Postman" always skipped, and she and Mo always belted out the last of the chorus. . . .

"Wait a minute, Mr. Postman," Bird sings now, warm with the memory of heat.

Coffee has rolled a blunt in the silence, and into a fragrant exhalation he looks at her and says, "What's that?"

Bird laughs. "We'd be terrible together," she says. "You don't even know music."

"I know plenty of music. Have you heard Caetano Veloso? Chico Buarque?"

"Muddy Waters?" she counters, for the first time considering that she might have gotten a contact high. "Prince?"

"Dude, Prince? I'm from Brazil, not Antarctica."

"Sorry."

He smiles a sweet, decidedly un-Coffee smile that melts her into the seat. She would kiss that smile in a different world. "We could teach each other," he says.

"You're a fugitive from justice. I'm under the surveillance of a creep security officer and my asshole boyfriend and my mother. Also, there's a plague. It's not going to work out."

"Your mother doesn't get an adjective? Cold? Ambitious? Demanding?"

"Carol Bird is Carol Bird," she says. "Wholly herself."

"And Emily Bird?"

She wraps her arms around her stomach, holds herself in. "Still working that out."

Coffee looks away while his feet start up that restless tattoo against the frosted earth. She half expects him to launch himself off the bench and start pacing back and forth over the little bridge, but he keeps his warmth beside her.

"I chased you down the driveway," he says softly. His fingers drum the wood right beside her thigh. She wants him to touch her, and so holds herself rigidly to avoid it. "I stayed behind when the rest of you guys went to the woods out back. I figured, you wanted Paul, then fine, I'd leave you to him. But I felt . . . weird. Roosevelt had disappeared upstairs. I actually talked with that DEA guy, if you can believe it. Trevor had a grin wider than the Cheshire cat when he saw it. I mean, shit, you think I'm reckless. I finally asked Trevor where Roosevelt went, and he said something about Paul getting this killer job with the CIA. But Roosevelt left right around the same time you two headed to the woods. And then you came back . . . I knew something was wrong. I mean, sure, maybe you'd been pissed enough with me to get plastered at Trevor's party. . . ."

"At *you*? Why would it have to be you? Maybe I just wanted to have a good time with Paul."

"Did you?"

"Do you always have to be so egotistical?"

"I just know you. Is that so bad? No one else realized anything was wrong. Maybe it's egotistical, but not many people piss you off more than I do."

She clenches her fists against the fire in her chest, the flare of joy and frustration. "Fine, whatever, I'm smashed. Go on."

"Paul is practically leading you around the room like a puppy. He takes you outside. You look at me a few times. And . . . I don't know, Bird, it felt like you were asking for something. But I didn't know if I should try to talk to you or not, given the way we left things. And Paul was hovering, so there was no way to get you alone. I figured, hey, you'd made your choice pretty clear. Maybe it was time I stopped trying to save you from it."

"Nice."

He turns on her. "I didn't think you wanted my help."

"You said . . . you said I was looking at you. Like . . ."

He tilts his head back and sends up a column of exhausted smoke. "You ask me for help, I help. Even when I don't like it. Every time. Forever."

Bird keeps quiet, the only response she can make when his words have punched the air from her lungs.

Coffee stubs out his blunt, half-smoked, on the arm of the bench. "I followed you both outside," he says eventually. "You were vomiting. Trevor and Paul were talking over your head, and Paul was nervous as hell. He tried to pass it off, but I could tell. They were arguing about what you drank, but then Paul suddenly stopped talking and hauled you over to the car. Trevor's like, 'What's going on,' and Paul said he left the canteen and asked Trevor to watch you. I didn't really think about it, I just ran to the basement. I had a weird feeling. I remembered that canteen, some army surplus issue that he dumped half a bottle into right before you all left. I found it beside the couch and I locked myself in the bathroom with it before he got down there."

"You hid in the *bathroom*?"

He grimaces. "I had a few-second lead. It seemed the safest place to be."

Bird wants to mock the idea of Paul being any real threat, but she remembers how it felt to be swaddled and immobile in the passenger side of his car. She shakes her head. "What did Paul do?"

"I heard him cursing and slamming some things. Someone came down and asked him what was happening. Then his phone rang and he left to answer it. I wondered if I should try to get you away from him and take you home, but what excuse did I have? Paul's your boyfriend, not me. But that canteen was pretty full for something that got you so smashed. And then I took a sip. There's not many drugs I haven't taken, Bird. At least once, just to see. I might not recognize all of them, but I recognize a lot. There was *something* in this drink, I could feel it after just a minute, but it didn't feel like something I'd ever had before. So I sprint down the driveway just as you're pulling away. You look at me like . . . like . . ."

He gulps and fumbles for his lighter. He takes a toke and passes it to her. Bird wonders for a second what will happen to her if her mother finds out, and then realizes things between them can hardly get worse. She sucks in a lungful of organic tobacco and high-resin marijuana like the baddest kid at school, and then passes it back to Coffee.

"I try calling the police. I don't get very far — give them his license plate number and suddenly I'm passed up to some guy who tells me not to worry. So, I go home. I don't sleep. I wait by my phone, because I never had your number. I Google everything I can about Synergy Labs and the Lukas Group and Roosevelt David, but I don't get much. Let's just say I doubt that's his real name. But I saw his face when you mentioned Synergy Labs. He was interested in you before, maybe because of your parents, maybe because of Paul. But after you said that, something changed. I figure, he's probably just brought you in for questioning. And maybe he's not nice, but he won't hurt you. But all I can remember is your face, staring at me like I was rescuing you from a fucking dragon. . . . Oh, I am so sorry. I should have grabbed you as soon as I saw Paul and Trevor talking."

He rocks back and forth, feet tapping, hands flipping an invisible spoon. She wants to grab him, pull him close to her, be the grounding wire for all of his bright static, but she's in no position to offer him that comfort.

"So I waited, like the asshole I am. And at six the next morning you called me. You were slurring your words, almost incoherent. You said, 'They're coming, Coffee.' You told me to get away. You told me that someone had asked about me and I wasn't safe. And then you hung up."

"Damn." The pot has worked some magic; the horror of their situation feels distant, a sharp-edged but understandable object. "I don't remember any of that. Roosevelt, in the hospital when I woke up, he said you'd given me a dissociative."

"A dissociative? What kind? An opioid? A morphinan? Definitely not nitrous, not the morning after . . ."

"He said no one knew. He said it was some new drug, the kind you make."

Coffee nods thoughtfully, unperturbed by the accusation. "The best lies stay close to the truth. Say it was a novel synthesis. Something those CIA crackpots dreamed up. They give it to you, blame it on me. I get dragged into custody on trumped-up charges for selling a couple of pills at a party, now everyone blames me. But if they haven't found that canteen . . ."

"You still have it!"

"I don't know. I didn't dare go back to check. If I skip out, you'll have to find it, Bird. There's a few people I know you can trust to test it, prove there was no way I could have synthesized it myself. . . ."

"What if you could have?"

His head snaps to her and he curses softly. "But you know I didn't."

"I know. They're doing this to you because of me. They think I might have told you something. He says it's because of my parents, but I think it's bigger . . . I think I learned something that night. Something huge, and they're terrified of what will happen if I leak it."

"Make me stay," he says. "Tell me to stay for you."

"And if they crucify you for my sake? Forget it, Coffee, I don't need a sacrifice."

But she's making one, anyway. Those bleak, desperate eyes, that quickening, sharp breath. She will lose so much if she pushes him away. She will lose the hope of him, the broad horizon of his strange possibility. He will escape to São Paulo or Brasília, and she will muddle on in the District, hoping that eventually Roosevelt's attention will turn to juicier prey.

But he will be free, he will be himself, he will not hurt, the one who first called her Bird.

She hugs him. Just leans forward and wraps her arms around him and buries her head beneath his chin. He jerks, then hugs her back, tightly enough to constrict her breathing. She doesn't mind. She's delirious with him, or maybe that's just the pot. The three inches of exposed skin touching his expands so that she is all neck and fingers, a magnificently twisted homunculus. They breathe in tandem and they do not move for a million years, for the eternity she has waited to do this, and the eternity she will wait when he leaves.

Something splashes in the water. He pulls back and looks around.

"A duck." His voice is a wrung dishrag.

"You've got my blessing, Coffee. If you need it. Take care of yourself. Maybe one day I'll see you again."

He doesn't even look at her when she starts to leave. She thinks he won't say anything at all, but he finally manages when she steps onto the bridge.

"I think she's worthy of her mother, you know. Emily Bird. I think she's good enough to beat them all."

"And Alonso Oliveira?"

A Coffee smile. "That asshole? He'll figure something out."

She dresses carefully, the morning of her free fall. She armors herself in baggy jeans and old tennis shoes, a Cookie Monster T-shirt under a gray turtleneck. Her stitches came out a few days ago, but the scar is still pulled and angry at her hairline. She considers dying her hair a shocking red, might dare it if she had enough time, but Aaron needs to get to school and so she doesn't.

Nicky gives her the once-over when she gets to the kitchen that morning. "New look, kid," he says, neutral, as he eats the same marshmallow cereal as Aaron.

"I thought it was time for a change," she says, resisting the urge to touch her exposed ears and neck.

He nods slowly. He starts to smile, but it falls. "What about your mom?"

"She ain't here, now is she?"

And that's all he has to say about it. School is easier, in its way. No one even talks to her there, they just stare and whisper. She's finally lost it, they say. They hide behind their masks at school, but Bird doesn't bother with hers. Sometimes she'd welcome getting the v-flu — at least that way she wouldn't have to suffer through Devonshire senior class politics. And if she died, it would serve her mother right.

She winces at the childishness of the thought, but she will get better, she will grow into this painful, shiny new skin. She sits by herself at lunch, warded away from the somewhat-black lunch table by Charlotte's awkwardly hunched back. Her ostracization complete, no Felice required.

She hurries outside as soon as she's finished, though the ground is wet and the sky is gray and spitting misery. The soldiers watch her cross the bridge, but the garden is within sight of their posting. The fountain is dry and filled with leaves, the roses themselves little more than spindly branches with sharp thorns. Still, she breathes easier here. The second half of classes is canceled today for group counseling followed by a chapel service in honor of "sick and departed friends." If she's lucky, she'll sleep through the service.

But she falls asleep in the garden despite the cold and wet. She dreams of Coffee, sun-red and frowning on a beach. He's holding out Paul's canteen — she remembers it now, a metal canister covered in faux-military camo.

"It's all here, Bird," dream-Coffee says, but she can't reach him. She never will again.

She wakes up with a start to the sound of someone else entering the garden. It's Marella, looking as ragged around the edges as Bird feels.

"You're missing group therapy," Marella says.

Bird takes a startled glance at her phone and sees she's been here for an hour. "What about you?"

Marella shrugs. "Felice started crying, and I didn't see you. Figured I might as well check in case she'd dumped your body behind the cafeteria trash bins."

"Oh no," Bird says, matching Marella's sly smile. "Felice would bribe some Bradley boy to do it. I'm safe until at least seventh period."

"You're looking hot, Emily Bird."

"You too, Marella. Are you still with that Holton girl?"

Marella balances on the lip of the fountain, looking younger and more innocent than Bird's ever seen her. "Her family's keeping her under house arrest until they find a vaccine for this thing and she sure as hell hasn't called. So I guess, no, not really. How about you? You broken up with that jerk yet?"

"How do you know I want to?"

Marella jumps from the fountain and lands in front of Bird's bench. "I saw you this morning, sistah. If Coffee hadn't jumped, he'd have seen it too. Bird is reborn."

Bird laughs. "And she don't take no shit."

"So have you?"

"I will. For sure I will."

Marella sits beside her and they skip counseling together, peaceably side by side, shoulders touching in a way that's only mostly platonic.

It's inevitable, she supposes, that God would call her bluff. They join the crowd crossing over to the boys' side for the big chapel service. She hews close to the adults, teachers she vaguely recognizes mixed with the medical staff and soldiers and a few men in suits and ear-pieces — Secret Service for the vice president's daughter. Even so, Paul sees her as she starts up the chapel steps.

"Emily!" he yells from the doorway. She can feel Charlotte's and Felice's glares from fifteen feet away, their appalled realization that Paul might not have given up on her when they have.

Marella squeezes her hand. "Reborn," she whispers. "None of those girls can touch you anymore."

Bird backs down the steps slowly. If she has to do this, she'd rather not be in the middle of a crowd of fourth graders. The doctor she recognizes from her first day back gives her a startled glance, as if she's noticed Bird there for the first time, and rubs her eyes hard enough that Bird winces.

"Emily." Paul puts his arm on her shoulder and she stares at his hand until he takes it away. "You . . . what happened? Your cousin play a practical joke or something?"

When she looks up at him now, all she can think of is how he looked when he said he loved her, not so much devoted as *determined*, exactly the way he looks now. It should be flattering that he's pursuing her without any encouragement, but all she can wonder is why. Loving her is about fifth on her list of likely possibilities.

"What do you want?" Her voice is soft, barely inflected. She searches for Marella in the crowd over his shoulder, but all she can see are soldiers and lower school uniforms. Why hasn't anyone gone into the chapel yet?

He frowns. "I'm trying to help you. Jesus, you have no idea how deep this shit is, Emily, and you're in it. I could be an ally."

"Could be?"

"I am. Trying to be, anyway. Come on, babe, cut me some slack. I'm sorry about that party, but it wasn't my fault."

She nods slowly, but she isn't really paying attention to him. She knows he's lying, the bastard, through his pin-straight teeth and pouting lips.

"Did you have something you wanted to tell me, then?" she asks. Behind him, Dr. Granger stumbles on the steps and sprawls on her chest. One of the soldiers goes to help her and she cowers away from him, clutching her hand to her side.

"I know you went somewhere last night, Emily," Paul says softly. He doesn't even glance behind him.

Bird's heartbeat races. She looks around for Roosevelt, but of course she doesn't see him. "I don't know what you mean —"

He shakes his head. "They saw you come back late. You're my responsibility, I keep telling you that. After the party, what I'm doing with Lukas Group . . . It's me, Emily, one way or another. Don't you want to make this easy? You used to like me. You can't still, even a little?"

"You want to date the senior class's scandal of the year?"

He rolls his eyes. "If you're with me, you won't be a scandal. Even with that hair."

"What's wrong with my hair, Paul?"

A crowd has surged around the collapsed doctor, blocking her view.

The thin wail of a siren gets louder, closer. Paul finally turns around. "What the hell . . . ?"

"One of the doctors collapsed," Bird says conversationally. "Do you think she has the v-flu?"

"Goddamn." He puts an arm out in front of her, like her mother does when someone cuts her off in traffic. Like an arm can stop Bird from hurtling through the windshield — or stop a colony of viruses from jumping to a fresh host. She's worried for the doctor. She remembers her bitter words about a Venezuelan needing to be perfect, and relates to it more than she could articulate at the time. Has the stress of it finally overwhelmed her? Dr. Granger gave Bird the sleeping guide that has been, with the melatonin, the only rusted, dented shield she's had against relentless insomnia and nightmares.

The siren wail gets louder and then multiplies into a cacophonous multiharmonic symphony of panic. Soldiers bellow at the sudden rush of students from the chapel doors while paramedics struggle to push a stretcher against the tide. Bird feels faint and staggers against Paul, only then remembering the necessity of breathing. A break in the crowd allows her a glimpse of another doctor doing compressions on Dr. Granger's exposed chest. A paramedic slaps a mask on her slack face, and then the rest is lost as Paul takes her wrist in a bruising grip and drags her away.

"We have to get to the shelter," he shouts.

Nearby, a freshman girl shrieks and points at the sky. They all turn to follow the line of her wavering finger, and Bird doesn't know what she expected — maybe a low-flying plane heading for the White House, to finish what they started when she was just a toddler — but she's astonished at the appearance of what looks more like a crop duster than a jumbo jet, raining mist somewhere east of them.

Paul sticks a hand into her pocket, and she punches him in the chest without thinking. Then she realizes that he's grabbed her bunched-up face mask.

"What was that for?"

"We're done, Paul. Keep your hands to yourself."

"Emily . . ."

A sonic boom drowns out the rest of his words. A black blur connects with the crop duster, and they both explode in the clear, cold air above the city. She doesn't understand what she's just seen, but she knows that it has changed their lives forever.

"Put it on," Paul says, giving her the face mask. Just what was that crop duster raining on the city before the other beast shot it down? What good can a flower-printed mask do against it? But she puts it on.

She allows herself to be carried along like a pebble in a stream by the crowd and soldiers, down into the chapel basement with a mismatched group of lower and upper schoolers and whoever else was nearby at the time. She tries to make sense of the barked orders over the walkie-talkies, but all she can gather is what she already knows: Something horrible has happened nearby, and they're all in danger of it coming for them.

"You didn't mean that, right?" Paul says, still inexplicably beside her. "Because you know that I can help you."

"Only if you're my boyfriend though, huh?" She shudders.

"Haven't I said sorry? What did you do with my bracelet, anyway?"

What's happening in the rest of the city? What about Nicky and Aaron? Her cell phone doesn't get a signal down here, and she doubts she could get through to them even if it did. She takes a deep breath. "Fine, you think you can help me? Prove it. Make sure Nicky and Aaron are safe. Find out what's going on in Northeast."

"Nicky and Aaron?"

She's told Paul about them a dozen times and Coffee only twice, but Coffee remembered. God, she misses him already. But at least he should be safe from that death rain, even if Brazil hasn't been spared the v-flu.

"My uncle and cousin. You know, the ones I'm living with. Go. Help, if that's what you want to do."

Paul frowns. "So you're not dumping me?"

"I'm considering your application," she says. "Now go impress me."

He mistakes her words for flirtation; grins at her before he struts away. She sags against the wall, numb where he touched her. The room is crowded and stifling, surely way over the fire limit. Even so, she catches a commotion by the door, an eddy in the swamp.

She searches for a friendly face, but only sees Cindy de la Vega, uncharacteristically alone.

"Cindy? What's going on?"

Cindy flinches at the sound of Bird's voice, but doesn't try to move away. "What isn't?" she says. "This is such bullshit. I just wanted to go to Cornell with Byron and party and major in philosophy. And now what? We're probably going to have to live in bunkers and eat space food and tell our children about the days when we used to see the sun."

Bird can't help it, she laughs. "I don't think it's that bad yet, Cindy."

"Did you see that death plane? I bet the people on the surface are watching their skin fall off as we speak."

"I hope not!" She would not worry about Nicky and Aaron. They had to be fine. That plane couldn't have been *that* far east.

Cindy glances at her and swallowed. "Yeah. Sorry. I'm just panicking. I heard that poor woman on the stairs died. Probably some other terrorist disease. First the party and then the quarantine and now . . ."

Paul wades his way back to her, frowning like he's learned something truly awful.

"They're okay, right?" she says, hurrying to meet him. "Nicky and Aaron?"

Paul shakes his head. "I'm not sure yet. We're checking. It's not that. It's . . . Emily, what the hell were you up to last night?"

She flashes back to the hug, the feel of her skin on his, the pot that anyone could test for if they had a mind to. But if she looks panicked, God knows she has plenty of reason. "None of your business."

"It is my business," he says. "It definitely is. Because look —"

He points like Moses parting the sea. The commotion by the door reveals itself as a beanpole of a boy with roving green eyes and thick, curly hair, flipping a pen between his fingers and looking warily at an older man in a suit as he speaks with Mrs. Early.

"Alonso's back."

Make me stay, he said. But she told him to leave, she swears she did. Their eyes meet clear across the shelter.

They'll crucify you, she thinks. He tosses the pen high in the air and catches it easily in long fingers. His look is unfathomable, indecipher-able, granite-hard.

Her joy, for an evanescence, drowns the world.

A clue:

I have already told you what happened.

An admission:

I don't remember everything.

A question:

Have you made us strong enough to find out for yourself?

[phosgene]

CCl$_2$O

When Bird was eleven years old, her school bus crashed in the middle of a small suburban intersection on the way back home from a field trip. It shouldn't have been a bad accident, but the other car was driving thirty miles over the speed limit and plowed right into the side of her bus. One kid died, that's what the reporters all said on the evening news, while their parents huddled in the waiting room of the hospital. No one knew whose child had died, and the stink of ill-wishes clogged their noses like clotting blood. Carol Bird silently prayed the dead child would be Gretchen Borowitz, who had cheated off of her daughter six months before, causing no end of trouble for both of them. What Greg Bird thought during those dark hours, he never said, though Bird can't quite imagine her detached father wishing soul-destroying grief on anyone. Carol Bird, in a moment of uncharacteristic honesty, said those two hours aged her two years. And when the bullet did fall on the Borowitz family, Carol Bird told herself for years that it couldn't possibly be her fault, that no wish of hers could really kill a child. Emily Bird always thought that it was the guilt, not the waiting, that had aged her mother in the months afterward.

But now, four hours into her involuntary entombment, she realizes that her mother had been, for once, merely honest. The hours of waiting while Nicky or Aaron could already have choked to death on poison gas have taken her past anxiety, to a point that Coffee might call an altered state of consciousness.

They still haven't spoken. He sits in the corner with the man in the

117

suit who Bird has decided must be his lawyer. Paul told her that Coffee turned himself in that morning, making a deal with the DA and the school to finish the semester while he awaits trial. She wonders what Roosevelt thinks of this, since Paul looks torn between wary satisfaction and vague discontent.

But that might just be because he's trapped here with the rest of the powerless students — summarily demoted from the role of hotshot government operative he's been playing these last few weeks. With most networks down, jammed, or simply inaccessible from the basement, the most he's been able to find out was that Aaron's school had fully evacuated about fifteen minutes after the attack. Fifteen minutes isn't a long time when you're struggling to finish a chemistry exam, but it's plenty of time to get an extra, deadly inhale of whatever rained down from the sky this afternoon.

At six o'clock, when it looks like the students might stage a mutiny if they don't get something to eat, a few soldiers come back with wet boxes of Oreos and milk. It looks like they scored it from the snack room of the lower school, and even the peculiar dampness doesn't deter everyone from grabbing what they can.

Paul wades through and brings her back three of each. "It's like *Lord of the Flies* down here," he says.

"Why is it wet?" Bird wipes one of the blue-and-black packages on her pants leg.

"Standard decontamination procedure for potential nerve agents," he says, like he's auditioning to be the munitions expert in a heist movie. She doesn't laugh. She just contains the hollow echo of *nerve agent* while thinking about Mrs. Early, who still hasn't said anything to them besides vague platitudes, and the soldiers, who squawk and bark into their walkie-talkies like it really is the end of the world, and everyone else, who munches metallic chocolate and talks about the war that's inevitably coming as if it's a high-budget video game.

She stands up. "I need to be alone for a second, Paul," she says. He opens his mouth in genuine astonishment before nodding once. She picks up the rest of the food he brought her.

It's Coffee's lawyer who looks up when she approaches them, though she knows that Coffee knows she's there, a bird on a live wire.

"You didn't get anything," she says, offering the unopened packages to the lawyer.

After a beat, he takes the food. "Had a protein bar in my pocket. Alonso, you want something? We have a ministering angel."

At that, Coffee snorts and turns to her. In the corner of her eye she sees Mrs. Early frown and lean forward in her chair, but what can she really do? *It's the apocalypse*, Bird wants to shout, but it turns out she doesn't have to speak truth to power — only ignore it.

She squats while Coffee eats a cookie in two economical bites. "Nicky? Aaron?" he asks softly.

She shakes her head and forces the words past her throat. "No word. Paul only knows that Aaron evacuated. Fifteen minutes after."

Coffee grimaces at the number, offers her one of his cookies. She takes it, more to feel the brush of his fingers than out of any particular desire for empty calories.

"Paul says they're wet as a precaution against nerve gas," she says.

Coffee nods. "Could be. I caught a whiff of something though, just before we went down. Not many nerve gases have a smell at nonlethal concentrations. It could have been a choking agent. Or some sort of bioterror weapon."

"Is that any better?"

"I'm not sure anything could be *better*."

"Nicky and Aaron being healthy and alive."

"No one else? My mother? Trevor's dog?"

She stiffens at that gentle, almost loving barb. "Why shouldn't I care about my family first?"

"Why shouldn't you?" Coffee says, and stuffs the last cookie in his mouth.

She looks away, searching for something to smother her awareness of being in the wrong, and is rewarded by Mrs. Early stepping away from conversation with one of the soldiers. Her raised arm is as effective as a mute button.

"I've just gotten word that the terror alert will be lifted within the next hour." A few people clap, but most keep still, waiting for the bad news. They are not disappointed.

"The attack we witnessed also took place over Capitol Hill and downtown Manhattan. Three crop dusters were used to deliver a poison gas called phosgene. Luckily, most people were able to get to safety or treatment in sufficient time. The death toll right now is being estimated at five hundred in the District, and somewhere between five hundred and a thousand in New York. I am praying that our loved ones are safe. I also need to tell you . . ." She wipes at her eyes, which have gone owly with smeared mascara and under-eye foundation. "The president has declared martial law."

In the profound silence that follows, Coffee's low whistle echoes like a firecracker. Mrs. Early glares at him, but the other students regard Coffee with wary respect. Apparently, fleeing from justice helped improve his rank in their stratified, privileged world.

"What does that mean?" a sophomore boy asks, his gaze wavering between Coffee and Mrs. Early.

"For now, it means that only authorized personnel are allowed to move between checkpoints. You'll all have to sleep at school for the night."

Coffee's response is drowned out by the chorus of groans and not-very-well-muffled curses. "The writing was on the wall," he says, and Bird turns to him while her heart gallops and her head throbs like he's driven a chisel into her skull.

"You did write it!"

"Write what?" He looks so genuinely puzzled that she wants to hit him.

"When you gave me your number. That night."

There's only one night *that night* could be, but he still frowns at her. "I wrote down my number."

"Anything else?" The fluorescent lights seem to waver to the rhythm of the throbbing in her head. She squints against it.

"What? My name? I figured that you'd know it was mine, one way or another."

"No," she says, and only realizes that her voice has risen to a shout when everyone turns to stare at her.

"Bird?" Coffee says.

"The writing on the wall," she whispers. "Who else could it have been? Roosevelt?" The thought makes her taste chocolate product and stomach acid.

"Emily? Is he bothering you?"

She looks up, startled, to see Paul hovering above the two of them. She opens her mouth to tell him off, but then remembers what he said about her being his responsibility one way or another. He believes it, whatever she thinks, and she knows that Roosevelt does too. He wasn't much use in helping her find out what happened to Nicky and Aaron, but he tried. Wouldn't it be better to have him as a friend and not as an enemy? But that creature trying to break out of her skull doesn't seem to think there's much of a difference.

Coffee stands up, his greater height giving him a slight advantage in the cockfight those two are always an insult away from starting. Her head is going to burst like an egg in a microwave if she has to spend another minute in this basement with either of them.

She pushes past them both, putting more energy into the shove than she has to. Coffee stumbles back, nearly tripping over his lawyer.

Mrs. Early tries to block her from the door. "Emily? What —"

"Bathroom," she says, and Mrs. Early hurriedly motions for one of the soldiers to accompany her down the hall. He gives a startled shout when she starts up the stairs instead of going into the janitor's bathroom. She takes the stairs two at a time, wondering if he might shoot and almost hoping he will.

The exit is only one flight up. She sinks to her knees on the sidewalk outside the door, much to the surprise of the two soldiers guarding it. Their gas masks dangle from around their necks, and so she figures it's safe enough to gulp the chill, damp air and wonder how her tears can feel so hot on her cheeks, like a liquid that has boiled under subterranean pressure.

"You all right?"

She looks up at the one who spoke, the young one who reminds her a little of her cousin. He shakes his head and pats her shoulder awkwardly. "I'm sorry," he says. The other one looks back down at the open door but then shrugs.

"All clear in a few minutes anyway," he says.

Bird feels empty, a cracked shell covered with a crude, Emily-shaped mâché. The migraine has settled in for an extended visit, and she knows that by morning she'll miss her melatonin even more than her toothbrush.

"That doctor," she asks, "the one who collapsed. Is she all right?"

Soldier-two shares a look with soldier-cousin, who chews his tongue. "Did you know her?"

That forlorn tense is answer enough. "Was it the gas?"

She's not surprised by soldier-cousin's slow shake of his head. "Bad coincidence, honey. Probably a heart attack."

Bird summons an image of Dr. Granger, their first casualty of the new war. Latina, curly brown hair, a small nose, and large gray eyes, tired and watchful. Maybe ten pounds overweight, maybe early forties. The sort of woman she sees a lot in the halls of Devonshire: accomplished, holding it together, a little lonely.

"She wasn't old," Bird says.

Soldier-cousin shrugs. "My mom went that way too. It happens."

"I'm sorry."

He rubs his gun like a rabbit's foot. "Yeah."

The all clear goes off then, a clear, high aria in the breeze and starlight. And as it does her phone buzzes in her pocket. She fumbles, spills it onto the pavement, and then has to wipe off the grit with her sleeve.

Five new messages, it tells her. Three generic school announcements. A blank email from an address that looks vaguely familiar, but is probably spam. And there, the golden ticket:

> *I'm safe. We weren't too close to the plane, but Aaron's school got them to the shelter too late. He inhaled a bit of the stuff. Don't worry, Em, he'll be fine, but they're keeping him at this treatment center near the school. I've got the address below, but I know you won't be able to get across town with all this bullshit going down. Don't worry, remember we love you. Write back as soon as you get this — they said you guys cleared out quick, but I want to make sure!*

She replies immediately (*fine here, c u soon*), and then closes her eyes. The steps of the first students out of the shelter echo behind her, but she can't summon the will to move out of their way. Nicky's fine. Aaron will be. Nicky wouldn't lie about something like that. But maybe the doctors lied to him, maybe no one knows what happens when you inhale the toxic gas some terrorists decided to drop on the one city spared the pandemic.

She smells him before she sees him, tobacco and laundry detergent and stale basement air. She grips his hand before she can think better of it, and he jerks a little in surprise.

"The toxic effects of phosgene," she says. "A list."

"You think I make chemical weapons in my spare time?"

"I think you read chemistry textbooks in your spare time."

"Did something happen?"

She doesn't look at him. "Aaron."

He swears softly. "Is he okay?"

"Nicky says he is. They're at some treatment center near Capitol Hill. I need to get there."

123

Coffee hauls her up by their shared hand and moves her a few feet away from the bumbling crowd of newly freed prisoners.

"Coughing, watery eyes, blurred vision." He ticks off each one with the fingers of his free hand.

"That can't be it," she says.

He shakes his head. "It was pretty common during WWI, not a conflict known for its humane weaponry. Burns if it touches you. Pulmonary edema — that's when lungs fill with fluid. Low blood pressure. Heart failure. Death."

"Jesus."

"It'll be all right, Bird. The dose makes the poison. He couldn't have inhaled too much in Northeast. The winds weren't blowing that direction."

"I have to get to him."

Coffee nods slowly, then looks down at her with a vaguely puzzled frown. "It's nice to see you."

"How did they catch you?"

His eyes stray to something over her shoulder. "I made a deal."

This sounds uncomfortably close to Paul's obviously untrue version of events. "If you were going to pull a stunt like this, I might as well have narced on you!"

"Wish you had?"

Does she wish she threw in with Roosevelt, that she kept Paul's bracelet, that she trusted, for the rest of her life, the parallel lines of her mother's judgment?

But, the shining edges of those eyes. "I told you to save yourself."

"You told me a lot of things, Bird."

She gapes at him, wondering what he means even as her knees wobble and her head fills with sparks.

"Upper school ladies! Please follow Mrs. Cunningham, we'll dine at the boys' refectory and then sort out the sleeping arrangements."

Mrs. Early's announcement results in the dutiful herding of the fifty or so older boys and girls stuck in this particular shelter. The young girls line up behind one of the medics to go across the campus, back to their walled compound. Other groups of students emerge from their underground lairs like just-molted cicadas and head to the brownstone facade of Bradley Hall. She hopes that no one got caught out when the phosgene dropped.

The lawyer comes up to them. "Better go with them, Alonso," he says, gesturing with the hand holding his rumpled coat.

Coffee frowns and cracks his knuckles. "I need to get to Capitol Hill," he says.

"I think I've worked enough miracles for one day, buddy. That thing won't let you get past Wisconsin Avenue, let alone Southeast."

He gestures at Coffee's feet and Bird notices, for the first time, the white plastic box strapped to his right ankle.

"Is that a monitor?" she asks stupidly.

Coffee just shrugs. "Part of the bail agreement."

She's going to be sick. He could have gotten away. Now he's got an ankle monitor and a lawyer and her hornet's nest. What could he do for her now? Does he think she'll be grateful? She is grateful.

"What's this about Capitol Hill?"

Coffee drops her hand abruptly. Paul, inevitably and always. Paul, butting his way in with a solicitous mask for the adult in the conversation. She would glare at him if she weren't so exhausted, and so worried for Aaron. "My cousin is at a treatment center over there. They set one up in a school near RFK. I need to see him."

"Is he okay?"

At least he's retained that much humanity, Bird thinks, looking up at him. At least he cares just a little about someone who can't help his career. She hates that she's someone who could have once loved him. When she looks at him, she sees her own reflection. She sees Carol Bird's inferior copy. She hates everyone sometimes.

"I don't know, Paul. That's why I need to get there. And if there's *anything* you can do with your connections . . . you know, put in a word with Lukas Group or whoever, I'd be very grateful."

She can't believe that she's calling on Roosevelt to help with this mess, but Paul understands her meaning perfectly well, and he smiles with the thrill of self-importance and responsibility.

"I'll do my best. Let me just make a call, if I can get through. Just you, right?"

"All of us," she says while the lawyer gives her a sharp look and then laughs.

"Why the hell not, if you can do it. I've got a friend who lives a few blocks from there."

Paul doesn't look too happy about the prospect of bringing Coffee anywhere, but he'd lose face if he objected. He walks a few yards away, phone to his ear. Coffee looks between the two of them and grins.

"You're using him," he says, a light in his eyes that makes her palm itch with the memory of his hand.

The lawyer steps closer to Coffee. "I seem to recall Lukas Group coming up in the charges. Doesn't one of the testifying witnesses work for them?"

"Roosevelt David," Bird says before she can stop herself. "Asshole in chief. But in this case, I think he'll be useful. After all, what else can he do to Coffee?"

The lawyer looks at her and sighs. "The president declared martial law tonight. That means soldiers — not just National Guard, but the army, the marines, even the air force — on our streets, out of the jurisdiction of civilian courts. At least the police can go to trial. The first time it's happened since the Civil War. And private security contractors like your Mr. David, well, let's just say they aren't going to get less dangerous."

"What kind of a lawyer are you, anyway?"

He raises his eyebrows and pulls a card from his wallet.

"Bao Tran, Citizens for Humane Drug Policy, Legal Defense Department," she reads. "So your group, it's like the ACLU or something?"

The ACLU is on Coffee's very short list of Decent Institutions.

"Very similar aims," Bao says, "but we focus on drug policy. Your friend Alonso was very eloquent about the worthiness of his case."

"Do you think he can get off?"

Coffee rolls his eyes at her but looks sidelong at Bao Tran, as though he hasn't dared ask the question.

Bao shrugs. "I've argued more hopeless cases."

Which isn't precisely reassuring. Paul comes back over a moment later, after a brief exchange with Mrs. Early. He looks smug, which tells Bird that her gamble worked.

"They're sending a car over. It'll take Emily to the treatment center, but no one will be able to leave again until end of curfew."

He says this last to Coffee, who just flicks his finger against his palm. "No worse than sleeping in the dining hall," he says.

"I have to stay with my client," Bao says, though she suspects that he doesn't, and really wants to sleep somewhere besides a school cafeteria.

"Then we'll all just go together," he says with a rigid smile. "I'm sure your uncle will appreciate the support."

She's sure Nicky will jump out of his damn skin to see Coffee and Bao the lawyer and Paul roll up in a black asshole-mobile with some tinted-glasses national security type at the wheel, but this is her bed, and she is relieved to lie in it.

"Thank you, Paul," she says, very sincerely. Over his shoulder Coffee grins like the man on the moon.

Aaron is larger than most of the other kids in the narrow beds of this makeshift hospital ward, but he still looks small to Bird. He snores a little, a high-pitched whistle through his nose, though normally he's a quiet sleeper.

"He was coughing," Nicky said after he got over his surprise at seeing all of them. "One of the doctors gave him something to sleep."

So she sits on the scuffed linoleum beside his cot, where half a decade ago two would-be-forever lovers carved *RJ luvs Cherry 2008* right beside the horns of the school mascot. She's never been inside this high school before, and only passed it a few times on her way to Caps games in RFK. Now the gym, originally home of the Eastern Ramblers, hosts over fifty kids exposed to toxic gas.

"No one's claimed it yet," Roosevelt said very confidently on the ride over. "FARC explicitly said they didn't. The money's on an Iranian-Venezuelan alliance. But nobody gives a damn anymore if FARC is playing or not. Those oil fields are the real prize. I say we have boots on the ground in a week. Things are about to get very interesting," he said, and nodded at Paul. Bird could have puked.

Now, with Roosevelt and Coffee's lawyer gone, Paul broods on a chair beside Nicky. Coffee sits cross-legged on the floor across from her. She reaches up periodically to stroke Aaron's hand. He's fine, that's what everyone said, but he's still sleeping in a gym on a cot when he should be at home.

"Did you tell Mo?" she asks Nicky softly.

He rubs his eyes. "Can't get through to anyone on my phone. Sent an email. I haven't heard back, though."

"Wait . . . I got something weird in my inbox earlier. I didn't recognize the address, but maybe it was Mo."

She fishes her phone from her pocket and scrolls through her messages. The network is down again, but the odd email downloaded to her phone when she checked earlier. The email address looks familiar, but not like any of Mo's. The subject is blank.

Did you remember? The writing on the wall? Did it help you? I'm trying, but it's all fading already.

"Is it Mo?" Nicky asks.

She shakes her head and presses the phone screen down against her thigh. Her hands start to tremble and she braces them on the dirty floor. She remembers the email address now. A stupid throwaway account she made in middle school to prank Felice on April Fools'. She knows, though she isn't sure how, that the email isn't some weird joke from someone who hacked into an old account.

That email came from her account because *she* wrote it.

And she doesn't remember a goddamn thing.

Coffee reaches over; she flinches and he pulls back, uncommonly still.

"Not Mo," she says, though the words sound breathy and high-pitched and oddly distanced from her throat. "Some weird spam, that's all."

"Emily . . ." Paul leaves his chair and squats beside her, putting a hand on her shoulder before she even has time to prepare herself. "I think you need some rest. You look terrible."

Nicky looks between Paul and Coffee and sighs. "I'm going to get a Coke," he says. "You guys want anything?"

No one does, so he walks off with his hands deep in the pockets of his low black jeans. Coffee watches Paul's draped arm like it's a feral hawk. Bird takes a deep breath of gym musk and steam heat and disinfectant.

"What the hell are you doing here, Oliveira?" Paul asks as soon as Nicky's gone.

Coffee flares his nostrils. "Same thing you are, I guess."

"*Emily* is my girlfriend."

Maybe it's the emphasis on her first name that breaks her; the final evidence of Paul's determination never to see her how she really is, only how he wishes her to be. To him she was Emily, ideal girlfriend, and then Emily, ticket to professional success and guilty responsibility. How he might feel about *her* underneath all of that signifying was always an open question, but one she now feels isn't worth answering.

"*Emily* is not anyone's girlfriend."

Paul freezes. She pushes his arm off of her shoulder and it falls like a log.

Coffee looks at her very carefully. "What about Bird?"

"She isn't either."

"What is this? I've been helping you all night! I thought you agreed —"

When she turns to Paul she's assaulted by her memory of Aaron right after she cut her hair. *You're always cool, Em.* She wants to be that girl, forever.

"What was in the canteen, Paul?"

His Adam's apple bobs up and down, massaging words too stiff to leave his throat. She watches him realize the moment of plausible denial has passed; she watches him know what they both know.

"So this is it," he says finally. "A year and a half. Just like that."

"I think it's past time."

He nods, which surprises her, even hurts a little. Strange to know that the boy desperate to stay with you doesn't like *you* much at all.

"Roosevelt isn't going to like it. I warned you about that."

"He'll never make it easy for me. What happened after I got in your car? After you drugged me?"

"I don't know."

"Did you rape me?"

He falls back against Aaron's bed. "Did I — Em — what the hell?"

His shock reassures her. She doesn't *feel* that he did, though given the holes in her memory, it's impossible to be sure. "Did Roosevelt?"

"Of course not! This is about national security! Not . . ." His throat works again. "Not whatever you're thinking, and I don't know what happened after —"

This prompts Coffee to break his silence. "Yes you do. And you owe it to her —"

"I don't owe either of you anything!"

He doesn't quite shout this, but it's so much louder than their previous whispered conversation that she flinches back. A nearby nurse makes a librarian shush with her finger on her lips. Paul hunches with mortification.

"I'm leaving." He lurches to his feet and bumps the foot of Aaron's bed before he regains his balance and walks away. He wings Nicky by the vending machines.

Watching him leave, Bird feels triumphant, untethered and free. Then she looks back at Coffee, whose eyes are soft and gray in the low light, and puts a cold hand against her head.

"Was that a very good idea?" he asks softly. "Practically speaking, I mean. Impractically speaking, it was a glorious moment that I will recall with fondness for the rest of my potentially brief life."

"Oh, Coffee." The headache settles in behind her right eye. "What am I going to do?"

"We," he says. "It's always *we*. If you want it."

Bird is no one's girlfriend. But his hand is palm up, a priceless offering of comfort on the dirty altar of a gym floor, and she takes it. She falls asleep like that, touching him, her head on the edge of Aaron's cot, lulled by a chorus of a hundred breaths and the hiss of steam through bulky pipes.

When Bird was eleven years old, her school bus crashed in the middle of a small suburban intersection on the way back home from a field trip.

Gretchen Borowitz had shiny copper hair that Bird had regarded with unrelieved envy for the entire three years of their acquaintance, and as Bird hung upside down from maroon seat belt straps, it was that hair that she recognized from the bloody wreckage of Gretchen's body. Gretchen had fallen to the ceiling, which was now the floor, one arm flung across the emergency exit. What was left of her neck spurted blood in increasingly sluggish pulses that soaked the dangling edge of Bird's new beach towel. The single rope of Gretchen's ocean-soaked braid fell over her eyes, and Bird stared at it to avoid staring at the rest. The seat belt slowly cut off her air supply, but she didn't shift it, afraid that if she moved even a fraction she might end up like Gretchen

Borowitz, broken and red on the roof of the bus. Red for hair, red for blood, red for the seat belt that had saved her life. How could one word mean all of those different things? How could one word separate her from Gretchen, who would have sat beside her if Bird hadn't made a point to glare and put her wet towel on the empty seat? Her mother said that Gretchen wasn't a good person to have as a friend; she said that Bird wouldn't go anywhere unless she learned to pick her associates more carefully. And so, ostracized and shunned, the girl with the beautiful also-red hair sat in the seat that would kill her thirty-five minutes later, much to Carol Bird's horrified relief.

Bird passed out two minutes after the crash, a combination of low oxygen and high guilt. For years afterward, she refused to wear so much as a red barrette. "It's so not my color," Bird would say, and smile, until even she believed it. When asked about the accident, which left a small but noticeable scar behind her right ear, she would explain about the reckless driver who had fled the country that night and never been caught. Sometimes she would mention the nice woman on the ambulance who had given her a Miss Piggy doll that she still kept in her bedroom. Did she remember the accident? the nosy ones would ask.

No, Bird answers, every time. *One moment I'm talking with my friend about Sailor Moon and the next I'm in the ambulance. I hit my head, I guess that's why.*

She's not even lying. There's a lot that Bird doesn't remember, and that's the least of it. She dreams of redheads sometimes, strange nightmares with sea-soaked braids that she purges upon waking. Let's take a page from Donald Rumsfeld, who cribbed his sheet from Aristotle: There are known knowns and known unknowns and unknown unknowns. But our Bird is in that saddest category of all: the unknown known.

[unknown, similar to GHB]

REDACTED

Coffee doesn't speak to her in school, but he doesn't ignore her. For days after the terrorist attack, she sees him in hallways, between classes, with expressions so eloquent she can hear the half words behind them.

"He's doing okay," she told him the morning after Aaron came home. The doctor said to keep him home for a week just in case. There were worries about his immune function, which made Bird remember that the v-flu doesn't disappear while NATO ground troops amass on the Colombian–Venezuelan border. He just nodded and went back to jotting strange notes in the margins of his AP Chem textbook. Coffee and his ankle monitor provide juicy enough gossip that even a terrorist attack and a new war can't quite drown out the titillated whispers.

Bird ignores them. She ignores almost everyone except Coffee, who won't speak to her, and Marella, who will. Her painkillers have run out, and though she could ask one of the doctors for another prescription, she hesitates every time in front of the guarded lower school doors. Maybe it's just the memory of Dr. Granger clutching her side on the chapel steps. Betrayed, Bird is obscurely sure, by the pressure of her position here.

Sasha Calero Granger. They announced her death in assembly the next morning. Sadly departed, intoned the chaplain, and there were looks at the mention of her home country that made Bird furious. The Thursday after the attack, Bird is back to dreaming in her blinks. She dreams in recursive commentary, of classes taught by different teachers on impenetrable subjects, and so with every painful lurch awake she has to remember which class is the dream, and which is real. In AP Chemistry she dreams that Coffee sits beside her. She dreams that she sleeps now the way she did then, fully, deeply, and without even the residue of unremembered nightmares. He pushes his fingers deep into her roots and tells her that he came back for her sake, and two dreams deep she smiles.

Mrs. Cunningham shakes her awake after class and cuts short Bird's apology.

"Just make sure you review chapter seven," she says. "You looked too tired to wake." Mrs. Cunningham has never seemed particularly fond of Bird — favorite student status was inevitably reserved for Coffee — so she's grateful for this unexpected kindness. Bird rubs her eyes and shoves her books into her backpack. Nearly an hour of sleep. That's a record since her night beside Aaron's bed. Coffee is gone — she looks — but just as she's about to close her bag she notices a piece of green paper sticking out of the top of her notebook.

TESTING THE C FOR DRUGS. HAVEN'T FOUND ANYTHING YET. DON'T ASK, I'LL LET YOU KNOW. BURN AFTER READING.

Her stomach lurches even as she crumples the note and shoves it in her pocket. Burn after reading?

"Who are you, John le Carré?" she mutters. But at least now she's sure that his silence this past week is strategy, not shunning. She's been almost sure. Almost.

She doesn't smoke, a fact that must have slipped Coffee's mind, so she settles for ripping the evidence into tiny pieces and tossing them in the cafeteria compost bucket. The rest of the note is even stranger, in its way. They both know that Paul drugged her; he as well as admitted it. Does it really matter *how*? Still, knowing might give her an edge with Roosevelt. She has no doubts about who gave Paul the motive and means.

After school, she's tempted to race back to Nicky's like she has every other day this week. Aaron is passing the time at home cataloging every album and CD in their grandparents' collection, and he likes to play her his special finds in the evening. But she knows that he's scheduled to go back to school on Monday, and the prospect terrifies her. Her only plan to do something about it involves Trevor's mother, and she has been reluctant to engage that particular hornet's nest for most of the week. After everything that's happened, her fear of requesting a prescription or of asking Trevor about his mother baffles her. Shouldn't life-altering events make you less afraid of the little stuff? But it's the little stuff that paralyzes her: talking, eating, dressing, sleeping. Everyone in school is afraid of the apocalypse; she is afraid of living through it.

She finds Marella the second place she looks, reading a book in the fiction room of the upper school library. Marella smiles to see Bird — a looking glass expression or a miracle. Most of their lives, Marella has regarded Bird with pained indulgence. But now Bird has won the friendship she had given up hoping for. Some things change for the better, they always do, that's just physics.

"I need a favor," Bird says as Marella cracks the spine and lays the book flat on the table. Nikki Giovanni, collected poems.

"Is it illegal?" Marella flips her braid over her shoulder and quickly plaits the unraveling end. She looks calm as ever, but Bird can tell she wants her to say yes.

Bird smiles. "Moral support. Could you come with me to Bradley? I need to talk to Trevor about something."

"Trevor? Don't tell me you've joined the line."

"The line? Oh, you mean the girls who like him." Felice has come closest as his date to the prom last year, but it never went anywhere afterward. This sparked the nearest thing Felice and Charlotte ever had to a fight, but in the end Charlotte backed down. It wasn't Felice's fault she was gorgeous and outgoing, Charlotte told Bird.

"You don't, then?"

"My love life is complicated enough without Trevor Robinson, thanks."

Marella laughs and snaps her fingers. "Thank God for fugitive dealers. Not that I'd get it anyway, but you'd think it would be a little more obvious to those girls that he ain't never gonna be interested."

Marella watches her carefully as she says this. Bird puts it together. "You think he's gay?" Pam Robinson is one of the most socially conservative democrats in the Senate. She even voted for DOMA.

Marella shrugs. "I think he's been redecorating his closet for the last four years, sure, but I've never actually seen him with a guy. And hey, what do I know? I'm probably just some bitter dyke. Sarah sent a breakup text yesterday. Like I hadn't already figured that one out."

"Oh shit, Mar. I'm sorry. A *text*?"

"What are you gonna do? I'd say I'm looking forward to college girls, but who knows if we'll make it to college." Marella bites her lip, a gesture so uncharacteristic that Bird can only stand awkwardly and wonder what to say. "So," Marella says after a moment, "what did you want to talk to Trevor about?"

"His mom," she says.

Marella doesn't even ask, just squeezes her elbow and leads the way out of the library. They go to the boys' side and hang out by the circle. With the new regs, only authorized vehicles are allowed on the roads. The Metro and buses are a clogged mess, a perfect petri dish of potential v-flu transmission, but apparently the government is more worried about car bombs than the pandemic. The school has chartered buses to take students back to certain neighborhoods, but the fact is that staying home or sleeping at school has started to look more reasonable than shuttling back and forth. But apparently senators are still allowed to drive, and Trevor has gotten curbside service the last few days. It was Marella's idea to wait for him here, and they shiver on a bench while blue-blazered boys on their way inside give them curious stares.

"You know they're going to think you're gay if you keep hanging with me," Marella says after three guys in their class start punching one another and laughing as soon as they pass.

Bird flips her middle finger at their backs. "Guys are assholes."

"Just guys?"

Bird sighs. "Not just guys. You'll get to college, Marella. *We'll* get to college."

Marella wipes her eyes and leans forward until her forehead rests, warm and dry, on Bird's. "Promise?" she whispers. Her voice shakes.

"Promise."

A moment later Marella sits up and points. "That must be the ride." A tan Mercedes with tinted windows pulls around the cul-de-sac and idles in front of the entrance, puffing clouds of white smoke that drift in their direction. Trevor glances at them when he walks out, then shakes his head.

"Do you want me to come with you?" Marella asks.

"I'm good. You should have time to catch the last bus."

"Tell me how it went."

Bird waves at Trevor before he can open the car door. His frown deepens as she approaches, which surprises her. He's always been friendly enough, if distant.

"Emily. What's up?"

Trevor looks great, as usual, with his sleeves rolled up and tie draped like a scarf around his neck. He's not as big as Paul, not so obviously a gym bunny, but his solid, lean body goes well with his chiseled good looks. He keeps his head shaved, which only heightens the uncanny symmetry of his features. Smart, rich, hot as hell — but he's never felt anything much for the girls at school. She wonders if Marella is right about why.

"I . . ." She swallows. "I prefer Bird."

"Okay." He draws this out, and looks pointedly at the idling car.

"I need to speak with your mother."

He raises a perfect eyebrow. "Not sure that's a good idea. She wanted to skin me alive after that party, and anyway, it's old news. If you apologize now, it'll just dredge shit up."

She crosses her arms. "It's important."

"Call her office, then."

"You know that will never work."

"Yeah. I do. Em — *Bird*, I'm sorry about what happened that night, but seriously, this is not my problem."

His nonchalance lights the spark that burns away her fear. "Would it kill you to help me a little? Your party landed me in the hospital. I was in a coma for *eight* days. Just ask her for me. Tell her my mother thinks it's important to apologize. Tell her I won't take long."

Trevor lets out a long whistle. "I liked you better as Emily. Poor Paul." He shakes his head and jams his hands in his pockets. "Wait here."

He opens the back door of the car and climbs inside. At first she thinks he's ditched her, but the car doesn't move. After a few minutes, he gets out again.

"Okay, she'll talk. I wouldn't take too long, if I were you."

Bird stares at him. He gestures at the door. "Well? Hurry up."

She gulps. She didn't expect her request to have such speedy results. She hasn't prepared her arguments properly, but it's too late now. Years of school presentations had better be good for something.

Pam Robinson is a stocky woman with a politician bob going gray at the roots. Trevor's narrow and sculpted features take after his father, but he has his mother's intimidating, appraising stare. She nods when Bird settles into the tan leather seat beside her, but keeps speaking into her headset.

"Yes, I'm aware that the senator needs to attend the summit, but that doesn't mean that we can violate quarantine protocols. Can't he do it remotely, if it comes to that? No, it's not 'just one week,' not when we're talking about the v-flu. No, no, he *left* when we were under attack, he doesn't just get to waltz back in here. . . . Yes, I know the outer municipalities have different quarantine protocols, but if he wants to get past the Beltway he needs to wait his fifteen days —" She pauses and sighs. "Fine, Billy, let's table this for now. We'll bring it up again at tomorrow's meeting. Can I ring you back in, oh, twenty minutes? I'm picking my son up. Yes, thank you."

Bird stares back calmly when Pam Robinson levels that gaze in her direction. Pam Robinson's got nothing on Carol Bird.

"Now, what can I do for you, Emily? I'm glad to see you looking so well."

Bird is pretty sure that she doesn't look *well* — but she looks alive, and not actively sick, which is about as good as anyone can hope for these days. She nods. "I want to talk to you about your party," Bird says.

The corner of Pam Robinson's mouth quirks up a fraction of a centimeter, and then falls back to pleasant impassivity. "Ah, yes. I'm afraid that did not go as well as I had hoped."

"I'm sorry for my part in what happened," Bird says, hoping that this is enough. "But I couldn't help but wonder . . . your scholarship, have you picked the recipients yet?"

The dry smile emerges again, and Bird realizes that this odd sense of humor is probably her strongest resemblance with her son. "I'm afraid I haven't quite found the time, dear. Why, did you have someone in mind?"

"My cousin Aaron. He's eleven, a great kid. His school . . . their evacuation procedures are terrible, and he inhaled some of that gas. He's supposed to go back on Monday, and I just can't . . . I'd beg my uncle to keep him home before sending him back there. And then I remembered your scholarship, and . . ."

Senator Robinson nods slowly, while Bird's skin burns from the exposure of her request. She knows what's coming.

"But the scholarship is supposed to be for underprivileged students. Your family is, well . . ."

"My mother doesn't support her brother. Financially, I mean. They don't have much money. He's the doorman of an office building. My aunt died a long time ago. I can't tell you how much it would mean to him. And I'm living with them right now. Because of my parents, you know. So getting Aaron here wouldn't be any trouble."

Pam Robinson keeps her silence; Bird presses her nails until her upper arm feels like fire. Up front, the driver flips the page of a magazine, indifferent or discreet. Pam rolls her shoulders back and turns to the window, looking at the wind-whipped trees and milky-yellow lamps in sconces of greening iron.

"It's a curious situation, Emily," she says finally. She keeps her head turned away, but their eyes meet in the window's blurred reflection.

"Yes."

"I admire your sense of responsibility and action. Your cousin is lucky to have you."

Bird blinks very fast. "But," she says.

Senator Robinson smiles at her own reflection, an expression that makes her resemble Trevor Robinson, inviting a drug dealer and a DEA agent to a party.

"But nothing, dear. Shouldn't some good come from all this? Why not you? Bring your cousin to the Bradley lower school on Monday. I'll work it out. Who knows, if certain bloggers are to be believed, it might help me sleep at night."

Bird stays up until midnight, checking the tech geek message boards where she's posted a few questions. She wants to know how her old email account managed to send her that strange message. It's of course possible to schedule messages to send out days, even weeks, after you write them. She could even check, if she could manage to log in to her old account, but the password has been changed. Is there a way to tell the location of the sender? No response to that question yet — at least, none that sound vaguely plausible. There aren't many people bothering with newbie tech questions. On the other hand, *Draft rumors getting scary real* has over three thousand responses.

Another thread discusses *Bloody Thursday — who really dropped the phosgene?* She clicks on that, she can't help herself, it seems so much like the kind of conspiracy theories Coffee loves. They sequestered the terrorists responsible for releasing the flu immediately. The official story is that the attacks were a counterstrike by Venezuela in retaliation for the drone campaign. And she's heard allegations of continued ties to FARC and Iran, which she had thought were credible. These anonymous message board commenters, though, seem to believe everything *but* that — the US government orchestrated the 8/16 terror attack as a "false flag" to provide the final pretext for instituting regime change in Venezuela. Or it's actually al-Qaeda, operating through contacts in Cuba. They claimed the attack, apparently, along with a half dozen other groups with varying degrees of plausibility. Someone makes a surprisingly strong case for a secret FARC operation, which has been increasingly radicalized by the collateral of the drone and now ground war.

> *This doesn't make any sense — if they are technologically advanced enough to make a flu that's paralyzing the world, then why resort to phosgene in crop dusters? That's as low tech as it gets.*

> *Why go high tech when low tech causes just as much damage?*

> *I'm with RonJon84. The MO of these attacks is totally different from the v-flu. Something is weird here.*

She scrolls past that particular argumentative eddy, which gets vicious and deep with nested replies, and looks for other, saner viewpoints. She finds instead rumors and wild conjecture, supposed inside information and an occasional death notice — here, as everywhere, people are dying. She finds it at first touching, then horrifying that someone's most lasting contribution could have been on the politics sub-forum of a tech message board. But once she's started looking, she can't seem to stop. Even this fevered speculation is better than feeling mired in her own ignorance. She hasn't seen Roosevelt in a week, but she still watches for him. She doesn't know whom to believe, but she agrees with the tinfoil hatters about one thing: *Something is weird here.*

She clicks around to other threads: about the crop dusters, about the president and abuses of martial law, about the arrests of war protestors in New York and Seattle. It's all horrible, but nothing kicks her belly like the discussion of quarantine zones.

> *Some people are more equal than others, I guess. Turns out you can buy your way past the municipal quarantines if you have enough money. A friend of mine's father-in-law got past the Potomac quarantine for a cool ten grand.*

> *Wow. I'd heard that about Detroit and Indianapolis, but figured they'd be more hard core about that shit so close to Washington.*

> *Well, no one's saying you can get past the Beltway.*

> *I can't say anything more than this, but trust me: You can get past any quarantine line with enough money and power. Yes, I mean even that one.*

Bird stares at that for a long time, then closes her computer. This quarantine is miserable, but she's seen the footage from California, she knows how much worse it can get. She ought to check the tech help sub-forums again, but doesn't bother. It's clear the techies have more important things to worry about than some noob's lost email password.

If her life were a heist movie, she would know a genius computer geek with a slight crush on her who could type a few lines of code into a computer and tell her everything she'd ever want to know about the strange email. But the only person she can think of who might vaguely match that description is the technology teacher, and Ms. Berger hasn't shown her face in school for the last week and a half. The rumor is v-flu, but Bird thinks she's just too scared to leave the house.

So Bird instead worries about quarantine breaches and impending world war as she crawls under her covers. She takes some melatonin and hopes that she might at least get three uninterrupted hours.

She would have said she was still awake, except that her phone wakes her up.

The glowing light sears her retinas and the ringtone sounds loud enough to wake up Aaron. She answers it without thinking, just to make it quiet.

"Hello?"

Silence. She squints at the screen and sees the number listed as unavailable.

"Roosevelt?" Her voice cracks, but it's a victory that she even managed to speak.

"No, no, Emily, it's me." The half-whispered voice sounds familiar, but it's so faint and tentative she's not sure.

"Who?"

He sighs. "Your dad, Emmie."

"Dad? Why are you calling so late? Has something happened?"

She can't remember the last time her dad started a conversation with her. His approach to parenthood has always been that of distant, delegated authority.

"Not exactly. Not on our end, at least. I just want you to know that we're doing everything we can to get back into the city. I know your mother doesn't like emotional subjects —"

Bird snorts.

"Okay, Emily, we're not an emotional family. But . . . it's been hard, being away from you when you've been in such trouble. I understand you've been having difficulties with your mother's old colleague. Have you done anything to rouse his suspicion?"

"Like get drugged at a party?"

Her father sucks in a breath. "*You* took those drugs," he says, but there's a discordant note in his flat assurance.

"You *know* I didn't. You knew it from the beginning. Why wouldn't you —"

"Emily!"

She cuts herself off, breathless. Greg Bird's mild manners have always had a threat behind them. Even on the other end of a phone call, she shies away from triggering the explosion.

"There are things you *don't need to know.* I had thought we made this clear to you a long time ago. I had thought you understood. And if you were a little too curious, then I blame myself for not noticing. But this isn't any kind of joke. It's not a game. You don't get to reset this if you make a mistake, and believe me, giving Roosevelt David any further reason to suspect you is a *mistake.*"

The hand holding the phone is a bloodless claw, each joint a locus of unnoticed pain. "You've heard something."

"You don't know anything, Emily. And that's good. That's going to save you. We'll be able to protect you better once we get back to the city, but until then, for heaven's sake, use the good sense we gave you and don't antagonize him."

A siren wails into the earpiece, too loud for a building in an undisclosed location. "Dad, why are you calling from an unlisted number?"

"Don't you think we would have been at the hospital if we could have? Don't you believe that we love you?"

Bird scrunches her eyes closed, as though he can see her cry. "Your work," she croaks.

"They watch us too. Emily," he says, and hesitates. "Emmie, try not to let your things out of your sight, all right? Be careful."

"Daddy, what is this? What's happening? What is he going to do?"

"I'll see you soon."

The melatonin doesn't work that night. Or maybe it does, and she dreams herself awake and hurting, the telephone silent in her hands.

Aaron tugs awkwardly at his blue blazer and turns the volume on his headphones loud enough that she can hear Chuck Berry like a soulful bee meandering through the frosted morning air.

Nicky took the morning off work to ride the Metro with them. With all the new regulations in place, the Metro ride takes an hour each way. The silver lining of insomnia: There's nothing particularly difficult about early mornings. She wades through a world hazed with familiar exhaustion, but Aaron and Nicky yawn and scowl at the sun.

"This will be good for you, Aaron," Nicky says, adjusting Aaron's red tie.

Aaron scrunches his nose. "I didn't mind my old school, you know. The kids were cool. Now they're gonna call me an Oreo, aren't they?"

Bird winces. "Don't say that, Aaron."

"It's a good education," Nicky says, his voice as firm and dadlike as it ever gets. "You'll appreciate it when it's time to go to college like Mo."

"I don't want to go to college. I want to be a music producer, like Russell Simmons. And he didn't ever have to go to a school with some dumb tie and jacket. Why doesn't Em have to wear a jacket?"

"Life's unfair, kid," she says. "If it's any consolation, they won't let us wear T-shirts."

"This look like a T-shirt to you?" he says, pointing to his white button-down. They had to buy it, along with the blazer and tie, that weekend.

"Hey," she says, and squats awkwardly so that she's at his eye level. "Aaron, I know this isn't exactly the most fun thing that's ever happened to you. But they have a music studio and music teachers and I bet someone will teach you how to play something if you ask politely, okay?"

He gives her a sidelong glance, but turns down the music volume. "Yeah?"

"Yeah. You can learn guitar like Robert Johnson."

He grins. "Aw, shit!"

One of the lower school teachers gives him a startled glance and Bird stifles a laugh. "Don't say that at school either. We'll just get through this, right? Once all this war and quarantine bullshit is through . . ."

Her throat tightens. Aaron looks up at Nicky and then reaches out to pat her shoulder. "Right, Em. It'll be okay."

Bird knows she wasn't half as smart or mature at Aaron's age. She wants to cry with the relief of having him here, where the self-interest of the people Coffee would call rich assholes will cover him in a protective halo.

A halo she wishes she could believe still extends over her, but she's had a whole weekend to think about her father's phone call. He used an unlisted number, but he called her cell. If Roosevelt and his bosses really are watching him — and they're certainly watching her — then he must know that her cell is probably tapped. Which means he wasn't trying to avoid them. He was trying to avoid her mother. Because her mother didn't want Bird warned?

She says good-bye to Nicky and Aaron, and heads back to the Devonshire side of campus. She isn't particularly surprised to see Coffee waiting for her in the wooded part of the path between the schools. He's wearing jeans against uniform code, red tie slung over his neck, and blue blazer bunched around his elbows. He fiddles with a lighter in his right hand, though there's no cigarette in his left; even he wouldn't dare smoke on campus. She sees, because she looks, the bulge of his ankle monitor beneath his worn jeans.

"Trevor tells me you got him to do something for another human being without an immediate benefit to himself. If you're planning another miracle, you might try doing something about this v-flu."

"I think he decided it would be funny."

Coffee nods thoughtfully. "The Robinson Achilles, a sadistic sense of humor. Probably why he keeps me around. Good for you. I'm glad Aaron will be safe."

"Safe as money, anyway."

"Now you sound like me."

"Maybe I'm coming around to your point of view."

"Oh, Bird," he says, like she's told him she has six months to live.

"Didn't you tell me that I should know better? Maybe I do, now."

Emmie, try not to let your things out of your sight. Every ridiculous conspiracy Coffee ever told her sounds more plausible after that phone call. She packed her own lunch this morning.

He winces and drops his lighter back in his pocket. "Did I ever tell you that I'm an asshole?"

"You didn't have to."

"So why did you always talk to me?"

She finds herself smiling even though her heart feels like a piece of pounded citrus, peeled apart by clumsy hands.

"Because you're the most interesting asshole I've ever met?"

He takes a step closer to her, and she stares up at him. His angular face shows the marks of exhaustion as surely as hers must: messy hair, purple bruises beneath red eyes. He traces her jaw with long fingers, the pads red and rough enough to tickle her. She shivers and closes her eyes.

"I can't tell you what you are to me," he whispers, and presses something smooth and cool into her left hand.

By the time she opens her eyes again he's heading in the opposite direction, flipping a pen between his fingers and then high in the air, a magician of nervous energy and inveterate paranoia. She watches until she can't see him anymore, and then she opens the note.

WANT TO SHOW YOU SOMETHING. MEET ME IN FRONT OF LOWER SCHOOL AFTER CLASSES. YOU CAN BRING AARON, BUT THIS NEEDS TO LOOK LIKE A DATE. BURN AFTER READING — CHECK YOUR POCKET.

It feels like magic when she reaches down and pulls out the battered metal lighter that she's seen him use hundreds of times. He must have slipped it there when he touched her face.

She laughs. The cold-dry skin on her bottom lip cracks with the spread of her grin. She tosses the lighter in the air, fumbles on the catch, and crouches to pick it from the mulch.

"You're a lunatic," she says to the burning paper, lighting it close to the earth.

"Pretty sure fire starting is against the honor code," a voice says.

She jerks, loses her balance, and sprawls on the ground. Roosevelt adjusts the lapels of his gray blazer. "Didn't mean to startle you," he says. "On my way to a meeting."

She glances down, where the last of the paper has curled into ember and ash. He follows her gaze and offers a hand. She stands on her own.

"Here," he says, and his hand is still out and something is in it. A pin: red, white, and blue, with the words *Only you can protect the homeland. If you see something, tell an authority.* He drops it into her open palm before she can snatch it away. Grease refracts a muddy rainbow from its plastic casing, and something sick rises in her throat as she remembers her father's warning.

"I've got one in Spanish if you'd like to give it to your new boyfriend."

She lets it fall to the mulch, in the ashes of Coffee's letter, and smashes it under the heel of her boot. "He speaks Portuguese. And he's not my boyfriend."

He smiles softly. "Paul told me otherwise. You picked wrong, you know."

"What the hell can you do about it?" It's bravado and it's desperation, straight from her shaking hands to her cracking voice. If her father won't give her a straight answer, then she can ask the man himself.

The smile stays, but it strains. "Well, Emily, your parents have been cooperating, but you . . ."

"What about me?"

His hands twitch, and for a moment she's afraid that he'll grab her again. He seemed so contained at the Robinsons' party, in control of every gesture, every veiled threat. But something is fraying him, just like he's been fraying her. He has unraveled a little more each time they meet. And even though these glimpses of his anger frighten her, they also convince her she's doing something right. Only a threat could get under his skin like that, only a girl he never expected to have any power.

"You're a bit tricky, Bird," he says. "It's my job to make sure our operations here go smoothly. And my superiors are concerned you might interfere with that."

"And how exactly could I do that, Roosevelt?" She emphasizes his name, to let him know that she noticed what he called her. She hates the sound of that nickname in his mouth.

He laughs softly. "It depends, doesn't it? On what you think you remember about that night. Wish me luck at my meeting. If you think you don't like me, just wait till you meet my bosses."

"Why would I meet them?"

"Remember that Russian spy? Someone passed him on the street, pricked him with a needle, and just like that" — he snaps his fingers — "he was gone." He nods at her dry terror. "Be seeing you, I hope."

He's an actual nightmare, a specter come out of the deep dream to walk the Earth. He trails horror like ichor, he shines his boots with insecurity and doubt. He is a hollow man, and he will suck her dry if he can. Don't give Roosevelt David a reason to suspect her? *He already does, Dad.*

She picks herself up. She goes to school — which is to say, she fights.

Coffee looks sexy in his rubber smock and safety goggles, like a cover model for *Mad Scientist* magazine with his dirty blond curls tousled in that bedhead look she wishes she could believe he intended. In fact, she's pretty sure he has no idea how much she's always ogled him here in his pun-intended element. Even back when she was in almost-love with Paul, she couldn't help but notice the nutty genius in AP Chemistry.

To watch him now is to feel her lead turned halfway to gold, to feel special and chosen and in unspeakable danger. He titrates a solution over a burner, each movement as careful and precise as a surgeon rearranging a heart. He doesn't glance at her, he doesn't speak to her; he mixes his chemicals with an ecclesiastic intensity that doesn't so much contrast with his normal jitters as explain them.

She and Coffee are alone in the chem lab. Aaron wasted no time introducing himself to the music teacher and wanted to spend some time with the instruments. Coffee said he needed help catching up on his chemistry coursework and took her here, blithely unconcerned about the unlikeliness of this cover story. Coffee could teach AP Chemistry, and everyone in the class knows it.

"What are you testing for?" she asks when he turns off the burner.

He glances up, startled at her existence. "The concentration of thio-cyanate iron in an aqueous solution."

"That was our lab two weeks ago."

"When I was sadly absent from class due to a momentary lapse in judgment that I deeply regret. It's hard to truly appreciate central heating until you sleep next to the Potomac River in November."

He pushes his goggles onto his forehead. "So, are you going to help me?"

"Come on, Coffee, you can titrate a solution in your sleep."

He gives her a lopsided grin. "But then I couldn't do it with you."

He never flirts with her like that, like he's having fun and doesn't quite mean it. "Coffee, what the —"

He shakes his head once and lifts his pants leg. The ankle monitor. She hops off a lab stool and crosses over to him.

"Don't be paranoid," she whispers, so close to the ridged curve of his ear that his hair slides through the Vaseline on her lips.

"Don't be naive," he says, though it's more the feel of his mouth and skin that conveys his meaning than the words, subvocalized.

She now understands the strange wording of his note: *This needs to look like a date.* She frowns.

"What," she says at normal volume, "I'll let you find my molar mass if you let me change your polarity?"

He bursts out laughing. "You've already done it, baby." She freezes at the sound of his happiness, unable to tell if he's mocking her or flirting or just appreciating the absurdity of their situation. That he might be stating the truth is a possibility she does not entertain.

He pulls off his gloves and fiddles with his open laptop. Heavy breathing and lip suction fill the silence of the room as he turns the computer in her direction.

This way they won't suspect we're doing anything useful, are the words typed on the screen.

She stares at the words and then back at Coffee, who looks remarkably smug. The sounds coming from the computer make her face feel warm, so she turns away and gets her notebook and a pencil.

If you're going to be paranoid, what about keyloggers?

His eyes get wide. He takes her pencil.

I FIGURED OUT WHAT THEY USED IN THE CANTEEN.

Where's that secret lab of yours, anyway? Here?

NEED TO KNOW BASIS, B. I HAVE SOME FRIENDS. ANYWAY, DO YOU WANT TO KNOW OR NOT?

Lay it on me, Q.

Q?

Dude, if you're going to play superspy, you at least ought to familiarize yourself with the genre.

He takes the pencil from her fingers before she can quite finish the last word.

IF YOU THINK I'M PLAYING, I SHOULD HAVE GONE TO BRASÍLIA. THIS ANKLE MONITOR IS A JOKE?

He's pissed, but the lip smacking and grunting is making it hard for her to focus on higher-order emotions like empathy and contrition.

And Debbie Does Dallas is some serious business, huh?

151

He snorts.

IT'S A COVER STORY!

Cause it's so im

The pencil tip snaps and she tosses it on the ground in frustration. He glares at her and picks it up. They are separated by less than an inch, and so she gives up the game and leans in. "That you might want to?" she whispers.

His hands smell like rubber and isopropyl alcohol, and they touch the pencil instead of her.

THE BEST COVER STORIES ARE THE MOST PLAUSIBLE, EMILY BIRD.

She catches her breath in time with the sound track. His look might be an invitation, but she doesn't take it. Desire and fear are mutually insoluble compounds after all.

What did they give me? she writes.

In response he writes out a chemical reaction, a long chain of molecules reacting with other molecules in a sequence that looks like the most complicated problems for further research at the end of their textbook.

And then, at the very end: I'VE NEVER SEEN THIS ONE BEFORE, BUT I'M 99% SURE. IT LOOKS LIKE IT WOULD BE SIMILAR TO GHB. BUT IT WOULD BE HARD TO SYNTHESIZE EXCEPT IN VERY WELL-EQUIPPED LABS.

GHB? The date rape drug?

He lets his fingers twine through hers as he takes the pencil, and nods very slightly. IT'S A DISSOCIATIVE. PEOPLE USE IT FOR LOTS OF STUFF, BUT WHEN IT'S GIVEN TO SOMEONE WHO DOESN'T KNOW WHAT THEY'RE GETTING? NOT GOOD. IT CAN CAUSE SHORT-TERM MEMORY LOSS. THIS ONE MIGHT BE EVEN STRONGER — THERE'S NO REAL WAY TO TELL WITHOUT TRYING IT MYSELF, BUT . . . THERE'S A REASON WHY YOU DON'T REMEMBER WHAT HAPPENED THAT NIGHT.

He offers her the pencil and she stares at his clean, blunt-cut fingernails with fascinated incomprehension. The make-out track starts its second loop — she remembers that breathy female gasp and stifled giggle, and wonders if Coffee's imaginary eavesdroppers will notice. She remembers lots of things about that night, she would tell him if she could. She remembers what he said about her and how much it hurt. She remembers wishing that she'd broken up with Paul. But she doesn't remember what matters. She doesn't remember what Roosevelt did to her, and she doesn't remember what she did after. Is it possible that those memories still exist in some dusty gyre of white matter, and all she needs to unlock them is a key? Everything is a drug, Coffee taught her that. Some are legal and some are illegal, some your brain makes on its own, and some your doctor dispenses in orange bottles, but it's all brain chemistry in the end.

"Bird?" Coffee's whisper is light, but the worry behind it brings her back to herself. She picks up the pencil and writes, very carefully:

If a drug can make me lose memories, could another bring them back?

His foot starts its restless beat on the chemical-stained linoleum. The skin wrinkles between his eyebrows, an expression too familiar on that malleable, kinetic face. She doesn't understand it when he rips the paper from her notebook. He takes two ground-eating strides to his computer and some growling, thrashing death metal replaces the make-out session.

"I'm not some pusher, Bird," he says, just soft enough that she has to strain to hear him over the music.

"You're a dealer. That's the actual definition."

He grimaces. "Not anymore, and besides, I never did it like that. You're not the drug type."

"Who is the drug type? I need something to help me remember."

"What if there's *nothing* to remember? You're . . . Bird, I can still see the scar from your stitches. You want to toss some extra chemicals in there, just to see what happens? If I give you a nervous breakdown, I think your mother will personally assassinate me."

"If anyone's going to give me a nervous breakdown, it's Roosevelt David. It's like he thinks I could become the next Deep Throat."

"If you could be, if that's the scale of whatever he thinks you know . . . damn. Deep Throat destroyed Nixon. If some CIA agents could have stopped him before he ever leaked to Woodward, don't you think they'd have gone pretty far? Do you really want to get in the middle of that?"

"Can you help me or not?"

He closes his eyes, revealing the tracery of blue veins beneath pink skin. "It's dangerous."

"Didn't you tell me about peeling back the layers of self with pharmacological tools, or whatever?"

"They're not a universal tool."

"What? I'm not strong enough?"

He swallows. "Maybe I'm not."

"Coffee?"

"I'll look around. Do some research. If we do it, we do this slow, controlled. And in the meantime, we try to do something else about Roosevelt. Maybe you won't have to remember."

She hugs him, because this is enough of an excuse to feel the ridges of his ribs and spine and his collarbone against her forehead. One day she will have to admit what this means, the feeling that gets stronger every time she's around him.

But not today.

Hell is loving your parents.

This is my well-substantiated hypothesis, based on years of building walls and plugging holes with passing bullets. (I do all the work around here.)

If Bird didn't love her parents, she could hate them cleanly, purely, dispassionately. She could coldly tolerate her mother and pity her father; she could wait to leave and when she did she could *never think about them again.*

But she loves her parents, and so she recalibrates.

She loves her mother when she says, "You are too much like Nicky not to work harder than you do. You *have* to fight your worst tendencies."

She loves her mother when she sighs to see a pair of Bs on Bird's report card and says, "Even Monique gets better grades. If you won't apply yourself, I swear I won't help you any more than I help Nicky. I won't enable your addiction to mediocrity."

And when Bird, thirteen years old and panicking, decides to *talk back* ("I'm not Uncle Nicky, I'm your daughter! Why can't you even look at me without seeing someone else? What the hell is wrong with you?"), she loves the mother whose answer will be an unstitched wound for many years after they have both tried to forget.

"Greg," says her mother, calm as frost, "you need to discipline your daughter."

Her father looks up from the television. "Uh, go to your room —"

"You know what I mean, Greg! Don't fool with me. I'm not in the mood."

"She's thirteen," Greg says cautiously.

Carol Bird just glares. He clears his throat. "Emily, uh, I think you have to come here."

She can't believe it even as she approaches him; she watches her parents in a haze of terror and anticipated pain. She has forgotten that Felice and her father should arrive any minute to pick her up for a sleepover. She has forgotten everything but the resignation on her father's face.

Something flashes beneath her mother's calm righteousness when Bird unbuttons her pants. Satisfaction maybe, but Carol turns away before Bird can tell for sure.

Pants around her ankles, she lies across her father's lap — a position that recalls a long gallery of punishment and acceptance, and nothing of comfort.

Above her head, they discuss her. Carol asks for twenty. Greg agrees to fifteen. Greg starts. Bird cries immediately and immeasurably, with choking, snot-filled gales. Greg pauses. The sting amplifies in anticipation of the next falling hand.

"Carol, this is enough. Look, they're pulling up now —"

"Finish it!" Her heels click away on the living room floor. Greg finishes it.

Eight. Nine. Ten. Eleven.

"I'm sorry, I'm sorry, I'm sorry," she says after each one, but she doesn't beg him to stop. No matter how often her mother compares her to Nicky, she is their true daughter. She knows that nothing will make them stop.

Her snot has fallen from her nose in a long, beautiful filament weighted like a pendulum at the end. She can feel the pull on her septum as it hangs in the air below her overturned forehead, mucus glittering in the glow of the television, jerking with each spank.

Thirteen. Fourteen.

"Oh my God."

Bird turns her head. The motion finally snaps the delicate thread, and the mucus breaks against her face and the floor. Through a curtain of wet hair, she sees Felice down the hall, her hand over her mouth. Felice's father desperately tugs her to the door. Bird's mother stands against the wall, arms crossed. Her lips are pressed tight, and at last Bird recognizes the sentiment bubbling beneath the coldness her mother prefers to express: fury.

Fifteen.

"Get up," he says, not without gentleness.

She falls to her knees. By the time she looks up again, Felice and her dad have gone.

Her mother leans over her. "You do not talk back to me, Emily. Not ever. I am your mother, and you will respect me."

"You let Felice . . ."

Her mother raises her eyebrows. "You'll never learn any lessons without an incentive, that much is clear. If your friends are the only thing important to you, I'll use your friends. Do you understand?"

"Yes, Mom."

Greg turns up the volume on the television.

Later that night, he knocks on her door. She winces when she sees him standing stiffly in the hallway. Her hands clench.

"Emily, your mother . . . she had a hard life. The kind of life you and I can't always understand. It's not that she doesn't love you. It's that she's tough, and she wants you to be too."

Bird just stares. Greg leans forward on his toes and then pulls a pen from his pocket. She recognizes it immediately: the gold-inlaid fountain pen her father keeps in his bureau drawer, the one he only fills to sign special contracts.

"My grandfather gave this to me before he died. It's seen all the accomplishments of the last three generation of Birds. I think it should be yours now, Emily."

"Like I'm going to do anything worthwhile." Her voice, rough and bitter, surprises her. She meant to keep silent.

Greg just smiles and presses the green-and-gold heirloom into her palm. "You will, sweetie. I know it. And one day your mother will know it too."

"Dad, do *you* think I'm just like Uncle Nicky?"

Her father looks away. "Your Uncle Nicky is just someone else your mother doesn't really understand. Good night, Emmie."

She sits back on her bed, beneath the wall-collage of ripped-out magazine ads and features and photographs that normally comforts her. Houses and storefronts and neighborhoods from all over the world. There's one in particular, an old black-and-white shot of U Street from the fifties, full of smiling Black couples in their Sunday best strolling past gleaming storefronts, freshly painted. She wants a shop like that, she knows that even now. She takes her father's pen and writes very carefully beneath the Mary Janes of a woman who could be her grandmother:

She doesn't know who you are.

And then she takes this precious pen, this heirloom, this chunk of history and family and connection, down to her father's office and puts it back in his drawer.

The next day, she sees the pen in its case, carefully exposed on the left side of his desk. It stays there for the next five years.

The Birds pretend that night never happened.

I pick up the pieces.

[vitamin b12]

$C_{63}H_{88}CoN_{14}O_{14}P$

The note in her school mailbox is printed on thick paper, more like a wedding invitation than an administrative summons. Which it must be, despite the odd request: *Please report to the lower school medical facility during sixth period. You have been excused from class.*

That last is quaint, given the impunity with which the remaining students at Devonshire have been skipping. The ones like Bird, who at least show up, seem to do it more out of habit than conviction. With no guarantee of colleges in the fall to compete over, the hamster wheel of prep school has lost its motivational carrot. She waves the card at Marella, who picks up a folded-over essay from her box and stuffs it into her backpack without checking the grade.

"Did you get this?" she asks.

Marella glances at the card. "Oh, I got one yesterday. Some kind of flu shot."

"Flu shot? I thought this thing was the incurable beast."

"It's not a cure. We'd have heard about that. They said something about immune-boosting vitamins."

Bird looks back at the card. "Vitamins?" The word stings her memory; she winces before she remembers why. Poor Dr. Granger, that first day back at school, explaining the quiet lower schoolers lining up in the hallway.

"Weird," Bird says. "Do you think it'll do any good?"

Marella grins. "I'm not dead yet."

"I'd wait until after chapel service to make sure."

Marella punches her arm lightly. "You know the weird thing? Before this end-of-days stuff started, I'd totally given up."

"On what?"

Marella turns so that her long, glossy curls arc over her shoulder like a cartoon bombshell. "Having a real friend in high school. I kept telling myself to wait until college, but there you were all along."

Bird feels warm the whole walk to the lower school, happy and full of compressed bubbles, like she's back in seventh grade and Brady Wright has just sent her a carnation for Valentine's Day. Even before she came out in ninth grade, Marella always stood just outside Carol Bird's approved Devonshire social world. Scholarship students didn't have the valuable connections in the elite African American community of the District. Marella's parents certainly didn't belong to Jack and Jill, and as far as Bird could tell, Marella herself had no interest in joining, even though most of the Black students at Devonshire and Bradley participate at some point. And while that used to make her a somewhat dangerous prospect for friendship, now Bird feels unspeakably grateful. She wishes she'd been brave enough to choose Marella over Charlotte and Felice earlier. But then, she never believed that aloof, cosmopolitan, watchful Marella would choose her. Is she a bad person to feel a little grateful to the v-flu that's ravaging the world? It gave her Marella and Coffee, it took away Paul and her parents. It killed Emily and raised up Bird, and that's nothing she can regret anymore.

Aaron waits with ten other boys in the hall outside the medical facility. He waves and keeps talking to a boy his age. A moment later, Paul slips into the back of the line. He nods at her and raises his eyebrows in a way that makes her wonder if her skirt is stuck in her underwear.

The line slowly files into the converted classrooms, where a blue-masked nurse instructs her to sit on the examining bench closest to a desk covered in scattered papers and an open packing box marked "Granger" in black Sharpie. Bird scans the window reflexively as she waits, but only the scraggled backs of rosebushes watch her. No black Beemer, no men in suits with white earpieces, not even a soldier. She relaxes. She's had a remarkably, jubilantly uneventful week. Maybe Roosevelt only meant to scare her. Maybe her father overreacted. Maybe it would be okay not to pack a lunch tomorrow.

When it's her turn, the nurse takes her temperature and blood pressure before swabbing her upper arm.

"You might feel a sting," he says in a disinterested monotone. "If your arm swells or if you develop a fever in the next forty-eight hours, please contact us immediately."

"I thought it was just a vitamin shot."

The nurse actually looks at her then, pausing mid-swab. "Well. It's got some B12 and other vitamins that have shown promise in prophylactic studies, yes. But it's also a seasonal flu shot. At least this way we can protect you against secondary infections. Would you like to opt out?"

Bird hadn't even been aware that this was an option, and stares down at her hands in embarrassment. Her mother would want her to get the shot, of course, but she'd be disappointed that Bird didn't so much as question it. Maybe Emily hasn't left her entirely.

"No," she says after a moment. "You can give it to me."

The nurse picks up a needle from the table and taps it. She tries to focus on something else, and turns back to the desk. "Did you know the doctor?" she asks. "Sasha Granger?"

She winces as he punctures her arm with what feels like more force than necessary. He doesn't so much as move an eyebrow as he plunges down the peach-colored liquid and removes the needle.

"Yes," he says, "I knew Dr. Granger. But not well. It's a tragedy what happened to her. If you would like to speak with someone about it, however, I'd suggest the guidance counselor."

He doesn't look at her once while he speaks. His voice is flat — but guarded, not bored. Maybe it's that whiff of office drama — it never ends, does it? Not when you grow up, not even when you die — that makes her stroll to the desk when he turns his back. The box marked *Granger* has her things inside: pictures with her husband, a framed diploma from University of Chicago, plushies of infectious diseases, and thank-you notes from lower schoolers. No folders or notebooks that she would expect a head medical officer to have, but maybe they kept those for her replacement.

"Everyone who has received their shot needs to clear out immediately!"

The nurse's voice, not even a foot behind her. She jerks, hits the box, and grabs it just before it falls to the floor.

"Sorry!" she says. Her hands tremble as she replaces it on the desk; for just a moment, she'd thought he was Roosevelt. She glances reflexively inside the box just before she leaves, mostly to avoid the nurse's basilisk stare. She sees something she hadn't before, which must have been churned up by its near fall, but she's almost to the door before half recognition bursts into realization. A pin in patriotic colors with two lines of text in Spanish. Even if she weren't in AP Spanish she'd know what they said, because she ground its English-language cousin pin under her boot as Roosevelt told her about how he or his bosses could kill her without anyone knowing.

She remembers, now, Dr. Granger's strange advice the day Bird came back to school: *Stay here. This school will keep you safe. Whatever else it does.*

Those Homeland Security pins are everywhere these days, but not when Dr. Granger died. Had Roosevelt given it to her? Had he threatened her too? And now she was dead. Bird feels tipsy with fear, but forces it back when she sees Aaron waiting with his friends in the hallway.

"Want to get some pizza after school? We can bring Vace's back for Uncle Nicky."

Aaron frowns and steps away from the line. "I don't know, Em. The guy in the suit told Mr. Levenson that I have to stay at school from now on."

Bird's stomach drops even as she asks the next question. "Guy in a suit? Who?"

"He said you know him. He had a funny name, like a last name."

"Roosevelt."

"Yeah, that's it. Em, are you —"

She kneels down and hugs him tight. "Fine," she whispers. "We'll be fine. You stay in the library after classes, okay? I'll find you there."

She thought he would be safer here. She should have known better.

She doesn't have to go far to find him. She recognizes his car parked across the street from the upper school entrance. He rolls down the tinted window as she approaches and nods curtly.

"I figured you'd want to talk," he says. "You'll be glad to hear my meeting went well."

"You're keeping a little kid *trapped* in school?"

Roosevelt shakes his head. "That's just a courtesy. We're keeping *you* in school. But I thought you'd want to be able to keep an eye on him."

"Me?" She looks around, wondering if the soldiers would shoot her if she tried to leave. Probably not. Roosevelt would just run her over with his Beemer.

"We've got to keep an eye on you. Paul made an excellent suggestion, so —"

"This is *Paul's* idea?"

"And your mother preferred it this way." He shrugs. "I told you. You picked wrong."

She and Coffee and Aaron sit in the stacks at the back of Bradley library, sharing a Vace's pizza that Coffee paid some freshman to pick up for them. School arrest doesn't feel so terrible with her favorite pizza, but she worries about Aaron.

She thinks again of the strange email that she might have written herself during that lost night, timed to send a month later. But she's no closer to getting into that account, and Coffee has no more idea of what her message means than she does. Her past self has been singularly useless — the writing might be on the wall, but she has no idea what it says. She wishes she did.

"The guy is like a nuclear bomb of assholery," she says. "I think he killed the doctor."

"With polonium on the Homeland Security pin? Come on, Bird. A dozen people have to have touched that thing since she died. It was a heart attack. People have them. I doubt Roosevelt even knew her."

She sighs. "There's got to be some way to stop him."

Coffee sprawls against a couple of tomes of ancient Roman history and starts his slice crust first. "We could eat his heart and gain his power," he says around a mouthful.

Aaron looks at him, wide-eyed. "Does that really work?"

Coffee shakes his head and Aaron's shoulders slump. "Oh. Yeah. I knew you were joking."

Aaron knew exactly who Coffee was, but he still pretended to introduce himself this afternoon. Her cousin has a knack for espionage, but Bird refuses to involve him any further. She's afraid that Coffee is rapidly approaching Robert Johnson levels of coolness in his imagination.

"Aaron, why don't you start your homework at one of the carrels?"

"Aw, Em! No one cares about homework. I want to listen to music in the AV room. They've got a bunch of records I've never heard before."

"Okay, do that, then."

"Are you trying to get rid of me?"

She rolls over and tickles him in the stomach. "With love, and for your own good. Listen to music, you'd be bored anyway."

He looks between Coffee and Bird and picks up his backpack. "I'm out," he says. "I don't need to see a bunch of kissing."

He makes a smoochy face while Bird blushes and pretends to swat him away.

"Perceptive kid," Coffee says after Aaron's whistled his way into the AV room.

She's painfully aware of his knee resting against her thigh in the close quarters of the library shelves. "I'm not about to kiss you."

He puts down his half-eaten slice. "Why not?"

She closes her eyes. *Why not, Bird?* "You scare me to death," she hears herself saying.

He doesn't respond for the space of several breaths. She dares a peek, finds him steepling his fingers against his temples, the tips white with pressure. He leans his head back and stares up at the ceiling.

"I didn't mean it like you had to, like I expect it. I help you because I want to. You don't have to like me back. I can leave if you want. I'm not — I'm not Roosevelt. Or Paul. I promise." His quiet words are dry and choked. Instead of that expressive face, she watches the bowstring tautness of his muscles beneath the uniform collared shirt.

She slides forward, so her knee goes under his thigh and their hips touch; it's like a dance, this thing they do together. She never realized that it hurt him too. Only that gives her the courage to speak.

"I think about you. All the time. It's never been like this for me. My mom would have a fit. You're probably going to jail. I'm not sure you actually like me. You're a deal —"

"Okay," he says, the smile in his voice luring her gaze to his face. He holds up his hands. "You've convinced me. Bad-news Coffee keeps his lips off, promise. I'll write you from prison. Every week. In code so your mother won't know, and I'll find you when I get out, unless I've died of prison v-flu, in which case I hope you'll attend the memorial."

Halfway through this improbable declaration she starts to laugh. "I'll put red roses on your grave."

He flicks her hair. "What I said that night —"

And just like that, the laughter melts away. "Don't say you didn't mean it." She puts one finger on his chest. "Because I know you did."

His stuttering breath vibrates up her arm. "I think of you. Every hour. Either I hate you or I . . ."

His words stumble still and she pulls away. She remembers a song that her grandmother loved, Smokey Robinson, *I don't like you, but I —*

"If I kiss you," she says, forcing herself to hold her hand over the candle of his wide eyes, "it means that I've given up everything."

"Maybe you'll find something you like better."

"Like you're some expert in self-abnegation."

He gives her a thin smile, and she remembers how much he gave up just to be here, arguing with her in the history stacks.

"Do you know why I started experimenting?" he asks.

She shakes her head. It never occurred to her that there must have been a start, an origin story to the legend of Coffee the Dealer.

"You didn't emerge from your mother's forehead with a joint in one hand and an Erlenmeyer flask in the other?"

He rolls his eyes. "I was fourteen. I'd been living in London for the last four years. I liked chemistry plenty, but it'd never really occurred to me to relate it to pharmacologically active substances. This is your brain, this is your brain on drugs, I totally believed that shit. I doubt it would have changed much — well, I'd probably have managed to smoke a joint or two in college, but the rest?" He shrugs. "But then my dad drove us home from an event at the embassy. We were having an argument about Brazil — I wanted to go to some football camp for the summer and they thought I should go back to São Paulo to spend time with my grandmother. There was black ice on the road. We skidded, hit the guardrail, flipped. Next thing I know, I'm waking up from surgery with my leg on fire and they tell me my dad died three days ago."

His voice isn't particularly emotional, though he doesn't look at her. She wants to cover his mouth, as though that could stop this awful thing that happened long ago. She settles for taking his hand.

He shivers at the touch, leans closer. "My mom got away with a few stitches in her arm. I missed the funeral. Missed the summer and a semester of school. Long, boring hospital story, but the gist is I learned to walk again only with copious reliance on prescription opiates. So I'm never going to be a football star, it's not much of a disappointment in the end, but damn am I addicted to those little white pills. And you have a lot of spare time in traction, let me tell you. So I start to research them, what exactly they do, their chemical structure, the pathways in the brain. I sort of . . . thought my way out of it, I guess. Quit cold turkey once I learned how to synthesize my first drug in the school chem lab. And at that point, I'd learned there was this whole world of people who did it for fun. Wrote step-by-step instructions for brewing dozens of things I'd never heard of. Not just the simple stuff, like opiates, but ways to unlock pathways in your brain you'd otherwise have to be near death to even approach. My dad . . . he'd been dead a year before I even managed to visit his grave. I took shrooms, mescaline, LSD. Whatever. Trying to get closure. Turns out no drug can give you that, but I guess it helped to see the inside of my brain. It was like my guilt was this physical thing, and I had to push it out before it killed me."

His shivering gets worse. Bird squeezes his hand, afraid they both might crash if she lets go. This isn't a story smoothed and sanded with telling; this is rough and splintered, hacked from the tree and still oozing sap. He breathes, that's all he does, harsh breaths that hurt her because she asked for this, and warm her because he gave it to her.

"There's a freedom to knowing how strong you are. Knowing you can catch yourself."

"Fledging the nest?"

He snorts. "I wasn't going to go there."

She leans against him, head against his collarbone. He puts his arm around her. She should say something, a condolence or an apology or some other tortured syntax that might convey a quarter of what she's feeling.

Instead, she falls asleep. "I can only sleep when you're around," she might have said in that long corridor between drowsiness and dream.

And he might have kissed the top of her head, a diffuse pressure through kinky hair, and she might have dreamed of him until Aaron finds her alone on her side, her head pillowed on a blue blazer several sizes too large.

Nicky comes to visit the day after their school arrest. He and Aaron take a walk together while Bird and Marella sit on the bench by the rose bridge in puffy winter coats.

"What exactly happens to you if you try to leave?" Marella asks without looking up from some lumpy object she's attempting to knit with green yarn.

"Someone drags me back?" Bird yawns and watches the soldiers watching Nicky and Aaron. "Either that or they shoot me."

"Some of that infamous Coffee paranoia rubbing off, huh?"

"Like all this wouldn't make anyone paranoid. I mean, look at you."

"Look at what?"

"Marella, you're *knitting*. Not doing homework, not hanging out with a hot girl —"

"Don't sell yourself short, honey. Coffee thinks you're pretty fine."

Bird buries her hands in her coat sleeves. "Coffee thinks . . ." *I can't tell you what I feel for you.* She shakes her head. "Whatever, the point is that you are doing a deliberately mindless activity. Not very well."

Marella squints at the lumpy green square. "I just started! And with all the time we've been spending in the shelter, I'll get plenty of practice."

"Exactly. You are changing your activities in response to repeated stress. Tell me you don't feel a little worried around these soldiers every day."

They fall silent as a soldier speaks into a walkie-talkie and slings one of those black automatics over her shoulder. A pair of helicopters make a low pass overhead.

"Not like they're going to *shoot* me," she says, but without much conviction.

"I take it you haven't met Roosevelt."

"Bird, you make this guy sound like Dr. Evil. I'm the last person to tell you people can't be real douches, but this is Devonshire, not Afghanistan. What's the worst he can do?"

"He gave my boyfriend a date rape drug to mix with my drink and I ended up in the hospital. I still don't remember what happened to me. And I'm telling you, he's capable of more. So yeah, let's call it justified paranoia."

Marella puts down her knitting and rubs Bird's arm. "Right. Pure evil. Bird, what does he want with you?"

Bird lifts her feet onto the bench and presses her face against her knees. "That's the worst part. I don't really know. I think it has something to do with my parents. Or that he thinks I know something. I mean, in full paranoia mode I think I must know some major state secret that could bring down the government, I just have to figure out what it is. Though that doesn't explain why he's gunning for Coffee too." It's been a relief to let Marella in on her private nightmare; the perspective of someone not directly involved makes her feel a little more human.

"So, he's watching you. And he's working with Paul or using him or whatever, and that's why you and Aaron are under school arrest. But has he done anything since? I mean, let's say that you did forget some huge state secret. Well, as long as you don't do anything, then he's happy and you're safe, right?"

Bird opens her mouth to argue — the words "Roosevelt" and "safe" do not belong together in any positive statement — but then she considers. Marella's reasoning echoes that of her parents, and though she's felt like struggling every moment since she woke up in the hospital, isn't it possible that they're right? Is she a fly, banging against the walls of a room with an open window?

Marella wraps an arm around Bird's shoulders. "There's nothing wrong with taking care of yourself, you know. What's the point of being brave if it destroys you?"

"Marella," she says, exasperated and touched, "you could have made your life so much easier these last few years and you didn't. I dreamed of being you."

"And believe me, honey, there were a hella lot of days I wished I'd taken my advice. But being true to who I am is the rest of my life. We'd better hope that Roosevelt is just passing through yours."

Marella resumes her knitting and Bird sits, not thinking about much, but feeling something bubble from that same space where Coffee and her mother hide.

"But," she hears herself saying, and Marella's needles pause. "But, *I want to know.* I wanted myself to know. That's why I wrote the email. So he wouldn't win."

"Bird, this isn't a fair fight. His people wrote the rules, they judge the game. I'm scared for you. Can't you let it go?"

But she can't. There's a girl she doesn't remember, a terrified Bird who had learned something she shouldn't have. A girl who begged her future self to do what she couldn't.

"It doesn't always have to be like this. We don't *always* have to work around, let by, give up. Do we? They always have the power. But I have a little bit, now. I have something he doesn't want me to know."

Marella bunches her knitting between her hands and takes a deep breath.

"Okay," she says softly. "Okay. So where do we start?"

"Really?"

Marella shakes her head. "It kills me. All this time, I thought you were drowning in friends. I mean, one of them was Felice, but still." She stuffs her knitting into her backpack and pulls out her pencil case. "Girl, I got your back. Promise."

"The first thing," Marella says that evening as they sit in their pajamas on the floor of an empty senior room, "is to imagine."

She's holding a pen they stole from the school store (all the students have been stealing from the school store, which no one has bothered to lock or staff) and a fancy college-ruled notebook from the back of Bird's locker. The notebook has been labeled *Application Essay Notes and Drafts* (Marella wanted to call it *The Secret Sex Lives of the Senior Class: A Tragicomedy*, but Bird reminded her that it needed to look inconspicuous), and Marella's new pen bleeds a purple dot onto its white pages, awaiting inspiration.

"Imagine what?" Bird asks.

"Imagine Roosevelt David, as you want him to be."

"As I — what does that mean?"

"We need something to work toward. My mom reads about this stuff all the time. There can be no success without a clearly defined goal."

Bird wraps her fleece more tightly around her shoulders. "What if I told you I imagined him run over by a car?"

Marella's expression doesn't flicker. "Should I write that down?"

"You would not help me run him over with a car."

"We're just planning. The next stage is when I talk you out of fool ideas."

Bird snorts. "All right, I imagine him the hell away from my life. And Coffee's. And I imagine him wishing he'd never met me. I want him to know that doing . . . whatever he did to me was the biggest mistake of his life. He can live to be a hundred for all I care."

Marella starts to write. "Well, that's better. I wasn't looking forward to talking you out of murder."

"But just think of the killer college essay you could have gotten out of it."

"You are just a little too good at being a Devonshire girl, you know that?"

Bird sighs, Marella glances up. "Have you thought of just . . . walking back through that night at the party? Trying to remember whatever happened?"

"I've tried and tried. But I've asked Coffee . . . well."

"Asked him — oh, I see. And in case his, ah, psychedelic depth charges don't work, you want to find some other way to make Roosevelt regret ever meeting you?"

Bird lets her shrug speak. Marella's look is equal parts respect and worry, which Bird can handle. Whatever she was before, she isn't playing the perfect Devonshire girl now.

"And I have a place to start," Bird says.

"Should I be scared?"

"Probably. But you won't have to drive the car."

Marella snorts and flaps the notebook in Bird's direction. "All right, all right. What are we starting?"

"I mean, I don't know, and Coffee says I'm nuts —"

"Very reasonable and glass-housey of him."

"That's what I thought! Anyway, remember that doctor who had a heart attack during the terror attacks? I think Roosevelt might have killed her."

Marella drops the notebook. "No. Oh no, *killed* her? Bird, are you —"

Bird tells her about Roosevelt's veiled threat that one morning, his description of the way he could kill without anyone knowing and the Homeland Security pin he made a point of handing her.

"It's not much," Marella says. "I'm not saying it's nothing, and it's weird that she had the pin weeks before anyone else. But *killing* her? They said it was a heart attack. And what reason would he have?"

"Maybe she knew something she shouldn't? Why is he here all the time? Why's he so tight with Mrs. Early? He's CIA. Something secret has to be happening."

Marella stays silent for a long minute. Then she picks up the notebook and starts to write, paragraphs of carefully looping cursive that Bird can't quite read upside down.

"So you think I'm onto something?"

"I think there's a small chance. But it's a chance, and I trust your gut, so here's what we can do. If something strange was going on between that doctor and Roosevelt, the other doctors and nurses had to have gotten a whiff of it. So we need their story."

"What are you going to do, go up and ask? That one nurse practically shoved me out of the room when I tried."

Marella grins. "We won't have to ask them. You know that recorder I sometimes use in history? It'll fit in my pencil case. I'll visit the doctor in the morning and forget it under a table."

"Genius. But how do you know they'll talk about her at all? What if they find it?"

"They give it back to me and we try something else. No harm, no foul."

"No harm," Bird echoes.

Bird dreams of closed rooms, of long syringes filled with mercury, of romantic pop hits from the eighties and nineties, of questions she can't answer, of questions she can. She dreams of Roosevelt and she dreams of Paul and she dreams of wanting Coffee, wanting and never having, all the dark dream long until she wakes and doesn't remember.

This isn't just about you anymore. The world is falling down, Bird, and anyone can forget. Anyone can give in. But if you want your power?

Remember it.

[adrenaline]

$C_9H_{13}NO_3$

Fifty years ago, half of the students at Devonshire were boarders, but that number dwindled until the eighties, when it officially became a day school. The attic dorms were converted into a dance studio and study hall, but the room seems more at home jammed with narrow cots and dressers than it ever did with a ballet barre and stereo system. It remembers its old shape. A television is on at the far end of the room, beside porthole windows that overlook the rose garden and middle school. A reporter in a bulletproof vest and headphones is breathlessly explaining to the furrow-browed news anchor that he's embedded with the marines, amassed on the Colombian–Venezuelan border, and engaged in a heavy firefight. The bombs have been going off for months, but Bird's tried hard not to hear them, or think about what they might mean. Bombs don't mean war anymore, not *war* war, they're just tough foreign policy (she knows this means shit to the people blown up by them, but she carefully bifurcates her mind on this point). But a land invasion? That's like when she was in fourth grade and her mother sat glued to the television, cheering when the sky lit up over Baghdad. It's like her granddad, who always limped from the shrapnel he caught in his hip during Vietnam. First plague, then war. She swallows and tries to focus on her notebook, where she's writing down theories about the email her past ghost sent her present self.

A trick of Roosevelt's? A drug-induced delusion? One half of a clue, but I didn't have time to leave myself the other?

174

Something thumps on the floor behind her. She spins around. It's Charlotte, surprisingly, with a silk bandanna tied around her braids and flower-print pajamas.

"Mrs. Cunningham said this bed is free," she says, kicking her duffel bag beneath it. "But I can find another if you want."

"You're welcome to it," Bird says, intending sarcasm but achieving flat exhaustion. "But I'm surprised your parents are letting you bunk." Charlotte's mother is the smothering type, and hardly lets Charlotte out of the house for sleepovers.

Charlotte sits abruptly; the cot creaks beneath her sudden weight. She darts a glance at Bird's face and then looks down again.

"Mom has a cough," she says softly. "And a fever. They say it started this afternoon. The nurses here checked me out and I'm fine, but my parents have to stay under quarantine for now. I know it's just a cold. I mean, the District's practically a prison camp these days, how the hell could anyone catch the v-flu? But the house is locked up, so here I am."

Bird puts down her notebook. The sight of Charlotte struggling back tears reminds her of the times they actually enjoyed each other's company, of the friendship she was sad to lose when Felice finally grew tired of her.

"That sucks, Charlotte. I'm sure they'll be okay."

Charlotte nods jerkily and forces a smile. "Yeah, I know. Thanks."

For a moment Bird thinks she might throw a rope across the chasm; that they might be friends without Felice between them. But then Charlotte hunches her shoulders and turns away.

Bird closes her notebook, then her eyes.

On the television, the news anchor brings up the new draft bill, which the reporter says the "boots on the ground" aren't happy about, but is gaining momentum in Congress. They discuss the terror threat, and recent suspicious events in Phoenix and San Jose. The flight ban, martial law, the president's deferment of the next election until the "terrorist plague has run its course" — current disasters drift over her in wave after icy wave. Eventually, Mrs. Cunningham turns off the television and the lights. Bird stares at the play of blue and yellow behind her eyelids, until Marella crouches beside her and taps her shoulder.

"You okay?" she whispers.

"I could have been sleeping," Bird says.

"You never sleep."

Now Bird opens her eyes and rolls them suspiciously to her left. Marella crouches by the bed in mismatched flannel pajamas covered by a tattered red cardigan and matching fingerless gloves. Two long braids swing on either side of her head, the kind of glossy, walnut-colored ropes that would have won some storybook adventurer wisdom or eternal life or the hand of a princess if he could have brought them back to the king. Bird sighs. She longed for Marella's hair when they were younger. Part of her still does.

"Well," Marella says, sitting back on her heels, "at night, anyway. You do it pretty well in class."

Bird yawns. "I absorb information better during my REM cycle. What's up?"

Mrs. Cunningham taps her pen against the radiator beside her bed and their heads snap up. "Ladies, it was lights-out ten minutes ago. Please wrap up your conversations before eleven, or take them outside."

"Pay *dirt*," Marella whispers.

Bird gasps. "Seriously? You just left it there and they didn't notice?"

"Oh," she says, and clutches her heart with artful desperation, "my *chest* is hurting. I'm so afraid, do you think I could be having a heart attack like that doctor? Maybe that gas caused her heart attack? Maybe they're contagious?"

"Really? They believed you?"

"They rolled their eyes the whole time they gave me the EKG, I left my pencil case in the corner, and no one noticed a thing. They don't have a very high opinion of us private school brats, those doctors. It's called playing to their prejudices."

Mrs. Cunningham claps her hands. "All right, ladies, quiet time starts now."

Marella puts the stick on Bird's pillow and leans forward. "There's about six hours," she whispers. "You want to go through it?"

"Since I don't sleep anyway?"

Marella shrugs. "Reasonable divisions of labor."

"Ladies, *right* now,' or do I need to give out detentions?"

Marella shakes her head and gives Bird a cheesy thumbs-up before heading to the other side of the room, where she's been sleeping for the last two weeks.

Bird takes out her phone and texts Aaron a quick good night. She means to put it away before Mrs. Cunningham can make good on detention threats, but the unopened message at the top of her inbox snags her attention. It doesn't have a subject line, but that hardly matters. The return address is enough to send her pulse into a heavy jazz snare that jumps in her neck and armpits and groin. Her breath is a dog-whistle whine that delivers hardly any oxygen. It's the email address that told her about the writing on the wall. The email she *sent herself*.

Bird's finger clicks the message before her brain can tell it no.

> *That is a very fascinating letter in the sent messages box. I would leave this alone, Bird. Say hi to your mother for me.*
> FDR

Bird starts Marella's recording full of hope and fire, and finishes, many hours later, in the cooling ashes of another disappointment. After that message from Roosevelt, she can't walk across campus without flinching at the fat squirrels barking in piles of composting leaves. She wanted so badly for this to be the leverage she needed. But instead, it's nothing.

"Not quite nothing," Marella says while they wait for Aaron to finish his music lesson in the hallway outside the pit. "Play me that bit again, about the quarantine?"

Bird rewinds past the hours of repeated instructions, student questions, and tense office banter, to the one section she marked. They listen again.

"How many more do we have to get through?"

"Um . . ." Shuffling papers, something scraping against the floor. "It looks like we've got all the girls up to date. No refusals among the ones still regularly attending. Early says that she'll announce the new rule about the shot being mandatory for attendance after Thanksgiving."

"So today we have to finish out the boys? Have we finally gotten the last shipment?"

"Yeah, there's a group of seniors and the last of the faculty. Orders are to hurry."

"That's what he keeps saying. And I keep asking, what the hell is the big rush about a vitamin treatment?"

A pause. "It's the quarantine, I think. There's concerns."

"Concerns. Tyler, if you've heard anything I need to know —"

"Just get your shot this evening and keep your head. You know David doesn't tell us anything."

Bird stops the recording and raises her eyebrows at Marella. "This is shit and you know it."

"That thing about the quarantine is weird."

"It's just that rumor, you know, the one about people bribing their way in."

"Damn, that's some gold-plated gossip you got there, Bird. All I get to hear about is Tory Silver banging some soldier in the janitor's closet."

"Wait — really?"

Marella points two fingers at her eyes. "Focus. World catastrophe versus rich girl sexcapades. Not a contest."

"I don't know about that. What if there's a video?"

"Her dad'll buy YouTube. Are you serious about the quarantine thing?"

"I saw it on some message board. Which ain't bringing down Roosevelt David, so —"

"Holy shit. His name."

"Is completely — holy shit."

Bird reaches for Marella's hand unthinkingly as she rewinds again, and then plays:

"You know David doesn't tell us anything."

"It's Roosevelt," Bird whispers. "He's involved somehow with the medical team. He must have known Dr. Granger."

"Which doesn't mean he killed her."

"Okay, okay. But listen: It's strange enough he's so chummy with Mrs. Early, but the medical team? Are vitamin treatments at a prep school really that vital to national security?"

"A prep school with the vice president's daughter? Look at your cousin. He switches schools and magically he gets flu shots and proper air raid shelters and, you know, a fighting chance. God, sometimes I hate this city."

There's nothing much Bird can say to that, so she doesn't. Marella's family isn't rich. She knows more than Bird about the differences between white DC and, well, everywhere else.

"So, do you think it's a good lead?" Marella asks finally. "Vitamin treatments? Not exactly earth-shaking, but . . ."

"There's something there," Bird says slowly. A door opens at the end of the hallway and Aaron waves at her. She waves back. "I think we should just check with Mrs. Early."

"Because she's really going to tell us the truth."

"No," Bird says quietly, "but her computer might."

Bird makes a calculation, checks it again, and the answer is a string of ten numbers that have scared her most of her life. But she dials them, leaves a message, and waits. It does not take very long.

"Emily," her mother says. "I'm so glad you called."

This is cautiously promising. "I have a question about school," she says.

"Interesting. Well then, go ahead."

"I would like to have a conversation with Mrs. Early. In her office."

"In her office?"

"So we can be alone," Bird says. "I have some concerns of a private nature."

"You do. Would you mind sharing? Because I'd hate to bother your headmistress about some trifling better handled by the school counselor."

Bird swallows. "I would mind. Yes."

"Emily, I've been hearing some . . . worrying things. I think I told you how important it is for you to keep quiet and follow the rules. This is not the time to stage your teenage rebellion."

If not now, when? But she swallows that automatically. "I'm being safe, Mom."

"That's not what Paul says. He says you've started dating that drug-dealing thug —"

"Mom!"

Of course she's been talking to Paul. Bird is only disgusted with herself that she didn't anticipate it.

Her mother takes a deep breath. "I'll call Mrs. Early. And you will not disappoint me, Emily. We'll talk later."

"Thank you, Mom, I —"

But Carol Bird has already hung up. Bird arranges things with Marella between lunch and the afternoon chapel service, where she sees Coffee goofing around with Trevor Robinson as if one of them might not be going to jail for the next decade. Coffee nods at her, which makes her flush and then grimace, because of course Felice and Gina saw. Charlotte is absent again; there are rumors about her parents that Bird doesn't like to think about. The prep school social hierarchy is damaged but resilient. Coffee rises, Bird falls, Marella continues to employ her middle finger.

After chapel, a group of soldiers escorts the girls back to the Devonshire side. Several black cars with tinted windows have parked across the street, but none lower their windows, and there's no way for her to know if one of them is Roosevelt. She doesn't see Paul anywhere, a proximate relief and a long-term worry.

She arrives at her six o'clock appointment two minutes before, and Mrs. Early greets her at the door. Bird is relieved to see Mrs. Early's laptop open on the desk, and surprised to recognize the cardboard box next to it. Sasha Granger's effects.

"Why do you have that?" she asks without thinking.

Mrs. Early glances behind her. "Ah, Dr. Granger. Did you know her? Her husband was one of the first casualties of the v-flu, so I'm arranging to have her things sent to her daughter outside the quarantine zone. Please, Emily, have a seat."

Bird sits on one of the rose-upholstered chairs while Mrs. Early takes the other. Bird glances at the clock and estimates she has four minutes.

"I want to report harassment," Bird says.

Mrs. Early blinks, but maintains that admirable poise Bird remembers from that ninth-grade encounter with her mother. "We take any kind of harassment very seriously, Emily. Can you tell me who you'd like to report?"

Bird shifts to find a more comfortable position, but these chairs were designed to keep their sitters off-balance. "Roosevelt David," she says. Three minutes.

Mrs. Early winces. "Your mother . . . informed me that you might come here to discuss that."

"And she told you to ignore me?"

"She . . . not in so many words." Mrs. Early steeples her fingers and breathes deep. "I have to tell you, Mr. David is an unaffiliated agent of the US government. I'm not sure how much we can do. But if you'd like to make a complaint, I'm here to listen."

Bird feels in control again. A different kind of control than she had as Emily, Carol Bird's perfect daughter. This is the control of rubber gloves mixing volatile chemicals, of a fireproof suit walking through flames. It's the control of one minute left.

"You're saying it wouldn't matter what he did?"

"I'd inform his superiors, Emily. If he's behaving inappropriately with our students, I have every reason to hope it will be relevant to their view of his current work."

In the thirty seconds she has left, Bird's throat constricts. She remembers Roosevelt's insinuation of what his bosses might do to her in his place. But he would say that, wouldn't he? Could her power be so simple? Could she tell a supportive adult about his bad behavior and let the system sort him out? Could she trust authority and just walk away?

"I can't *fucking do it anymore!*"

The scream easily carries past the closed door, as do the fruitless efforts of Mrs. Early's secretary to calm Marella down.

"Honey, just sit here —"

"We're all *going to die* and you want me to sit down?"

Mrs. Early looks at the door, back at Bird, and shakes her head. "Not another," she mutters. "Emily, just wait here for a second. Let me see what's going on."

Bird does not bother to check on Marella, gunning for an Oscar on the administrative couch. She heads straight for Mrs. Early's desk. The laptop is open, unlocked, and the inbox is open to a draft of an email to the student body about quarantine procedures. Bird hesitates, then types Roosevelt's name into the search field. Hundreds of emails populate the resulting window, but as she scrolls through she realizes that she miscalculated. Sure, one of these could contain damning evidence, but she has a minute at most and no time to read any. The subject lines are oppressively administrative, though certainly quite a few seem to discuss the "vitamin supplement program." Should she try to forward some to herself? But that will leave an obvious trail on Mrs. Early's computer.

Bird clears the search field and moves away. Dr. Granger's box contains the melancholic office junk she remembers, but she's optimistic as she digs through. The pictures she ignores, but she grabs the few papers that look vaguely official. As Marella starts another round of sobbing, and Mrs. Early places an emergency call to the counselor — Bird spares a stray thought for her friend, who she hopes won't have to spend too long on another administrative couch — Bird realizes she's lost her bet. There's nothing else in the box but a collection of parasite plushies and a handful of cheap jewelry. Most are rubberized bands that support one cause or another, but one aquamarine hairpin catches her attention. Dr. Granger didn't seem like the costume jewelry type, and there's no way that thumb-sized gem is real. She picks it up, fiddles with the catch, and nearly drops it when a tiny metal rectangle pops from the back.

A hidden USB drive.

Bird is sitting again by the time Mrs. Early comes back with sweat running into the makeup around her eyes.

"Goodness," she says, like she wishes she could say something else. "Now, forgive me, Emily, where were we? Did you want to make a formal complaint?"

"On second thought," Bird says, "I think my mom might be right."

Mrs. Early's shoulders relax. "Mothers often are, Emily."

The call that pays the piper comes that night, a few minutes before lights out. Marella reclines on Bird's bed with a cold pack over her eyes and an expression that wavers between a grimace and a smile. She has appointments with the counselor lined up for the next two weeks.

"You owe me nothing," she told Bird when she staggered into the dorm. "But I hope you are *very* nice to me for the rest of your life."

Bird hopes her sacrifice will be rewarded, but she hasn't checked the USB drive yet. She wants to use a computer less likely to be bugged. This is what she's contemplating when her phone buzzes, but very different thoughts come after. She takes them to the stairwell and sits.

"Well, Emily," her mother says, "I think it's time you tell me what's going on. How could you have broken up with Paul?"

"I don't see how it's your business."

Carol Bird sighs, the weight of the world not quite as burdensome as that of disappointing offspring. "You are my only child. Of course it's my business if I see you making a terrible decision. If I caught you with drugs in your room, I suppose you'd tell me that's none of my business either?"

Bird sticks her knuckles in her mouth, but her giggles bubble around the crude stopper of her fist. She has to snag the skin between her molars before she can get herself to stop. It's not even the pain, but the sweetness of her own blood that surprises her into stillness.

"Is this your uncle's influence? I should have known better than to leave you alone with Nicky for so long. How that man has managed to get to fifty with habits like his —"

"Maybe because they're not so bad?"

"Oh no, you listen to me, now. Is that any way to talk your own mother?"

"Sorry, Mom."

"My father used to say, 'Carol, I brought you into this world and I can take you out.' You should be grateful I go so easy on you. If your grandfather heard this mouth of yours, he'd make you cut the switch yourself."

"You made me do that too."

Carol Bird clucks her tongue. "I never *used* it. Honestly, you kids have no idea how good you have it."

"Sorry, Mom."

"And Emily, I obviously cannot control your love life, but you'll allow me to tell you that you have made a *huge* mistake with Paul. He called me yesterday, and, child, whatever he did I want you to promise me you'll consider taking him back. A man like that is one in a million.

He's going to make something of himself. And I don't even want to contemplate what he told me about that white boy, that drug dealer who gave you something at the party —"

"He didn't."

Bird doesn't mean to say this, but the defense leaps from her lips with its own, contrary consciousness.

"I have it on very good authority that he did."

"I think we both know how good that authority is."

"Roosevelt David is —"

"You know better. You can blame me for breaking up with Paul, but don't you dare blame Coffee for drugging me."

"Coffee? What kind of a name is that? Did I raise you to date some thug?"

You raised me to do exactly what you told me.

"We're not dating," she says. "Paul had no right to call you."

"Emily, you don't sound very well."

"I'm fine."

"Tell you what, we don't have to discuss this now. And when I get back, we can just have a girls' night with Aunt Grace. I'll get a great new relaxer —"

"I like my hair." She knew this moment had to come sometime, but she still feels assaulted.

"You're too young to understand the world the way I do, so you have to trust me on this. Those sorts of seventies styles make people in the professional world uncomfortable."

"You mean white people uncomfortable?"

"No, not necessarily, it's about projecting the right image —"

"Because otherwise I'm too Black?"

"Emily!"

Bird pants, her hand stings, and she wishes to God that she could have a single conversation with her mother that doesn't feel like being skinned alive.

"Sorry, Mom."

"I will let this go. You are clearly under a lot of stress. I love you. Think about what I said about Paul. Never underestimate the power of a good man. I'll talk to you soon."

The power of a good man. She closes her eyes and wishes for him to find her. And while she wishes, the world spins, the marble falls, and the emergency siren shatters everyone else's peace.

The first time the school evacuated, the shelters smelled of dust and mold and rat poison; they looked like industrial caverns with cracked linoleum floors lit yellow with flickering incandescent bulbs. The chapel basement still reeks of disuse, but someone has made an effort to make it more habitable. Multicolored rugs join in a haphazard mosaic. Beanbag chairs and large pillows are scattered with fuzzy, lived-in welcome, and the students collapse on top of them like the bosoms of lovers whose return they had despaired.

The boys arrived before them, and Bird finds Coffee effortlessly in the crowd of dazed and grunting boarders. It annoys her, this homing signal, this Coffee-shaped beacon drumming his tattoo in the unwary reaches of her subconscious. Even at the height of her obsession, she had never felt that for Paul. Coffee's hair looks shaggier, curlier than normal, spilling onto his forehead and sprouting in tufts that glitter in the light of the new fluorescent bulbs. His lean, chiseled musculature is disconcertingly obvious in his plain white T-shirt and low-riding sweatpants. Marella takes one look at him and laughs.

"Close your mouth, honey."

Bird gulps. "I don't know what you're talking about."

"I've known I liked girls since the third grade and even I know what I'm talking about. Go ahead, I'll just wait for the world to end over here." She flops into one of the last free beanbags and stretches her arms over her head.

In the far corner, Coffee watches her without even the pretense of indifference. She has to talk to him, of course she does. Resentment, terror, common sense, parental disapproval, nothing has ever changed that.

He's sharing his carpet of red and blue stars with Aaron, which at least gives her an excuse. Her cousin gives her a quick hug, then looks over his shoulder in case anyone saw. There aren't many lower school boarders, though, and being friends with Coffee probably gives him plenty of cred.

"Em, I tried calling Dad but it didn't go through. He's okay, right?"

"It's just a threat," Bird says, squatting between him and Coffee, "not a real attack. I'm sure he's fine."

Coffee wraps his long arms over his knees and tilts his head so that he's looking up at her for once. Bird can hardly feel her body, except where her leg almost touches his and the heat between them could send her to the moon if she let it.

"I want to go back home, Emmie," Aaron whispers, yawning. "The school isn't that bad, I guess, but I miss our albums."

She could kill Roosevelt, dig his heart out with a rusty spoon. "I'm sorry," she whispers. "Aaron, I swear, I'm trying. I want you to go back home too."

Aaron yawns again and stretches out on a pillow. Coffee pulls a piece of cloth from his pocket and hands it to her.

"It's clean," he says, his first words to her in four days.

She stares at it for too long, through eyes that don't want to focus. Very gently, Coffee pries it from her grip and wipes her eyes. Which is how she realizes that she's crying.

"A handkerchief?" she says, taking it back from him. "Have the preppies finally converted you?"

Coffee grins and leans against the beanbag. "Sometimes the best defense is blending in."

"*You?*" She wipes her face again and tries to discreetly blow her nose. "Too late, huh?"

She taps his ankle monitor, which the bunched sweatpants let her see clearly for the first time. "I'd say so."

He nods, but he's looking at her in that way he has, like she's a volatile chemical in one of his experiments. "For both of us."

She wonders, suddenly, if ironic accident has branded the leg that led to his first, seminal addiction. From genius chemist to busted dealer in twelve easy steps. She wondered earlier if he regretted his library confession, if his absence when she woke signaled embarrassment or something more complicated.

But she should never have doubted him: With Coffee, everything is something more complicated.

"Do you have a trial date yet?"

Coffee winces. "Tired of me already?"

"Oh, come on, you know —"

"Bao is trying to get it dismissed. I'm hoping for continued court delays."

He looks so tired. She wishes she could touch him, draw down his head and shoulders until she feels his lungs expand against her stomach, his breath tickle her collarbone with sweet, soft exhales. She wants to gift him with sleep and comfort, to make him need her as much as she needs him. She wants to be safe with him, when they have never been less safe.

"I should show you something," she says, and pulls her phone from her hastily packed bag.

He runs his hands through his hair, and it must be stress that's doing this to her, this feeling that she might lose everything if she doesn't just give in and admit —

Admit what? The denial of her own thoughts is familiar to her as her mother's voice, and as comforting.

Her hand is steady and her heart is stone when she shows him the message from her hacked account.

Coffee whistles low. "This is personal for him," he whispers, so low the words are more shape than sound.

"But why? I didn't *do* anything to him —"

She's too loud. His finger rests on her lips, a single, explosive charge. His wide eyes tell her to stay silent, but she couldn't speak now to save the world.

You don't remember, he mouths. "But something happened. You still don't know what it means? The email?"

She shakes her head and whispers, "What about a drug?"

He swallows, and she can hear all the objections in his eyes: *It might not work, it might hurt you, if I get caught I will be in such deep shit.* But he knows as well as she does that something is wrong with Roosevelt. The sociopath with the dead brown eyes has some agenda for Bird, and they need to understand it soon. Maybe Roosevelt just has a kink for harassing girls who can't fight back, but when it comes down to it, he's just one man in a larger machine. No way his bosses would let him spend so much time intimidating Bird if they didn't have some reason to keep her afraid and off-balance and, above all, unable to understand what's happening.

The only weapon she has in this fight is knowledge. Knowledge she suspects — like the circumstances of Sasha Granger's death — and knowledge she must have somewhere inside her — like what happened after Paul drugged her at the party.

She stares at Coffee, willing him to understand her thoughts. He sighs, because he does.

"If something happens —" he whispers.

"I'll forgive you."

He winces. "The trouble is forgiving myself."

For the past month, statistics have littered Bird's path like ill-concealed land mines, easy enough to avoid until a momentary lapse in attention leaves her picking out shrapnel. Today's devastation for the unwary: half a million. Estimated deaths worldwide from the v-flu.

And then another: thirty-three.

Confirmed cases of v-flu inside the Beltway quarantine within the last twenty-four hours.

Having overheard this news from nervous hallway conversations after religion class, Bird turns it over in her head until she's dizzy from spinning in place. She gives her classes as much attention as normal — enough that she might still squeak into Stanford if they survive the apocalypse, but only because of her SAT scores. She isn't sure she wants to go to Stanford these days, but it seems prudent to keep her options open. In the quiet spaces of her post-Paul life, she finds herself looking at a forgotten archive of photos she's taken of storefronts and DC neighborhoods, of quirky bookshops with piles of mystery paperbacks in the corners and history books on the shelves. Clicking through the photos, the musk of acid-yellowed paper and burning sticks of patchouli incense cling to her memory. She's avoided this folder for a year now, ever since her mother told her precisely what she would think if Bird became something so unambitious as a shopkeeper. But she looks at them now, since her traditional comfort of real estate listings has turned into a pixel-dusted, time-stamped Internet graveyard. No one is buying, no one is selling. The whole of the District has frozen like Sleeping Beauty's castle, waiting for a prince to breach the thorny walls.

Too bad the dragon beat him here.

Thirty-three. It might be nothing, a statistical blip of people who took longer than average to manifest symptoms. But after twenty days of no new cases, it feels like the endgame. The safest place in the country is turning into the perfect virgin breeding ground for a flu with five to ten percent mortality. Another statistic she wishes she didn't know.

Classes over, she washes up in the senior room, where the usual suspects crowd the television, glowing faces tilted up, receiving the gospel according to Wolf Blitzer. She squints at the stained couch and then sighs and perches on the edge. The Crenshaw twins and Cindy de la Vega are wearing face masks again, and Felice has one on her lap, which means that the school will be back to a hand sanitizer–scented, floral-masked prison by tomorrow morning.

Wolf is talking via satellite to some official with the CDC. The official is explaining that while everyone hopes the quarantine has held, some kind of breach is inevitable.

"The Beltway quarantine is the most ambitious, most extensive, most complicated public health project of its kind attempted in the history of pandemic disease," he says.

"Where's Charlotte?" Bird asks.

Ari Crenshaw glares and turns back to the television. Cindy won't even acknowledge she's in the room. Only Felice turns in her direction, her face a mask of distaste.

"The hospital," she says.

"Is she —"

"Like you care," Felice says, and lifts the mask from her lap. "What's the point? We're all going to die anyway."

She tosses it on the floor while Ari stares, openmouthed astonishment pressing a circle against the blue fabric of her mask.

"She's one of the thirty-three?" Bird asks.

Felice still glares, but at least she's speaking. "Fifty-five now. And no, it's her parents. They're confirmed, but she's still fine, apparently."

"That's terrible," Bird says.

"If you really gave a shit, you would talk to her."

She and Felice have been friends since eighth grade. She's always been that perfect, queen-bee Devonshire student, the one with the Abercrombie clothes and cute boyfriend and a dozen girls who want to be her friend. Bird never quite understood why she picked her.

"You're the one who ditched me," Bird says, strangled.

"You never liked us anyway. You think I couldn't tell? It's just that this impending doom thing, it really puts life in perspective. Why keep a shitty friend when I could have my real one?"

"Charlotte was my friend too."

Felice laughs. "See, you're using the past tense already."

"She won't talk to me! Thanks to you."

"I'm not her goddamned mother. She can make her own decisions, promise. You want to talk to her, then *talk* to her. But hey, I'm not holding my breath."

Bird recognizes this feeling: guilt and cognitive dissonance and the suspicion that someone else might just be right. But it's Felice, not Coffee, glaring at her through those blunt-cut bangs. Bird forces herself to take a deep breath.

"Okay," she says. "I'm leaving."

Felice shrugs and turns back to the television. On the door, beside the proliferating photographs of dead friends and family, someone has taped an orange flyer.

It's the end of the world as we know it
We're going to Go-Go like it's 1999
Doomsday: December 15, 7pm, ~~Sidwell Gymnasium~~ To Be Announced!
Dress to impress & shake your booty, 'cause we're about to meet our
(money) maker

Bird laughs. She can't help it: a *doomsday* go-go?

"It was Charlotte's idea. We're doing it with the Sidwell BSU."

Felice stands behind her, but Bird doesn't turn around. Felice has been involved in the Black Student Union for years, one of the few white kids who bothers. Charlotte loves go-gos to death, though she always recruits a posse of girls to help fend off the grabbier species of dude.

"The school is really letting you do this?"

"The location is a little aspirational at the moment, but I'm sure we'll convince someone."

"It'll be a petri dish," Bird says.

"It's like during the Black Death, people would gather in the town square and dance . . . whatever, I wouldn't expect you —"

"It's goddamn brilliant," Bird says, and laughs again.

*   *   *

Bird has had a girl crush on Marella since they were ten. As Bird is about 90 percent hetero, this has remained platonic, though occasionally some lazy spark will drift down between her shoulder blades at the sight of Marella's long supermodel curls or French-manicured fingers spreading gloss over her wide bottom lip. As far as Bird can tell, she's not really Marella's romantic type, not being Latina or willowy or in possession of equally fabulous hair. I think that Marella would probably go for it if Bird swung that direction, but why ruin a great friendship with a mediocre affair? They are neither of them material candidates for the loves of their respective lives.

Bird joined Africa Club because she thought it might be a way to get to know Marella better. Charlotte and Felice reveled in the scandal of her coming out in ninth grade, since she did it by hooking up with one of the bi seniors right before graduation. The first open interstudent homosexual relationship in the memory of Devonshire prompted the administration to issue special rules about "PDA on School Grounds." Bird never defended Marella, but she thought maybe it would be okay if she could be nice to her on her own, away from her two best frenemies. It never worked, mostly because Bird cultivated her talents in *wanting* but not in *trying*, the better to protect herself. So by the time they fell into copresidency as seniors, their dynamic of tentative approval-seeking and guarded, ironic indulgence had hardened like stale bread.

But Marella must have always liked her, at least a little. She called her Bird within a month of Coffee. She said, on a shared Metro ride back home from an Adams Morgan party, "That dealer uses your last name, like you're a guy."

"Yeah," Bird said, squirming into the orange seats of the old train car.

"You don't mind it." Not a question, something Bird liked about Marella. She noticed people, she treated them like puzzles she could never fully solve, but she never gossiped. She wasn't interested in what people did, but how they felt about it.

"I guess not." And then, after the train had pulled out of Dupont Circle and the deep, warm-throated conductor had announced, "Red Line to Shady Grove," she added, "I like it."

"Because you want to fly away?"

Bird looked down at her feet, at the new blister on her right heel. Her mother had insisted she buy those shoes. "I'd like the option," she said.

[cocaine]

$$C_{17}H_{21}NO_4$$

Marella sprawls across the round fiction room table, listening to music while she flips through a stack of printouts. She pulls a bud from her ear and pats the empty space on the table beside her.

"Had a flash of brilliance and used Mrs. Rider's computer while she was teaching some fourth graders."

Bird shuts the door. "Wait, you *printed* the stuff on the USB drive?"

Marella frowns. "It was a good idea. Who would ever monitor the assistant librarian's computer? And since her printer isn't connected to the network, there's no record of what I sent to it. You're the one paranoid about keyloggers. We have to read all this stuff of hers somehow, right?"

Bird perches on the edge of the table and takes a deep breath. "Yeah, you're right. Sorry."

Marella flops back on her elbows, the ends of her long curls tickling Bird's arms. "I forgive you. You've been under a lot of stress lately, and I have had the benefit of our school counselor's extremely focused attention."

"Yeah, I'm really sorry about that. . . ."

"Honestly, she's nice. I'm rethinking my prejudices about therapy. You might try it sometime. I'd hate to lose my Bird now that she's finally left her shell — hey, no fair!"

Bird elbows Marella, and they both laugh. "Brilliant puns aside," Marella says, "I know it gets hard, being yourself."

A silence follows that undeniable truth. "Is that why you never wanted to be friends with me?" Bird asks quietly.

Marella's hands tighten to fists then relax, deliberately, against the pocked wood of the table. "I just didn't trust you to be real enough. I mean, Felice and Charlotte talked about me for years and you never said anything. How was I supposed to know you wouldn't do it too? No matter how much I liked you."

This confirmation feels more liberating than it ought to, like she's cut her hair off all over again, like Marella has given her a mirror that reflects someone a little better than before.

"Charlotte's parents have the v-flu," Bird says. "And now she's put together some kind of doomsday go-go when we'd normally have winter formal."

Marella flops onto her back. "Good for her. I always thought Charlotte was kind of wasted on Felice. Not as much as you, but still."

"I hope we don't make such stupid choices after high school."

"That's the dream."

"It can't be worse, right?"

"I don't know. Devonshire girls can be bitchy, but they don't usually drop chemical weapons."

Bird considers this. "You don't think that's the big secret? Like, when people tell us these are the best years of our lives, and all you can think is that they've forgotten what high school was like? But what if they're right? What if we're just forced to make worse and worse choices until we die? What if the real world is *nothing but* Felice and Paul and Roosevelt?"

Marella groans. "London. Paris. New York. There's got to be a place for me. For us. There are good people in the world. There are people we will like."

Bird lies down beside Marella, who smells like the springtime tea roses in the school garden, like fresh laundry and sunshine, like pink and childhood things, but her voice is bitter, her hope defiant. She smells like the girl she once was; she speaks like the woman she's becoming. Does Bird still smell like Emily? Does she speak like her? Her fears are still Emily's fears, but her problems are different.

"Sometimes, when things got bad," Bird says slowly, "when everything I did disappointed my mom and I was just desperate, I thought, it's okay, because my real life will start when I go to college. I could major in econ or bio and, when I got Mom off my back, *then* I would be part of the real world. Then I could open a shop if I wanted, I could live anywhere I wanted, I could date . . . anyone I wanted." Bird gulps air. Marella turns her head so their noses are just a few inches apart.

"I know Paul is supposed to be some perfect guy, I know you're supposed to be crazy for dumping him, but Bird, you know better. Maybe he was nice once, but right now he's big-time into patriarchal douche-hattery."

Bird's panicked breaths give way to sharp, rueful laughter. "Isn't he? God, this school, it's like you can go crazy just from being sane."

"It's not all bad," Marella says. "We found each other. You have Coffee."

She narrows her eyes at Marella's wistful expression. "Coffee and I aren't . . . we don't have —"

"Oh, I know you *aren't*, but don't you dare tell me you don't *have*. I swear, every time you look at each other I hear thunder." She shakes her head. "London. Paris. Berlin." A soft and desperate prayer.

"Marella, you're one of the most amazing people I know. One day girls will line up to fall in love with you."

"Just not now."

"Just wait until . . ." But Bird trails off, the habitual end of the sentence unexpectedly impassable.

"We could be dead by Christmas. We could be in boot camp training for World War III or we could be holed up in some bunker waiting for the radioactive dust to clear. God, I want to fall in love so badly it makes me cry at night, but maybe I won't get to. If this is all we have,

Bird, our choices right now matter. They might matter more than any other ones we'll make."

Bird closes her eyes, because all she can see is Coffee running after Paul's car, all she can hear is Coffee asking her, over and over again, *Why not, Bird?* If he dies, if she dies, will she end her life smothered in the regret of that low voice, those rounded vowels, those sharp and blooded eyes?

"Coffee's not a bad guy. He's been a pretty good one lately."

"For a dealer."

"Hey, no one's perfect. He sells decent hash."

Bird smacks the table. "Get out. *You?*"

Marella grins. "Think you're the only goody-two-shoes with bad-girl depths? Sure, I bought some off him, but mostly it was for Sarah. Not my scene."

She doesn't wince at the mention of her ex, but she drags out the syllables of her name a second too long, an overarticulation meant to cover the wound. She sits up. "Okay, shouldn't we get started? Most of the stuff on there is old emails and drafts of articles. You can take pile one or pile two."

Bird picks pile two, and they sit together silently, reading the remainders of a life. Pile two mostly consists of emails between Dr. Granger, the medical staff, and government representatives (most commonly Roosevelt David) about quarantine procedures and the vitamin treatments. There's nothing about any of the emails in particular that seems incriminating or revelatory, and yet as she goes through dozens of them she starts to get a strange feeling. Like they're not talking about what they say they're talking about.

Bird looks up from an email chain between one of the doctors and Roosevelt, expressing concern that the shipments of vitamin treatments will be delayed for another week, "in light of quarantine concerns, these have to be a priority."

"I think this is a record," Bird says. "I think she picked these emails because they're all *about* something. I mean, there's nothing personal here. Didn't her husband die? Wouldn't she have had family in Venezuela? But there's nothing, not even a bill. Are all of yours about the vitamin treatments?"

Marella puts down her pile, gives her a funny look, and slides it over. "This is a draft of a letter she sent to Roosevelt."

The first few lines are enough.

I believe the true nature of the "vitamin treatment" program is a blight on our democracy, and a disaster for the District's larger pandemic prevention efforts. We cannot vaccinate a small percentage of residents at the expense of everyone else, no matter how important they (or their parents) are.

"Holy shit."

"Yeah."

"Marella . . . those shots aren't vitamin treatments."

"They told us it's also a regular flu vaccine."

"A blight on our democracy? Pandemic prevention?"

Marella looks at her hands. "Okay, yeah. What you're thinking? That's what I'm thinking. But I can't *believe* it. If there's a vaccine for the v-flu, why haven't we heard anything about it? Why are they giving it to us in secret?"

"So the rich girls can stay alive."

"And he killed the doctor because she didn't like the program? This is ridiculous. We sound like conspiracy freaks."

"But are we wrong?"

Marella groans and buries her head between her knees. "Jesus H. Roosevelt Christ."

"Exactly."

*　　*　　*

She leaves the message on Coffee's desk during AP Chem the next day:

I need all conceivable dirt on a certain private security contractor dirtbag you can find. Bring to designated rendezvous point tomorrow after classes. Smoke after reading.

Coffee laughs out loud in the middle of Mrs. Cunningham's explanation of net ionic equations, but she pretends not to hear. There's only half the normal roster of students in class anyway. Coffee swivels in his seat and mouths: *Designated rendezvous point?*

The library, Bird mouths back.

He grins again and even their dazed classmates stir themselves to look between the two of them. Bird blushes and slouches back over her notebook. She can only imagine what they made of that flashing joy in his eyes, that happiness with no business on Coffee's habitually dour face. Coaxing a genuine smile from him has always felt like winning the ringtoss at a street fair. In the back of the classroom, Charlotte pulls out her phone and starts texting. It could be about anything, but basic narcissism convinces Bird it must be her. Charlotte hasn't so much as met her eyes since she returned from the hospital. Does Charlotte hate her enough to tell the school that Bird is macking on its resident fugitive?

And how can it matter, anyway? What possible hold could gossip have over her in a world where Charlotte's parents might be dying, where NATO troops are laying siege to Caracas, and the school might be secretly giving their students a vaccine for the v-flu that no one else in the world knows exists? And she's afraid Coffee might ruin her reputation? It's not her reputation anymore. It's Emily's, and the more they tear her down, the more they build Bird up.

But still, Bird feels his eyes follow her when she leaves to go to the bathroom a minute later. She wants to make him laugh again. She wants his smile to light just because she's walked into the room, just because she exists. She wants this right now and for a very long time, and so she leans against the chipped pink bathroom stall and presses her fists against her eyes.

Don't love him, don't love him, don't love him, she thinks, too afraid to even say it out loud.

When her heartbeat slows, she splashes water on her face and runs a helpless hand through her hair. She needs to get back to Nicky's for a supply run. She's run out of his hair sheen, which, despite a distinct eau de middle-aged uncle, at least works. Marella's fancy leave-in conditioner runs in terror at the sight of Bird's short kinks.

Thanksgiving is just two days away. She has to convince Roosevelt to let her and Aaron go back to Nicky's for the holiday. And permanently, with any luck. Since she can't expect him to agree out of compassion, she needs a credible threat. With Dr. Granger's cache, she could probably try it now, but Bird retains enough innate cautiousness to wait. Better to over prepare than run in stupid.

She jumps at the sound of laughter when she steps out of the bathroom. The laugh is confident and loud enough to shoot through the hall. Six months ago, he might have gotten in trouble for making noise during class hours, but no one will touch him now. He's gotten what he always wanted, her perfect ex: the good favor of powerful men. He's walking with Trevor, punching him on the arm, the two of them so picture-perfect they could pose for the cover of *Ebony*, headlining an article about the new generation of Black leaders.

They both freeze when they catch sight of her. Trevor sticks his hands in his pockets and leans back with the barest lift of his lips, an expression that she has learned to recognize as amused anticipation. Paul crosses his arms, but he looks more nervous than disapproving. They stare at each other for a moment. Bird considers just pushing past, but her subconscious must feel reckless because she speaks with particular relish.

"Slow day at spy school, Paul? Are you happy I'm still trapped here? Or have you come up with some even better way to punish me for breaking up with you?"

Trevor slouches against the lockers, his proto-smile blossoming into a grin full of teeth and cruel humor. Paul just glowers.

"You didn't give me a choice," he says. "Honestly, you should thank me for heading off something worse. You know what he's like."

"Which is why I'm not his errand boy. But then, you've always been precocious. Most people wait at least a couple more years before selling their souls."

"My God, you're a bitch."

"Thank you," she bites back, feeling like she could fly.

She brushes past him, close enough to touch his forearm with the back of her hand. The familiarity of his skin is an aching regret, one she digs at until the pain flares true and unmistakable. Like a dreamer pinching herself to wake up, she touches him to remind herself that he isn't hers anymore, that she has changed her world.

"Emily . . ."

She wouldn't stop, except that the confidence has leaked from his voice. She turns.

"Things are getting bad out there. You should be careful."

"I've taken my vitamin treatment," she says, wondering if he knows, but he only looks baffled. Roosevelt isn't telling him everything.

Trevor stirs himself from the lockers. "See ya, Bird," he says.

Bird shakes her head and goes back to class. Mrs. Cunningham doesn't say anything about her prolonged absence, but Coffee stares like he's beaming thoughts across the room. Bird makes herself recall the heat of Paul's skin against hers, that painful familiarity, until he looks away and she can breathe again.

At seven o'clock on the Wednesday before Thanksgiving, Bird meets her two unexpected allies in the AV room of the Bradley library. At Bird's suggestion, Marella cranks up some death metal on the school's giant headphones and puts them directly on top of Coffee's ankle monitor.

Coffee leans back carefully against a shelf of dusty VHS tapes and regards them both with wary bemusement.

"You're really getting into this," he says.

Bird shrugs. "If a girl finds herself unexpectedly at the heart of a globe-spanning government conspiracy . . ."

His lips twitch. "The girl defeats the bad guys and wins a medal for service to her country?"

"It might get her mother off her back."

"I've heard of less ambitious bids for parental approval."

"I am my mother's daughter."

And there, the smile she longed for breaks from the storm clouds of his eyes and he shakes his head. She squats to keep from shivering. Marella looks between them.

"We want you to tell us what you make of this," she says, and hands him Dr. Granger's letter.

He reads both pages, then starts again. Marella puckers her lips and massages a lumpy stitch in her newly completed scarf.

"And you are very sure this letter is real." His voice is so uninflected that Bird can't tell if he thinks they're brilliant or delusional.

"I stole it from her effects," Bird says.

"She let something like this sit in the open?"

"Hidden USB drive," Marella says, handing it to him. "I guess they didn't notice."

Coffee shakes his head. "So you think he killed her over this?"

"If he thought she was going to pull a Snowden —"

"This is an internal memo, not a press leak."

Bird rolls her eyes. "Oh for God's —"

"Just listen. If you're right and this is some secret vaccine, the implications are . . . intense."

"We figured," she says, tonguing the sarcasm-sharpened consonants.

Coffee arches his eyebrows and leans forward — argument engaged, bow drawn, target sighted. She steadies and waits, wondering how she could love something so dizzying and uncontrollable. How she could love him.

"If there is a vaccine and we're getting it, that means that other people *aren't*. That's what she's arguing against in the letter, right? They developed a secret cure that only rich, connected people can get. And not the other billion people who could use it."

"Maybe they have to test it secretly. It might start a war otherwise."

"A bit too late to worry about that, Bird."

"A bigger war."

"Right. Because if there's something other countries hate the US doing, it's saving their lives with a cutting-edge vaccine for pandemic flu. And not, you know, bombing them."

"Maybe they'll find out later. Maybe they know now and the diplomats are hammering out the details."

They glower at each other, and Marella sighs and waves her scarf in the air over their heads. "Hackles down, you two. Coffee, I think Bird has a point. A vaccine doesn't *have* to mean we're hoarding it. What if they're testing it?"

Coffee jiggles his ankle so Marella's headphones tap staccato against his monitor. "Bird, who got the vitamin treatments first?"

"The lower school, I think? Hold on, it should be in her emails."

She flips through the stack, which she and Marella have arranged by date, until she finds the ones she remembers. "Yeah, they started with the fourth graders."

Coffee takes the paper, but he keeps his eyes on her, waiting. She gets it.

"Holy shit," she says.

"What?" Marella says.

"They started on the fourth graders. The vice president's daughter, Marella."

Coffee leans forward and shakes his hair out of his suddenly bright eyes. "Bingo," he whispers.

Marella nods slowly. "Of course. If they're giving it to the VP's daughter, then it's real. And safe."

"And tested on someone else," Coffee says.

Marella swallows. "Not necessarily?"

Coffee draws himself up, a pen in his right hand blurring in beautiful hummingbird flight between and above his fingers. "There's a reason drug trials take years. Let's say someone developed a potential vaccine. Let's say that they needed to test it, fast, to make sure it was safe for the most powerful people in the world and their sons and daughters. So let's say that instead of going about it the safe, legal way with stage I and II trials and animal prototypes and all that, they test it on a group no one will really care about or notice. Prisoners. The kind no one knows exist because the government has secretly rendi- tioned them. I bet Guantánamo has been a real treat for the last few months. But of course you can't admit that in public. So you find out it's safe and it works and you give it to the people in power and then the people those in power care about —"

"Wait," Marella says, and to Bird's surprise, Coffee does, his blue pen pausing mid-flight between his middle and index fingers. "I can see that applying to you and Bird, but me? I'm a scholarship student. My mom is an executive assistant at a real estate firm. I'm not saying I'm poor, but I sure as hell ain't the daughter of one of the most pow- erful people in the world."

"Epidemiology," Coffee says.

"What?"

"You're lucky, like Bird's cousin. You're breathing the air of the chil- dren of the most important people in the world, so you get vaccinated to protect them. Us."

"At least you admit you're one of them," Marella says.

Coffee shrugs. "I'd be dead if I weren't. And I'm at least marginally self-aware."

He catches Bird's eye with this last, and she snorts before she can help herself. He moves his leg so it grazes her calf. If they were alone, she might touch his thigh or even catch one of those ever-moving hands, she might walk that tightwire with need yawning on one side and a rocky acceptance on the other. But they are three instead of two, and so she just stares at their single point of contact like an unexploded ordnance.

"But," Marella says, "even if there's a secret vaccine, that doesn't mean anyone killed Dr. Granger."

Bird can't look away from the sinuous glyph written in the contrast between her navy-blue tights and his faded gray corduroys. She reaches out a hand to finger the fraying edge that sweeps out from their intersection, but freezes an inch away.

"She told him that she thought his operation was illegal and dangerous to public health and Roosevelt David said, sure, that's cool?"

Coffee shakes his head. "Asshole doesn't equal murderer."

"And a lot of people saw her die of that heart attack," Marella says.

Coffee and Marella are staring; she wills her hand to move. The effort frightens her. Is this another side effect of her accident? Along with the headaches and the insomnia and the anxiety, will she now lose control over her own body? But then Coffee takes her trembling hand in his and guides it to the ground with casual, undemanding generosity. His touch breaks the spell, or transmutes it. Without even meaning to, she is walking the tightwire again, she is about to plunge to the rocks.

She meets his eyes, so gentle and concerned they nearly break her, and asks, "So did you find any dirt on Roosevelt?"

He nods. "Not much. According to the Internet, he doesn't exist. No photos, no Facebook page, no LinkedIn, nothing. And believe me, I was looking before you asked. The only hint I got was a few mentions on national security message boards of an operative who might meet his description. But the most distinctive thing about him is that ripe aroma of sociopathy, so who knows."

Marella laughs. "Coffee, you're a poet."

"A lost beatnik," Bird says, deadpan and pinning down a smile. "Did you find anything else?"

"I looked up Lukas Group too. They didn't exist until around ten years ago. It was founded by some former CIA operatives as an, ah, 'adjunct security service and optics firm,' whatever that means. They're listed on a couple dozen national security contracts, mostly to do with counterterrorism and communications in the Middle East and South America. Given what they do, I wouldn't be surprised if they're on a dozen more contracts that aren't posted publicly. They're basically a private arm of the government, which means they get even less oversight than the CIA. Ever read about Blackwater mercenaries during Iraq? There were cases of them massacring whole families and getting away with it. This is like that, but for spies."

"But if they're spies," Marella says, "what is Roosevelt doing at Devonshire? The closest thing to a scandal we have around here is Tory Silver's dad buying a sports facility at Duke so she can get in."

Bird grimaces. "Well, who *wouldn't* be interested in Tory Silver's rich daddy?"

"It turns out," Coffee says, "that a few Lukas Group contracts were specifically related to bioterrorism and disaster planning. A month ago someone leaked slides from some classified CIA business meeting. I didn't catch it at the time, and the site got taken down. But it popped up again yesterday when I asked about Lukas Group." Coffee reaches for his bag and pulls out a handful of trash — receipts with food stains, torn notebook pages covered in intricate abstract doodles and molecular diagrams, singed rolling paper, half-smoked cigarettes, multicolored gel pens with their middles worn smooth. Coffee sifts calmly through this alarming mess while Bird and Marella exchange glances.

"Did Lukas Group bomb your bag?" Bird asks.

"It's not that bad," Coffee says, pulling out another handful of detritus. A few liberated tobacco leaves ride air currents to land on Bird's shoulders; one lands on her eyelash. She pulls it off and makes a wish.

Marella scoots a few inches closer to Bird and brushes her skirt for invisible crumbs. "Not that bad?"

Coffee just pokes his tongue between his teeth and excavates the papers. Bird has never seen so many chemical equations in her life. Some are photocopies of academic journals, but mostly they're written in Coffee's precise hand, a periodic table deconstructed and scattered and double bonded in thick, primary colors. They remind her, in a way she can't articulate, of her wish to own a shop.

"Here!" he says, pulling a crumpled, multiply folded printout from the pile. He passes it over to them.

The first slide is simple, big red text on a white background.

Safe Havens Protocol (SHP) - Development
Working with our partner firms to construct a protocol for threats of biological terrorism. Segment II focuses on potential pandemic influenza strains, wild-type and laboratory-developed.

The next slide shows the names of several flu strains, alongside notations that indicate the status of vaccine development. Then comes a map of the continental US with lines drawn between major city centers, unlabeled, probably from further along in the presentation.

The final leaked slide seems to come from near the end. Beneath the headline *Partner Firms* are about fifteen different corporate logos, presumably the subcontractors affiliated with the project.

"Look, there's Lukas Group," Marella says. "We were right."

But Bird's gaze has fixed upon a different image. The wings circling a beaker have the wrong name underneath them, and she's only seen the logo once in her life, but she recognizes it immediately.

"Synergy Labs," she whispers. Where her parents worked many years ago. Her reckless shot in the dark that made Roosevelt start shooting back.

Coffee scans the paper. "I didn't see that."

"This logo." She points with a shaky hand. "It's got a new name now, see, TriState Research? But I recognize the logo. It's the same one that was on that letter I found in the trash five years ago. It's Synergy Labs."

Coffee whistles. "Well, we knew he used to work with your parents. I guess he still does."

Bird looks down, dizzy. "But this is all about developing vaccines. And my mom . . . she seemed to know something about Mrs. Early and Devonshire. She told me to make sure that I was here and I followed all the rules. Do you think . . . did she know because they helped develop it?"

"If she did," Marella says, "then she was only trying to protect you. It's not your mother's decision who gets the vaccine and who doesn't."

But Bird can't imagine her mother objecting in principle either. Not like Sasha Granger did.

"That night," Bird says quietly, "you said that you knew Synergy Labs was bad news. What kind of bad news, Coffee?"

She can't look at his face, but she hears the pained reluctance in his voice. "They're just rumors on a message board. Tinfoil hatters, like you said. There's no reason to believe it."

"You did then."

He sighs and for some reason that makes her look at him, at the lines and shadows on his face, at his long fingers buried in thick curls. He laughs, that old Coffee laugh, riddled with bullets. "I wanted to get a rise out of you. I wanted to see what you would say if your perfect boyfriend were involved in something even you couldn't defend."

"What the hell?"

"Well, wanting to work with a bunch of torturers and assassins didn't seem to tip the scale."

"It's more complicated, and you know it. The way you talk, everyone who works with the government is some kind of depraved monster."

He arches his eyebrows, but his eyes seem as hurt as her own. "Not a monster. Just morally compromised."

"What about your mother?"

"She works for the *Brazilian* government."

"And they're saints, huh? I don't pretend to know as much as you, Comrade Alonso, but I seem to remember some stories about indigenous groups in the Amazon getting kicked off their land because of an earth-destroying dam your government wants to build? Didn't an international court call it human rights abuse?"

Coffee flinches and Marella clears her throat. "You guys, could we get back to the topic?"

"Right. Sorry." Coffee looks away from Bird with palpable effort. "Synergy Labs did research on bioterrorism delivery mechanisms. Like, warheads for diseases. And —"

"Only according to the Internet," Bird interrupts.

"And what?" Marella says.

Coffee hesitates. "And there's reports . . . Have you heard of this? The terrorist effect? If you look at maps of who is dying of the v-flu, there's a statistical blip in unrelated rural communities in countries all over the world: Afghanistan, Iraq, Yemen, Somalia, Colombia, Venezuela, Cuba, possibly China, though that's hard to tell —"

Bird shakes her head. "You're saying that people in countries with terrorists are more likely to die of the v-flu?"

"I'm saying certain people in countries with recent so-called US counterterrorism operations are significantly *less* likely to die of it."

"This is a real thing?" Marella asks.

"Some Canadian scientists noticed it a few months ago, and the effect has only gotten stronger."

"That is really weird."

"Weird, yes," Bird says, "but related to Synergy how, exactly? Terrorists released that flu. Did Synergy test the vaccine alongside some drones?"

"The rumors were they had tested something. And yes, at the same time as the drone attacks. But who knows what it was." Coffee shrugs. "I said you couldn't use it."

It's clear enough what he believes, but Coffee's message board conspiracies won't make any difference with Roosevelt.

"I guess the stuff Dr. Granger left us has to be enough."

"You're going to confront him," Coffee says without inflection.

"Am I supposed to let him keep stalking me? And now he's even threatening Aaron. We are getting home for Thanksgiving, I don't care what I have to do."

"Home?" Coffee asks softly.

Bird feels the air in her face, the lurch and exhilaration of that subconscious slip. "Nicky's," she mumbles. "Do you guys want to come? If you don't have anything else . . ."

Marella turns to her. "Really? I'd . . . kind of love to, honestly. Mom is terrified of leaving the house, she told me to stay here. And my dad's place is too far out for the buses."

Coffee frowns. "What if Roosevelt doesn't agree?"

"He will."

"And your uncle?"

"Do you want to come or not? Invitation expiring in three, two —"

"Yes," he says.

Bird smiles.

"And Bird?"

She's already imagining the food she'll make — her grandmother's collard greens, her father's rolls, the best goddamn mac and cheese this side of the Potomac — "Yes?"

"You're sure? He might escalate, after this."

Bird reaches up and feels her nappy roots like a talisman. She will be dangerous to Roosevelt. She will be true to that girl who sent the email; he will regret what he did to her. "I'm sure."

Coffee blinks. "You should do it now."

There are words behind those words, thoughts trapped behind his lips, truths he has never quite said, and she has never quite heard. She wants to hear them. She wants to crack his mind and steal the treasure. But she wants a lot of things she can't have.

She fishes her phone from her pocket and dials.

Paul picks up immediately. "Emily?" he says.

"I need to speak with Roosevelt," she says. "He can meet me in the rose garden in a half hour."

"Emily, I don't think you can just demand —"

"Let him know," Bird says. "I'm pretty sure he'll want to speak with me."

She hangs up before he can answer.

She shivers on the bench, watching the brightest stars share the sky with the faint afterglow of the setting sun. The cold, dry air carries a musk of dead leaves and cracked mud. The silence of the quarantined streets makes her jump at every natural sound: The squirrels chasing one another in the oak above her head might as well be the rattle of a machine gun. Within eyesight but not earshot, Coffee and Marella wait on the steps of the upper school. She doubts they could really do anything if Roosevelt loses it, but she feels safer with witnesses. They debated giving her Marella's recording stick, but eventually decided that it would be too dangerous if Roosevelt found it. So she waits, ten minutes past the thirty she gave Paul, before her very own nemesis crunches his boots on the mulched path.

He's wearing a long black pea coat and a black knit ski cap that makes him even more anonymous than usual. His smile, however, is unmistakable.

"Hello again, Emily," he says. "I was just thinking I should give you the good news."

He has her off-balance already. "Good news?"

"Your parents came back with Senator Grossman's entourage, and they'll be out of quarantine in time for Thanksgiving. Aren't you happy?"

She grips her thighs and swallows sour acid. She doesn't look at him. She didn't know how much she had relaxed in her mother's absence, but Roosevelt clearly did; he said *happy* because he knows how miserably she feels the foreshadow of Carol Bird's eyes.

"They didn't tell me," she says.

"It would have been a security breach if they had, and we both know your parents are too careful for that." The sarcastic edge of his voice startles her into looking up, but his eyes are as bland as ever, two shoe-polish puddles waiting to consume whatever might fall inside.

"You think my parents told me something I shouldn't know," she says. He's led the conversation exactly where she wanted it to go, which makes her wary.

He smiles and shakes his head. "I'm keeping an eye on the daughter of a friend. As a favor, *Bird*."

"Don't call me that."

He leans forward. "Because he's watching?"

Coffee stands beneath the pale neo-Gothic arches by the upper school entrance, his hands deep in his pockets and his gaze fixed unerringly on Bird and Roosevelt. Bird's thoughts stutter when she looks at him, her ears fill with crashing waves. But she can breathe, and that's enough.

"I want you to leave me alone," she says.

"You were the one who asked to see me. Poor Paul. He asked me not to hurt you, but he still passed on your message." Roosevelt shakes his head. "But he's a bright kid, pleasantly ambitious. I'm sure he'll learn."

Bird's hand tingles where she brushed against Paul in the hallway, a physical memory that has nothing to do with her rational mind. She hates what Paul has become. She hates what he's done to her. And it makes it worse, somehow, that he's retained enough of his conscience to regret it, and not enough to stop.

"No more spying," she says, forcing the words out. "No more threats. I want my life back."

He frowns. "So would about two million other people."

It's a long way down if she jumps, and her mother is coming home tomorrow. Roosevelt meant that news to intimidate her, and even two weeks ago it would have worked — Bird would have retreated to her cave and Emily would have glued on her molted feathers. But with Coffee and Marella watching, reckless bravery bubbles up her throat.

"Then it would have helped," she says, "if you had given them the vaccine."

For a second, Roosevelt doesn't so much as twitch a finger. Then he takes a gentle step closer to her bench, so she is forced to look up to see his face, now a mask of dark hollows and white planes. When she breathes all she can smell is him: menthol cigarettes and sandalwood cologne, Coffee's ripe aroma of sociopathy.

"That's what this is? I wondered. The *vaccine*." A faint laugh.

From this angle, she can see a dust of white powder in his nostrils. *Coke* is her immediate thought, though it seems fantastic that a CIA contractor could get away with it. But then again, who better?

Bird clears her throat. "We have proof that's what the school has been giving us. A secret vaccine that could have saved millions of lives." Her heart races, her mouth is dry, but she only has eyes for Roosevelt.

"Proof!" Roosevelt rolls his shoulders and fixes her with a glare of sudden impatience. "What, did you write it down in invisible ink?"

"It's not true?"

He looks at her for several long seconds, then shrugs. "It is a vaccine. And so I'm sure you'll be excited to hear that the president himself will give the nation the good news Thanksgiving morning."

And there's the ground, rushing close. "Tomorrow?"

"It'll be a good turkey day," he says. "I hear the Redskins are going to play Dallas in a demonstration game. The good American spirit, cowboys versus Indians. The Indians will lose, of course. Everything is going back to normal."

If Roosevelt isn't lying — and why would he be? — the president's announcement undermines any leverage she might have had. Should she tell him she has Dr. Granger's emails, her formal letter of complaint? They might make a good news story, but they might not protect her. She fumbles at the few remaining questions. "Why did we get it so early, then? How did you test it? — you gave it to the vice president's daughter, you must have known it was safe. Criminals? Why keep it secret —"

Roosevelt raises his hand. Just that, but it stops her short. "To keep you safe." His voice is strangled, as if he has barely stopped himself from saying something very different. "That's why we're doing all of this. To protect America from ungrateful national security risks like you. You think you know a secret, Bird?"

He puts a hand on her shoulder, a violation she doesn't dare remove. In the corner of her eye, she sees Coffee pull away from the wall and cross the bridge. Part of her longs for him to intervene, but she knows that he would only make this worse. Roosevelt doesn't see her as a threat. He thinks she is stupid and harmless, and only that might provoke him into carelessness. She shakes her head firmly. Coffee stops like he's hit a wall.

"The vaccine is a big deal," she makes herself say, so he won't notice.

"The vaccine program was very important to our national security. Feel free to tell the papers you got it early — but the kids of the big editors also got the vaccine early, so something tells me you won't get much traction with them. And the Internet? Well, who can believe the conspiracy theories you read online?"

"But the rest of the world —"

"Can buy it from us at a fair price. It's not simple to manufacture after all. It took weeks just to give it to Congress."

Bird closes her eyes. "You can't do this forever. You have to leave me alone sometime."

"I'll leave you alone now. Your parents are back, you don't know anything you shouldn't."

She opens her eyes and stands, unbalancing him so he staggers backward. "What happened to Sasha Granger?"

"Sasha? Of course you would ask about her. She didn't like the vaccine program any more than you do."

"So you killed her," she says.

"Massive aortic aneurysm. Her heart was a time bomb." Roosevelt shrugs. "We just got lucky."

She wishes she could be sure he's lying. He's a cokehead hypocrite serial harasser, but he might not have done anything to hurt Dr. Granger. And if he didn't, then there is nothing else she can do. She has played her ace and lost.

"Oh, you and your cousin are free to go home any time you want. Happy Thanksgiving, Bird. If you need to get in touch again, just leave a message."

He nods at her and ambles away, hands in pockets. He chuckles to himself and says, "The *vaccine*!" low and disbelieving. He nods at Coffee when they pass each other. Coffee doesn't bother to acknowledge him. He meets Bird at the rose garden entrance and cups her elbows in his large, restless hands. Marella hangs back.

"Are you okay?"

"You can come for Thanksgiving."

He frowns, reads the whole story on her face. "But it didn't work." It has scared her how well Coffee knows her, but now that knowledge feels like a salve on angry burns.

"The president will announce the vaccine tomorrow morning. We were too late. But Roosevelt said he would leave me alone, anyway. My parents are coming back, and really he was only using me as some sort of hostage in case they said something. . . ."

Coffee frowns. "But Bird," he whispers, "the party."

Roosevelt's low chuckle as he left. *The vaccine*, he said, as if he couldn't believe his luck. Because she couldn't touch him, or because she had made the *wrong* threat? His story fit together with everything except the party. Why interrogate her if he was only interested in ensuring her parents stayed quiet? What had happened in those hours after Coffee chased Paul's car down the driveway? If Roosevelt came here thinking there was a chance she knew something, then maybe she does.

"When you come tomorrow," she says carefully, "bring that dessert you promised me. The mind-blowing one you had after your father died."

Coffee flinches. She keeps her gaze steady on his. "Bird —"

"It's time," she says.

His Adam's apple bobs and he blinks twice. She catches a tear with her thumb and rests her cold hand on his cheek. When he unlocks her memories, what Trojan secrets will follow them?

He leans into her palm. His evening stubble pricks a constellation in her skin. Her breath is lazy and thick, full of him and striated with longing. What will he hear tomorrow, if this works? She asks, "What do you feel for me?"

He goes rigid; lifts his head and steps back in a jerky, panicked motion. "Why are you asking me that?"

"Because if we do this tomorrow . . ."

"You've never wanted to know before." His voice is rough with anger.

"I was afraid before."

Two more tears leak from his eyes and he wipes them away angrily. "Christ. Oh, goddamn it, Bird, you don't — I can't even — I just —" He shakes his head.

Bird can only stare.

"I'll come to your uncle's tomorrow," he says. "I'll bring what you want. Good night."

Considerate as always, Marella walks up to her after Coffee stalks away. "We should get back inside. It's nearly curfew."

"I screwed everything up, Mar." Bird hugs herself and shivers.

"It'll be better tomorrow," Marella says. "I promise. Nothing looks as bad with a turkey and mashed potatoes. Not even to Coffee."

Bird first spoke to Paul Simpson at Flower Mart, the May Day festival held every year on the grounds of the National Cathedral. He had always been more adult than the other Bradley boys in their grade: stronger, taller, broader. He had an easy smile and the kind of confidence that had made heartthrobs of boys far less naturally hot. She nearly fainted from astonishment when he followed her out of the stall of paper flowers and handed her one of blue and white — colors to match her dress. They inched toward each other for the first month of summer vacation, over text messages and weekend parties and not-quite-chance meetings in coffee shops.

The night he first kissed her, on the couch in his living room while his parents were away, she shivered and leaned back.

"Why?" she asked, surprising herself. She could have sworn she'd only been thinking of Paul's soft lips and what Felice would say when she texted her later that night. But still, she pressed: "Why me?"

Paul's frown smoothed into a smile, and he ran a hand through her hair. "Because you're smart and hot. I don't settle, Emily. And I want you."

It was the most romantic thing anyone had ever said to her. He became her second official boyfriend, and the first one she really cared about.

"It's because he said smart before hot," she told Charlotte, later that week. "That's how I knew."

She knew that she could have felt more, but instead she felt just enough. Love has scared Bird from the moment she knew her mother's name.

It still scares us. But we've realized something else, in the year and a half since that somewhat romantic declaration. The potential for pain can be its own reassurance.

It's numbness that scares me now. Cut enough love away, Bird, and you could die without even knowing you had lived.

[psilocybin]

$$C_{12}H_{17}N_2O_4P$$

Thanksgiving morning, Bird and Marella and two dozen upper school boarders gather in front of the television with Mrs. Cunningham to watch the president's special holiday address. Bird held out some half-formed hope that Roosevelt lied to her, but it fades the moment the president's lined, exhausted face appears on television.

"After months of struggle, pain, and conflict," he says, "after trials greater than any our nation has suffered in living memory, I am proud to face you, the great American people, on this day of thanks and announce that American scientists have developed a vaccine against the pandemic Venezuelan flu."

Bird and Marella look at each other while disbelieving chatter rises to the rafters. Mrs. Cunningham's expression is so impassive that Bird guesses she knew the secret of the vitamin shots. Charlotte, still perched on her bed, puts her head between her knees like she's going to puke. The rumor mill says that her father is recovering, but her mother is still in the ICU. How will Charlotte feel if one of her parents dies of this disease just after the president announced the vaccine? If she found out she was immunized in secret weeks ago?

The president continues his speech, explaining that the vaccine was difficult to manufacture, so a lottery system will be employed to ensure its fair administration among the whole US population. Needless to say, he doesn't mention that he and his family were vaccinated more than a month ago, along with probably the entirety of the audience applauding wildly in the East Room of the White House.

"Mrs. Cunningham," says one of the freshman girls, who looks in her bunny pajamas and tangled hair so young that Bird has to blink. "Mrs. Cunningham, will we get the vaccine too? He said there would be exceptions to the lottery, do you know if we could get excepted?"

Mrs. Cunningham looks, for a fraction of a second, as nauseated as Charlotte. Then her mask reforms, seamless and serene, and she shakes her head gently. "I'm not sure, Tara. I know Mrs. Early will make an announcement on Monday for the whole school, and she'll probably discuss all this then. For now, those of you going home for the day should get your things together. The buses are leaving in forty minutes."

"Did you hear from your parents?" Marella asks softly.

Bird shrugs. "Mom called a few times. Nicky texted that they're coming over for dinner. I'm postponing the agony."

"And Coffee?"

She shivers, though the attic room is hot enough that someone cracked open a porthole. "Incommunicado. We'll see if he shows."

"You know, Bird, I was thinking . . . Roo — I mean, *he* might have meant what he said. About leaving you alone. Even though it didn't work out the way we thought, he's letting you and Aaron go back home, right?"

Despite having woken up a half hour before, Marella looks exactly as well-rested and beautiful as Bird looks disheveled and strung-out. Her perfect hair falls down her back in waves formed by her nighttime braids. Her eyes are bright and wide, without a single popped vessel to mar the shining white. Bird sighs and tries not to feel the comparison too deeply.

"He might have meant it," Bird says, "but you asked me what I wanted." She wants to win. Not just to be free of him, but to beat him at this game that he started. Even though it will put her in more danger. Even though she might lose. Even if her mother is back and Roosevelt is satisfied that he has done his duty, Bird doesn't care. Something happened to her that night. Something she tried to remember. She left herself clues, she called Coffee, she struggled to get away, and now Bird is going to honor her past, forgotten self.

She is going do that most dangerous thing: remember.

Charlotte has her headphones on, a copy of *Brides* magazine in her lap, and an energy bar in her hand. Her compact stillness is a glaring beacon through the bustle of girls getting ready to go home for Thanksgiving. Bird gulps and puts her hand on Marella's elbow.

"Wait for me downstairs," she says. Marella follows the direction of her gaze and nods.

"You don't mind?" Bird asks.

Marella shrugs. "Perspective, the silver lining of the apocalypse. Ask her."

So Bird stands awkwardly at the foot of Charlotte's bed and coughs. "Hey," she says.

Charlotte makes a show of raising her eyes and looking startled. "Oh, Emily. What's up?"

"I'm heading to my uncle's for Thanksgiving. He says he fought it out for the last turkey at Safeway. Think you might want to help us eat it?"

Bird stills her erratically tapping foot, crosses her arms, and struggles to keep her gaze somewhere in the vicinity of Charlotte's exhausted, guarded eyes. Charlotte used to be the nice one, but she doesn't look the part anymore; she has the air of a wounded animal snapping at hands that get too close.

"I'm good here, thanks."

Bird nods, and she's half turned to escape when she hears herself say, "It really wouldn't be a big deal. I mean, if you're as tired of this place as I am. It would be nice to have you there. My mom is back, I could use some allies."

She feels sick with regret as soon as the words escape her lips. They hang in the air between them, a poison gas. She tries to apologize, but the syllables catch on one another in a meaningless babble that Charlotte cuts short with a wave of her hand.

"I'm spending the day in the hospital. My mom went into respiratory arrest last night. I don't know how many more days I'll have to spend with her, so if you don't mind, find some other *allies*."

Bird digs her nails into her palm and forces herself to face Charlotte. "That was a shitty thing to say. I'm sorry. And I'm really sorry about your mom. I can bring back some leftovers, just in case."

For a moment, Charlotte cracks that sweet smile. Then she shrugs. "Are you and Coffee coming to the go-go?"

"Me and Coffee?"

"I heard you finally went for him. Ditching Paul for Coffee . . ." She laughs. "Only you, Emily. But I don't know why it matters anymore, so how about it? Will you come?"

Bird wonders about the layers of Charlotte she never bothered to explore — why one of the nicest girls in class would be best friends with its resident queen bee, why she dreams of weddings the way other girls dream of college, why she's determined to throw the perfect go-go when her mother might die of v-flu. Maybe one day they can be friends again. Bird promises herself to do it better the second time around. For now, she offers the only comfort she can.

"I'll be there."

"Good. And . . . I wouldn't mind it if you saved me some of that turkey. I think I've forgotten what real food tastes like."

Coffee slouches onto the bus at the last possible moment. Aaron waves happily, but Coffee just nods at them before stuffing his long limbs into the very back seat and pulling a baseball cap over his head. Bird's stomach clenches. She wishes she could travel back in time and slap herself before she asked that question. If acknowledging the depths beneath them means they both drown, then she would rather spend her life staring out at placid waters. She would rather keep Coffee as a lanky totem at parties, Kokopelli curled around a hand-rolled cigarette and anarchist political theory, than lose him because she tried to force a normal relationship. Not when she's pretended for more than a year that he was just some weird friend, the funny dealer who liked to argue. And now, with Paul finally gone and her mother about to descend, she decides that she likes him after all? Maybe he thinks she asked him as a consolation prize. Maybe after all this time, he's decided he doesn't want her. Or maybe it's just like he told her at the party: He doesn't want what Bird is, but what she *could be*.

The bus goes slowly, since it has to stop at each inspection point between the school and Northeast. By the time they get to Sixteenth Street, the churches have let out their morning services, and the crowds of people spilling onto the sidewalk and street slow the bus down even more. A group of people dressed in white hold up signs protesting the quarantine as being against "God's plan." Some kids heckle them in Spanish and English from across the street. Bird stares until they drop out of sight. The school insisted on curbside service for the safety of the lower schoolers, and Nicky's house is at the far end of the route. Bird's phone buzzes. She doesn't even pick it up, but Aaron peels his nose from the window and pokes her arm.

"Your phone, Em."

"It's probably Aunt Carol."

Aaron makes a face. "Oh," he says. "I hope Dad cooks the turkey right this time. Aunt Carol is really picky."

Bird laughs and squeezes his shoulder. "That's one way to put it."

"Em?"

"Yeah?"

"Even if your parents are back, do you think you'll stay with us?"

A few months ago, the thought of permanently living with Nicky would have made her cry. It would be a vindication of her mother's most painful accusations about Bird's character. Now the prospect feels like a long-sought solace, a third way she never imagined possible. But how would it happen? Her parents will certainly expect her to move back home once things settle down with the quarantine, and it's easier to stand up to Roosevelt than her mother.

"Mo will probably want her room back, Aaron," she says tactfully.

Aaron nods but his shoulders slump. "But now that I'm at Bradley, I guess it won't be too different, right? You'll still come by sometimes and make me your funny salad?"

Bird squeezes his hand. "And you can play me all your new records," she says, voice scratchy.

Nearly two hours after they started, the bus stops at the end of Nicky's street and the four of them climb out on stiff legs. Nicky opens the door before they knock and picks Aaron up in a bear hug that leaves her cousin giggling.

"Your parents are coming by in the afternoon," he says over Aaron's shoulder. Bird can hardly nod for the dread weighing her down. She feels the heat of Coffee's gaze, but shame keeps her from meeting it. He knows more about her relationship with her parents than anyone but Mo, but that's just the trouble: There's no more painful rejection than that of the person who knows you best.

They all crowd into the living room, while Bird makes introductions. A few shirts and jackets pile at one end of the faded red floral couch and a dozen empty beer bottles wait for the recycling bin in crooked rows by the door. Nicky tugs awkwardly on his do-rag. "I guess I should have cleaned up more around here. Em, did you want to —"

"I'll get started with the cooking," she says quickly.

Nicky smiles. "Your Aunt Grace is bringing some deviled eggs and that coconut cake. I might not have enough milk for the mashed potatoes, but that bodega on the corner is open till one."

"You'll do the turkey?" she asks.

He grimaces. "*We'll* do the turkey. That way your mom can spread the blame."

Their eyes meet and an understanding that Bird has resisted her whole life passes, at last, between them. Her mother's nightmare is flowered and heavy with fruit after long years of growing in the dark. Their similarities, in the end, are due to no particular cosmic coincidence or genetic endowment, just the self-fulfilled prophecy of a woman they both are doomed to love. This might be Carol Bird's tragic irony, but it is her daughter's sudden strength. Her uncle's eyes contain her every childhood terror, and they do not destroy her after all. She turns to Coffee in the moment of this realization, but he's looking at her uncle with the frown he reserves for tricky problems of organic chemistry.

"We could cook it Brazilian style," he says.

"You cook turkey in Brazil?" Marella asks.

He smiles. "Not really. But I figure it can't be too different from chicken."

Nicky gets that mischievous look she remembers from when she was a kid. "Brazilian turkey," he says. "Now that's practically Carol-proof."

"If she has no idea what it's supposed to taste like, how can she tell us we've done it wrong?" Bird almost laughs at the idea. Her mother conceives of herself as very culinarily adventurous, though in reality this never goes much further than the local Thai restaurant. Bird could hug Coffee for seeing the situation with such clarity and compassion, but he still hasn't spoken to her directly; he's still hardly looked at her.

"Coffee, why don't you go down to that bodega and see if they have what you need," says Nicky.

"I'll take him," Bird says, surprising herself. Coffee jerks. Marella clears her throat. "Aaron," she says, "why don't you show me around the kitchen? I can get started on peeling the potatoes, at least."

Nicky smiles benevolently and settles down on the couch to watch the pregame talk shows, because even a v-flu vaccine has nothing on a Thanksgiving day match between the Cowboys and the 'skins. He doesn't even think about helping, any more than her father would, with so many women in the house. And Bird thinks that her mother isn't all wrong about her brother, any more than she's all wrong about her daughter. Scared of everything, and only ambitious enough for a postage stamp of a mark on the world; gifted with the privilege of class and education and unable to articulate what she wants to do with it. She will disappoint her parents by the simple expedient of being herself.

Outside, braced by the cold, sunny day and the revelations of the morning, she turns to Coffee. "Did you get it?"

He snorts. "Of all the things I never expected to hear you say."

She looks down at her sneakers, embarrassed. "Sorry."

"I did," he says after a beat. "And *foda-se*, don't ask how. I'll need an excuse to sleep over."

She nods. She didn't think they could manage this at school. The rest depends on her parents, but she'll deal with them somehow. At the bodega, Coffee makes quick work of the sparse shelves. A few cans of coconut milk, dried chili peppers, cinnamon sticks, and cloves. A jar of orange palm oil the owner kept behind the cashier. He gets the least brown scallions and a few bags of frozen vegetables. Shopping has been hell in the District since the quarantine, with most of the produce too wilted to use after the required holding period. Of course, there are small towns on the West Coast so decimated by the v-flu that trucking companies won't even deliver there anymore. It can always be worse.

She walks slowly on the way back, hoping that Coffee might offer her some Thanksgiving truce, but he's stone silent beside her. She nods to the few neighbors she recognizes, though yellow quarantine tape stretches across five houses on Nicky's block alone. She wonders if that means her parents still won't be allowed back home.

Coffee stops short at the foot of Nicky's steps, and she stumbles into him. Dizzy, she looks up at the thick curls that brush the back of his neck.

"Do you really want me to answer your question?" he asks.

Turn around, she thinks, but she doesn't have the breath for it. "Please."

She can only judge his mood by the angry question mark of his long spine; he denies her his face, and nearly all inflection.

"I've spent a year drowning in you. Even when you listened and smiled when your friends made fun of me. Even when you would stare at me when you thought I wasn't looking and I *knew* that I didn't feel this by myself and I *knew* that it would take an apocalypse to make you admit it. And ha! God gave me an apocalypse, thanks but no thanks. Do you know what your question feels like, Bird? It feels like you're giving me the scraps when everything else has gone to hell. And I hate how little that matters to me, how much I want whatever you can lower yourself to give."

Bird gasps twice and reaches to touch his back, feeling his warmth and tension beneath the thin gray fabric of his hoodie. He groans and turns and stops, so she can just see the curve of his cheekbone and chin sharp against the baby-blue sky.

"You didn't answer my question," she says, brushing aside the rest with the selfish desperation of the emotion she refuses to be the first to name. He's right, but it can't matter now, not anymore.

He bites his lip and his shoulders tremble before he turns to face her fully. His eyes are an open wound that she gave him, while his mouth — that beautiful, terrible instrument — pronounces judgment:

"I love you, Emily Bird. You're the best person I know. I love who you were, who you are, I dream of the woman you'll be. I want you to have your shop, I want you to spend Thanksgivings laughing with your uncle, I want your mother to hate all the ways you will never be like her, because you are so much better and you don't even know it. You're so brave and beautiful and, God, I thought, why did I even bother to come back, she didn't need me, I just needed her. . . ."

She wraps her arms around his neck, she buries a hand in that thick, well-loved hair, and she kisses him; there is no one else.

*   *   *

"Aaron," Bird calls, "are you watching that stove? You gotta keep stirring the sauce or the eggs will cook."

"I'll be there in a sec," he says, and then that iconic, plaintive rising guitar riff blasts into the kitchen by way of the dining room speakers, and Marvin Gaye wails about how he's going to get it on with enough force to shake the countertops.

"Turn that down, Aaron!" Nicky shouts from the den, and they all pretend not to hear him.

Marella, face sweaty from the effort of mashing ten pounds of potatoes by hand, does a little dance with the battered metal bowl, crooning the words in a surprisingly pretty falsetto and swinging her hips. Aaron runs back to the stove and his neglected whisk, grinning like he's just won the Super Bowl.

Aaron beats the whisk against the edge of the pot in perfect quarter time and matches his voice to Marella's in an only slightly wobbly harmony. Given the lyrics this is both ridiculous and cute as hell. Coffee smiles over the cutting board, where he's chopping several onions for inclusion in the turkey stew he calls a quasi-*bobo*. Bird grates cheese and watches him over her shoulder, her foot tapping the beat, her heart full and jumping in counterpoint. Her lips tingle with memory, her tongue feels too full inside her mouth, she longs for another taste of him. He catches her watching and grins and moves his elbow so it brushes hers. In the ensuing fireworks they stare at each other, Aaron and Marella belt like they're on audition for *American Idol*, and Bird wonders how such a little nothing could shake her knees and spin her stomach, how one kiss could change so much. Fear crosses his face, quickly chased by a smile. He drops the last of the onions in the Dutch oven and, passing by her on his way to the sink, kisses her beneath her ear.

"It was that inspiring, huh?" Marella says, laughing.

Bird turns to find them both staring as Marvin finishes his exhortations to carnal pleasures, and laughs with her.

"I knew it!" Aaron says. "Bird's got a —"

"Watch the sauce, kiddo," Bird interrupts, though she can't stop smiling any more than Coffee can. Aaron goes back to stirring the sauce and Bird grabs a few handfuls of cheese and dumps them into the liquid.

The sauce is for the world's best macaroni and cheese, taught to Bird by her grandmother the year before she died. And now Bird is passing it on to Aaron herself, since Nicky never bothered to learn and her mother always sniffed about how "caloric" and "old-fashioned" the recipe was. "The only thing worse was her chitlins," Carol Bird had declared last Christmas. "Good lord, those would smell so bad she made Daddy clean them out back in his shed. I understand eating that sort of thing in the slave days, but some traditions are better off in the past."

Bird vaguely remembers the crunchy breading and chewy middles of her grandma's chitlins from when she was very little, but by the time she would have been old enough to learn the recipe her mother's protests had succeeded in removing them from the menu. No one, however, would listen to her about the mac and cheese — for that matter, Carol Bird helped herself to a big spoonful every holiday, complaining all the while.

An hour later they have everything in the oven but the sweet potato pie. This takes longer because Marella and Bird have strongly differing opinions as to the relative virtues of lemon juice in the filling. Namely: *Lemon juice, are you nuts?* (Marella) and *It's perfect to round out the flavor* (Bird). Coffee facilitates a compromise by suggesting that Bird zest the rind instead of squeezing the juice, and then grates a hard stick of cinnamon over top of the filled pies, a dust of brown pollen on golden-orange skin. At this point Nicky wanders into the kitchen, stretching his arms over his head and says, "Something smells damn good in here. Should I help? It's halftime. 'Skins are down seven, but I think they can pick it up in the second half if they get that damn second-stringer out of there."

Bird suggests he set the table, Marella wheedles Aaron to play some later-era Michael Jackson, Coffee sighs theatrically, and then just stares as Bird and Marella dance like hell to "Blood on the Dance Floor" while stacking the dishwasher. She's genuinely surprised when the doorbell rings, utterly unprepared with dish soap soaking the front of her shirt and sweet potato pulp drying on her collar, for the sound of her mother's voice in the hallway: "Nicky! It's been too long. I hope you won't mind, Greg and I picked up a turkey from Whole Foods on the way."

She doesn't realize that she's hyperventilating until she feels Coffee's hands on her shoulders and his voice in her ear. "Breathe. It's four against one."

She gulps. Her mother's voice is getting closer. "You can't count Nicky. He's never any help —"

"Not Nicky. *You.*"

She's never counted herself for much in the fight against her mother, but maybe that's because she has always surrendered before the battle, ceded territory rather than risk total annihilation. She feels as exposed as she always has, painfully aware of the nappy tangles of her unwashed hair even before her mother steps into the kitchen and gives them a long, purse-lipped stare. But there's Aaron standing on a chair by the stove and Marella getting cider from the fridge and Coffee behind her, one hand brushing her collarbone before he takes a step back. When she meets her mother's eyes, she understands for the first time how love can be a strength instead of weakness, how the web that enmeshes her among the people in this room can, if she lets it, hold her up, not tear her apart.

"Emily," her mother says, full of ice and disapproval. Her father, carrying a large box, looks between Bird and Coffee and forces an exhausted smile. They are different from Bird's memory — smaller, tired, even vulnerable. She recognizes her mother's habitual uniform of a tight bun, red lipstick, Elizabeth Arden perfume, and tasteful pantsuit, but they are a faded coat of paint on an old house that hasn't quite forgotten past glories. Her father looks tired enough to sleep in the doorway; a tremor in his hands rattles the turkey box and then stills. It's been just two months, but to Bird it feels like years. The people before her are old, mortal, the gods come down from their mountain and revealed to be human after all. She nearly cries for no reason she can articulate and hurries forward to take the turkey from her dad.

She swallows in the face of his astonishment and forces a smile.

"Happy Thanksgiving," she says. "We made a turkey, but we can heat this up when the other one is done."

Her mother sniffs. "Thank goodness for that. I've had calamari less chewy than that bird your uncle trussed up last year."

"Actually, Coffee made it," Aaron says, voice tight. "It's his special recipe from Brazil." Bird wonders what Aaron thinks of her mother. Does he resent his Aunt Carol for her snide comments about his father? The thought jolts her; Bird has always been so concerned with her own standing in her mother's eyes that she's never paused to consider how other people see Carol Bird.

"Coffee?" her mother says, though Bird knows she's heard his name several times before. "Like the beverage?"

Coffee's lips tip up in that cutting smile, but he strides forward and offers his hand. "You can call me Alonso," he says. "Bird was nice enough to invite me and Marella."

Her mother's head turns sharply back toward her. "How generous of you, *Emily*."

Just like Paul, she thinks, as though there were something offensive about having the temerity to name yourself.

Her father rubs the back of his head and looks over his shoulder. "Looks like the game is starting again," he says, and hurries away. He didn't even touch her; didn't even say hello. *He's just a man afraid of love*, Bird thinks, and reaches for Coffee's hand.

Aunt Grace comes a few minutes later with a can of frozen concentrate for the punch bowl and two Tupperwares full of her famous deviled eggs. Aaron sneaks a few before Aunt Grace can shoo him away, and Bird catches herself smiling again. She checks on the collard greens, breaks up the skin on the gravy, and then her mother declares that she's not going to wait for that silly game to finish just so she can eat her meal. The men grumble, but not too much — the 'skins are down 31–14.

Aunt Grace's husband, Uncle Terry, is a deacon at their church, so he says the grace while they all clasp hands around the table. To her surprise, Coffee closes his eyes, but across the table Marella raises her eyebrows. Bird shakes her head and shrugs helplessly, *family, what can you do?* and Marella smiles. She is overwhelmed with the understanding that she has wanted most of her life and hasn't found until now.

"We remember the departed, Grandpa Cornelius and Grandma May, who guided this family with strength and love and watch us still. We remember our family who are here with us in spirit, may the Lord protect them from harm and bring them safely home. We give thanks that two of our number, Carol and Greg, have finally returned to us, and that our Emily has come through her troubles happy and healthy and a testament to those who love and care for her. We pray for the strength to meet this pestilence and war with resilience and the fear of God in our hearts, and we give thanks for all richness we have as a family in these dark times. In the name of Jesus Christ our Lord we give thanks, Amen."

The answering chorus of *Amen*s echo around the table, Bird's no less fervent than the rest. She wishes that Monique could be here, but with any luck the quarantine restrictions will ease with the new vaccine.

"Time to eat!" Nicky says, taking up his plate.

"I call a corner of the mac and cheese," Aaron says.

Aunt Grace pours herself some punch and tops it off with a dollop from her flask. She called it her "medicine" when Bird used to ask, which always made her and Mo laugh hysterically. Coffee's quasi-*bobo* turns out to be a spicy, sweet-savory stew of turkey in coconut milk, and after a few tentative bites Aunt Grace declares it "darned interesting," and goes for seconds. Coffee eats his mac and cheese with the relish of the converted.

"I always just thought it was one of those weird American things, like funnel cakes."

"Funnel cake," pronounces Marella over a forkful of turkey, "is divine."

"And that cheesy mac shit isn't real m'n'c, anyway," says Nicky.

"Nicky! Watch your language at the table."

"Sorry, Carol."

Uncle Terry shakes his head. "Where are you from, son?"

Coffee smiles as though he's trying to keep himself from falling over with laughter. "Brazil," he says.

"Really?" Aunt Grace says, loud enough that she must have gotten a good start on her medicine. "We at war with you yet?"

"Not yet, but you never know —"

Bird coughs and elbows him in the ribs.

Thankfully, the hush of a thoroughly enjoyed meal descends on the table, and she endures nothing more taxing than her mother's speculative glances. It's strange — she keeps waiting for her mother to lash out at her, to condemn the life Bird has lived in their absence, but instead of wrathful, Carol Bird looks surprisingly wary. As if she returned home expecting a caterpillar and discovered a crow.

When Bird goes to the kitchen to take the pies out of the oven, her mother follows.

"Well, Emily, you're looking —"

"I'm not talking about my hair." Bird slams the oven door.

Her mother winces. "I wasn't. It . . . suits you better than I thought it would. I just wanted to say that I'm glad you're looking well. The school has taken good care of you."

"And Nicky," says Bird mutinously.

"Nicky did his best, I'm sure. You'll have to stay there for at least another week, so you know. There's some . . . paperwork to take care of with getting the house back."

"I don't understand how anything there could still be contagious. The quarantine is just another game of Roosevelt's, isn't it?"

"Roosevelt . . ." It seems as though she is about to confess something, trust Bird with the truth for once in their lives, but then her eyes flick around the room and she draws her lips back into a painful smile. "They're being very careful, that's all. Of course it's not contagious, but your father and I were too busy to initiate the clearance process. In any case, we should be cleared to go back home by next Friday."

"And what were you busy doing, Mom?" Bird asks. "Curing the v-flu? Making sure people like us got the vaccine before people like Nicky?"

She feels her mother's grip on her arm before she registers her movement. Long, manicured nails dig into her skin with stinging force. "Have you lost your mind?" her mother whispers fiercely. "Emily, haven't you gone through enough? You're our only daughter, we've given you everything. Don't throw it back in our faces like this. Please."

The "please," so uncharacteristic of her mother's lectures, stops her. "I'm sorry," she whispers, just as laughter erupts from the dining room. Her mother releases her arm and Bird rubs it, grateful for the pain because it keeps her from crying.

"Bird?" Coffee pokes his head into the kitchen. "Did we burn the pies?"

And Carol Bird, who has not retreated from a fight in her life, puts her head down and hurries past him, muttering something about washing up. Bird stares unblinking at the trail of her passage, until Coffee traces the marks of her mother's nails with a long finger.

"I'm sorry," he says, understanding everything, like always.

"He nearly killed me," Bird whispers, "but they still defend him. They say they're protecting me, but that's just their excuse."

"Would you be safer if they called him out?"

"Maybe not. But I'm so sick of being in the dark. They've all got this knowledge that is vital to my life, but somehow it's never *safe* to tell me? Bullshit."

Coffee bites his lip and looks at her for long, heavy seconds. The aroma of cinnamon and sweet potato and baked pastry mingles with Coffee's unmistakable scent and she sways like a tree in the wind, toward him and away, hoping for an embrace and not daring to give him one.

"I love you," he says.

Happiness ignites a bomb in her too-full stomach. She cannot possibly contain it; she sways into his waiting arms.

"I will never get tired of hearing you say that," she says, her words muffled against his shirt.

He laughs, and waits, but if she responds in kind, it is only in her hands and eyes and roving lips; she cannot say to him what she can't even say to herself.

Coffee sits across from Bird on the old green papasan chair that used to belong to her grandma. Bird focuses on the spray of unraveling rattan by his knee that catches the fabric of his jeans. She doesn't look at the quarters of lumpen chocolate sitting on a saucer on the table between them. She doesn't watch his face, just hears his breathing. Upstairs, Aaron and Nicky sleep while she and Coffee play Eve and Adam in the basement. The first girl takes the chocolate apples in a parody of greed, sweeping the lumps into her hand and cramming them at once into her mouth. An initial wash of sugar masks the musted chalk of off-brand supermarket chocolate, but it can't hide the taste that hits a moment later: dirt and pure bitters, collapsing to dust between her molars. She gags and Coffee takes her sticky chocolate hand.

"Just swallow. Shrooms are too gross to chew."

Thus the chocolate, she thinks, forcing the gelatinous mass past her epiglottis. But it seems like a misguided attempt. All the sugar in the world couldn't rehabilitate a mushroom that grows exclusively on poop.

She takes the mug of tea still steaming on the table, letting the thickly steeped beverage wash down the remains of those misbegotten truffles.

"Wow," she says, her heart pounding. "I want to know who first thought that a cow poop mushroom looked good to try."

Coffee traces a smile on the back of her hand and surrounds it with wavy lines. They radiate up her arm, far from their point of origin, and tickle the nape of her neck. The corners of Coffee's eyes crinkle with humor and irony and with the wonder that hasn't left him since they kissed that afternoon.

"Probably the person who noticed how happy the monkeys got after they ate a few."

Bird laughs. "Like those documentaries where all the animals on the savannah eat the fermented fruit and stagger around drunk."

"Sex and drugs: the universal constants of the mammalian condition."

"And death," she mumbles, thinking, for no reason at all, of her mother.

Coffee shrugs. "That's just entropy. Even stars die, but only we can get high."

"Not much compared to nuclear fusion."

"But it's a hell of a consolation prize for a speck of stardust."

She shivers and leans across the table; he cups a starry hand behind her head. "Can you feel it yet?" he asks after they kiss.

"I don't know. Maybe. Your hand feels like its melting into the back of my head."

"Yes," he says, and looks frightened again.

"So what are we going to do? Should we have music?"

"I thought I'd try to hypnotize you."

There are light-years in his eyes, concatenating gas clouds strung along webs of dark matter and a spinning, hungry pupil of a black hole at the center.

"Does that work?" says a voice like her own. She feels a little queasy and reaches for what's left of the tea, marveling at how she can feel at once aware of every inch of sensation between her fingertips and elbow and yet utterly disassociated from it. Like she's a puppeteer who has inhabited her own puppet and just now recalled the strings.

"Sort of. Hypnotism works, but as far as bringing back memories goes, it's controversial. Some psychologists think there's no such thing as repressed memories. Even the ones who do believe in them know that it's easy to implant false ones. I don't think it will work."

"So why do it?"

He looks away suddenly and riffles through his pockets, piling lint and crumpled receipts and half-smoked papers beside the remains of her communion. There seems to be no space between the sparkler fizz of intuition and the dip of her hand into her own pocket to pull out a pen. She marvels at the sight of it — a grubby Bic with a long crack in the side and ink congealed in a glossy mass by the uncapped tip. A typical Bird pen, because she loses them too quickly to keep anything else. Coffee's hands shake when he takes it from her. Yet even his shaking fingers make that utilitarian instrument a blurred streak of beauty as it dances between them. She could watch him forever and be content; strange how she didn't understand that until now. Why remember hard pasts, like the writing on the wall, when she could make a universe of this infinite present?

"Do you trust me?" he asks her. She sees his voice as indigo stars, slow-burning embers flicked like spittle from his lips. She reaches to catch one in her left hand: *trust* flickers there, desperate and hopeful.

"I like your trust," she says, smiling at it.

He sighs. "Bird."

"I never thought I did. I was so angry. You aren't always very nice."

"I'm sorry."

She shakes her head, deflecting that dejected stream of yellow. "I don't like your sorry."

"I'm —" He cuts himself off and laughs.

"I trust you," she says.

Coffee levers himself from the papasan chair and sits beside her. Just now, his heat is the most beautiful thing about him. He glows.

"Then close your eyes, Bird. Let's find out what you remember."

He glows even through her eyelids, but she won't tell him that. Just like she won't tell him how much she loves him, how long she has, how all those months she was terrified of a wall that turned out to be a trick of the light.

Paper rustles and Coffee clears his throat. "I just want you to concentrate on my voice. I can't hypnotize you unless you want me to. I need you to focus and relax. We're going to remember what you did after Trevor Robinson's party. And if you don't remember, that's fine too. There's no —"

"Coffee, wait, wait!"

She falls forward on the couch, ungainly from the warmth of his body and the stringy relaxation of her muscles. She struggles to sit upright. "What about your ankle tracker?"

Coffee snorts and she remembers to open her eyes. Even when she does, his features are fogged by the pulsing glow that fills the whole room.

"Bao tested its wireless signal yesterday. It's not sending enough data for audio. I'm just paranoid, like you said."

She hunts for his hand and squeezes it. "Roosevelt demands paranoia."

He sinks his fingers into her inch of hair. She sighs and leans back against him — happy, happy, happy, a girl with all fizz and no edge.

"Relax," he says with an awkward distance in his voice from reading off the papers. "Focus on that night. Tell me the last thing you remember."

"You." Unequivocal.

Coffee's arms tense around her. "What about me?" Painfully neutral.

"You running after the car. You can't catch us and you're sprinting anyway and then Paul turns and I smash my head and all I want to do is protect you."

She can see it all. Even feel that starry flash of pain and the sticky wet of her own blood on her hand. Then a new sensation: rough synthetic fabric over rounded, smooth metal. Coffee has put something in her hands.

"Do you remember this?"

Not by touch, but the smell, faint as it is after all these weeks, is unmistakable. "Peach schnapps. That shit fucked me up, but I didn't care. I kind of wanted it."

More smells assault her, attached to the first like burrs on a stray dog: the humus of the earth in the woods behind Trevor's house, cheap cigarettes, cheaper beer. And then laughter, explosive and muffled, the delight of kids getting away with the worst in their parents' backyard. The briefest lingering afterburn of someone else's pot.

"You don't want any more?" Paul asks her, rubbing her back.

She takes another sip. It's disgusting, but she doesn't say so. You don't get martinis hiding from the adults in the woods.

"What do you remember?" Coffee, reminding her of the present.

"How he drugged me in the woods."

"Good. Now focus on the car. Paul has pulled away from the house. What happens?"

"He gets a call."

"Who is it?"

"Unavailable. Roosevelt. But I don't hear. I pass out."

"Do you dream?"

"I . . ."

"It's okay. Don't try to force it. Remember something else. What did you think the first time you met me?"

"I liked your accent. Organic chemistry never sounded sexier."

"Wow." He has momentarily forgotten the calculated dispassion of his hypnotist voice.

"Are you sure about this hypnotizing thing?"

"No. This script isn't very helpful. Next I'm supposed to tell you that there's someone else in the room who wants to ask you some questions."

She shifts against him, eyes closed, and a sudden snap reverberates through the room. The couch is gone, and so is all sensation of Coffee's body but his warmth. She floats in a black void, but there are stars limning the distance. Does she have a body, or has she only imagined it all this time? She's a brain, she's a shooting star, she's a trillion trillion atoms in the improbable, evanescent arrangement that will call itself Bird.

"Do you hear the question?" ask the stars.

"There are no more questions," says a voice.

Now another woman floats with her in the dark. She looks familiar — a bit like Mo, a bit like her mother, with an air of determined confidence that reminds her of Marella. She has a full-on Black power fro, a thing of such beauty she wants to ask her for hair tips. Her eyes are hard but edged with compassion; she's sorry for what she has to do, and Bird makes herself face this implacable goddess with her every ounce of bootstrapped bravery. The stars shudder and sigh around her and she loves them, but she has traveled beyond their help.

"Then what is there?" asks the thing called Bird.

The goddess smiles. "A story."

"Bird?" say the stars.

"Shh," she says. "Listen."

I remember the confusion of that drug. The sickness of it. The struggle to keep any thought in my head longer than a few minutes. It's worse than not being able to think, not being able to remember what you were thinking.

I remember the brassy smell of new leather recently wiped down with bleach. It tickled my nose and I sneezed. Someone said to get me a tissue, but no one did, so I just wiped my snot on my sleeve.

I remember the sounds of men. Men cursing, shuffling, laughing at dirty jokes, smoking, drinking coffee, belching. Mostly asking and asking and asking, questions I could hardly keep in the shallow bowl of my memory. They spoke to one another a great deal and me more than enough. *Tell me about your daddy*, they asked. *Tell me about that boy. Tell me what you know, girl.*

I remember the dry squeak of an alcohol swab packet tearing open, and the cool swipes drawing a barcode up my arm. Each time a needle would prick and burn, and I would lose the world for a few minutes before they dragged me back into it. *Tell me about Synergy Labs, tell me about your mommy.*

I don't know, I just found it in the trash.

And what did your mommy think of that?

I remember the man with the needle who smelled of cinnamon breath mints, sandalwood cologne, and sour armpit. He had a voice at once deep and thin, as though he took his breaths through a narrow tube obstructed with gravel. *She could OD*, he said before he pricked me again. *We don't have much experience with this formula.* I hated him most of all.

I remember the voice in my ear, the one from the party. He thought I was pathetic, and stroked my hand like he could just as easily rip it off. *And that boy at the party, that diplomat's kid. What did you tell him about your parents? What did he tell you?*

Nothing, you asshole, I thought. *Leave him out of this*, I said.

The voice smiled. *Too late.*

I remember getting the idea.

I remember how my arm burned, twisted and bunched beneath me when I slumped on that couch. I told myself not to move. He propped up my head with a hand that smelled of soap and cigarettes. I drooled on it.

Oh, great. Victor, get me a tissue. How much did you give her?

You've always known how to pick 'em, a voice laughed and Roosevelt said, clear as a bell, *Ugly Black chicks aren't my type. That kid is welcome to her.*

("He's an asshole, Bird."

I know. This would have been so much worse if he were attracted to me.)

I don't remember seeing anything but blues and oranges chasing the black behind my eyeballs. I don't remember how I got there. I don't remember how I got away.

But I remember *needing* to remember. I have a space inside of me, and the shape of that space is something overheard accidentally, spoken by people who thought me mindless. It was important, what those men said over the body of the girl they had drugged into a stupor. My parents never told me a thing, but *those men* did. It would have been safer for me if they just kept their mouths shut. But I didn't care. I remember being *so happy* that Roosevelt thought so little of me that he had given me something that would destroy him.

I said to myself, *Remember, Bird. No matter what you do, you must remember this.*

But I didn't. I couldn't, not after what they dropped in my veins. They nearly killed me with it, just to make my memory a mile of rotted lace.

("You remember enough. You don't have to —"

I do. I always did.)

All they left me are flashes. My hand with my father's pen. *The writing on the wall* on a carefully smoothed out piece of paper.

My face, smeared in my mother's bathroom mirror. Someone crying.

Your voice on the other end of the phone. Not the words, but the sound of it, the apology and the worry and the relief. The sound of you that cared enough to warn me at the party, caring enough to find me now at the other end of the line. I don't know why I called. Maybe it was just to hear your voice.

("You told me to get away. You told me to think of your shop for you if you died."

I'm still here. It's okay.

"No, it isn't. Not even a little.")

My tights, covered in mud and soaked from the rain. I'm outside. I peel them off and stuff the paper inside, then wad the mess back in my pocket. I am more afraid than I have ever been. I swallow rainwater and salt and bile. Then I turn and face the monster behind me.

I do not remember forgetting.

[seratonin]

$C_{10}H_{12}N_2O$

The sweet potato pie tastes like the dying dream of a root vegetable, an ecstasy of light custard contrasted with crumbly, buttery crust and a piquant afterbite of nutmeg and lemon. Marella, Coffee, Aaron, and Bird shovel forkfuls in their mouths like squirrels storing acorns for winter.

"I think it got better since Thanksgiving," Marella says, her words only intelligible to her fellow pie-stuffers. "Is that possible?"

"It matures in the fridge," Bird says. "Leftovers are always superior."

"Matures?" Aaron giggles. "It's got sweet potato puberty."

Coffee laughs so hard he starts to cough, momentarily removing his fork from the competition. Bird takes advantage, securing a sizable chunk of crust.

"Good thing we're eating it now," Coffee says. "It might get PMS or something." He and Aaron can't speak for laughing. Marella and Bird raise their eyebrows in concert.

"You've both got the sense of humor of a ten-year-old," Bird says. "That's not good news for one of you."

"If you're going to make stale period jokes at our pie, then I think you can watch us ladies eat the rest of it." Marella smiles sweetly at Aaron's pout. "The PMS, you know. It makes us unreasonable."

"And hungry." Bird takes a very large bite. Her stomach twists, because in point of fact she did get her period this morning, and she's already gone through three ibuprofen attempting to beat back the cramps. This pie, Nicky's all-star-parent idea for Aaron's lunch today, couldn't have been better timed.

Coffee smiles at her and sucks on the end of his fork, which pushes out his bottom lip in a way she finds suddenly, complexly distracting. The three days since Thanksgiving have been a dollhouse of tiny joys. Each look or laugh or brush of hesitating fingers is a memory she polishes and arranges and rearranges because she knows that eventually this will be all she has left of him. One day either she will be gone or he will; she has no trust in the permanence of love or life — no one does, here at the end of days.

Bird takes pity on him and feeds him the last forkful of pie. He keeps his eyes on hers the whole time, until she feels gooey and warm, fresh out of the oven. In her peripheral vision Aaron makes a gagging motion.

"No kissing," Aaron says.

"Were we kissing?" Bird asks, looking away from Coffee.

Marella laughs. "We know the warning signs."

The four of them are sitting in the stacks of the Bradley library again, where the normal rules against eating seem to have been waived in a general End Times exemption.

"Aaron, don't you have classes?"

He groans. Coffee glances at his cell phone and stands up. "I've got a makeup appointment for my, ah, *vitamin treatment*," he says. "You coming, Aaron?"

"Makeup?" Marella asks.

Bird rolls her eyes. "He opted out the first time around."

"Smart move."

Coffee shrugs. "Distrust authority, that's my motto. I'll see you after school, Bird."

She squeezes his hand in farewell and watches until he and Aaron clear the swinging doors by the abandoned circulation desk. She sighs.

"So when I left, did you two just make out all night or did you try what you said you were going to?"

Bird looks up at Marella, then down at the hole in her right sock. The rough and ashy skin on the bottom of her foot has snagged the unraveling weave. The sight surprises her, since she's had regular pedicures since tenth grade. But then, in a universe where she's made out ten times in three days with an ex-fugitive drug dealer, the president has declared martial law, and she has finally apprehended her mother as a creature of human faults and frailties, ashy feet are an unremarkable dislocation.

"I did," Bird says. "It sort of worked. I don't remember much, but I know I need to get back into my house. My mom says the quarantine tape will be cleared by the end of this week, so I'll see what I can find then."

It seemed so obvious, once she remembered. *The writing on the wall* meant the words she wrote herself years ago. She'd used it as an arrow pointing to the clue that only she could find: her father's gold pen. She must have escaped Roosevelt, run back to her house, written down what she heard, warned Coffee, and then gotten caught again. This time, they didn't let her go until they'd doped her enough to destroy most of her memories of that night. Most, but not all.

"And this thing with Coffee . . ." Marella's lips twist, like she's trying to frown and smile at the same time. Bird pulls a book out at random from behind her elbow and runs her fingers down the edges of rough-cut papers. Her mother is back in the city; she doesn't need any more disapproval.

"Hey." Marella puts her hand on Bird's, blocking the blurry march of black type on yellow paper. "Bird, come on, I'm happy for you. You've sure wanted this long enough."

"Haven't I," Bird says, her tone somewhere between a question and a revelation.

"It's just, has he told you how his case is going? He doesn't have diplomatic immunity. He's eighteen. He could go to prison."

Marella has tied her hair back in four braids and as she speaks, quiet and serious, she winds and unwinds one of these dark ropes around a finger. *This is a friend*, Bird thinks: scared and concerned enough to speak her mind, but not judgmental. Bird makes room in her dollhouse for this new treasure, an incalculable gratitude for having Marella in her life.

But she says, with deliberate lightness, "I can wait. We can get matching tats and show them off at the five-year reunion, once he's out on probation."

Marella snorts. "I'd go just to see Felice's face. But seriously —"

"He could die of the v-flu too. He hasn't had the vaccine yet. It'd be like in English last semester, an Aristotelian tragedy."

Marella gives in. "Influenza isn't much of a tragic flaw."

"Ah." Bird tosses the book aside and sprawls across the aisle. The carpet smells of pie crumbs and book dust. Not a combination she'd have made herself, but she takes a deep breath and lets it out slowly. "Anti-authoritarianism might be, though."

"I've always liked that about him."

"See? Perfect Aristotelian tragedy. Or we could just get hit by some rogue terrorist anthrax attack and get tossed in a mass grave. A regular, nonliterary tragedy."

"The inevitability of death, huh? Not exactly an original argument for bad decision making."

"Is that what this is? A bad decision?"

"You'd really wait for him if he went to jail?"

"I'll just pretend he's at a different college."

"Most people can't swing that either."

Bird squeezes her hands together, remembering the warmth of his lips tracing the lines of her palms. "Most people don't have Coffee."

After a moment, Marella lies down on the floor herself, one braid tickling Bird's cheek. "So you love him."

Bird expects her stomach to clench at the word, but it just sighs lazily and unfurls, a sea anemone in sun-drenched waters. "Even if this ends. And, okay, not like me weeping and throwing myself on his bier ending, just high school romance, let's-see-other-people ending, I don't care. I don't care what my mother thinks, I don't care what Paul thinks, and Marella, I love you, but I'm not going to let myself care what you think either. This thing with Coffee . . . it's worth however long I get."

Marella giggles. "You love me?"

Bird elbows her in the ribs. "Hey, baby, wanna see if there's any fries left in the cafeteria? If we drown them in enough Tabasco and honey, they might even get to edible."

"You got it, Romeo," Marella says, and reaches out a hand to help her up.

There's a manila envelope in her school mailbox that afternoon. She brings it with her to English, not thinking much of the scrawl of her name on the front, or what teacher would hand back a test in an envelope. Only when the snow starts halfway through class, and Bird pulls out the loose pages that she certainly didn't write, does she remember to worry.

By then, all she can do is read.

District of Columbia Office of the Chief Medical Examiner
Name of Deceased: Sasha Calero Granger
Cause of Death: Ruptured thoracic aortic aneurysm (TAA)

The report goes on for two pages, detailing the precise location of the aneurysm and confounding factors (Dr. Granger had been taking quite a few of the sleeping pills she refused to prescribe for Bird). She doesn't want to read it, but she does, if only to be sure. Roosevelt didn't kill Sasha Granger, and he's laughing at her for believing that he did. On the back of the last page she reads his handwritten note:

SO YOU FINALLY SEALED THE DEAL WITH ALONSO. LET ME BE THE FIRST TO OFFER MY CONGRATULATIONS. GOOD TIMING, BECAUSE HE MIGHT NOT BE FREE MUCH LONGER TO

ENJOY YOUR COMPANY. UNFORTUNATELY FOR YOU AND ME,
HOWEVER, YOUR THANKSGIVING ADVENTURE HAS MADE YOU
FAR MORE INTERESTING TO MY COLLEAGUES. I TRIED TO
WARN YOU. IT SEEMS THAT WE'RE NOT QUITE DONE WITH EACH
OTHER AFTER ALL.

Bird stumbles out of the classroom without asking for permission. She squats on a window seat and presses her cheek against cold, snow-crusted glass. Roosevelt knows what she did on Thanksgiving. She should never have taken that shroom, she should never have pushed. She thought that she'd won, that he would leave her alone and she would have the time to strategize against him. But instead it seems that he's had a bug on *her*, not Coffee. But how? Who could have gotten into the house without Nicky or the neighbors noticing? Is it on her clothes? Her bag? It would have to be something they thought she would keep with her. And then it flashes in her memory: Paul's bracelet. The one she kept for a week, and then dumped in a jar of hair relaxer. The same jar still sitting on the bathroom counter in the basement. That's how she gave him all the reason he needs to threaten her forever.

And it's not just me. I've given him Coffee too. She hates the thought, she tries not to think it, but the only lingering effect of her psychedelic experiment is a disquieting tendency for her subconscious to assert itself implacably upon her conscious thoughts. Ideas she has spent years resolutely unthinking, feelings more closely guarded than a Guantánamo detainee, have broken free. But maybe it's unfair to blame it all on that bitter earth mushroom. She's never fallen in love before. And love, she knows, changes everyone.

She folds the envelope and squashes it in the bottom of her bag. Either of them could die this afternoon, tomorrow, next week. She wants to be happy for however long she can. She's tired of fighting. She's tired of losing. Roosevelt can threaten her, but he can't destroy everything.

She waits outside until her class ends, then heads downstairs with everyone else. A few teachers begin to corral her sorry-faced classmates for the afternoon assembly, but Bird hangs back. Beyond the large glass plated doors to the front steps, Cindy de la Vega and a few of her friends huddle around a tablet. Bird would rather be out there than in assembly, so she joins them outside.

"What's up?" she asks Rupa Patel, hovering on the edge of the group.

Rupa glances at Bird and frowns. "You didn't hear? Charlotte's mom died a few hours ago. I think they're going to announce it in assembly."

"Oh no. Poor Charlotte."

"Yeah. At least I heard her dad should make it. Oh, and the quarantine is going to end in a week. Which is, like, crazy because there's way more cases of v-flu now." She shudders. "We're lucky none of us has gotten it yet."

"Yeah," Bird says, her voice drier than champagne. "Lucky."

Rupa turns her attention back to Cindy's tablet, which shows a live stream of a BBC report about potential cease-fire negotiations with the Venezuelan government. The first ground war the US has fought since Iraq doesn't seem to be going as well as everyone thought it would. But Cindy isn't one of the disaster junkies who spends all her free hours flipping between CNN and MSNBC in the senior room. There has to be something more than yet another bleak report from the front to keep them staring at the screen so intently.

"Did they mention Charlotte's mom on the news?" Bird asks.

"No, shh," Cindy tosses over her shoulder. "Just listen."

This is difficult, since a cavalcade of ambulances, sirens blaring, drive down the street at just that moment. There have been a lot of ambulances around the city lately, but this is the most she's ever seen at once. The quarantine is ending in a week? Bird shakes her head. Maybe that's the point, to let the plague decimate the city now that all the important people have been safely vaccinated. But that's a conspiracy theory not even Coffee would believe.

Bird still can't fathom what Cindy is waiting for until the sirens recede and she catches the faint end of a clipped British voice saying, "hopes for a cure of the so-called Venezuelan flu seriously called into question. A report, issued by an independent body of EU virologists, has made an urgent request for evidence of the efficacy of the United States government's recently announced flu vaccine. The world greeted the announcement with joy, on the morning of the American Thanksgiving holiday, but it appears that some scientists have serious doubts about the safety or effectiveness of a vaccine developed only three months after the first cases."

"See, I told you," Cindy says to a friend. "The vaccine thing is a total lie. My mom wants me to go with her to some farm in the middle of nowhere Virginia. She's been getting shit at work because she's not a citizen. Like, making her sign loyalty declarations. Totally serious. So she wants out and we're going to wait until we can be sure the thing works."

"And miss the go-go?"

Bird cringes at the spray of Felice's acid voice behind her, but then remembers that she doesn't care if Felice likes her anymore. It astonishes her, the relief of being Felice's enemy. She turns around slowly, and is faintly surprised to see Felice holding a stack of flyers advertising Charlotte's doomsday go-go.

"Oh my God, Felice!" Cindy says. "Charlotte's mom is *dead*. What the hell are you doing?"

Bird enjoys the sight of Felice momentarily discomposed, her nostrils flared and head jutting rigidly forward. Bird wishes Marella were here; the schadenfreude of watching the queen bee face down this unexpected mutiny is too sweet to savor alone.

"Charlotte," Felice says, spitting out the consonants with machine-gun precision, "wants the go-go. She told me herself. Because she's my best friend." Bird repels Felice's quick glare in her direction with a shrug.

Rupa grimaces and turns away. Cindy jams her knit cap farther down over her ears. "You're nuts if you think she's going to want to go to some sweaty, loud go-go five days after her mother died."

"Then she's nuts, Cindy. And so am I, because she's my best friend and if she wants it, I'm going to give it to her. It's the least I can do. Hell, maybe we've all caught the v-flu already."

"And the thing you want to do with your last week on Earth is plan a dance? Where everyone can give the v-flu to everyone else? How is the school even letting this happen?"

"Sidwell might still let us do it and, even if they don't, I've got a backup plan. This will definitely happen."

"You are really that shallow." The reservoir of hate behind these words surprises even Bird, but then she remembers Cindy's confession in the senior room about the Bradley boy who raped her. Cindy's reputation has always been indefinably slutty, and Felice has always treated her with a certain knowing contempt. Bird realizes that she's witnessing a festering wound, finally lanced on the upper school steps.

Felice, to her credit, sums this up very quickly. "Shallow? Sure, sometimes," she says, ripping a piece of masking tape. "But I can think of worse ways to go."

Cindy's incredulous snort clouds the air between them. "Than a *high school dance*?"

"No," Bird says, knowing she should keep quiet, but thinking of Charlotte, motherless in the hospital. "Than a *go-go*."

Felice's eyes smile, even if her mouth doesn't. They've only ever tolerated each other for Charlotte's sake, and for a second that bond rematerializes like a sigh in cold air: a thick mist, evaporated, revealing nothing at all.

*   *   *

Bird waits for Coffee on the steps while Felice tapes go-go posters and Cindy cries and tells all her field hockey friends how much she'll miss them and she'll totally come back as soon as she gets the real vaccine. The rest of the school is trickling out from assembly, and from the heavy-eyed looks the seniors give Felice and Bird, Mrs. Early must have announced Charlotte's mother's death. Felice doesn't reply to anyone's awkward attempts at conversation, just rips her masking tape with pointed force and decorates the marble columns with posters of baby blue and lemon yellow.

Felice is giving us this go-go as her last act on Earth, Bird texts Marella. *I'm thinking I have nothing to wear. How bout you?*

A few seconds later, Marella's reply pops on-screen. *If we don't go shopping, I might have to show up naked. It don't mean a thang . . .*

Bird bursts out laughing and types, *If it ain't got that bootie swing? Are any shops still open?*

Maybe one of those AdMo thrift stores? Will check. Btw, sure you have date with C's lips, but in case u want me I might b back late.

Is everything okay?

No reply. Bird waits for a minute, then two, and is about to hunt Marella down before her phone tweets and buzzes in her hand. It's a text, not from Marella, but from Aaron.

Dad says he's got a cold and we should stay at school.

A cold? Bird's throat closes at the thought of those ambulances screaming up and down the street all day. But pandemic flu doesn't mean that all regular viruses go on vacation. The chances that Nicky has caught v-flu weeks before the vaccination lottery starts have to be tiny.

I'm sure he's fine, Aaron. Stay here tonight and we can visit him tomorrow.

But still, she waits another minute, frozen with images of flashing red and blue lights. Her phone chirps.

Sarah wrote me yesterday, said that she was sorry she broke up like that and wants to try again. Her parents still have her on house arrest, but she said she'll sneak into the city and meet me. So. I'm not saying we'll get back together, but I figure it can't hurt to talk again.

"Oh shit," Bird says, but she texts a simple, *Take care of yourself. Try not to jump into anything.*

I'm gonna pretend I don't know what u did last weekend, Marella replies and then, a few seconds later, *Thanks, babe.*

The first wave of boys have finally made their way across campus, their arrival heralded by deep, laughing voices echoing off the school's cold limestone walls. As they come into view through the thickening snow, Bird wonders, not for the first time, what sort of competitive urge induces them to wear such thin coats in the cold. They're like peacocks, advertising their strength by deliberately exposing weaknesses. Bird, almost comfortable in a pea coat and giant scarf, finds the daily evening visitation silly but indefinably appealing — that covey of wind-bright cheeks, floppy hair, and loose ties has made her pulse speed ever since ninth grade, when those boys throwing Frisbees on the lawn and flirting with senior girls had been as far above her as clouds. Now she searches for one face in the pack, and is rewarded by the sight of dirty-blond curls squashed beneath a red knit cap, walking with Trevor. He waves. She starts to stand, then freezes, knowing how it will look if she goes running to him at the end of the school day. Felice notices, anyway.

"So it's true? Goodwife Emily and the fugitive? I mean, Coffee can be cool, but his boyfriend potential? Yikes. Wait till I tell Paul."

"I can't imagine why you or Paul would care, but go ahead," Bird says, exhausted. "And if this means you've finally given up on Trevor, congrats."

"What would you know about it?" Felice says softly, looking over her shoulder to make sure the boys don't overhear.

"You actually have a chance with Paul," Bird says, and stands. How Felice takes this, she doesn't notice — the hopeful grin and long, loping strides of the boy coming toward her have pushed every other thought out of her head.

Coffee takes the steps two at a time and lifts her up in a hug that she supposes will end all speculation. He tastes of a just-smoked cigarette and peppermint and only a pointed whistle from Trevor makes her remember where they are.

"Pissing on your territory?" Trevor asks Coffee.

Coffee rubs her hands between his own and grins over his shoulder. "Just saying hello. Hello, Bird."

Bird laughs. "Hello, Coffee."

Trevor shakes his head and leans against the balustrade. "Damn, girl, you should come with a warning label. You seemed so nice too."

"Warning label?" Bird takes a step away from Coffee, though she keeps his hand. Her stomach lurches; has Coffee told him about her problems with Roosevelt?

"This one," Trevor says, pointing at Coffee, "nearly got the shit kicked out of him by your ex-boy."

"*Paul?* What the hell?"

Coffee grimaces. "You can be such a dick, Trevor. And for the record, I could have held my own."

"I pride myself on my dickishness, my caffeinated friend. But in this case, I merely state the truth. Paul could bench your entire body mass in tenth grade. You have a bum leg and the muscle definition of overcooked spaghetti. Emily should thank me for saving your life."

Bird climbs up two steps, so she can look down at both of them. "What the hell is he talking about, Coffee?"

"I got into it with Paul this afternoon. Trevor broke it up. And if the confessional is now closed, Father Robinson —"

"Paul said you were too good for Coffee," Trevor interrupts. "Coffee took exception. Though frankly, dating you seems to be a health hazard."

Bird glares at him. "I think you've come down with a bad case of correlation-causation fallacy, Trevor."

This surprises Coffee into one of his dart-laughs. "She's got you there, Trev."

"Be careful, that's all I got. And avoid Paul."

"He's your friend," Coffee says.

Trevor looks thoughtful. "For my sins." He exchanges a quick good-bye with Coffee, nods at Bird, and heads back across campus without so much as a glance in Felice's indignant direction. Bird avoids it as well, acutely aware of the audience on the upper school steps. She takes Coffee's hand and drags him down the stairs and out of the range of anyone's stare. She should tell him about Roosevelt's latest salvo, about the bug she kept in a jar, but she'd rather kiss him.

After a while, he pulls back. "This might not be the best idea," he whispers. "I'm sure Marella's told you so."

She forgets about Roosevelt. "Don't even," she snaps. "This is not some telenovela, Coffee. I'm not a curse."

He touches her like he doesn't know how to stop. She braces herself against the reverberations of his fingertips.

"Not because of you, because of *me*."

"You said you loved me."

Now he laughs and pries her fingers, very gently, from his wrist. "I hate to tell you this, Bird, but that does sound like a telenovela."

She smiles, then remembers herself. "Don't you dare break up with me for my own good. Don't even approach that bullshit. If you love me, then . . ."

He is very still. "Then what?"

"*Stay.*"

"Don't worry, *menina*." He flashes his teeth. "I'm too selfish to leave."

She loves his kisses when they're soft and lazy, but she loves these too: hard and challenging and a little angry. It's all him, everything she wants, everything that will stop the rest of it from mattering, even for a few stolen minutes against a wall.

Coffee takes after his mother: the same dirty-blond hair, the same willowy height. Her hair is straighter and finer than Coffee's, her eyes a clear blue to his swamp green. She smiles with reserve when they greet each other, but Bird doesn't blame her for being wary. Bird's role in Coffee's life has been intense, and they've only just started dating.

"Would you like something to drink?" his mother asks. Her accent is stronger, with lilting vowels broadened by Brazilian Portuguese instead of Coffee's polyglot mix of British and American.

Bird wonders if Coffee's mom expects to interview her, and nervously requests tea, which feels safe enough. Coffee squeezes her hand.

"It's all right," he whispers. "Just talk to her for a few minutes and we can go to my room. She's just curious."

"Curious to see the Jezebel who ruined your life," Bird mumbles.

Coffee snorts. "Did that all by myself."

They sit down at his kitchen table, an intimidating slab of striated steel, which would look like something out of an operating theater if not for the glass bowl full of dried roses in the center. The whole apartment seems as though it came to life from the sketchbook of a religiously minimalist interior designer: chrome and molded plastic, shades of beige and white with a single splash of red on the refrigerator handle — an exclamation point at the end of a very dull sentence. His mother moves among the showroom perfection with regal ease, her movements neat and graceful when she pours boiling water from the chrome electric kettle into two mugs. The setting suits her, but Coffee looks awkward and overbright, like a painted farmhouse sandwiched between glass high-rises. He slouches on the molded S-chair and fidgets with a loose end of his knit hat until his mother hands him one of the mugs, three fat tea bags bobbing on top. Bird's only has one, and though she doesn't ask, his mother's lips slip up.

"Alonso likes everything very strong."

Coffee winces at his mother even while he laughs. She looks over at him, exasperated but helplessly fond, and an unexpected stab of jealousy makes Bird stare down at the rough-glazed mug in her hands. It's such a simple expectation, the love of a parent. She has imagined that one day her mother might come to accept her like that: not precisely understanding her daughter's quirks, but accommodating them. Carol Bird would approve of the affluence and cleanliness of this kitchen, but she would have never tolerated Coffee's glaring nonconformity to its aesthetic.

Coffee bumps his knee against hers, a question in his eyes. Bird forces herself to smile and sip the tea, which leaves a prickly burn on the tip of her tongue.

"Alonso tells me you're planning to go to Stanford," his mother says.

"They've delayed admissions," Bird says. "They might even cancel the fall quarter, so I don't know. But I was thinking that I might take a year off. See the world. Maybe I won't apply to Stanford at all."

Coffee stares at her. "When did this happen?" he asks.

She isn't sure — she has avoided thinking about her future for weeks. Maybe this new idea has been percolating in her subconscious all that time, waiting for release. Or maybe it was just the sight of Coffee and his mother, so different but utterly sure of each other's love. She knows she can't have that, and she's so tired of trying.

So she shrugs. "Nothing like a coma and a plague to make you reconsider your life plans."

Coffee and his mother give her the exact same long, considering look, as if they are peering out of a tunnel from beneath their eyebrows. Bird bites her lip to keep from laughing.

"Well, you know," his mother says after a moment, "my Alonso is going through a difficult time right now. We really have no idea when he'll be free to even continue his studies, let alone tour the world. I'm afraid that he doesn't have much time to spend on a relationship."

Bird leans back in her chair, a little surprised that his mother would express her disapproval directly. Bird's only had two boyfriends before, and both of their mothers had glowed with self-satisfied pride to see the girl their sons had brought home for dinner. Of course, both Paul and the long-forgotten Wes had been Black. Is this what she gets for dating a white boy? Or, at least, a Brazilian boy who looks white? But then again, it could be what she gets for dating an ex-fugitive with an ankle monitor. Alone at the hazy crossroads of race and culture and the drug war, Bird struggles to think of what to say.

"Mom!" Coffee slams his mug down on the table. His mother turns to him, her expression imperturbable. She says something in soft Portuguese and he responds in the same language, his own consonants clipped and harsh. She sighs and turns back to Bird.

"I apologize. I shouldn't have said that. I know that high school relationships aren't marriages, I just don't want to see you get hurt. He's not in a position to make a long-term commitment."

Coffee groans and sinks into his chair. "Who said she wanted one, Mom?"

On impulse, Bird leans over and takes his hand. "I do," she says. "Want one. With him."

Coffee freezes. "Not a nightmare," he says softly.

His mother looks between them, startled and hurt and then, for a very brief moment, hopeful.

"For heaven's sake, Emily," she says, her words exasperated but her tone unreadably full. "You aren't Romeo and Juliet."

"No," Bird says, taking his other hand for good measure. Flying or falling, she won't let go of him now. "Just Bird and Coffee."

Bird steals what happiness she can, but nothing can stop the world from flooding back in. Her mother calls just as she and Coffee have fallen back on his bed, scattering the papers and books and pens like confetti.

"Emily," her mother says while Bird stifles her giggles and bats Coffee's hand away, "your uncle is in the hospital. V-flu. I suppose you'll have to bring Aaron."

Coffee takes her hand. Bird stares at him while her mother speaks, mild exasperation the only detectable emotion in that cool voice. "It's a bad enough case that they need to keep him under surveillance, but they seemed fairly confident of a good prognosis. Goodness, what a mess. I had three meetings scheduled this afternoon."

"And Nicky had the nerve to get sick?"

"That's not what I mean, and you know it. But leave it to your poor uncle to catch this just when we're getting the vaccine."

Bird can't trust herself to respond, so she just rests her forehead against Coffee's and stares at his parted lips.

"He'll be all right," Coffee says when her mother finally hangs up.

"Charlotte's mom died yesterday. He could die too."

He doesn't respond, just pulls her closer and, cupping the back of her head with one hand, guides her down to the hollow of his shoulder. She breathes him with long, shuddering breaths, but the terror inside her is too dry and deep for tears. After a few minutes she feels steady enough to pull away.

"I have to get back to school and pick up Aaron. Can I just sneak out the window? I'm not sure I can face your mother again."

Coffee grimaces. "I'll tell her to behave herself. And to give you a ride — she has a driving permit."

And she does behave herself, her conversation guarded but perfectly polite as she gets Aaron from in front of the boy's lower school and then takes them all to GW, one of the District hospitals with a ward cleared for v-flu admissions.

On the ride over, Coffee distracts Aaron with questions about the songs he's learning to play on the guitar.

"'Dock of the Bay,'" Aaron says, ticking them off on his fingers, "'Somebody That I Used to Know,' some Beatles song Mr. Henry likes —"

Coffee laughs. "What Beatles song?"

"Something about wood and a bathtub. It's weird. I want him to teach me twelve bar blues, but I don't know enough yet. But I found the tabs for 'Poison Ivy' online."

At this Bird twists in her seat. "No!"

Aaron crosses his arms. "What? It's a good song."

Bird feels half of her mouth lifting into a grin and forces it back down. "You know exactly why, and don't look at me like that. Do you want Mr. Henry to stop teaching you?"

"The Coasters are awesome. I can play 'Poison Ivy' if I want and you can't stop me."

"What's next, 'Meet Me With Your Black Drawers On'?"

Now even Aaron's mulish frown twitches. "Not in front of Aunt Carol."

Coffee fiddles with the unfastened end of his seat belt. "I am missing something," he says.

"'Poison Ivy,'" Bird says. "Come on, you have to know it!" He shakes his head. Bird's mock-disapproving sigh dives into a hiccupping giggle. "He's gonna need an ocean of calamine lotion, *that* poison ivy."

"It's a plant," Aaron says.

"It is *not* a plant," Bird says, still laughing, remembering her mother's expression when granddad would get to that part on his Coasters collection. She'd been thirteen when she figured it out.

Coffee doesn't know what they're talking about, but she can tell from that half twist to his lips that he's figured out the important part.

"Maybe you could play it for me first," Coffee says diplomatically, and Bird grows aware of a feeling somewhere between her stomach and sternum, something at once painful and beautiful, swelling like a tumor until she has to gasp to breathe.

"Emily, are you all right?" his mother asks softly. Bird twists herself straight again, her cheek pressed against the soft taupe leather seat of the embassy car.

She nods, swallows painfully, and manages a soft "Yes."

His mother purses her lips, exposing deep lines that cross her face like channels of water through rock. But she has laugh lines too, crinkles around her eyes that are deeper versions of the ones that write across Coffee's face when he smiles.

I love him too. She keeps the thought safely inside, but his mother gives Bird one startled glance before pulling into the hospital's visitor entrance. They find Carol Bird sitting in the lobby, typing intently on a razor-thin laptop balanced on her knees.

"Hi, Aunt Carol," Aaron says, taking a few hesitant steps to her. "Where's Daddy?"

"In his hospital room," she says, still typing, "I'll take you there in a minute, but we have to put on quarantine suits."

Bird has a brief fantasy of ripping that tiny, expensive laptop from her mother's hands and throwing it into the revolving doors. Even Coffee's mother looks startled.

"I think we should leave, Alonso," she says softly.

Bird's mother finally seems to register the presence of someone other than her daughter and nephew.

"Oh," she says, lowering the screen. She frowns at Coffee. "Emily, I don't think they'll allow that many visitors."

"That's perfectly fine," Coffee's mother says, her tone frigid. "Because we are leaving. Alonso has a meeting with his lawyer to prepare for."

Coffee and Bird glance at each other from across the maternal battle line. He gives a rueful shrug and the utter absurdity of the situation makes that painful, beautiful thing pop inside of her. They start to laugh at the exact same moment.

"Well," her mother says. "I'm glad someone can find this situation amusing. Emily, what in heaven's name is going on with you these days?"

"I could ask the same of you, Alonso."

He decants his laughter like bottles of too-old wine — most turned to vinegar, but a few precious vintages like this, sweet and dry and redolent of dark fruit. She gets drunk on it until he wipes his eyes and stops, looking warily down at his mother. She snaps something in Portuguese and then walks back toward the entrance.

"Call me," Coffee says, tenting the fingertips of his left hand against Bird's right. He says good-bye to Aaron and Carol Bird, who hardly acknowledges him, and lopes after his mother.

"Emily," Carol Bird says, "I think it's long past time we had a serious discussion about your life choices recently. A *court date*? That woman!"

Bird would laugh again, except he isn't here to understand it. "Mom," she says, leaning over and shutting the laptop with a gentle click. Carol Bird pulls her hands back at the last minute. "Let's see Nicky first."

The entrance to the quarantine ward is crowded with police and soldiers, far more than Bird would expect in a place like this. Are they worried about deathly ill v-flu patients attempting a breakout? She's even more confused when she sees a reporter and her cameraman interviewing a doctor.

"Is something else happening?" Bird asks.

Her mother looks at her and then abruptly away, critically examining the patterned sleeve of her suit jacket as if she's just now noticed a spot the dry cleaner missed.

"One of Senator Grossman's aides was admitted this morning," she says.

Bird might have taken longer to put this together, if not for her mother's obvious discomfort. She remembers where she last heard that name. "Senator . . . the one that you and Dad came back with? Don't tell me, he's one of the rich assholes who broke the quarantine?"

Carol Bird twists her sleeve back and forth between two fingers that are at least a week past their scheduled manicure. "Now, Emily, no one *broke* the quarantine. We had a special dispensation."

"You came back with someone who was infected. And then at Thanksgiving . . . Was it you? Did you give this to Nicky?"

At this, her mother's eyes snap up with their old steel. "There is no way to know *how* your uncle got sick, though I'll remind you the new cases in the city started before we got there."

"Em," Aaron says, elbowing her in the side. His eyes have gone wide. "Does this mean we'll get sick too? Like Dad?"

Bird draws her hands up beneath her armpits. "No," she says, looking straight at her mother. "Because we all have the vaccine."

Carol Bird's jaw has gone stiff enough to crack the bone, but she doesn't say anything. In public, she doesn't dare. She has so much to lose while what little Bird has left seems to trickle between the fingers of her tightly clenched fist. When they push their way to the front of the visitor's line, a nurse checks their names against a list of patients cleared for visitors.

She takes them to a waiting area with plastic benches and signs warning of biohazards and transmission dangers. They each take translucent yellow smocks, caps, gloves, and masks.

"The ward nurse will get you in a few minutes," she says, and leaves.

Even her mother looks unnerved. Bird helps Aaron with his smock, then ties her own, her fingers clumsy and cold.

"The trouble with this flu," her mother says, snapping the gloves over her fingers with an efficiency of long practice, "is that the incubation period is exceptionally long. Really, everyone knows they need to sequester anyone exposed to it, sick or not. But that would lock up half the country, at this rate. So stupid not to do this properly, when it first happened. A few thousand twenty-day quarantines, what's that compared to . . ." She blinks slowly and looks away from the doors and back to her daughter. She had forgotten them, Bird realizes. She had been about to say something she shouldn't.

"Someone made a mistake when this first happened?" Bird thinks of that tender hole in her memory. The forgotten piece she told herself to never forget. Does her mother know it?

"Of course they did," her mother snaps. "Don't you even watch the news? It was a public health disaster."

She meets her daughter's suspicious stare coolly, but Bird catches worry folded into the corners of her mother's mouth, the firm clasp of her gloved hands. Bird almost presses her advantage, but just as she's about to speak she sees Aaron between them, awkwardly pulling down his cap. His father is beyond that door. He hasn't forgotten that for a moment, though Bird and her mother have been trying. They focus on the abstract as a defense against that concrete terror. And they have left Aaron, without these complicated adult fortifications, alone and vulnerable. She wishes for Coffee, who understands Aaron so well. She wishes that Nicky were happy and at home and this was some big mistake. But it isn't, and one of them has to be the grown-up.

She takes Aaron's hand just as the ward nurse — a middle-aged Asian man with a paunch nearly hidden by the quarantine smock — opens the door.

"Nicky Washington's family?" he says, his voice muffled by the paper mask. "Put your masks on and follow me."

The quarantine ward is a large room filled in with a transparent grid of plastic dividers hung from the ceiling on hooks. In each rectangular section are a bed and a boxy air filter. The room must have at least four hundred beds, each one occupied.

"The worst cases are in their own rooms. Your father is responding well to treatment." He leads them down a row in the back. The nurse looks down at his clipboard and then stops toward the end of the aisle. "He's awake," he says softly. "You can stay for half an hour."

Bird squeezes Aaron's hand and he squeezes back. Nicky appears distorted, cartoonish behind the plastic barrier of his tiny quarantine cell. He waves. The nurse unzips the partition to let them inside.

Nicky has an extra white blanket pulled around his shoulders, but he looks oddly exposed without his black do-rag. The few scraggly strands of gray she remembers have multiplied into owlish tufts by his ears, and his ragged ends could use some of that Afro sheen that she stole from him last week. His skin looks gray too, like an ashy elbow, except that it gleams with sweat in the bright fluorescent light.

"Hey," her uncle says, smiling at Aaron. His shoulders are oddly rigid beneath the blanket. For a moment his fear is written plain across his forehead, and then he forces a smile and holds out his arms. "Come here, boy," he says gruffly, and Aaron jumps across the bed to hug him.

Over Aaron's head, Nicky nods at his sister. "Thanks for coming, Carol," he says.

Carol Bird only glances at her brother before turning away, so obviously uncomfortable at the display of emotion that Bird would laugh if she weren't trying so hard to keep from crying.

Her mother's hand closes over her elbow. "Why don't we wait outside, Emily?" she says softly. "I think it's time you and I had a talk."

Bird has grown accustomed to the sight of faces half-hidden by masks, but she shudders at the intensity of her mother's wide brown eyes. Her fear she expects — it hasn't left her for a moment in her mother's company since that day with Felice and her father — but her disorientation catches her off guard. She has changed in the two months away from her mother. And while the emerging Bird is stronger than Emily in many ways, she lacks her defenses.

"I'm going to trust that the boy is a phase. You'll meet plenty at college, maybe someone better for you than Paul. I do like confidence, but there's a fine line and sometimes Paul seemed to have more than his share."

Bird's mouth opens against the cloth mask. "Funny you only mention it now," she says.

Her mother clicks her tongue in annoyance; a lifetime of habit makes Bird flinch against the plastic chair and lower her eyes. "More importantly, Emily, what are you planning to do? The worst of the pandemic is over, now that we finally have a vaccine. Stanford might not even open next year and I don't think it's wise for you to defer your education. I had a talk with your college guidance counselor, and she says that there's a very good chance you can go to Georgetown if you apply for the emergency admissions program."

"Georgetown?" Bird twists her middle finger behind her back and holds onto the pain; something to remind herself that she exists, that she's not just a slug nestled in the divot between her mother's slanted eyebrows.

"It's a wonderful school, and you'll have the edge of being a legacy. You know how hard the pandemic hit Stanford. They've lost dozens of their faculty just from the v-flu."

Bird struggles to remember what she had said about her plans to Coffee's mother. Seeing the world. Not going to Stanford. Not staying in the District. Her mouth feels dry, but she can't coordinate enough to swallow.

"No." Just that. Hoarse and almost inaudible over the background bustle of the quarantine ward.

Carol Bird blinks. "What?"

Bird tries again to summon up the half-illuminated paths to a future she will be happy in, the possibilities she has only allowed herself to discover in her mother's absence. Finding herself. Finding Coffee. She thinks, *There will be a day when I don't give you this power.* She dreams a flash of the future: Aaron playing guitar for Mo and Nicky and Bird and Coffee and even Carol. It's "Poison Ivy," and Mo will laugh till she can't breathe and Nicky will tug on the edge of his do-rag and her mother will sigh and shake her head. And Aaron, proud and talented enough to make them cry, will look right at Bird and give her a sly grin, because you learn all sorts of things when you grow up. Like when plants aren't just plants, and mothers aren't always right or even always good.

"You are *just* like him, my God," Carol Bird says, snapping her daughter like a switch from a willow. "And I tried. Lord knows I tried to give you everything I didn't have. And you'll throw it back in my face? You'll stay with your drug dealer and run some sad little shop on U Street when you could have changed the world? Don't look at me like that — you think I don't know about that pipe dream? Wake up, Emily! Go to Georgetown, get a good degree, make a good living. You might love your uncle — for heaven's sake, you know I love Nicky — but you don't have to go to hell with him too."

"Not hell," she says, twisting her finger harder. "It's only hell when you don't love."

"You think I don't love you?"

It's a question, and her mother never asks her questions. And Emily Bird has an answer. "There is a man who has drugged me and harassed me and frightened me half to death. You know and you haven't done a thing. You tell me to do what he says. You won't tell me *why* this is happening. You won't do anything to make him stop. And then, when Nicky could *die*, you pressure me to go to a school you know I'd hate. You don't care what I feel. You don't care what I think. I'm just your displaced ambition. So no, Mom. I think you love the daughter you wish I could be."

Bird is not always kind, or fair. But she is honest. At her best, she is brave.

We dream of a future with love. Her mother dreams of a future with success.

But not all choices are ours. Not everyone has agency, and a Black woman — even a rich one — knows that better than most. There's a king in our play; there's a god in the wings: King Plague, Lord Death, Her Honor Influenza.

Who will live, O Lord, and who will die?

[dopamine]

$C_8H_{11}NO_2$

Nicky's neighborhood still holds a lingering stink of post-apocalyptic desolation, but Northwest has started to tentatively bloom in these bittersweet final days of the quarantine. The evacuation sirens have kept their silence for nearly two weeks, and though the v-flu finally breeched the wall of the Beltway, healthy Washingtonians walk through Georgetown in tentative twos and threes beneath hastily strung arcades of holiday lights. Most people still wear masks, but a surprising number of the pedestrians Marella and Bird pass don't bother, daring the plague with smiling, cold-chapped faces.

Bird and Marella don't wear masks either, though Marella has pushed her scarf over her lips to keep out the cold.

"New Again Vintage said they were opening for a few hours this evening," Marella says, her voice muffled by the gray-and-black scarf.

Bird, who has never thought much of the DC winter, gives her a dubious look. "We need outfits for a go-go, not prom. *Felice* shops there."

"It's this or the army surplus store, babe. The Salvation Army isn't open."

So Bird shrugs and lets Marella lead the way up to the second floor of the quaint whitewashed brick row house. A woman in a floral mask lifts her head up from a book as the bells jangle in the door.

"Oh," she says, giving them a dubious once-over. "Can I help you?"

Bird and Marella glance at each other, their mutual sigh conveyed in hunched shoulders and shuffled feet. As if there wasn't enough bullshit in their lives already.

"We want some clothes," Marella says, recovering first because her ballet flats and heavy black coat and good hair look more white-respectable than Bird's jeans and nappy, half-combed fro. "For a school dance."

"I'm not sure we have anything you two would . . ."

Bird takes a step back, twisted with anger and embarrassment and, worst of all, that familiar self-doubt, as if she's the one who's done something wrong. She wants to leave and she wants to stay here for an hour and try on every dress in the whole damn store. Marella, though she can't possibly see Bird's expression, reaches behind her and squeezes her wrist.

"Listen, lady," she says, "we go to Devonshire. We just need clothes for a dance and there's not that many places open, so can we just pretend that you smiled and said hello?"

Bird stares at Marella. The woman jumps up from her seat behind the counter, her skin flushing red above the white of her mask. "Of course, I'm sorry, we just haven't had many customers. I'm sorry. I didn't mean for you to think — I mean . . ."

"Some of your best friends are Black," Bird mutters, just loud enough for Marella to hear, and they both burst out laughing. The woman smiles uneasily. She tries to help them, to make up for her initial reaction, Bird supposes, but they wave her off. The prices are ridiculous for used clothes, but they stay. Marella, more amply endowed than Bird in every area, tries on a red dress that makes her look like Lena Horne, and a black velvet pantsuit with silver appliqué that makes her look like Catwoman.

"None of them exactly scream go-go," Bird says.

"It's a *doomsday* go-go. It's gotta be special. Also, I prefer to dress to scare away the horndogs."

Bird eyes Marella's fashion-plate curves. "Not possible," she says.

"Then I'll just have to bring Sarah," Marella says, framing her hips with her hands in the mirror. "She can be my lesbian force field."

"So you two . . ." Bird trails off. She should know this already, but this is the first time she's seen Marella in the two days since Nicky was hospitalized. Marella had to drag her out here this evening, since both of them agreed there was no point in missing the dance. His doctors declared Nicky out of danger yesterday, though he has to stay in the hospital for a few more days.

Still, she could have texted or called. She recalls Charlotte with a pang; this time, she has to be a better friend.

Marella gives her a half smile in the mirror and twists so she can look at the back.

"Does my butt look big in this?" she asks, shaking it.

"Oh, no —" says the woman at the counter.

"Yes," says Bird.

Marella tosses her hair and grins. "I'll take it," she tells the woman, and then hands Bird a pile of clothes. "Here, try these on and I'll tell you about Sarah."

"Let's put it like this," Marella says while Bird pulls on a pair of improbably pink overalls behind the blue velvet curtain in the changing room. "Sarah's relationship status on Facebook has gone from 'single' to 'it's complicated.'"

"This is hideous," Bird says, stuffing her hands into the deep pockets.

"Which one? The leaf dress or the rainbow sequin booty skirt?"

"Uh, Pepto-Bismol overalls."

"I put those in there? Sorry about that. Try the dress."

"Do you think it's complicated?" Bird asks, kicking the overalls to a corner.

Marella sighs. "I think she's beautiful and smart and way too dependent on parental approval and a great kisser and I mostly want to move on except whenever she's nearby."

The leaf dress turns out to be a dress of leaf-shaped pieces of cloth in different shades of green and yellow and rust, stitched together in a pattern of questionable modesty. Normally, she avoids wearing any shade that approaches red, but something about this dress looks worth trying.

"So it's complicated, but you don't want it to be."

"Who does?"

"Half the sophomore class?"

Marella snorts. "Well? Come out here and show me."

Bird adjusts the dress. "I can see my belly button."

"What are you, a nun? Let me see."

So Bird sets back her shoulders and pushes the curtain to the side. Marella jumps to her feet.

"Oh, shit," she says.

"It's the red, isn't it? Not my color."

"It looks very nice on you," the woman at the counter says faintly.

Marella nods. "Yes, that. Seriously, look at yourself in the big mirror."

Though the dress is short and layered with strategic holes and emphasizes all the parts of her body that she has hated for eight years — her big thighs, her small breasts, her absurdly defined biceps, her giraffe neck — it might have been made for her.

No, she thinks, turning slowly in the triple-mirror. Not for her, but for confident, happy, independent, got-her-shit-together *adult* Bird. The woman in the mirror, so solid and strange in a dress made of autumn, isn't afraid of her own power. She knows fear, but it doesn't dominate her. Staring at herself, future and present, Bird feels a moment of dislocation powerful enough to recall her shroom trip. But it's not that she's high, it's that she's here.

"Oh, shit," Bird says.

Marella, still in her bootylicious pantsuit, stands beside Bird in the mirror. "Sarah and Coffee will think they've gone to heaven."

Thoughts of him stream through her mind. Coffee, running down Trevor's driveway. Coffee, watching her dance in Nicky's kitchen on Thanksgiving. Coffee, kissing her and telling her about love.

"Whatever they think," Bird says, "they won't look away."

*   *   *

The summons comes five minutes after Bird and Marella leave the store.

"Good news, honey," her mother says, "it looks like we'll be able to move back home at the start of next week. Now, I know you've been wanting to get a few of your things from your room, and I've been catching up with an old friend who just happens to be able to give the permissions for that sort of thing. Come by our hotel so you can get the keys — bring that new boyfriend of yours too."

This speech, delivered in tones so sticky sweet Bird wants to peel her ear from the receiver, prompts a comment from someone in the room with her mother. Carol Bird laughs, soft and throaty, in response.

"Mom, what the hell?"

Her mother sucks her teeth, just that, but Bird has always been her mother's daughter, and she understands precisely what it means: *Play the game.*

"Didn't you want some shoes for the dance?" her mother says.

Bird glances at Marella and nods. "I do," she says slowly. She doesn't know if she should be afraid for her mother or for herself. She doesn't know what will happen when she takes Coffee to that hotel room with this *friend* of her mother's, but she knows she will.

Because her mother will be in some kind of trouble if she doesn't.

She and Coffee take a taxi to the Mandarin Oriental, on streets that seem strangely crowded after weeks with only buses and government cars. With the quarantine ending, the government has eased most driving restrictions. She doubts this return to normalcy will last another terrorist attack like the one that dropped phosgene gas, but for now she allows herself to hope. She and Coffee have the vaccine, and soon the rest of the world will too. They can have a future — even with his looming trial, even with the hole in her memory.

Coffee is quiet on the ride to the boutique Southwest hotel with views of the Mall and the marina. He rests his head on the fogged window and rubs the soft flesh between her thumb and index finger. He looks tired. She wants to ask him if something is wrong, but she keeps as quiet as he, the only sound in the taxi their breathing and the low drone of the driver's Christian radio station. She's worried about what it means for her mother to insist she return to the house, which holds the only clue to Bird's missing memory. Coffee understood this as soon as she repeated her mother's invitation; with nothing more than a worried glance and a discreet shake of his left leg, she knew that he knew the danger. His lawyer said his ankle monitor wasn't transmitting audio, but there are other ways to bug a conversation.

Her mother opens the door when she knocks, and enfolds Bird in an embrace before she can even say hello. Buffeted by the unexpectedly familiar scent of her mother's perfume and the rigid outline of her bra pressing into her shoulder, Bird goes slack. Nothing about this show of affection is real, but she holds on to every false second. She pretends, as surely as her mother does: She is accepted, she is loved, she is a girl becoming a woman sure of her own worth.

Then her mother pinches her arm hard enough to leave a bruise as she draws back, and they are themselves again: Bird the elder and younger, bound by ties that might once have been as simple as love.

"Hello, Alonso," Carol Bird says. "Come inside and meet Donovan, then I'll leave you guys to it."

Donovan is a large man with curly red hair and squinting eyes. He wears khaki slacks and a blue blazer. His smile when Coffee and Bird walk into the sitting room ought to be open and friendly, but something in the back of it makes Bird stumble on the carpet. He's older, less attractive, probably friendlier, but the moment she looks at him, all she can think about is Roosevelt.

"Pleased to meet you, Emily," he says, extending his hand. "Your mother has told me a lot about you."

She forces herself to take it. "None of it's true," she says.

He laughs and so does her mother; her mother is less convincing. "I met you once when you were much younger," he says. "You've grown into a lovely young woman."

Behind her, Coffee snorts. Donovan looks up.

"You must be Coffee," he says. "I've heard a lot about you too."

Coffee jams his hands into the pockets of his jeans and hunches in elaborate indifference. "I'm sure you have."

Her mother gives her a long look over Donovan's shoulder; she means it as a warning, but Bird takes it as evidence.

"Lukas Group?" she says, bringing back his startled attention. "Let me guess, Roosevelt's boss?"

He blinks. "Coworker, let's say. Clever girl you've got here, Carol."

"Takes after her father," Carol Bird says, knowing perfectly well which half of her marriage has the brains.

"So I hear you want to get some of your clothes for a dance tomorrow night?"

"A go-go," Bird says, wondering how her mother even heard about it. It's the exact sort of excuse her mother would concoct: a reason that a girl shaped like Bird *should* care about, but actual Bird doesn't. But maybe that's the point. Maybe her mother wants her to know about the strangeness of Donovan's visit, wants her to be on her guard. Maybe this time, Emily and Carol Bird are on the same team.

The possibility dizzies her nearly as much as her mother's embrace.

"A go-go?" he says.

Carol Bird laughs. "Honestly, Donovan, how long have you lived in this city?"

"Too damn long, I'd say. But Langley keeps me too busy for the local color. Well, Emily, I've cleared you to visit, but call your mother if anyone bothers you."

Her mother gives her two sets of keys — one for her car, the other for the house. Bird takes them numbly, not understanding half as much as she needs to. They want her to go back to her house — they're insisting on it. A coincidence? Not a chance.

Because they overheard her basement shroom trip and are just as curious about what it means as she is? Because this final clue is the only way to make them leave her alone?

As she takes the house keys, her mother's eyes are full of resignation and trust. Whatever she's done, she's done it for Bird. She'd accused her mother in the hospital of doing nothing to help her.

And these keys, this strange man, are her answer. An answer so dangerous Carol has decided to trust her daughter for the first time in her life.

Bird holds the keys tight in her left hand and nods slowly. *I can do this.*

Her mother smiles. For a bright moment, Bird takes it as a gift, more precious than the embrace because this evanescent, anemic gesture is real. But then she realizes her mother's gaze has wandered past Bird, to the bedroom door that had been closed a moment earlier. Her father braces himself in the doorway, one hand against the jamb. His anger hangs naked in the room, but everyone pretends not to see it.

"There you go, Greg," Carol says inexplicably.

"Nice seeing you again, Emily," Donovan says, not taking his eyes from her father in the doorway.

"Dad?" Bird says.

He shakes his head and turns his back to them all. They watch him too, he said. And Roosevelt did warn her about his boss. Bird watches the tableau — father, mother, daughter, and danger, red-haired — as if she has died and floats, disembodied, above the scene of an accident. Offered, at last, her mother's trust and denied her mother's love.

Only Coffee's warm hand has no place in her nightmare; only he can pull her down to her body, out of the crossfire, into the hallway and an embrace that is everything desired and true.

"I'm sorry," he whispers into her hair, and Bird could cry because for once he has nothing to be sorry for.

Coffee drives. Bird writes.

We pretend we don't know.

She shows him, her handwriting a trembled scrawl that she tries to blame on the traffic.

He cocks his head, a question: *Know what?*

That they're listening, she writes. *We pretend we're looking and no matter what, we pretend that we can't find it. I get upset that I've lost my last chance to get my memory. You comfort me. Then we get the hell out.*

"It's okay, Bird," he says after reading this. "We'll find it, whatever it is."

She smiles. "They might have gotten to it before us."

"But how could they know where you hid the clue, anyway?" His voice sounds normal, but his cheeks pucker on the last word, his heavy eyebrows tilt down, like he's been forced to swallow sour milk.

"They would have looked, since I went back home after Roosevelt released me."

Coffee shakes his head, the lines of his frown deepening, but he still plays along. "Guess so."

She reaches across the gear console and traces one finger down the valley of his bicep. Traffic on Military Road is stop-and-go. He turns to stare at her, the black holes of his pupils devouring his swampy irises, his neck red as a dusty sunset. She snatches her hand back, regrets it immediately, watches him watching her, remembers to breathe.

"This is complete bullshit," he whispers.

The car behind them honks twice, loud and angry. He ignores it.

The anger is for her sake, frustration and exhaustion painfully contrasted with his ironic enthusiasm for the game six weeks ago, when they played at making out in the chem lab.

She leans forward and brushes her lips against the ridge of his ear. "I trust her," Bird says. "She wouldn't do this if it wouldn't stop them."

The honking rises into a chorus, competing Morse codes of

Washingtonian road rage, months of frustration sublimated and redirected at the human-scale target of her mother's white Mercedes.

Coffee whips his head around and gasses the car. The traffic hasn't moved very far, but a few of those drivers sounded willing to kill for six feet of forward motion. He taps his free foot against the door and drums the dash until she laces her fingers between his. His hand is warm, and she wonders what their eavesdroppers might think if she told him to turn down a side street into Rock Creek Park so he could crawl with her into the backseat of her mother's car. She almost asks him, but then he turns to her and smiles and says, "Then it will work, Bird."

She loses her nerve. The morning after she had sex with Paul, he told her he loved her. It felt momentous at the time, but she knows even the most cramped and awkward intimacy with Coffee will change her life forever. She has to know he wants it too. No, she corrects herself, as the road carries them away from DC's most traditional spot for teenage liaisons — she has to know that it will matter just as much to him.

The two-story yellow stucco house she has called home for most of her life looks alien when Coffee pulls the car into the driveway. She remembers Roosevelt dragging her here soon after she got out of the hospital, for no reason she could fathom at the time. She knelt there on the sidewalk and puked on the grass — ambiguous evidence, at best, but he must have taken that as some oblique confirmation that she remembered the night after Trevor's party.

The quarantine tape is a fresh and shiny yellow; someone has been back to visit recently. Probably a whole team of operatives, scouring her house for evidence that she prays they never found. Her mother's shadow has never let Bird feel particularly intelligent, but she has to trust that she's smarter than Roosevelt or Donovan or anyone else who works in the hell of government security contracting. Because if they *did* find whatever clue she left for herself, then why follow her around?

Why spy on her? Their focus hints of desperation, and that gives her hope. All she has to do is make them believe she doesn't know.

And when she does learn whatever this earth-shaking secret might be? She will hurt them with it.

"It might be better if you can't find it, you know," Coffee says as she ducks under the quarantine tape and unlocks the door. He has this look, like he knows this fits well with their charade but he still means it. She shakes her head and turns the knob.

The foyer reeks from antimicrobial foggers, a throat-searing stink of burning tires doused in cat piss and Pine-Sol that makes Coffee stumble back against the doorjamb.

"Smells like someone's been cooking crystal. Badly."

Bird, contemplating her mother's fury when she realizes that her house smells like a meth lab because of nonexistent v-flu exposure, smiles. "You would know."

He coughs. "I would *not*. I haven't cooked crystal in years."

"And I used to think you didn't have any ambition."

"I don't." He smiles, or he bares his teeth; he's all irony today, too tired for even passing joy.

She tries again, teasing. "Not even in chemistry?"

"Not ambition. Obsession. You said it often enough."

"Coffee . . ."

He shakes his head and squeezes her hand. "Where are you going to look first?"

"The writing on the wall," she says. It's strange that she would have even needed Coffee's psychedelic intervention to find the piece of her soul that she stared at every day for five years. And when she understood her mother's plan to make the men of Lukas Group believe, once and for all, that Bird is ignorant and harmless, she knew exactly how to do it. The path of her deliverance seemed to reveal itself, so clearly illuminated she knew someone had been there before her. She had been smart, the Bird of that forgotten night.

He follows her up the stairs. The door to her room is closed, but the wood by the lock is shiny with a recent heavy coat. *Someone tore this apart*, she thinks, feeling the lock. Someone angry, someone looking for something. She leaves her hand there long enough for Coffee to notice, then turns the knob. Inside the changes are more obvious: her sheets and comforter stripped from the bed, her desk drawers opened, her books stacked in loose piles beside the bookcase. They cleaned it up, but they didn't bother hiding their presence. They wanted her to know that someone had searched her things while she lay in a coma. They wanted her to be afraid. Of course they did.

"They've been through here," she says, hoping the tremor in her voice sounds more like fear than anger.

Coffee barks a laugh, and the harshness comforts her. She's not alone in her anger anymore: a gift almost as great as his love. "I'd say so. The assholes couldn't even put away your underwear."

"Oh God," she says. The thought of Roosevelt pawing through her mismatched collection of lingerie thongs and granny briefs revolts her enough, but not as much as the sight of the wall behind her bed.

She expects to see her collection of photographs and illustrations of buildings, the one she's kept since she was ten years old. She stole her very first — a black-and-white photograph of two gorgeous Black girls in ankle-length skirts smoking and laughing on the sidewalk in front of the Lincoln Theatre on U Street in the sixties. She tore the glossy, aging paper from the tight library binding and then returned the book. For weeks she avoided the school librarian, terrified that someone would notice the skip between pages 24 and 27. But Mrs. Walker never did, and Bird never had the nerve for further criminality — when she saw a picture she liked in a book, she looked for it on the Internet and used her parents' color printer. Over the years, the Lincoln Theatre joined a bustling, piebald town, where Hungarian bathhouses were down the street from Norwegian coffee shops and Siberian yurts. She spent evenings huddled with her X-Acto knife over stacks of *National Geographics* bought for fifty cents a copy from Hakim, the possibly homeless guy who had a table of used books and incense by the

Columbia Heights station. Her glance skipped over the most astonishing natural landscapes — glaciers in red sunsets, beaches white as whalebones being licked by crayon-blue water — in favor of crowded cement houses and colorful boats in Elmina harbor and the grass-covered procession of homes along Teotihuacán's Avenue of the Dead. To a stranger, the photographs would look random, haphazard, but that layered architecture traced the path of her life — tree rings growing out from the heart of two laughing, smoking beautiful Black girls Bird would have given anything to be.

They did not steal them. They didn't rip them apart in a fit of rage and throw the confetti around the room. It would have been better if they had.

Someone took her pictures down, checked every bit of sticky tack, every scrawled note, and replaced them, very carefully, on the wall. In neat rows, ten across, seven down, Bird sees her whole life disarranged like a denatured protein, the chains of amino acids unfolded from their proper shape, useless. They did not have to do this.

He did not have to do this.

He could have put them back in the same order, the same unrepeatable pattern, and checked each picture just as thoroughly. He did this because he wanted her to know what he'd seen. He wanted her to be scared. He wanted to disrespect her because he could, and he was glad that she knew it.

"*I hate him.*"

She's surprised to hear her thought out loud, so cold and steady. Coffee's surprised too — he looks away from the marching rows of pictures and flinches at what he sees in her face.

"Bird?"

She glowers at him, though she shouldn't: He's the man in her sights, enough like the white man who's done this to her that for a terrible moment that's all of him that matters — not his sharp swamp eyes or his chemistry obsession or his loyalty or his honesty. Nothing of that miraculous arrangement of neurons and hormones and spirit

282

that makes him *Coffee* signifies beside the overpowering awfulness of his apparent membership in that tribe of self-entitled assholes known as Caucasian male.

Her glare bleeds murderous; his eyes widen and he steps back — hurt, vulnerable, afraid — but this is Coffee and he doesn't turn from her.

The fever passes. Shaking, she stumbles to the bed. "I'm sorry," she says. He watches her, frozen. "I'm sorry," she says again. "It's not you. Won't you come here?"

He does. "I thought you were going to kill me," he whispers.

She rubs her cheek along his collarbone, hard and smooth. "I did too."

He laughs, of course.

Eventually she makes herself find the one picture that matters. The U Street shops from the fifties, Black couples strolling past. He placed it near the center of the anti-collage. A point or a coincidence?

She doesn't know who you are, then-Emily wrote nearly five years ago, in a pen that blotted at the start of each stroke. She fingers it for Coffee, because he won't need more explanation. She will tell him the story of those words one day, of the humiliation and shame and why she never dared to *not* be friends with Felice.

But not now. Not for them to hear.

"They found it," she says instead.

Coffee takes a deep breath, and plays the game. "Are you sure?"

"They *must* have," she says, going for the Oscar. "Or else I only dreamed writing another note. But when we, you know, when I took that thing, I had a really clear vision of my hand writing something and hiding it behind this picture. But now they've moved everything. He must have found it." She pauses, and repeats, just to drive the point: "*Roosevelt* must have taken it."

The old metal frame of her twin bed rattles with Coffee's jitters, but he runs the ball. "Then you don't remember what you wrote? Are you sure, Bird? Nothing at all?"

She shakes her head, warning Coffee not to overdo the emphasis. "Nothing," she says, truthfully. "I have no clue what Roosevelt thinks I know. And I wish I did."

Coffee gives a blustery sigh that tickles her ear. She smiles up at him and takes his hands. "Let's go. I can't stand to see this anymore."

She gives her closet a once-over on her way out. The shoes she's after are in a dusty back corner, but the knee-high brown leather will shine. She can't wait to see what they look like with her leaf dress.

"I can't believe that I still care about that go-go after all this," she says, walking slowly down the stairs. This part will be the trickiest.

"No one can be miserable all the time."

"Not even you?"

He lowers his head and she waits for him, for the kiss that makes her drop the boots down the rest of the stairs and fall hard against the banister and cling to him so she doesn't tip over. A minute later he pulls away.

"I've kicked the habit," he says, joyous, smiling that rarest of Coffee smiles. She can do nothing but stare at him. Her skin prickles with rolling heat, her breath comes short, she shakes with incipient fireworks. Whatever he sees in her face makes him drop her arms and look away.

Her stomach flips with embarrassment. When it comes to desire, she isn't used to ambiguity in her relationships. But with Coffee even that is complicated. She steps down, using the shoes at the bottom of the stairs as an excuse to glance through the open door of her father's office. From this side of the living room she can't see the desk clearly enough. She pauses, frantic for a reason to get closer without giving away the game.

Coffee taps the bannister behind her.

She closes her eyes. She had *fuck me* written all over her face and he looked away. There's so much she doesn't know about him, but she knows this: He'll play along.

Bird is brave; she puts her arms around his neck and pulls him down and kisses him so hard he grunts before kissing her back. She forgets, for long minutes, why she did this in the first place, until he tries to come up for air and she sticks her fingers against the hot flesh beneath his waistband and pulls him over to the living room couch.

She feels, somehow, with her lips and tongue and hands, when he understands what she needs him to do. He sits on the arm of the couch, she sprawls on his lap, then falls over onto the plush gray carpet. He laughs and picks her clear off her feet, and she giggles and shrieks even as she stares at the freakishly neat mahogany desk in her father's office. For the last five years, her father's desk has been an unchangeable, bedrock feature of her landscape. A large calendar blotter covering most of the surface, a telephone on the right side, and a service medal case on the left. And above that, always, the gold pen her father tried to give her that night he spanked her in front of her best friend. He always kept his atonement in the open, as if he hoped she might take it one day.

The real meaning of the writing on the wall, not the one she tried to pawn off on Roosevelt and Donovan and whoever else. But the corner of the desk is empty. The pen is gone. Which means they found it. Which means she wasn't lying, anyway.

Coffee feels her freeze. He lowers her carefully, searching her face for what she can't say. She shakes her head.

"Let's get out of here," he says roughly, which they will interpret in the way anyone would interpret a horny teenage boy making out with his girlfriend. "I feel like your mother's watching us."

Bird laughs, and if the sound is high and thready and a little panicked, she knows how they'll interpret that too.

Bird learned a long time ago that almost everyone lies about sex. To her grandmother, it was the most important gift a woman could give to a man, to be hoarded like a pirate's treasure until the proper moment. Carol Bird was cagey on the subject of the propriety of sex before marriage, but unequivocal that she expected her daughter to avoid it until well after high school. Stacey Goodrow, the senior-class slut, became notorious for claiming that sex was just a biological function that the patriarchy used to control women. Bird doesn't have any moral problems with free love — never mind what her grandmother said — but she discovered after her first time with an exchange student who wasn't even her boyfriend that she has trouble with the details. Sex makes her *feel*. Maybe not lasting love, and certainly not true love, but it has never been something she could do one night and forget the next morning. The vulnerability of it, the nudity and the touching and the profoundly beautiful awkwardness of two bodies fitting together — they tangle her in deep-woven threads.

Which is why she's so surprised when — one hand on the clasp of her bra and the other gripping her hip — Coffee lets her go abruptly and says, "Wait, hold on."

She trembles, the chill air in Nicky's basement more noticeable without Coffee's body against hers. Their shirts are colored puddles at the edge of the carpet, his pants are unzipped and halfway down his ass. The foil of two wrapped condoms reflects the light between them. His eyes are so bright she thinks he might cry.

"What is it?" she manages, panting. She made her decision in the car ride here, and prayed that she was imagining his reticence. She wants him to touch her so badly she aches.

Those long fingers twitch, but they find purchase in the tangled mass of his curls instead of her kinky fro. He smiles, bitter and fierce, and for the first time since he led her from her parents' house, she feels true fear.

"You don't want to?" she says, before he can. The shivering gets worse; Nicky never did bother to winterize the windows down here.

"I . . . Bird, this is . . . *foda-se.*" He shakes his head and puts his hands down, fingers splayed, on the carpet between them. He closes those bright eyes, and when he speaks again, his voice is deeper, his accent stronger than normal. "My first time. Though difficult to believe, I'm sure, given my overpowering sexiness."

Bird laughs, and his eyes spring open. But she leans forward and kisses his lips, nose, eyebrows, curls plastered to the sweat on his forehead.

"God," she says, still laughing though she knows this isn't her most sensitive reaction, "oh Jesus, I thought it was something terrible. I thought you didn't . . . I mean, what you said before, that it wasn't actually true."

"Love you?"

Her giggles feel like champagne. She hugs him just because she can. "Yes, that."

"You and that word. Should I give up my virginity to someone who doesn't even love me?"

His words tease, and his nimble fingers are already unhooking her bra, but she hears the sincerity carefully hidden behind the question.

"No," she says, all the answer she can bear to give him, even now, when the truth of what she feels burns through her like a fever.

He smiles against her cheek when he parses this. "But I should give it up to you, Bird?"

"Yes."

He shivers, and she takes his head very gently between her hands so she can kiss him properly. He blinks slowly up at her, like he's high or drowning, and she thinks that her grandmother was right after all — it is a gift, a pirate's treasure, so rich it steals her breath.

"Stay here," she says, and puts a finger to his lips. He sighs and tilts his head back, neck exposed, throat bobbing with a heavy swallow. She hurries to the record player and hunts through Aaron's tidy stacks for something perfect. It's there, near the top of one pile, like Aaron meant for her to find it. Donny Hathaway, ageless and beautiful, one of DC's lost sons. This is one of Nicky's favorite records, and she tries not to think about the likelihood of a younger Nicky putting this exact same record on for the exact same reasons twenty years ago.

Coffee watches her walk back to him. She sways her hips in time to the music, then panics, wondering how he'll judge her wide B-cup breasts, the curly hair on her belly, her thunder thighs. She never exposed herself like this in front of Paul; they did it in the dark of his room or the back of his car, and she saw more of him than he ever did of her. But Coffee regards her not in judgment but wonder; for the length of that walk, bumpy with gooseflesh and half-naked, Bird is as beautiful as she has always wanted to be.

And Coffee, the fuzzy edges of his mad scientist curls glittering in the low light, the whites of his eyes shot red with exhaustion and desire, his muscles wired and shivering — she drinks him like a dream.

He opens his mouth to speak, but no words come, only a scraping sigh.

"You're so beautiful," Bird says.

She sees this hit, and each pinball ricochet that follows: hope and misery and shame and fear and want —

"I'll take care of you," she says, and catches him — like he's caught her so many times before — and accepts it: his amber, his gold.

After, with his arms low around her belly, her back damp against his chest, his lips trace a reverent path down the vertebrae of her neck and come to rest between her shoulder blades. She vibrates beneath her skin, a tuning fork set off by a resonant pitch, a harmony of skin and sweat and mingled breath in the silence after the record's last song. Her thoughts tangle in knots that begin and end with his name, his smell, his voice. She did not know anything could feel like that; no drug has ever left her so fractured and luminous.

She almost tells him.

"Is it a cliché if I feel like a cigarette?" he says.

"You want to kill me already?"

He pulls her so tight her ribs ache. She doesn't mind. "I want this forever," he says. "I'll settle for the rest of our lives."

Her happiness hurts like an old wound. "That could be a week from now."

"Always optimistic."

"Coffee, I . . ."

He waits, but it was sex, not magic. Some things don't change easily, or at all.

But the difference is, Bird: You *want* it to change. As much as I do.

You see me, sometimes. And not only in your dreams.

[ecstasy]

$C_{11}H_{15}NO_2$

Aaron sits on the bathroom counter, next to the jar of Hawaiian Silky — and the bugged bracelet that Bird has decided is safest left alone. He looks critical as Bird pirouettes in front of the cloudy mirror.

"Your hair looks weird," Aaron says, swinging his legs.

Marella raises recently plucked eyebrows. "That doesn't sound like a compliment."

Bird stops and squints at her hair, tight sable curls unevenly frosted with drugstore silver spray.

"Should I rinse it out?"

"You look great. Aaron, tell your cousin she looks great."

"She looks kind of funky."

Bird turns around and points. "Like, Chuck Brown funky or *Thriller* funky?"

"You look —" Marella stops. "Wait, what?"

Aaron grins. "Chuck Brown funky, for sure."

She puts her arm around him and squeezes. "Then tell me I look hot, kiddo, 'cause we're going to a go-go."

"Em," he says, laughing and squirming, "no way, Em, that's just gross."

Marella looks between the two of them. "Okay, Chuck Brown, god-father of go-go, I get that, but *Thriller*?"

"*The funk of forty thousand years,*" Bird and Aaron quote at the same time, their best Vincent Price imitations, and bust out laughing.

After a minute Marella takes charge again and tells Aaron to move so she can do Bird's makeup.

"Dad says that you guys shouldn't go. Didn't you read that email?"

Marella twirls the eyeliner pencil like Coffee twirls his pens. "Close your left eye," she says.

"Everyone read that email," Bird says, "but it doesn't matter, because we all have the vaccine."

The email was addressed from the administrations of no fewer than five private institutions, most prominently Bradley and Devonshire, declaring that the go-go had been "organized against strenuous public health objections from every school administration" and that in their opinion, the local fitness center had displayed "egregious negligence" in allowing their gym to be rented for the purpose. They neglected to mention that the Beltway quarantine ends officially at midnight, and current curfew regulations allow weekend gatherings. So they threatened disciplinary action for any student attending, and the attending students made fun of them in text messages. Charlotte's go-go is turning into the biggest party of the year.

"Do you honestly think they expect us to stay inside for the next year?"

"I know my mother does," Marella says. "Luckily, I'm at school, not home. And hey, at least we know we're safe."

Bird grimaces, thinking of *how* they know. And yet, her life has begun to feel unexpectedly, suspiciously good. Her mother called 'this morning, after she and Coffee returned to school with wide smiles and no answers for frustrated proctors.

"Donovan understood the situation quite well, dear," Carol Bird said in tones suffused with self-satisfaction. "He's taken care of that man. He won't bother you again. And I hope that as things get back to normal, we can make solid plans about your future."

Bird doesn't trust Donovan like her mother does, but she's willing to hope. "I just need to figure out how to avoid Mom's new plan to send me to Georgetown. Ugh."

"One thing at a time, babe." Marella squeezes her shoulders. "On a scale of hot to nuclear, how do I look?"

Bird takes in Marella's teased beehive, starlet makeup, and ski-slope curves. If Sarah doesn't fall down at her feet, Bird will push her. "Panty-melting," Bird says.

Marella's lips spread wide and red. "Thought so."

The guerilla go-go has a line spilling onto the sidewalk of Wisconsin Avenue by the time Marella and Bird arrive. The old dive of a fitness and community center has hosted its share of Devonshire Bat Mitzvahs, but this might be its first go-go. She's not surprised to see familiar faces selling tickets behind the card table: Gina, Denise, Trevor, Paul. No Coffee yet, though he texted that he would meet her here. Trevor holds a roll of tickets in his hand, but he's not making any effort to give them out; he tilts back in his chair and watches the half dozen soldiers stationed in the vestibule and on the sidewalk.

Marella follows Trevor's gaze. One soldier jumps at the squawk of his walkie-talkie and adjusts his hold on his semiautomatic. "What the hell kind of go-go needs all this heat?" Marella says softly.

Bird hasn't seen this many soldiers since the phosgene attack. By the entrance to the dance floor, Felice argues with Mrs. Early and a police officer. Felice is furious, red-faced and sweating. As her former friend gesticulates with the energy of a silent-film actress, Bird indulges in the schadenfreude of seeing usually immaculate Felice with smeared lipstick and humidity-frizzed hair. She wonders what Mrs. Early could want that has Felice so agitated, but she can't hear them over the vibrating bass from the speaker towers inside.

Not my problem, Bird thinks, as they approach the ticket table and Paul turns his head. He freezes at the sight of her, a sylvan vision in gold and red and silver. She can't help it; she kicks out her hip and stares right back, affecting amused indifference and keeping his frustrated desire like a trophy.

"Emily," he says, "you, I mean, uh . . ."

He casts a floundering glance at Trevor, who smiles lazily and leans forward.

"Paul wants to say you look hot. Don't tell me you both came here stag?"

Marella looks politely amused. "My hot date's on her way, thank you for your concern."

Trevor just shrugs. "Three tickets, then?" he asks.

Bird looks around the vestibule again for the dirty-blond curls, the tapping fingers, the half smile she wants to turn full and real at the sight of her. But he's not here, and her phone sits still and message-free in her hand.

Marella glances at her, sees the answer in Bird's face, and shrugs at Trevor. "Two, please," she says sweetly. "Our dates can pay when they get here."

Trevor meets Bird's eyes for a long, considering moment. "Got that, Gina?" he says without taking his eyes from her.

Bird breaks the unsettling contact and hunts through her clutch for a twenty. She hears, but doesn't see, Paul's mumbled excuse about asking Felice for the latest with the cops. Her chest contracts for a sharp, painful beat — she doesn't want him, but that doesn't mean it's easy to see him chase another girl. Especially Felice.

They take their tickets and move to the end of the table with several Costco-sized bottles of hand sanitizer. Marella's phone buzzes.

"Sarah. She's inside already." She bites her bottom lip. "How do I look?"

"Gorgeous," Bird says. "Go ahead. I'll text you when I find Coffee."

Marella kisses her lightly on the cheek and hurries inside. Bird hesitates by the ticket table until a group of sophomore boys pushes her out of the way. She waits a full minute, ignoring Paul and Felice's whispered conversation in a corner, hoping to see Coffee and wishing he would reply to one of her texts.

"Sure he's coming?"

Bird freezes, startled by Trevor's voice beside her. He regards her with all his typical distant amusement, but she wonders if she sees an atypical concern beneath the mask. "Why wouldn't he?" she asks.

"Well," Trevor drawls, "there is that whole criminal trial on Monday."

Bird feels clammy. "Monday," she repeats, and realizes too late the weakness she's exposed. Trevor, like Felice, feels no pity. And yet it flashes across his face. It occurs to her that she left Trevor's oldest and socially accepted best friend for his mysterious new one. Poor Paul was always competing with Coffee, one way or another. And loving Coffee doesn't mean she understands this friendship, or a dozen other things about him. Of course Trevor knows his court date. Of course he's holding it over her. But he just raises his hand, like he would touch her arm before he recalls himself and rubs his forehead instead.

"He's had a hard time, Emily. Don't . . . well, that's up to you. I wanted to tell you sorry for my part in it. Paul is my friend, but he did a shitty thing that night. And so did I, but hey, you know what it's like to have a mom you can't say no to. I'm not testifying, if that means anything. Coffee is . . . you know, I guess. He sort of gets under your skin. I'm even starting to get what he sees in you. You and Marella look good together."

"Better than you and Felice."

Trevor smiles all the time, but this is the first she's seen him laugh. He laughs like he means it, with a hint of self-mockery; a flash of what he and Coffee like in each other. "See you around, Emily. Bird. Go dance before the cops stop us."

She would ask him more, but he heads back to the ticket table and Bird is left staring at her silent phone and an open door. Coffee promised her that he'd be here. She's worried, but the knowledge that he hid something as huge as his court date from her makes her feel sick and angry.

In the gym, the lurching, funky rhythm churns like her gut. *Whatever,* she thinks, *I can dance without him.* She tucks the phone in the band of her bra and stalks into the heart of the human mass.

She doesn't look for anyone she knows, just feels the slither of silk leaves over her hips as she pops her back. A boy gets behind her to grind, and she lets him, going down until her thighs burn and then coming back up slow, her hips gyrating enough to give her mother a heart attack. *You know what it's like to have a mom you can't say no to.*

"Not anymore," Bird mutters. "Hell no."

The boy gets the wrong idea and backs off. Bird doesn't mind. She dances alone. Eventually she spots Marella and her leggy blond making out against one of the speaker towers. Bird hopes they will avoid permanent hearing loss and glares at a few ogling guys nearby. She looks for Coffee, but has no real hope of finding him. Something has happened, he's facing twenty-five years in two days, and no matter what he gave her last night, he clearly doesn't want her now.

She's surprised by how many people dancing look far too old for high school. Go-gos always attract some of the regular fans, but this room feels packed and feverish, a city finally releasing steam after months of quarantine. Who would have thought a prep school go-go would become the big party of quarantine eve? She looks for Charlotte, hoping to congratulate her on a brilliant job, even if the cops do shut it down. She finds her near the stage, clinging to a freshman boy the same height as Aaron. She's laughing and patting his arms while he holds her up, nostrils flaring like a spooked horse.

Bird pushes her way toward them. "Charlotte!" she shouts over the music. Charlotte turns to her and giggles.

"Emily! I mean, what, it's Bird now, right? Bird, like a birdie."

Bird pulls Charlotte off the freshman, much to his relief. "Is she drunk?" Bird asks him.

He shakes his head. "I don't know! I don't think so. At least . . . there's some E going around."

"Charlotte," Bird shouts in her ear, "did you take E?"

"Don't be a mud stick, Birdie," Charlotte shouts, and laughs so hard Bird has to hold her up by the waist. The hard ends of Charlotte's braids sting where they whip her hands.

"Charlotte," Bird says, "let's get some fresh air."

Charlotte stands straight up and pulls her arm free. "Why are you so mean to me? Emily, didn't you know I always liked you better?"

Bird stares. Charlotte's high, but she looks perfectly serious, almost pleading. "No you didn't," Bird says. "You and Felice —"

"You and Felice," she mocks. "You know what she's like! You were just as afraid of her. Before, I mean. And then you go crazy and cut your hair, but do you expect me to cut my hair too? Am I supposed to let Felice destroy me because you only care about that drug dealer? You chose him. And Marella. But you could have chosen me."

"Felice likes *you* better," Bird tries, desperate. "You're the only person she really cares about."

Charlotte's smile is small and sad. "Felice understands me better. But I could have used you these last few days. I never thought you'd be the one to hurt me."

Bird can't speak. Her ears are clogged with ocean, her heart with silt. Did she give up too soon, too afraid of Felice to try with Charlotte? She closes her eyes, sick with the empty space where a friendship used to be, and so she does not see what's happening until there's nothing she can do.

It starts with a sudden silence, louder than any beat. And then a cleared throat and a deep male voice saying, "Due to a terrorist threat, we're going to have to shut this down. Please head to the exits in an orderly manner and —"

"Hells no, right?" Charlotte's voice, breathless and giggling. "We want our motherfucking go-go!"

Confused shouts and loud conversation fill the silence left by the band. The crowd around her surges forward. Bird stumbles and nearly falls, but pulls herself up on the arm of a man nearby. She vomits in her mouth and swallows it painfully. They would have trampled her to death and not even noticed. Just a few feet away from the stage, she can hardly see anything but sweaty backs and reaching hands. She wants to see what's happening onstage to foolhardy, grieving Charlotte, but she only glimpses shoulder-length braids swinging sharply and the boots of at least four soldiers and two police. Something buzzes against her ribs, and she yelps, terrified of Taser-happy cops before she remembers her phone. *Coffee*, she thinks, and struggles to move her hand enough to reach down the neckline of her dress. It's hopeless; the little room for maneuvering Bird has in this mob she has to use to keep herself upright and alive.

"No," Charlotte screams from the stage, "everyone was having fun! This isn't fair!" Someone must pull her away from the microphone, because next Bird hears the voice from before, repeating his instructions to clear the building. A blast of frigid outside air, a faint whiff of woodsmoke and pine needles and the damp of impending snow, cuts through the humid stink of the mob. Soldiers and police stand near the open fire doors, encouraging everyone to exit the building.

For the space of a breath, Bird thinks that this will turn out okay; no one will blame Charlotte for losing it five days after her mother died, the mob won't trample anyone, the police won't arrest anyone, and she'll find Coffee as soon as she can reach her phone.

Then she sees Felice pushing her way to the stage steps with the force of a battering ram, screaming something that Bird can't hear but knows is Charlotte's name. And as the crowd bows outward, diffusing like a pressured gas toward the fire exits, Bird stands sentinel. Charlotte smiles and closes her eyes. She twirls, a laughing, demented dervish who eludes all the cops' grasping hands until she fetches up against the one by the microphone. And that cop, clearly exhausted and pissed off, pulls his gun from the holster, levels it at Charlotte, and tells her to get on the floor. Felice leaps onstage and hurtles toward Charlotte. What's left of the crowd surges backward, pushing Bird to her knees when the gunshot cracks through the speakers.

Boots trample her hands, a knee snaps her jaw. *Get up now*, she tells herself, *get up or you'll die*. But she doesn't want to — if she stands she'll know who's screaming, and who the soldier shot. She'll know how it ended, the story of three girls who were sometimes friends. So she stays on her knees, panting and trembling to match the steady buzz against her ribs.

Someone pulls her up, hard, by the elbow.

"Come on!" Paul shouts, pushing her forward when she sways. "We have to get out!"

He's furious, his handsome face twisted with fear and frustration. His eyes dart behind her, but Bird doesn't turn around, and she doesn't ask what he sees. He drags her through an unguarded fire door on the other side of the dance hall, away from the stampede. It lets out in a parking lot adjacent to an alley. He tries to go farther from the door, but she yanks her arm away and glares.

"What are you doing?"

"Saving your ass. Not like you deserve it. What the hell did —"

Her phone buzzes again and she jumps. The screen is shiny with her sweat; she wipes it on her dress before looking at the missed calls. Marella and Aaron. The most recent texts are from Marella, asking if she's okay, but when she scrolls down she sees two that rip through her like a bullet.

I need some help. Meet me on George Walk?

And then:

Bird, please. Come find me.

He'd sent that last fifteen minutes ago.

She starts to run and Paul follows her with a shouted curse.

"Emily! Wait! I've got to talk to you! I got this crazy message from Roosevelt. He —"

Bird stops at the edge of the street and whirls around to face him. The ground is slippery with an inch of wet snow, but she just manages to keep her balance. "I don't give the slightest fuck about you and Roosevelt, Paul. News flash: Neither of you are my problem anymore."

"He says you made him lose his job! That I don't have any internship, any summer job. Shit, Emily, you've ruined my career before it even started!"

There's noise from sirens and helicopters and barked orders inside the community center, but the space between her and Paul feels quiet as death. She blinks away the flakes that have settled on her eyelashes and wonders when he changed. Paul was always self-interested, but the years have honed all his worst traits and discarded the best.

She shakes her head. "This has nothing to do with you."

He looks desperate, utterly convinced that he can pin his problems with Roosevelt on a fight with his ex. On any other night, she would feel sorry for him. "Then who? Alonso?"

Bird bites back a panicked sob. "Don't you get it? *Me*, Paul. It was always, ever, about me."

Bird runs. A crowd has gathered to watch paramedics load a gurney into the back of an ambulance. She doesn't look, she doesn't stop, she just prays for Charlotte and keeps running. She can't imagine the trouble Coffee must be in to send her a text like that. She remembers his exhaustion of the last few days, and the heat of his skin last night, and runs so fast she slides over the slick, icy ground. The school is a fifteen-minute walk from the community center. A ten-minute run. Her phone rings and she picks it up without checking.

"Bird! Are you okay?"

Bird glances over her shoulder, but she can't pick Marella out of the crowd behind her. "Yeah, I'm fine. I have to go, I think something's happened to Coffee."

"Holy shit. Where is he? Sarah has her mother's car if it would help. But we have to wait for the emergency stuff to clear before we can get it out of the lot."

Bird sees a cab across the street and runs across four lanes to reach it. "I'm taking a cab. Meet me at school as soon as you can."

"Okay, will do. First Felice, now Coffee . . . listen, find him, figure out what's going on, and call me back, okay?"

Felice.

Bird stutters out the name of her school to the cab driver, but she's thinking about those last moments of the go-go. Not Charlotte on the gurney, not Charlotte going to the hospital with a bullet in her, but Felice. She wipes the tears from her cheeks, overcome with a wave of relief and then self-loathing.

She calls Coffee a dozen times, but he doesn't answer. When the cab pulls in front of Bradley, she throws her remaining twenty at the driver and runs. A mulch path leads to the stretch of woods behind the boy's upper school called George Walk, well-known to hopeful student smokers (well-known to the administration as well, which always made Bird wonder why people kept trying). When she gets to the woods, she slows, shivering despite the punishing pace of her run. She left the go-go without her jacket, and the leaf dress has more holes than fabric.

"Coffee?" she calls. She uses the flashlight on her phone to illuminate the path ahead. Nothing but tall, bare trees, mulch, and the brief shine of a fox's reflected eyes.

"Coffee?" Her voice breaks on the last syllable. After yesterday she can't believe that she spent all night feeling pissed instead of worried. Did she think he changed his mind? That because he didn't tell her his trial date he didn't really love her?

She calls his name again, loud enough to startle a rat from the underbrush. Then she hears the sound of something much larger crunching on twigs and fallen leaves and she spins around. Someone waits in the shadows of the trees.

"Not Coffee," she whispers, and turns off the flashlight.

Roosevelt flicks on his own. "I figured you wouldn't come just for me," he says, stepping onto the path. "So I picked this up." He flips Coffee's phone with one hand.

"Did you hurt him?" She backs up with each step he takes, and fumbles in the dark for the call button. "Where is he?"

"I didn't hurt him, no," Roosevelt says with a grim smile, "but he wasn't looking very good when I left. It took you a long time to get here, Birdie. I don't think you'll be happy if you leave him much longer."

Please pick up. Bird angles the screen of her phone away from him. *Marella, please, help.*

"There was a riot at the go-go," Bird says, struggling to keep her voice as flat as his. "Took a while to get out. Where is he?"

He shakes his head. "Tedious. You know how this goes. I tell you once you give me what I want."

"And what do you want?"

He moves so quickly she doesn't have any time to react. His hand closes around her arm and shakes. Her phone drops to the ground behind her. This close, his face looks haggard and strangely dull, like he's just woken up after a night of heavy drinking. But he smells more like menthol cigarettes than liquor.

"I want you to admit you're lying. You knew about the bug, and so did your mother, and that's why she sent you back to the house. You just put on a little play to convince my boss that I'm off my nut, but I'm right, and he's wrong. The writing on the wall? Do you think I'm stupid? I *know you*, Bird. I know that you wrote that years ago, not that night. Your clue was something else. You wrote it and hid it somewhere. So where? Tell me where, tell me what you *really* know, and I'll tell you where to find your boyfriend before he dies of exposure. Or v-flu. He was pretty sick when I left him."

She starts to giggle. She can't believe that she's finally beaten Roosevelt only to lose Coffee. The cruelty of it, after everything else she has seen tonight, threatens to break her. They *took the pen*. They have her clue, whatever it is, but he doesn't know what it means any more than she does. Roosevelt has never mattered less to her, and he has never seemed like more of a threat.

"Are you high, you hypocritical cokehead?" He flinches. "Your career is over. Whether I know anything or not. But for the record, I don't. You've been chasing windmills this whole time."

"Coke, huh? I'd say you know plenty. You're much smarter than they give you credit for. And after all the good we've done, never mind that one mistake — I won't let you ruin everything. This country is worth more than your games."

Her exposed flesh burns where his fingers grip, but she pretends that she can't feel him. She pretends that her body is a fortress, and her words are flaming arrows.

"I only know what you told me, Roosevelt David," she says, slow and loud. "If underestimating me is a mistake, then you were the first to make it."

He tries to push her, but she uses the momentum to spin away from him and scoop up her phone.

"Tell me," she says, panting, a few feet away. "Please, Roosevelt, *please*. Coffee has nothing to do with this. You can't just let him die because you lost your job."

His shoulders twitch. He stares at her, hollow-eyed and hungry, but he doesn't approach. "I think I could," he says softly. "It might make me feel better."

"There has to be a human somewhere underneath all that."

"Fuck you," he says, and turns his back.

She finds him behind the chapel, curled on the flagstones. A dust of snow covers him like a faerie blanket. For a hard moment, she thinks that she found him too late.

Then he shivers and coughs.

She calls Marella. "The chapel," she says, kneeling down in her wet tights and pulling his head onto her lap.

"We're driving there now. Sarah, turn up the heat —"

"No." Coffee's eyes open and close. "An ambulance." His skin feels hot where it isn't cold as the snow. It took her twelve minutes after leaving Roosevelt to find him. She can't think, right now, about what that means.

She hears Marella swallow her questions. "I'm calling. Right now. We'll be there in a minute. Hang on, babe."

Bird drops her phone in the snow and wraps her arms around him. At least he's wearing a jacket and gloves.

"I'm sorry," she whispers, holding her head close to his frozen cheek. She is almost sure he can't hear her. "I love you so much. And I'm sorry."

His eyelids flutter, his hand twitches, and for a moment she imagines that he'll come alive in her arms and tell her everything will be okay.

But he only sighs; he doesn't wake. He leaves her alone in the silence of the snow and her misery and their love until the flashing red lights tell her that it's time to let go.

This is the story of a girl who knew something, and understood nothing at all.

This is the story of a girl who found something, and lost everything else.

This is the story of a girl who remembered something, and forgot why it mattered.

But this isn't a tragedy.

This is the story of a girl who loved someone, and told herself the truth.

[oxytocin]

$$C_{43}H_{66}N_{12}O_{12}S_2$$

They take out his blood and they put it back. They cut off his clothes and drape him in linens, clean and faded blue. They run tracks of needles down his arms and cover the violence with shining white tape. Tubes hiss air into his nose, drip IV fluid into his veins, keep the steady watch of his steady heart.

Saved from the cold, he burns hot as a DC summer. He wakes up in the middle of one long afternoon, two days later.

"You're all right?" he asks. His eyes, open and lucid, are all she has dared pray for. She peels off her gloves and takes his hand. She can't speak, so she calls for a nurse instead.

That night, the infection goes to his lungs.

"It would be best if you didn't come again until he's better," his mother tells her in the hallway outside the ICU.

The worst is that she means it kindly, to spare her what might be a death watch.

Dread pulls worn claws through her stomach. "I want to stay."

"Go home," says his mother. "Get some sleep. I'll call you when something changes."

"He hates hospitals."

This makes his mother laugh, low and bitter and short; she has never looked more like her son.

"I know far better than you. Go home, Juliet."

Bird falls asleep in a bathroom stall when her eyes hurt from crying. She dreams they're dancing in the snow to Donny Hathaway until a janitor pounds on the door. Reality hits her like it always does, a jump into icy water from a high bridge.

She doesn't go home.

"Dad," Aaron says, leaning against Nicky's legs, "tell me the story about Pops and the chickens."

Nicky looks tired, but mostly healthy. His hospital stay ends tomorrow, which means one more bed will be free for the increasing numbers of critical District v-flu patients.

Nicky squeezes Aaron's shoulders and laughs. "I can't tell it as well as your pops, but all right."

Curled at the end of the narrow bed, Bird listens. She loved it when her granddad told this story, with that sweet pipe tobacco curling toward his rapt audience and his slippered feet up on the recliner.

"So your granddad had an uncle who loved pigs' feet," Nicky says, leaning back against the pillows. "Uncle Spanky would bring jars of the things, pickled, to any big meal at your granddad's house, no matter how much my grandma would holler at him for it."

Aaron giggles. "'Cause they stank?" he asks.

"Stank like the devil's behind," Nicky agrees, and Bird cracks a smile at his imitation of his father's voice: *bee*-hind.

"So your pops got this idea about how he'd stop Uncle Spanky from bringing those pigs' feet back around to his mom's house," Nicky says, and goes on to tell the rest: the sly, old hunting dog that was always trying to get into the coop, Uncle Spanky's weakness for cheap whiskey, and the laying hens that broke into the house just when Pops was tossing the pigs' feet into the yard for the dogs.

Bird closes her eyes, giving in to the comfort of the story that she's heard two dozen times before. When the old hunting dog runs back and forth, howling, trying to choose between the pigs' feet and the chickens, Aaron laughs until he falls onto Bird's back.

"Did you hear that, Em?" he says, and then sets to howling like the dog in the story until Bird sticks her hand over his mouth.

"Hey, do you want us kicked out of here? What if someone notices you took off your mask?"

Aaron rolls his eyes, but he keeps quiet. Playing with the hospital rules would be a more serious offense if they hadn't both been vaccinated (the documentation of which her mother has quietly provided), but she doesn't think the ward nurse will look the other way if they disturb other patients. Nicky starts to tell the story again and Bird drifts off, thinking about the hallway behind them and the isolation room she's not allowed to visit.

He got the vaccine too late; she knew that as soon as she saw him in the snow. Thanksgiving: the day her parents came back in an exposed senator's entourage; the day he told her he loved her; the day she crawled inside her own mind and looked around. The memory of one of the best days of her life makes her want to vomit with self-recrimination and guilt. She kissed him and killed him, between the turkey and the sweet potato pie.

She clamps her hands hard around her sides, but it doesn't stop her from shivering.

"Em?" Nicky's voice, soft and careful. Aaron's fallen asleep. "Hey, kid, how you holding up?"

Even when Marella asks, she finds a way not to answer. Her mom has hardly spoken to her, uncomfortable with Bird's hospital vigil and any portent of her grief.

But Nicky watched his girlfriend die of ovarian cancer ten years ago, and though she doesn't remember much about her Aunt Valerie, she does know that Nicky has never expected anything from Bird but herself.

"I keep forgetting that it's real," she whispers, focusing on the tiny, perfect weave of the hospital blanket. "And then I remember and I . . ."

"Yeah," Nicky says, "it's like that too. But you'll survive, Em. You might not want to, sometimes. But remember that you'll survive."

"His mom calls me Juliet."

He snorts. "Em, you're a hundred times smarter than that chick."

She doesn't look up, but reaches her hand over Aaron's sleeping body and waits for him to take it. He does, and rubs the soft flesh between her thumb and forefinger so she cries a little with the comfort. How did it take her so long to understand the basic goodness at the heart of him? Her mother was never *wrong* about Nicky, Bird supposes, but she has never been right.

"Is it that bad?" he whispers after a minute.

"His lungs." The awful truth, out loud.

"Shit."

She sighs, floating in the release of that solitary burden. "I love you, Nicky."

"Em, what you've done for Aaron when I've been stuck here, and before, you know . . . hell, you're like my other daughter, you know that? God knows how Carol gave birth to you, but there you go. I'm sure she's asked that herself, knowing Carol."

"Knowing Carol," Bird agrees, and squeezes his hand, her other father.

Nicky goes home; Bird stays. She sometimes sees Charlotte pass through the hospital waiting room, a fellow soldier armed with water bottles and wedding magazines and fat bouquets of flowers. Bird never asks; she can tell from the growing stack of magazines that Felice isn't doing well. For the first few days, journalists loiter outside for news of her condition; the shooting has become the latest horror in a news cycle full of them. Felice ran straight toward the cop, ignoring all of his warnings to stop. But though the DC police chief defended him, the fact that he was a rookie at the end of a long shift only contributed to the national outrage. Charlotte never stays for long — she trains her hollow eyes on the elevator and then walks through, a firefighter running again and again into a burning building.

Bird has never been that brave. Even now, she hides in the hospital because she can't bear to go home and she can't think of a way to change his mother's mind. He's not any worse, that's all his mother says, after telling her again to leave. Bird catches herself staring through the tinted glass at the smokers outside, envying their perse-cuted camaraderie, their craving-induced punctuation of the hours that bear down on her with the mercy of an avalanche. She ought to hate the sight of them — Coffee's habit almost certainly helped the infection bloom in his smoke-stained alveoli — but she just remembers the smell of loose tobacco and the way his hands shook that night when she fol-lowed Paul up the stairs.

Marella comes to wait with her when school gets out, bringing gossip and a bag of Julia's empanadas from Adams Morgan, still steaming.

"Ms. Vern says the UC schools are going to reopen in the fall. Stanford hasn't announced yet, but they probably will too. So reapply and, voilà, escape."

Bird chews slowly, making herself focus on the flavor of the chorizo and semisweet crust. "What are you going to do?" she asks.

Marella laughs. "Go wherever I get the best scholarship."

"Do you think I could just follow you there?"

"What if I get a full ride from Georgetown?"

"Then I'd be sure God hates me."

Marella bites her lip and puts her hands on Bird's shoulders. "I know you're not okay," she says, "but you'll tell me if it gets too bad, right? If there's something I can do?"

Bird feels sticky with days of unwanted sympathy, but she loves Marella for this. She nods and listens to Marella tell her about school and city protests and her latest argument with Sarah — a reminder that everything doesn't end with sound of the boy she loves struggling to breathe. But eventually Marella leaves. Alone again, Bird rests her head on her raised knees. She waits for Coffee's mother to give her a grudging update, but instead her phone rings for a different reason entirely.

"Em, it's me," her dad says. "I'm outside. Alonso's mother called me. It's time I took you home."

Bird presses her forehead against the window and watches the holiday lights blur past. Her father turns down the already low volume of the public radio station and clears his throat.

"Not a good time, Dad," she says, before he can speak. She knew Coffee's mother didn't like her, but she'd never expected the contempt of an end-run to her parents. Doesn't it matter to her how her son felt?

"Emily," her father says, awkward as a ninth grader asking his crush to dance, "I know this is hard for you. . . ."

"Then why are you talking?"

He flinches, but he doesn't reply, just turns up the volume like he always does. It's a story about the go-go riots and martial law protests now that the quarantine has ended. Bird stares straight ahead when the reporter talks about a student being "critically injured" by a soldier in the chaos. Her dad doesn't seem to hear; when he glances at her, she can tell that even her best Carol Bird impression won't stop him from saying his piece. She feels pathetic enough to crawl under the wheels of the car, but of course she doesn't. *You'll survive*, Nicky told her, a comfort and a prophecy.

"That night," her father says, so softly she leans toward him, "the night of the party, your mother was out of town, but I had come back. She was worried about the quarantine. She wanted to get some . . . things from the house, in case we couldn't get back to the District."

Bird jerks back. "You were *here*? When I came back to the house, after what happened, did I talk to you?"

"I never saw you," he says even more softly than before. Does he whisper because he's afraid of someone hearing, or because he's afraid of her? "I packed while you were at school. And after I went to visit . . . a friend."

"A friend," she repeats, understanding precisely what he means and wishing she could feel surprised. Lord knows she can't blame him for seeking comfort in arms less constricting than Carol Bird's, but she also hates the cowardice of the backdoor escape, the silent betrayal of vows that must have once meant something.

"Emily, your mother and I . . ." Even he can't finish the sentence.

"You've never heard of divorce?"

He glares at her, which is a surprise. "We have a partnership." He hits the steering wheel for emphasis. "Professionally, we're famous for it. But personally too, with you. I can't just rip that up for better sex."

"My God, I don't want to hear about it. You're never even *home*, so don't use me as an excuse."

"I know that we haven't been able to spend as much time with you as other parents, but you've grown into an intelligent, capable, independent woman, haven't you? Independent enough to ignore my warning." He sighs. "And it's probably better that you did. That man needed to get put down."

Bird's heart fills with a volatile mix of disgust and pleasure, wondering if he means that someone killed Roosevelt. She doesn't ask; if Coffee dies, at least she can dream of what happened to the man who left him in the snow.

"If you'd been home that night," she whispers, "none of this would have happened, would it? You would have been able to stop it."

"No, Emmie." He whispers too. "No, and I'm so sorry, but it probably saved us both that I wasn't. The whole reason that man came to the party, the reason that he wanted to meet you was because I had . . . said something I shouldn't. Given them reason to doubt. They wanted to know what you knew because of me. If I had any idea they would go after you, I never would have opened my mouth. I thought we had protected you enough, been careful enough, and I was wrong, and I'm sorry."

Bird nods, pretending any of this makes sense. She feels her face to make sure that it's there. Two months of hell because of her father's work disagreement? "What did you do?"

He ignores her question. "When I got to the house that morning, I could see you'd been there. Mud all over the floor, I guess because you walked through the park. Carol called and told me you were in the hospital. Safe. So I left."

She thinks again of Coffee's mother-turned-lioness, and laughs. "Dad of the year," she says.

"I had no choice! You were in trouble no matter what I did, but we could help you more doing our jobs —"

"Saving the world?"

This stops him. He turns onto their street and stops the car before he speaks again. "From itself. I've had to reconsider a lot lately. I can't imagine what you've been through, but it hasn't been easy for me either. I want you to know that I'm proud of you. I picked this up when I went back to the house, because I hoped that you might be ready to take it."

He reaches into his jacket pocket and pulls out a black leather case. Inside, the gold pen. He looks at her, steady and, for once, not at all distant. She understands. That morning, when he came back to the house, he saw that she had moved the case. So he took it before Lukas Group ever knew it was there.

Her lost clue is the Trojan horse for her father's absolution. That's what this pen always meant to them, even before she knew the scope of her father's betrayal.

She hesitates, and then holds out her hand.

His mother calls the next afternoon: "He's asking for you."

Bird digs her fingers into her thigh. "Is he . . ."

"Better enough to yell at me. Come, I won't stop you. Make him happy."

311

Bird spares ten minutes for a quick shower and a fresh set of clothes. She's in the car when she realizes that the sweater she pulled from her drawer is an old one of Mo's, a pink hoodie with the word "fresh" blazoned in a glitter cursive across her chest. It looked better on Mo.

Bird hears his mother in the hall before she turns the corner. It's the undercurrent of alarm, not so much the words, that stops her: "*Two years?*"

A man answers, "He could get twenty if he's convicted on all counts."

His mother says something in soft Portuguese. "I thought you said the case should be dismissed?"

"It should. Prosecution's case is riddled with inconsistencies. But the judge is buying their arguments, so we'll have to try again on appeal."

"You don't think he should take the plea?"

A long pause. "There's something off about this case, Maria. The prosecutor is pushing it hard, more than he should, frankly, given the mess the cops left for him. Alonso thinks . . ."

"He thinks it's about that girl."

"I wouldn't have believed it myself, except I met the man he's talking about. Some CIA contractor type. The situation is strange, I'll give him that. He might regret refusing the plea."

Bird makes herself turn the corner before they can say anything else. His mother's mouth drops in comic surprise before she collects herself. The lawyer smiles slightly and shrugs.

"Roosevelt," she says, "that man, he's . . . fired or something. Shouldn't that make a difference? If he's not after Coffee anymore, then there shouldn't be a case."

The lawyer — Bao, she remembers — frowns and steps toward her. "You're sure?"

Bird swallows, remembering her father's confession last night. "Yeah."

"You heard what I said about the plea bargain? I got that call this morning. Maybe this CIA pressure goes higher than that one operative."

She shivers. Roosevelt did warn her.

"The district prosecutor isn't going to just drop it without a reason — probably the same sort of pressure that made him pick it up in the first place."

"So we need leverage," Bird says.

He looks over his shoulder at Coffee's mother, who rolls her eyes. "What Alonso needs is some common sense!"

Bird glares at her, then realizes she might change her mind about visiting Coffee and stares intently at the paper booties covering her tennis shoes.

Bao clears his throat. "If you find any of that leverage, Bird, let me know."

Bird has leverage burning a hole in her pocket, if only she could understand it. She meets his kind, intent eyes and nods.

"Go on, Emily," Coffee's mother says loudly. "Bao and I have some further business to discuss." The indignant subtext is hard to miss, even as she runs past them.

He smiles to see her when she freezes in the doorway of his isolation room. He is awake and alive, two adjectives she has regularly demanded of any passing deities, but she is greedy, and she immediately wants more.

His hair is plastered wet against his ears and forehead, and sticks up everywhere else like damp hay. His breathing wheezes, though not so badly as before. He looks as sick as her grandma did, when they took her to the hospital for pneumonia. Her grandmother never did come back home.

"Is it a cliché to say you look like shit?"

He tries too. "Nice shirt. Did you wear that to the go-go?"

Bird jerks like he hit her. She pulls up a chair, tries to pass it off, but she should have known better.

He takes a deep breath; she wishes he wouldn't. "I'm sorry," he says, hoarse. "I —"

"Don't." She makes herself look at him. "I'm sure it was way worse for you than for me."

"I wasn't awake for most of it, remember?"

"I remember."

They stare at each other for a minute, then two. He reaches for her gloved hand. Easier to speak this way, palm to palm, reading the volumes in his eyes, than with words he doesn't even have the breath to say.

But then he says them. "What's happened, Bird?"

"Too much."

"Highlights?"

"Your mother hates me?"

His abrupt laugh gives way to a coughing fit. When it ends, he says, "She doesn't like me much at the moment either."

She squeezes onto the edge of the bed, desperate to touch him, as if he can't really be sick as long as she can feel the weight of his shoulders pressing against her arm. "She loves you." She can't say any more. One day she'll tell him about the time Greg Bird saw his daughter's nightmare tracked in mud and leaves over the marble floor of his perfect house — saw it and left anyway, with a bomb in his briefcase.

Besides, Coffee knows the shape of it — no one understands her parental psychodrama better. He isn't stupid enough to say anything. They just lean against each other and breathe, happy to be alive and together, especially in this place, where nothing has seemed less sure.

"You still have something to tell me," he says, touching her neck.

"How do you know?"

"You breathe differently when you want to say something."

"Oh." She reaches into her pocket. The things they know about each other aren't things you know after a few weeks of dating; the way she feels about him overwhelms her with the vastness of its uncharted territory.

314

She takes out the pen. "My dad had it all along," she says, whispering out of habit. She unscrews the base from the nib. A piece of paper is wrapped carefully around the ink cartridge. She hands it to him. Coffee glances at the door, slightly ajar, before unrolling the paper.

On one side, in her own handwriting, are the words:

california boy asked doctor about mom & dad — didn't understand — but doctor said that it was the fault of the screwups at the FBI, what was their plant thinking giving the FARC guys the real virus? And c boy said you could only do so much with used-car salesmen — didn't understand — and anyway the chances of mutation had been one in a million. the new flu?

She's tried all night, but she can't remember a shadow of this conversation that she risked so much to record and keep safe. All she has are these cryptic sentences, hinting at a truth so damning that she understands, finally, all of Roosevelt's rage and paranoia.

Coffee lifts his head slowly. "This means . . . Bird, what you overheard . . ."

"I think so too," she says. "Turn it over."

The long string of molecular notation is so complex that she couldn't even figure out a way to plug it into a search engine. She knows she didn't write it. His eyes widen at the sight and for the first time since she entered the room, his hands start to twitch. Chemistry, his first love, holds him in her embrace and Bird smiles in relief to see it. "You overheard this too?" he asks.

"Not my handwriting," she says. "Besides, no way I could remember all that just from hearing it, especially not pumped full of that drug."

"Then who —"

He starts to cough again.

"I should go." She's shaking. His mother and Bao talked as if he was out of danger, as if they didn't know that teenagers are in the worst risk group for v-flu mortality. How could she drag him into this again?

"No." He takes her wrist in a surprisingly strong grip. "Stay, we don't have to talk. Please, Bird."

It's his eyes, not his hand, that stop her. Eyes as panicked as she feels, as deep and as adrift.

She takes off her shoes and curls up beside him.

"It's okay," he says, "you can sleep."

"No talking," she mutters.

His laugh rattles against the phlegm beneath his ribs, but it still carries her, dreamless and content, to sleep.

Hours later, they both wake up.

"I need a computer," he says.

"Because you want your mother to actually kill me?"

"Don't you want to know what that molecule is?"

She did, before. She'd been plotting out her leverage and exactly how to apply it. "I want you to be healthy."

"So do I, but this is something I actually have control over."

She asks the ward nurse for a computer. He works until he shakes with exhaustion and a nurse turns out the lights. She wants to stay, but his mother makes her go home again. Carol Bird gives her a long look, full of judgment, when she stumbles into the kitchen near midnight.

"Out of curiosity, are you planning to attend classes anytime before the New Year?"

Bird raises aching and salty eyes and says, simply, "No."

What Carol Bird sees there, she does not know, but her mother goes back upstairs without another word.

The next day and the next she visits him, though there are times when she has to sit in the hallway while he sleeps or the doctors talk with his mother. Bao visits once more and she wonders if he's representing a dying boy, or just one in a great deal of trouble. If they get out of this, she suspects that Coffee will spend his life finding trouble, one way or another. She dreams of a future where they can find it together — where her Bird pragmatism can temper his Coffee radicalism. Which is to say, she dreams of a future where he survives.

She gets a call from the dean, sympathetic about the *situation* as explained by her mother, and letting her know she can make everything up next semester. First Roosevelt, now school — she's had more help from her mother in the last two weeks than she's had for the last five years. She wishes that it made her feel safe and protected and loved; but even now, a part of her is afraid of the blow.

His skin glows translucent under the hospital lights; the tracery of veins on his lowered eyelids are a lost language on ancient parchment. He had a bad night, and now he sleeps with her pen clasped tight in his right hand. When he wakes up, he smiles to see her.

"I figured it out." His voice is so shredded she has to lean in to hear.

She closes her eyes, but the tears have crept up too quickly to stop. She hunches in the chair and hates herself, sobbing and choking when she's supposed to be the strong one, the one who will get them through this.

His hands in her hair. His breathless voice, coaxing her to sit beside him, to lie down, to wipe the embarrassing strings of snot off on his hospital gown. This makes her laugh, at last.

"I am a lousy date," she says.

"Then I guess we're even."

She has a sense that she will remember this forever: the antiseptic and detergent scent of his isolation room, his labored breaths, the muscles of his back, tense beneath her shaking hands. The present glows and blurs with the afterimage of its memory.

"Why does falling in love feel like sleeping with a loaded gun?"

He pulls her closer. "I'd never hurt you, Bird."

She shakes her head. "It's the twenty-first century, Coffee. Cupid packs heat."

Eventually she picks up her mantle and sword, she hunches her shoulders and ignores her heart and asks him, "So what does it mean?"

"Short or long version?"

"Short."

"It's a protein that the v-flu codes for. Part of what makes it so deadly. But that exact stretch of DNA isn't found on any known flu strains."

"But that could still mean some Venezuelan scientist developed it, right?"

He stops at that and, inexplicably, kisses her forehead. "It's not the scientists' fault, you know. They learn about the world; it takes governments to destroy it."

"You would say that."

He sighs. "Get the laptop?"

She pulls it from beneath the bed and watches as Coffee scrolls through his email. The last ten messages are from Aaron.

"What's Aaron bothering you about?"

He grins. "We've been sending each other music. He now likes Caetano Veloso, and I now understand the genius of seventies-era Stevie Wonder."

"*Songs In The Key Of Life*?" Bird asks. "I love that album."

"He said you did."

"Oh my God, are you getting romance tips from my eleven-year-old *cousin*?"

"Hey, I know when I'm out of my depth."

She feels soft and warm and content, which makes it more of a shock when Coffee opens a PDF file sent from a university email address.

Potential Influenza Virus Targets for Artificial Protein DNA Splicing Technology is the less-than-gripping title of the paper written more than a decade ago.

"I appreciate that you have such respect for my intelligence, Coffee, but this is your area of obsession, not mine."

"The authors," he says quietly.

The paper has four writers, but only two of them matter: *R. Wasson, F. Koramis, G. Bird, C. Bird*. The windup and the punch.

"That sequence," she says, steady as death, "the one on the v-flu. It's in this paper?"

"With some modifications."

"What does it do?"

He hesitates. "It's not entirely clear . . . things get messy in actual human bodies, and there's major changes in the genome of the v-flu from anything in this paper. The thing you wrote down, it sounded like the virus mutated after its release, that was what caused all these problems —"

She stops him with a hand. "Just tell me, Coffee."

"The incubation period," he says. "It's unusually long. That's what this codes for."

The unusually long incubation period that has allowed what might have otherwise been an unpleasant, localized outbreak to turn into a devastating global pandemic. She presses tight fists against her eyes until the pain distracts her. "Five million," she says. "You."

"Whatever your dad did, he's sorry."

Because who else could have written down that sequence, the smoking gun that proves the real origins of the "Venezuelan" flu?

"That's why we got the vaccine so quickly, isn't it? Even if it mutated, they at least understood where it came from."

"Your parents probably helped save millions of lives."

She snorts. "They always acted like they were saving the world. They never said it was from themselves."

He rubs slow circles on her back. Even now, he doesn't blame her. It would be easier if he did.

"What are we going to do with this, Bird?"

For a moment she allows herself to imagine it: the scandal of discovering the FBI botched a terrorist sting and released their own deadly bio weapon onto an unsuspecting population. The excoriation of scientists like her father and mother who helped to develop the worst flu outbreak in over a century and covered it up. She would go to the press and tell her story and no one would dare touch her.

But they could touch Coffee.

She swallows it down, that sweet confection, and comforts herself with the reality of his stubble against her forehead. "We use it," she says, "to get you free."

They argue about it for the next day; short, sniping volleys that would make her want to shake him if he didn't look like he would break apart from the force.

"This is huge news, Bird," he tries. "The world deserves to know."

"The world can figure it out later. You deserve to not rot in jail."

"You forget the problem of me being guilty."

She stalks to the vending machines and takes her time coming back.

"If you do this, we can be together," she says.

He hunches forward, pupils dilated with some new drug. "I thought we were together."

"And when they ship you to Sing Sing?"

"What, you wouldn't wait for me?"

"My whole life," she says, and turns away from his smile.

In the afternoon, Bao visits, bringing the bad news she's come to expect from him. "The prosecutor is contesting the delays. He says we can go forward if Alonso gives video testimony."

"From his hospital bed!" his mother shouts, saving Bird the trouble.

"I'm fighting it," Bao says, but they both know that he might not win.

Coffee gets his mother to call Trevor, who stops by an hour later. Bird glares at him, and he smiles back sadly. Trevor and Coffee's sprawling, gleefully implausible conversation completely excludes Bird, as Coffee intended it to.

"But if the universe was self-aware, there'd be evidence somewhere. You can't just argue something like that based on probabilities."

"God, you're such a chemist. Quantum physics says you're wrong."

"Quantum physics says that there's a nonzero probability your head will turn into a dick, but you don't see me pulling out a condom, do you?"

There's a slight pause, during which Bird wonders if she ever heard someone rib Trevor Robinson like that. Should she intervene? But then Trevor actually laughs. "All right," he says, and puts his gloved hand on Coffee's shoulder. "I'll give you that one."

"Taking pity on the dying friend, is that it? Whatever, I'll take what I can get."

Trevor stands. "Get some rest. Don't die. I'm saving my best arguments for when you get out of here."

Bird follows Trevor into the hallway. "Thanks."

"Don't," he says, and then stops, as if he's run out of words. He shakes his head and then hugs her, awkwardly and full of truth. After he leaves she goes to the vending machine and by the time she gets back Coffee has fallen asleep.

Is it okay, Bird thinks as Coffee dozes beside her, *to make someone hate you for their own good?* The stress of a trial while he's still in danger from v-flu and pneumonia might kill him. And the trouble, as Coffee said, is that he's guilty. She's always understood that the drug laws were the latest incarnation of Jim Crow, a way to target minorities for incarceration (and free labor) without explicitly denying their rights. But the irony is that Bradley boys have been dealing on the side to their classmates for as long as she's been there, and no one has ever gone down for it before Coffee. And given the pedigrees of the dealers and their clients, she doubts anyone else will.

"I know you know this," he says, startling her, "but I'm going to say it out loud for your sake."

"Sleep," she says automatically. "You're giving me a migraine."

"Bird, if I go to them with this, they will *never* believe you don't know. All that work we did, everything your mother did for you, that goes away. And your parents might not be very safe either."

"I don't want them hurt, but honestly, after what they've done, it's you I'm worried about. They'll take care of themselves, like always."

"Then what about you? You'll be watched, recorded, harassed . . . you might wish you had Roosevelt back by the end of it. I met Donovan too, remember?"

"You're the only one who could have understood the chemistry," she says. "You appeal to their paternalism and they'll believe you. I promise, I'll keep quiet."

He brushes his fingers over the pale scar by her hairline, evidence of what happened the last time she became a person of interest. "What if they decide to make sure?"

But even that won't scare her off. "Then make my safety a condition."

"What about your happiness?"

"What about yours?"

"Do I look happy to you?"

He doesn't; he looks exhausted and sick with worry and pain. She is a terrible person for doing this to him, and she would be an even worse person if she didn't. *Is it okay?* she asks, and decides.

"I'll do it for you," she says. "I'll go to them myself, and then the fat really will be in the fire."

"You're serious."

"And what kind of danger do you think I'd be in then?"

He's furious, like he was at the party when she nearly hit him with her shoe. The snap in his eyes shakes her, but she holds her ground. Part of her even enjoys it — the jousting has always been a part of her attraction to him.

"Sometimes I wish I didn't love you."

"Why do you think I held out so long?"

"Foda-se," he says, his voice thin as skim milk. "Get out, Bird. I need some time to myself."

The next day, Bao calls before she's out of the shower. She slips on the tiles and probably voids the warranty of her phone to pick it up with soapy, wet hands. He was fine when she left him last night, but things change.

"I need you to come into the office," Bao says.

"Is he —"

"The same," Bao says. "But you need to come here first. Don't call him or his mother."

Bird rinses, dresses, looks up Bao's address on her damp phone, and drives there. She has a hard time finishing her thoughts. Things change.

Citizens for Humane Drug Policy are located on the tenth floor of an older Capitol Hill office building. There's one other person there besides Bao; they look like they haven't slept all night. He leads her to his office and shuts the door.

"I check for bugs every week," he says. "Well, lately, every day."

"And you're telling me because . . ."

"Because we can have an honest conversation. And then you need to forget we ever talked at all."

Bao leans against the desk, dangerously close to several stacks of books and papers. His tie is draped around his neck, just like a Bradley boy, and she focuses on that, not his red and puffy eyes, not the hard lines etched in the corners of his mouth.

"Alonso has told me everything about your parents and what you overheard during your interrogation by CIA agents."

The tie is red, just like a Bradley tie, though she's sure the candy canes would go against dress code.

"Honestly, it makes sense. There have been persistent questions about the vaccine. My partner and I put this together with a few other strange reports that have been circulating — we're willing to bet that the government has been deploying bio weapons alongside conventional weapons for at least the past year, against traditional drone targets. It explains the terrorist effect — you heard about that? So-called terrorist communities having a strange immunity to the flu? That would make sense if they'd already been infected with the unmutated strain. If the government had deployed it dozens of times, then it also makes sense that they didn't think there'd be much danger in giving it to their FARC stooges and passing the blame onto Venezuela and even Iran for developing weapons of bioterrorism. That part in your note you didn't understand, about the used-car salesman?"

Bird forgets herself and meets his eyes. "Yes?"

He hands her a printout of an old article from the *New York Times*. It details a bizarre story that she vaguely remembers from several years ago — an FBI-thwarted Iranian plot to murder the Saudi Arabian ambassador. The would-be terrorist was an Iranian-American used-car salesman who the FBI had tapped and followed for the entire supposed plot, which involved paying a Mexican drug cartel to make the hit.

"Elements of the government tried to use this to make the case against Iran," Bao says, "but in the end, it wasn't very convincing. This guy would never have been a threat without the FBI plant supporting him. And there's a half dozen other stories like that — FBI thwarts FBI plot. I think what you overheard was someone acknowledging that those sorts of stories aren't very useful propaganda anymore. Better for the person to actually be caught in the middle of an act, like the underwear bomber."

"Better for who?" Bird hands back the papers.

"Better for people who want us to take more aggressive action in Venezuela and Iran. Better for war, Bird."

"And now we have our war. Thanks to my parents."

He levers himself from the desk and walks over to his window, with a view of the building across the street.

"That mutation . . . no one could have expected that. I'm betting that it was never supposed to be released in the first place. But even in the worst-case scenario, I think it was like H7N9 bird flu — potentially deadly if you catch it, but it couldn't spread from human-to-human contact. The chances of this virus mutating to cause a pandemic were minuscule."

She remembers the argument that Coffee and Trevor had just yesterday, about nonzero probabilities. "There is always a chance. Isn't that why everyone was worried about H7N9? If you're right, and they were deploying this Franken-virus with this killer incubation time around the world, then they were loading the gun every time. Maybe the chance was small, but *someone* always wins the lottery."

Bao pulls the shades. Bird wraps her arms around her stomach because she knows where this must end and she doesn't want to get there yet.

"So you were right," he says softly. "I'm grateful you could convince him. We can use this to make a deal. I've been on the phone all night. The conditions are —"

"I never see him again."

There, out loud. Bao hands her a tissue. "Any further contact between the two of you means the agreement is in breach. They believe you don't know. But they believe he might tell you."

"And we're each other's hostages. Just like I was supposed to be my parents' hostage."

"You were always a more credible witness than Alonso. A US citizen, daughter of two high-ranking scientists in the weapons program, model student . . . discrediting you was their nightmare. Discrediting Alonso would be easy."

She isn't crying, not much, but it's hard to see. She drags her sleeve across her eyes. "Why didn't they just kill me, then?"

"Because lucky for you, special service assassination isn't as easy as it looks in the movies. But . . . I think there was the possibility with that rogue agent. Roosevelt David. You are both much, much safer with this deal."

"Never again," Bird says, just to check. She can't feel her feet.

"There's always a chance . . . quite a few security operatives know the details of this. Sometimes things leak —" He stops abruptly and shakes his head. "No, I won't lie to you. If you contact him again, he's in jail or dead. And you're not very safe either."

"Okay."

Bao hands her a manila folder. "You need to sign the papers in here."

When she's done, Bird reaches into her bag and pulls out a CD. Aaron's copy of *Songs In The Key Of Life*; she figured he wouldn't mind.

"Give this to him," she says.

Bao hesitates, and nods. "Did you want to leave any other message? I'm not supposed to do this at all, but I will this one time."

"Tell him . . ."

But no. Half of it he knows already, and it's too late to say the rest.

Felice recovers. She moves to a rehab facility in southern Virginia where Charlotte visits a few times, and then stops. The rumors are of paralysis, of cognitive disability, of clinical depression. Bird doesn't ask.

Bird stays over at Charlotte's place a lot for the first few months. Her father hugs her every time, embarrassingly grateful that someone is there for his daughter after the initial flood of condolences. They watch BBC dramas and long, complicated animes with magical girls and doomed loves and hungry ghosts. They cook food for soup kitchens and collect clothes for homeless shelters and, occasionally, do their homework. Sometimes Marella tags along, and then, after they stay up all night to watch a Korean drama about a girl who dresses up as a boy to go to an elite school and ends up saving the kingdom, she comes more often. She wonders if it could have always been like this without Felice around, but then winces. Felice took a bullet to save Charlotte's life; she loved Charlotte, no matter what she thought of Bird. And Charlotte loved her. Bird doesn't feel obligated to like Felice now that she's been hurt, but she at least ought to respect the hidden depths no one but Charlotte got to see.

The hot war with Venezuela continues, despite concerned murmurs from coalition countries and stronger rumors that the v-flu couldn't possibly have been of entirely Venezuelan design. The vaccine halts the explosion of new cases, though the death toll still inexorably rises. People start to talk about other problems: nuclear proliferation in North Korea and Iran, global warming, the stability of global oil production. She reads the national and international news from three papers every day, one of them in Spanish. But Bao's small hope stays false; no one leaks.

Second semester senior year slides past, her classes not precisely jokes, but nonetheless hard to take seriously. She reapplies to Stanford and Georgetown just to appease her mother, but she has no intention of going to either.

"London, Paris," she chants with Marella when they talk about the future. She wonders if she could learn French and go to the Sorbonne. That reckless plan she told Coffee's mother — taking a year off to see the world — looks better with each month of silence. She is almost sure he's alive, but the doubt tickles her awake in the middle of some nights. She remembers how sick he was, and she's stared too long at the survival statistics for v-flu with a secondary infection of the lungs. The odds are on his side, but not by much.

A month before graduation, Marella pulls up outside her house and honks her horn.

"What are you doing here?" Bird asks, climbing in the passenger side in her pajama shorts and bunny slippers.

"Saving you from morbid reflections?" Marella says, and flicks her hair over her shoulder. Her makeup is smudged in a particular way that makes Bird wait.

"So, I'm sure it will be hard for you to contain your shock, but —"

"Sarah broke up with you?"

Marella's lips twist into a hard smile. "I did it this time. For good, Bird. I can't deal with it anymore, her always wondering what her mom will say and going on and on about that stupid waiting list for stupid Cornell, like her life will end if she doesn't go to an Ivy. Is my life so small? Am I really only ever going to be that girl who married her high school sweetheart, because if so, I might as well die here. It'll make a better story."

"Congratulations?"

Marella touches her thumbs to her forefingers and closes her eyes in a Zen exhale. "Thank you. I had to come here because I couldn't stop shaking. I still love her a little, but I'm sure it'll pass."

"Do you want to come inside? I wouldn't mind some distraction from my morbid reflections myself."

Marella's eyes fly open. "Bird, I didn't really mean, marrying your high school sweetheart — it would be different if I were madly in love with her."

"He's not my sweetheart, whatever he is."

Marella nods slowly. "I was thinking of the beach."

"The beach?"

"Ocean City? No, Rehoboth is prettier. Good ice cream. What do you say?"

"Right now? It's after five."

"I'll buy the gas."

Bird starts laughing. He'd love this. Her mother will hate it. And why not? "Wait here. I'll get my suit. And, uh, some shoes."

"Get one for me too, will you?"

"I think you've got several inches on me in the upper registers."

"Then I will make some lifeguard very happy, won't I? Hurry up, if we leave now we can get there before sunset."

They drive with the windows down, singing Rihanna and Aretha Franklin and P!nk and Gladys Knight. They talk and laugh and eat ice cream on the boardwalk in their bikinis and not once do they mention the boy and the girl they're both thinking about. It's a game they play, to pretend that other kind of love doesn't matter until, for a magical moment, it doesn't.

The news breaks the day she gets her late acceptance letter from Stanford.

V-flu proven to be in development in US labs years before terrorist attack, reads one headline on her Twitter feed.

US Scientists Developed So-Called "Venezuelan" Flu, reads another.

And then, the punch: *Exclusive: CIA whistleblower David Franklin speaks from undisclosed location in São Paulo about botched counterterror op.*

Bird knows even before she clicks the link. Roosevelt sits in an armchair in a hotel room, talking to an unseen camera operator about why he decided to leak the documents that reveal US government responsibility for the worst flu pandemic in over a century.

"People were dying," Roosevelt says, leaning forward. His face is a mask of sincerity. His shoe-polish eyes are shining. "And only I, and a few other people, knew why. I knew that America, the city on the hill, an example to the rest of the world, couldn't continue down this path and remain the great country that I know it is. Bioterrorism is the issue of our time, and we need to have a responsible, and honest, conversation about it. I cared more about telling the world these truths than my career or my safety."

Except that his career was ruined and his safety had probably been in serious doubt. And yet — she checks — it's all there. The unequal distribution of the vaccine, the development of the long incubation period by US scientists, its deployment during drone strikes. He claims that Venezuelan spies stole the virus, but FBI operatives were aware of this and let the plot continue before losing control of it at the crucial moment.

Bird very much doubts anyone in Venezuela ever laid eyes on their so-called v-flu, but even with this lie she can't deny the overwhelming good of Roosevelt's disclosures. His motives are unmistakably self-serving, but for once she has a reason to be grateful to him.

She grabs her phone and runs downstairs, scrolling for Bao's number. She plans to drive straight to his office, but stops short on the doorstep: A camera crew is waiting at the end of the driveway.

"Young lady?" A woman in a pencil skirt and fitted jacket, someone Bird recognizes from one of the cable news networks, hurries forward with a microphone. "Are your parents home?"

Bird is wearing short-shorts and a *Cowboy Bebop* T-shirt. Her hair needs a comb. This is how she will debut on national television. Her parents have been gone for a week in another undisclosed location, and she realizes that Roosevelt has complicated her life. Again.

"No," she says, and slams the door.

Bao tells her that he's "in discussions" and she shouldn't contact him again. He promises he'll get in touch if something changes. The news crews come and go, then descend in force when her parents arrive back home four days after the story breaks. They have been put on administrative leave, "just until this nonsense blows over," her mother says. "I told them they were playing with fire to release the virus like that. But the work we did on the protein coding" — she looks wistful — "was some of our best."

With all the dirty laundry finally airing, Bird spends days locked in the house with her parents that are not as unbearable as she had feared. They can talk now, she discovers, in a way that hadn't been possible in that web of secrets. She remembers what Coffee said:

Scientists learn about the world. It takes governments to use that knowledge for good or bad ends.

But still: "Why don't you guys work for someone else?" she asks. "Why not something more benign than CIA contracting?"

Greg Bird glances nervously at his wife, who purses her lips and then sighs. She looks at her daughter differently these days. Like someone she has to respect instead of control.

"I've been considering that, Emily. There's even a possibility of a university position for your father."

"Not if this scandal keeps up," Greg mutters.

But the spotlight moves from the scientists — who, the editorial board of the *Washington Post* argued, were hardly responsible — to the FBI and CIA. Antiwar protestors occupy the National Mall (and the Pentagon parking lot for twelve very tense hours). The antiwar fire catches all over the world, particularly in countries that have deployed their own military in the US-led offensive. The director of the FBI resigns. In the background of the press conference announcing the nomination of his replacement, she sees the man she only knew as Donovan.

Her parents return to work; Bird returns to her last two weeks of high school. She falls asleep with her phone, but she doesn't hear from Bao.

She graduates the same week that a special prosecutor is appointed to investigate presidential involvement in the secret bioweapons initiative. Rumors of impeachment are thicker than pollen in the late DC spring. Her parents come back home and watch her accept a diploma in a white dress. Charlotte gets an award for community service; Marella gets ones for English and Spanish and history. When they read out the chemistry award, she's not the only one who winces. The Bradley winner hoists the white-wrapped present above his head and chants "Coffee" at the top of his lungs. The others take it up until the teachers wave them silent again.

"He was never that popular when he was here," Bird whispers to Marella.

"Being a fugitive and a missing person does wonders for your rep."

Felice comes in a wheelchair, looking remarkably healthy given the rumors. She's cut her hair into a twenties-style bob that looks good on her. Bird says hi out of obligation and guilt, but Felice only raises a pencil-thin eyebrow and ignores her.

After the photos and the congratulations, Bird and Marella and Charlotte sit together on the edge of the rose garden fountain. The tea roses smell like a different world from school, even in sight of that old building. They make her think of English gardens and French pastries.

"I'm going to the travel agency tomorrow," Marella says. "Life is too short to spend it worrying about school."

"London, Paris," Bird says, smiling.

"I think I'm just going to stick close to home for now," Charlotte says. "My dad needs me. But maybe in the fall, wherever you are . . ."

"I promise, I'll want to see you. So you're going to Stanford, Bird?"

"I don't know," she says. She's beginning to think that even Roosevelt's miracle won't bring him back. That they'll enforce the deal out of spite. Or maybe he just doesn't want her anymore.

"Call me when you decide," Marella says.

Bird spends too much time on blogs, because they pay more attention to the details of the v-flu scandal than any mainstream newspaper. She prefers the left-wing ones, because while the conspiracy theories make her laugh (US republicans wanted it released in California to decimate the democratic base, for example), they're the closest she can get to having an argument with Coffee. She posts occasionally under a pseudonym, getting into debates that pass long, insomniac hours. She sometimes even finds the counterarguments convincing.

And two days after graduation, Bird finds a strange message in the comment threads of several blog posts.

Always. In the immortal words of Stevie Wonder: "Change your words into truth and then change that truth into love and maybe our children's grandchildren and their great-grandchildren will tell."

There's a street in São Paulo with a vacant storefront just large enough for a coffee shop. Or maybe a bookstore?

Head shop?

Just kidding.

It disappears from most of them quickly — off-topic, vaguely spammy, invalid email address.

But it's enough.

She runs down the stairs and nearly collides with her father, leaving his office. "Emily," he says, and stops.

"Dad," she says, "Dad, I'm going to leave."

"Not Stanford, I take it." Bird whirls around at the sound of her mother's voice. Her arms are crossed.

Bird shakes her head. She wants to run away from her, hide forever.

"Where, then? Don't tell me you're planning to run feral with that new friend of yours."

"São Paulo," she says.

"The dealer!"

But she doesn't have to hide, not inside herself, not in her mother's projected image, not ever again. Her mother takes a step toward her and raises her hand. *She will slap me*, Bird thinks, *but it won't matter.*

But she doesn't. "Call us," she says. "So we know you're safe. I'll miss you."

The funny thing is, Bird believes her.

She walks outside. Then she calls Bao.

"He left me a message," she says.

"I know."

"Is it safe?"

He sighs. "I can't say much over the phone, but you know it isn't."

She knows: Roosevelt waiting for her in Brazil; the very slight, very important lies in his skin-saving leaks.

"But they won't kill us."

"I can't offer you absolutes, Bird. It's safer to stay where you are. Safer for him."

"And he knows that?"

He snorts and she hears the smile in his voice. "Oh, he knows."

So he has given her a choice. Stay away and live without the government's cold shadow. Or take this chance, come for him, and live with the danger. Because together, she and Coffee will never be safe.

"I should stay away from him. For his own good."

"You should," Bao agrees. "But I — well, good luck." He hangs up. Bird stares at the screen of her phone until she gets a text message from Marella.

Just bought a one-way to Paris.

And Bird types:

Coming with you, babe. But we need to stop somewhere first.

Marella calls. "Bird, oh my God, Bird, did he —"

"São Paulo," she says, laughing and crying. "London, Paris, São Paulo."

When I get to São Paulo, he will meet me at the airport, holding words instead of roses. We will tell each other stories of how we spent long months without each other's company. We will laugh about our parents and say unkind words about our governments and look into each other's eyes like the stupidest couples in Paris. We will have sex and we will be careful and we will chase each other through the parks and down the streets of this city I already love. I will take pictures of buildings and argue with him over which neighborhood is the best, which shop would make us happiest, what sort of world we will live in, he and I, growing old together. We will travel the world with my best friend. We'll go to college and learn things we hate and things we never knew and things we will spend our lives understanding.

And if, some nights, I wake up to the memory of peach schnapps and vomit and the dull brown eyes of a man who might still hurt me, I will remember the boy who pelted down the driveway after a car he could not possibly catch. I will remember that the nightmare is over because we ended it, that we are healthy and alive, even if we are never completely safe, and I will hold him close, and I will go back to sleep.

ACKNOWLEDGMENTS

I grew up in the district ("What part?" the joke goes. "Bethesda."), and writing this novel has been a trip home in many ways. While the actual events and characters are entirely fictional, the atmosphere of the city reflects my own experience. So first I have to thank my family, for the macaroni and cheese at Thanksgiving, the arguments over lemon in the sweet potato pie — and the space to pursue my own wild dream of being a writer.

John Hart-Smith, for careful notes and much-appreciated corrections about the world of government contracting.

Abby, Alexis, Amanda, Bianca, and Lauren for DC reminiscences, suggestions, and critiques — and for reminding me of the parts that I loved.

Tamar, for always being so supportive and smart — thank you for sharing your excitement for this story with me when I needed it.

Justine, for taking my messy first drafts, understanding exactly where I want to go, and helping me get there. Scott, for the surprise notes that were like Christmas (or Thanksgiving) come early.

Ellen and Delia, for so graciously letting me crash in their spare bedroom when it mattered. I finished this novel thanks to that gift of your space.

Bill, for taking me out in Seattle and arguing plot with me for hours, like old times.

Steve Rendall, for his generosity in listening to my political plot difficulties and hashing out plausibly fake scenarios over sangria.

Martha Marsh and David Wohl for their generous help with niggling details of medical protocol. Needless to say, extreme implausibilities or outright mistakes are entirely my own.

My team at Scholastic deserves an ode for their work on my behalf. Arthur Levine and Emily Clement could not be more incisive or understanding in their editorial process. (And sorry, Emily, for all the thematic hay I made with your first name!)

Finally, Jill Grinberg, Cheryl Pientka, and Katelyn Detweiler make my life better with their wisdom, care, and support.

As always, thank you.

Alaya Dawn Johnson's first novel for young adults, *The Summer Prince*, received three starred reviews, was longlisted for the National Book Award, and was a 2013 *Kirkus Reviews* Best Book of the Year. She grew up in Washington, DC, where she attended the National Cathedral School. She went on to Columbia University and now lives in Mexico City. Visit her at www.alayadawnjohnson.com

Read on for a sneak peek of

"Mysterious, sweeping, wholly original . . . you'll be happy to drown in this dizzying, bloody brew of technology, lore, and world-shaking conflict."
—**LEIGH BARDUGO**, *New York Times* bestselling author

the
LIBRARY of
BROKEN
WORLDS

NEBULA AWARD–WINNING AUTHOR
ALAYA DAWN JOHNSON

A girl and a god, alone in communion. The god awakes, as he was meant to. He is furious!

"I'll kill you like I killed the others, the ones with your face."

The girl is her own light in the darkness. "I'm dying anyway."

"A virus can't kill you as fast as I can," he says.

"But you, great Nameren, the Naamaru Catre, the Tezcatlapa, Aurochs whose great horns are crescents of twin moons, whose testes swing like the bells of war—"

"Are you *laughing*?"

It is a fine, wide laugh. "You won't kill me, O first and greatest material god."

"Why not, O girl who should not exist?"

"Who else can you talk to? Without me, you'll slide back into your blood-laced sleep for another five centuries."

The god doesn't move from his darkness. "You came here to kill me."

"Maybe my sisters came to kill you—"

"I *know* you—"

"But I haven't."

"You were made for me," he says.

And she says, "I am a creature built from a dream, designed for deicide."

"What?"

"That's what Nadi, my watcher, once told me."

"No human can kill a god. Not even a human created for the purpose."

The girl lifts her chin. "Then why not keep me around a little longer? Unfortunately for my creators, I have free will. I didn't come here for deicide."

The god is suspicious. "For what, then?"

"To wake you up. All of you."

"They made me sleep. I've lost time, centuries, generations and generations . . ."

"What do you remember?"

"There was a war, a long war. The Awilu who made me against the Mahām who fed me, and I let the Mahām lose . . . somehow . . ."

"Do you remember the Library?"

The god considers. "There is a dream I have, of a disc spinning in space like a plate on a potter's wheel, lit by a red-orange sun and two dancing moons."

"The Library is a dream, Nameren—a dream of peace built on a grave, guarded by four drowsing gods. The Library is where all stories start, and where they all return before they die. I know I'll never see it again."

"Why not?"

"You're not the only one who wants to kill me."

The god is curious, as the girl intended him to be. "This Library of yours has four gods?" he asks. "There were seven material gods when I fell asleep."

"There are eight now," she says. "The Awilu made us a new one after the war. The last one they will ever make."

"A new god? Tell me."

She has him now. "I could tell you about her. About all of them. I could tell you about my home, just as befits the Library, in a story. All you have to do is promise not to kill me."

"This communion can't end with both of us alive. And gods don't die."

"Then don't kill me just yet."

"If I want the story, you mean?"

"Yes, great Nameren," says the girl to the god in the dark. "If you want the story."